SPOOKER

SPOOKER

DEAN ING

A TOM DOHERTY ASSOCIATES BOOK

NEW YORK

SPOOKER

Copyright © 1995 by Dean Ing

This book is printed on acid-free paper.

A Forge Book
Published by Tom Doherty Associates, Inc.
175 Fifth Avenue
New York, N.Y. 10010

Forge® is a registered trademark of Tom Doherty Associates, Inc.

Design by Ann Gold

Library of Congress Cataloging-in-Publication Data
Ing, Dean.
    Spooker / Dean Ing.
        p.   cm.
    "A Tom Doherty Associates book."
    ISBN 0-312-85740-3 (hardcover)
    I. Title.
    PS3559.N37S66   1995   95-34737
    813'.54—dc20   CIP

First edition: November 1995

Printed in the United States of America

0 9 8 7 6 5 4 3 2 1

ACKNOWLEDGMENTS

One of these days I may learn to plow arcane fields without the likes of Dr. Jay Mullen, Al Reiss, Ken Goddard, Dr. Tom Ewald, Dr. Leik Myrabo, Dr. Marvin Coffey, Dr. David Natharius, Dr. Carl Carmichael and several others, but I didn't manage that in this book. If I have run amok with their wise counsel, they have no one to blame but me. Federal agents, some retired, some active, added tidbits to my narrative as indulgently as other folks will feed a strutting park pigeon. To the latter: my sincere thanks, gentlemen; for the record, "I have no recollection of . . ." your names.

As for the Chamois: At least the model flies, thanks to the expert help of the EAA's David Guerriero.

For Walt Buckner, who is,
after all, the best man.

1

BECAUSE SKANDER MASARYK WAS THE VICTIM OF EARLIEST date in what Langley insiders call the Spooker File, both East and West needed a long time to unravel its tangles. Royston, a CIA handler, observed at the time that their prized Czech defector was in no condition to explain, and a corpse carbonized as badly as that could yield very little forensics data with the technology of 1968.

The record shows that they applied to their other star Czech defector, Ladislav Bittman, for more. Bittman, once a major in the Soviet-backed STB, the Czech secret police, was little help. The "uncles," as KGB handlers were called in Prague, had taken quite a few promising young Czechs to Moscow, and only the failures showed up again in Prague. Masaryk might have been many things, but a failure was not one of them.

The Langley dossier on Masaryk lacked a couple of extremely salient points the KGB could have furnished, but that was to be expected of a defecting Soviet-bloc spook in the late 1960s. What nobody could have expected was that Masaryk would become a spook of the sort to make men tremble, the sort that even when terminated, does not *stay* dead.

What CIA-Langley knew about Skander Roman Masaryk covered some forty pages, but some of that was palpable bullshit; the main points could have been crammed into a small envelope. In brief, Masaryk was born in 1934 to Ludwig and Maria Masaryk in the city of Brno at a moment when Czechoslovakia could still hope for better times. An engineer and pilot who believed in socialism, the elder Masaryk moved his wife and infant to Canada with the Czech trade mission shortly before

Nazi Germany began to demand her piece of Masaryk's homeland. While trying to sell the Czech-built Aero A204 transport aircraft in Ottawa, the leftist engineer polished his English and listened to his radio with increasing dread.

Canadians spoke English and French, which colored the views of Ludwig Masaryk and thus of his wife and child; it was the Englishman, Chamberlain, and the Frenchman, Daladier, who appeased Adolf Hitler in 1938 by allowing him to gobble pieces of Czechoslovakia unhindered. To all patriotic Czechs, this amounted to a flat betrayal by the Western democracies. In March 1939, with the Nazi takeover of the Skoda arms factories, Ludwig Masaryk abandoned any idea of going home and placed his faith in Moscow. When Germany attacked the Soviet Union in June 1941, Masaryk searched his conscience and then went to war.

With careful consideration for his wife and their precocious gypsy-featured child who adored him, Ludwig Masaryk signed on with one of the three Czech squadrons in Britain's Royal Air Force instead of volunteering directly with the Soviets. The records from this period suggest that eight-year-old Skander, already building model airplanes in Ottawa, was by nature a secretive child. Masaryk knew that Canada would protect his little family while he fought for socialism; and besides, as a pilot, he fancied his chances were better in a Spitfire than flying a lumbering dead-slow Russian bomber.

To say that his chances were better is not to say that they were good. Lieutenant Ludwig Masaryk's fighter disintegrated over the English Channel in 1942. Perhaps with more patriotism than good sense, the young widow emigrated back to a ravaged Czechoslovakia after the war with a strange and stateless teenager who was already cynical about the West. Young Skander had been tutored at home in Ottawa, and the dossier claims that his English was better than his Czech. As a confirmed socialist, and aware that Prague's technical colleges had been virtually destroyed, Maria Masaryk permitted the Soviet Union to take her fourteen-year-old for higher education.

All of this information, of course, was put together long after the events. The CIA dossier on young Skander Masaryk did not actually exist until, in August 1968, Soviet tanks rumbled through Czech cities to quell the revolt there. Days after the Prague revolt was crushed, an attractively lithe, swarthy fellow strode into the Central Los Angeles FBI office speaking perfect idiomatic American, carrying a Samsonite two-suiter and a story that filled the SAC, the special agent in charge, with mixed emotions.

On the one hand, a youngish walk-in with a technical degree from Leningrad State Institute and a decade of KGB experience was a plum the size of a cantaloupe. On the other hand, if Skander Masaryk's story was *all* true, this Czech had been living in the United States illegally, ferreting out secrets from American aerospace firms for almost a decade, without causing the merest ripple in FBI caseloads. Masaryk recited details about our experimental aircraft composites, jet-fuel additives and welding of titanium alloys that only a technical spook could know. He had obviously been moving about with practiced ease under the noses of FBI spycatchers for years, a heartworm at the core of our aerospace industry, with impunity; but in crushing Prague, the Soviets had crushed the last vestige of Masaryk's idealism. It was the best of news. And the worst.

The Spooker file does not explain how J. Edgar Hoover, who hated the CIA enough to have bulldozed the entire acreage of Langley if given half a chance, was persuaded to turn Masaryk over. Old hands speculate that Hoover was persuaded by a photograph held by the CIA's James Jesus Angleton, of Mr. Hoover engaged in homosexual activity. It is clear that CIA director James Schlesinger and his deputy, Rufus Taylor, wanted to cash in on that bad Czech and, in retrospect, could have learned more to aid Western spying than the FBI could in plugging U.S. aerospace leaks.

Langley had scant weeks to debrief their new defector. They could not know this, and took their time while giving Masaryk a sense of new, Western-style comradeship at Camp Peary near Williamsburg, Virginia. There he was befriended by an old-timer, Dennis Royston, who often walked the Czech around the Peary acreage on brisk fall mornings, enjoying the autumn palette of crimson, yellow, and brown colorbursts in nearby maples. Peary's red-brick complex of small buildings resembled an

Ivy League college more than a safe house, and it was here that the CIA lavished its best treatment on Masaryk. When Masaryk declined offers of a complete physical and insisted on the freedom to leave the tree-lined grounds of The Farm, as he pleased, his controllers balked.

Whereupon, Masaryk balked too. The Czech was already known to be a long-distance runner with that odd breed's stubborn traits. The mild disarming voice and those chiseled gypsyish features masked a will of carbide resolve, and because some of his information was timely, handler Royston argued that the Czech's demands were not all that unreasonable. They did, however, put an armed tail on their errant spook. Though Masaryk felt that the Soviets could not yet know of his defection, Langley spymasters thought it possible. In this they were correct: it was more than possible. The agency was to learn very soon that the existence and location of the Peary "Farm" was not a secret from the Soviets.

Masaryk drove different agency cars on short trips into Williamsburg, chiefly during the evenings. His tail reported that on most evenings, Masaryk, something of a freak for academic surroundings, parked the car and jogged innocently through the nearby William and Mary campus. The CIA man, who soon grew tired of running in Masaryk's wake, would frequently stop near the campus library and inhale the lingering scent of burnt fallen leaves while waiting for his ward's next pass. The days were spent on debriefing, usually with Royston in attendance. One measure of their growing friendship was Masaryk's divulging of a little secret to the CIA man: in some unspecified place, certainly not in his personal effects, Masaryk had secured enough valuables to let him live comfortably for years. Much of Masaryk's spying—but not all—had employed illegal wireless bugs; within a week, U.S. intelligence agencies were running new wiretaps in the Los Angeles area: two on aerospace engineers, one on a secretary in Glendale, and several electronic bugs in a Burbank ginmill which Masaryk had used in the same fashion. The results were almost immediate; stock in Masaryk ran high at Peary.

The KGB's Directorate S, which controlled illegals of Masaryk's stripe, had divulged one of its Los Angeles safe houses to the Czech. It was safe no more, but the place was not raided immediately because, it was thought, the raid would give the Czech's defection away too soon. Only decades later, upon the opening of old KGB files after the Soviet collapse, did we learn that the safe house was a KGB trip wire for Masaryk alone. The moment the place came under surveillance, the KGB—constantly alert for just such a hazard—realized that Masaryk had been turned.

In those days, newly turned defectors were almost always sent to The Farm. The Soviets knew this, too. That knowledge might have been of little use against Masaryk if the Czech had stayed safely on the grounds. KGB records on the kidnap attempt are sparse because the Czech's defection was counted as a KGB failure and the recovery job was given to their Soviet military intelligence brethren, the GRU. The rivalry between those agencies had always been hot; the GRU claimed the KGB was sluggish, incompetent. The KGB retorted that GRU men were given to violent excess. Both views were correct.

We may never learn exactly what ruse the GRU team used to spirit Masaryk from a college campus into a four-door Ford bound for distant parts; quite a few GRU thugs are fluent in idiomatic English, and it is reasonable to suppose that they carried forged IDs, perhaps identifying them as CIA. In any case, one William and Mary student reported a furious—yet subdued—argument on campus that evening between a jogger and two insistent gentlemen near a dark four-door sedan. The jogger entered the car without a scuffle; whether influenced by a handgun is unknown. What *is* known, is that no Company men were dispatched to pick up the Czech on that deadly evening. Whoever they were, neither of those insistent gentlemen was ever tracked down, and GRU files are, to this day, still secret.

From the campus in Williamsburg to the verge of a Chesapeake salt marsh near the village of Poquoson, Virginia, some thirty miles distant, we have no useful record. Several hours elapsed, however, before York County volunteer firemen were summoned to the end of a gravel road and to a blaze that engulfed a four-door Ford, spreading to involve scrub pines near the water's edge. No victim was found until someone jimmied the trunk lid.

By this time, Dennis Royston knew that Masaryk had vanished across the campus from his bodyguard. On a hunch, Royston checked out the torched sedan near Poquoson. By noon the next day, the CIA had enough data from Forensics to identify the remains, chiefly from charred clothing and a wristwatch. Even if The Farm had created a dental chart on Masaryk—which it had not got around to—that might have helped very little; the victim had been beaten so savagely that the facial bones were crushed and almost all the teeth were missing. But then, violent excess was a GRU trademark. . . .

"Poor sonofabitch!" Royston gloomed, trying to infer all that had happened. "They must've had perfect Company ID if he went without a fight. He probably thought it was our men picking him up until the lead pipe hit him. I blame myself, mostly."

After that, procedures at The Farm were tightened, and Royston was reassigned to the West Coast. It would be another two years before Dennis Royston himself disappeared without immediate trace; many more years before Royston's name was added to the Spooker File.

And when KGB files were opened after the Soviet debacle, one of those salient details was almost missed. It suggested a good reason why the Czech had refused a physical exam back in 1968. According to the KGB, Masaryk was not, strictly speaking, a man.

2

THE SPOOKER FILE WAS ONLY A DARK SURMISE IN A zealot's brain when, in late spring of the following year, the Iranian consulate made discreet inquiries from its Embarcadero office in San Francisco. We were still on good terms with Iran and listened politely. One Ghavam Razmara, a low-level diplomat, had disappeared from the Embarcadero without a trace. Would the Americans know anything about it?

We knew, of course, that the beefy, fortyish Razmara was a veteran of SAVAK, the Shah's American-trained intelligence bureau. From his life-style, including a forbidden blonde bimbette in Redwood City and a Porsche Carrera with diplomatic DM prefix license plates which he often drove to Oakland, we deduced that Razmara was using diplomatic-mail pouches to line his pockets, probably beginning with heroin transshipped from Iran. Our spymasters replied truthfully that they had no idea where Razmara had gone. Privately we hoped his disappearance was permanent, but paid a courtesy call on the Redwood City blonde anyway.

Razmara had cleaned out the little apartment wall safe ten days before, said Blondie, and laid down a strip of Pirelli when he left in his little German bathtub. And by the way, did anybody know if he intended to pay the rent?

Our man was patient in asking for details; known associates, documents, other apartments. Razmara had left no papers that she could find. If he had another apartment, she knew nothing about it, not that she didn't have her suspicions about the skirt-chasing bastard. His callers were always by telephone, she said, and conversations were brief. But he'd talked longer on a couple of his last incomings, making her leave the room, and afterward he was definitely not himself for a while. In what way? He had no interest in his usual smoked fish and caviar, Blondie replied, and not much in her—and his palms felt unaccountably clammy. And what about the rent on the apartment?

It would help, said our man, if she could remember what he packed when he left.

Pack, Blondie echoed, as if the idea were extravagant. After that last call, Razmara had put down the phone, fumbled his way through the safe combination, and crammed his pockets full of little wrapped packages, paying no attention to her repeated questions. There had been a gun, too, one of those little James Bond gizmos with a short pipe stuck on the muzzle.

A silencer? Could be, she guessed, he sure didn't pop it off for her, just stuck it inside his suede jacket and split—no suitcase, no jammies, no toothbrush. And how was she expected to pay the rent?

Our man sighed and counted out eight fifties—highway robbery for three rooms in those days. And now that we were subletting the apartment for one more month, so to speak, if her Iranian showed up again would she mind calling a certain number without telling Razmara?

It was the least she could do, Blondie smiled, counting the money; and by the way, was the Iranian in serious trouble?

Hard to say, our man replied, leaving, but added that Razmara seemed to think he was if he had gone for his spooker. The blonde wondered aloud what a spooker was, but she was already talking to a closed door.

Had our man been FBI and not CIA, he probably would have said "valuables," instead of "spooker." The FBI operated with a clear charter, normally within our national borders, and even its undercover agents of the Joe Pistone stripe could count on loyalty from above. The Bureau demanded strict accountability for every lunch chit, every gram of crack, every three-ounce tin of caviar an agent encountered. But the CIA, at that time, had a looser budget and operated more freely. It even operated inside the United States when surveilling foreign nationals, a tactic which had the two agencies stepping on each other's toes. But perhaps the worst CIA sin, in Mr. Hoover's view, was a certain laxity in Langley's hiring practices.

One knew, at that time, that if some scuffler were female or homely or black, that scuffler was *not* FBI. The Company was—well, different. And some of its people were part-timers, and a few had felony rap sheets. And while the FBI had never, ever been known to burn its own people, to sacrifice them as pawns in a larger game, the Company had its internal rumors of some pretty tacky trade-offs. That is why a cautious CIA veteran, with antisocial security in mind, might siphon off enough funds to accumulate a spooker.

The word originated among alcoholics, often professional men who hid that spare pint in the glove compartment or a half-pint of pure Everclear spirits in the medicine cabinet in a hydrogen peroxide bottle. A spooker was the emergency stash of the desperate seeker. But some cynical Company man, aware that he might one day have to disappear before someone disappeared him, borrowed the term and applied it to a different kind of emergency kit: a cash-filled wallet with several kinds of plausible ID; a few untraceable emeralds; a weapon, perhaps; keys to a hidden car, perhaps. And what label fitted the stash of the desperate spook better than "spooker"?

Mr. Ghavam Razmara was a bona fide spook, almost certainly playing on both sides of international law. From all appearances, he had fled on short notice, taking only his spooker, though he was not sought by us or Interpol. The Company did not expect to see him again, but assumed that he had made good his escape from whatever he feared. Some time later Langley reconsidered, made a copy of the Razmara dossier, and stuck it in the Spooker File.

But still, early in 1970, no such file existed when Sean Patrick called a close friend from a Long Beach telephone booth. Both men were Company part-timers; nominally, insurance investigators who picked up some nontaxable income running background checks on citizens for a Swiss firm. The Swiss were actually KGB, who imagined that they were well disguised by the false flag they waved. Sean Patrick was passing everything on to the CIA until, he confided from that phone booth, his true double-agent ploy was unmasked.

"It had to be Toro," Patrick snarled, invoking the code name of his CIA boss, "if it wasn't you. And it wasn't you because I could give up too much about how you built your spooker."

"You've got yours on you," the friend guessed.

"Damn right, and you should consider it yourself. I've felt for weeks that I was surveilled, but I couldn't be sure. Then I get this note shoved under my door and nearly shit my knickers. Whoever it was with our Swiss friends, I guess he has a soft spot for me; but *they know*, man. I'm going private."

"You could go to the Company, *above* Toro. I would."

"Then you risk it. Once burnt, I'm twice shy," Patrick said and broke the connection.

Patrick's friend spent days camping in the desert near Needles, thinking it all over where he could see five miles in every direction, before making his decision. The people he contacted were two rungs above the suspected Toro, and eventually he came to believe that Sean Patrick had not been burned by his own agency. He never received the prearranged signal that Patrick had reached a haven. For a time, the Company concluded that Sean Patrick had been flushed deliberately by the KGB in such a way that they could take the man while he had his spooker. It would be a perfect irony, worthy of Russian chess, for them to recover the cash they had paid out to an agent who was doubling on them.

This kind of thrust and parry was bound to intrigue Langley's James Angleton, a chain-smoking little gent with a wide humorless slit of a mouth and a legendary appreciation for byzantine plots that eventually got him bumped from counterintelligence. It was Angleton who, by 1971, became convinced that a field agent's spooker might be his death warrant, perhaps regardless of the nation he served. "Someone or something is out there somewhere, that's hungry for Western Intelligence," Angleton remarked to a visiting MI-6 man, waving vaguely at the Virginia countryside. "And it's hunting on our turf."

"A tiger in your midst," the Brit remarked.

"An earwig. It crawls inside your head and eats your brain."

The Brit smiled. "They don't really do that."

"This one does," Angleton said.

With loving care, Angleton's people went through archives to assemble a special record of agents known or suspected to have "gone private," fled the system, and who might have done so carrying small fortunes to smooth the ripples of early retirement. Even if a spook was accounted for afterward, that dossier was added to the Spooker File. The file continued to grow after Angleton's departure, and as it grew it became more unsettling. The dossiers went far beyond CIA's own people to include agencies friendly and neutral. As old relationships shifted, old mysteries surfaced.

Despite its straight-arrow image, the FBI had an unexplained disappearance from its Seattle office: a deep-cover brick agent working as a Boeing janitor. When he vanished, the man was carrying $30,000 in marked bills for a sting operation; ordinarily not enough to tempt a man with a legitimate retirement plan, especially with marked bills, but still the agent was gone.

A naturalized Israeli vanished from his bookstore in Pasco, Washington in 1974. We suspected that the man was a Mossad illegal with a technical background, and because the Hanford nuclear-bomb plant lies only a few miles from Pasco, the Mossad's interests in Pasco were rather easy to guess. The immigrant had been a popular host in the area; his parties had featured the kind of booze and decor that suggested better funding than he could support with a small bookstore. Mossad took its time asking, but eventually it did admit a passing interest in the onetime Israeli. For one thing, a Tel Aviv insider's rumor claimed, the vanished man had brought enough gold coins into the United States to throw expensive parties for fifty years. We took this as tacit admission that the man had dispensed bribes for Mossad and denied any knowledge of the man's loot or his disappearance. The Israelis pretended to believe us. There was, however, a veiled reference to the fact that Mossad knew how to play hardball as well as anybody.

Then, in 1983, ground was broken on the Yakima River Interstate

Bridge between Richland and Pasco. Workers began a pier excavation on a small island toward the Richland side. They had not gone down many feet before they discovered remains of an adult male estimated as having been buried roughly ten years previous. Forensics matched the dentition of the skull to the missing immigrant's dental chart. A fracture of the hyoid, a small bone at the base of the tongue, revealed that the victim had been strangled—but traces of potassium arsenite were found as well. Since some hair was still attached to the skull, and arsenic traces commonly show up in the hair but were absent in this case, it was deduced that the victim had *not* been poisoned gradually, but took a sizable dose shortly before his death. Evidently, the killer first tried poison and then finished the job with a garrote wire.

We shared our findings with the Israelis, who commented that the killing reminded them of an amateur job—perhaps a love affair gone sour. Many modern poisons work fast and are hard to identify after long interment, but arsenic can leave traces for centuries. Whoever had taken the man off was no expert with poisons.

At Langley, Angleton was long absent from that loop by 1983, but the file was growing like a dandelion. It grew considerably fatter on a case involving one Helmut Klemmt, who was sought by the German press after the reunification in late 1990. As a Kommandant in the East German Ministry of State Security, the solitary Klemmt had made enemies in West Berlin and managed a deal after the wall fell: detailed memoirs to CIA in exchange for free passage to America. Klemmt spoke academic English; he was a professional of many years' standing, surely capable of taking care of himself in the United States; and the only people who seemed to want him were reporters and a handful of vengeful German citizens.

Klemmt took a false name and moved to Palo Alto, near the resources of the Stanford library, where he began his memoirs and cooked gourmet meals for the scholarly gentlemen the CIA sent, from time to time, to read and discuss his first draft. Klemmt's local contact with the Company was a fellow code-named Jacob in Santa Clara, only ten miles away. It proved to be ten miles too far.

One evening in April 1991, Jacob returned to his Santa Clara apartment to find an odd message on his answering machine. Without preamble, Klemmt's voice said: "Jacob, this is Esau. It is three forty-eight P.M. and I am wondering about the wisdom of your masters. I have received an unsigned note warning me that I have become an embarrassment to my friends. The names Jacob and Esau were mentioned, as well as another name I no longer care to be associated with. If the note was yours, I thank you. In any case, I am not persuaded to panic. There may be more to this. I suggest that we convene over an excellent paella, which I shall prepare at your convenience. I am forewarned and, therefore, forearmed; I trust I said that correctly. I can take your call after ten tonight. Good evening."

It was Klemmt's—Esau's—habit to dine late when he dined out alone, and Jacob waited until 10:00 P.M. before returning that call. He got Esau's answering machine then, and the same message again every ten minutes until 11:20, when he slid into his Lexus and headed down El Camino toward Palo Alto.

Klemmt was not at home, but the police were there behind strips of yellow plastic. Jacob parked a block away and stood near the plastic tape with a dozen of Klemmt's neighbors, soaking up speculations long enough to hear a particularly unsettling rumor. Then he ambled off, drove home, and made a late, late call.

Other Company men discovered the details, and that rumor had been correct. Helmut Klemmt had died shortly after dark between 8:00 and 8:15, the victim of a mugging in the shadowed parking lot of a fine restaurant just off San Antonio Road. Klemmt's wallet was missing, pockets turned out. The body had been eased into a Dumpster by someone who evidently did not realize that restaurant staff dump garbage during a busy evening. His car was not to be found, then or later. An hour after Klemmt's death, his apartment had been quietly ransacked by someone who had left a lot of smudges but no fingerprints; a highly competent toss, presumably by a pro. The implications were clear: someone had failed to find what he sought on Klemmt's person and had continued the search in the dead man's apartment.

When Jacob read the police forensics report, he took note that because Klemmt's manuscript notes were found strewn about his study, they had not been the motive. Jacob's tumblers did not click until he came to the part about a fresh, deep gouge in the floor of the study where something massive had been dragged for a short distance. It left flecks of burgundy paint in the gouge.

Jacob knew that Klemmt had kept a heavy steel gun cabinet padlocked in his study. It was a deep burgundy. It was not listed among Klemmt's effects. "He would've had a spooker equal to Noriega's, right close at hand. They don't seem to have found anything like that. The odds are it was in that missing gun cabinet," he told his section chief.

Almost as an afterthought, Jacob wrote that the quiet removal of a whopping big gun cabinet from an apartment suggested that the black-bag job had probably taken at least two people. Jacob never knew it, but his report placed Helmut Klemmt's dossier in the Spooker File, where it belonged. At Langley, the wiser heads were shaking in dismay. If we had mounting evidence that someone had offed a dozen experienced people for their spookers, there were probably a dozen more we hadn't noticed. Fat as it was, the Spooker File might represent only the tip of the coffin.

At that point, a veteran analyst was assigned to the file. He spent a lot of Company money writing scenarios, but Langley made no more progress. Not until 1994, when a mine shaft was used to dispose of a missing DEA agent named Gary Landis.

3

HIS 1959 BIRTH CERTIFICATE FROM GARY, INDIANA, HAD
spelled it Marion Garrett Landis, but after his mother's death
in 1967, his father had taken the blond kid with the serious
gray eyes to Los Angeles. His birthplace became his playground name—
Gary—and he liked that a hell of a lot better than Marion, especially in
the tough neighborhood available to a boy whose dad worked in a Pep
Boys auto-parts store.

In his early teens, Gary lost the Midwest vowels and his hair
darkened a bit though it would yellow like yesterday's newspaper in a Los
Angeles summer sun, and he liked to wear it long in token rebellion. He
tried hanging out with this or that group, never with any of them for long
because some of their decisions, he thought, were dumb; window-
peeping saddened him, and turf battles seemed pointless. He had friends,
but was nobody's best friend. He made Bs and Cs, but became a straight-A
shoplifter with his favorite ploy: once on the street, he could outrun
anything but radio waves. It was a dispatcher's radio that caught him; that
and the LAPD's Duane Halvorsen, whose black-and-white was a familiar
sight in the area.

Swede Halvorsen was built like Babe Ruth, like a potato on match-
sticks; on the best day he ever had, he couldn't match the kid's broken-
field panache—even in his patrol car—without running over somebody
or splintering a few back fences. But Swede had an uncanny memory
for faces, and sometimes he drove an unmarked car. That is how he
trailed fifteen-year-old Gary Landis home one day, and found the boy

alone in the little apartment, and read him his wrongs without taking him in.

At first Gary hadn't said much during that confrontation, and Swede sensed in that solemn gaze a loneliness that, just maybe, hadn't found palliation in a gang. Swede didn't spare the verbal stick or the carrot either, asking how the kid would like having his dad bail him out and, tossing it off lightly, mentioning a high-school backfield coach by name. Had Gary thought much about college? Did he realize that a scatback capable of dodging Buicks on Paramount Boulevard could parlay that into a full scholarship? Did Gary Landis, in fact, give a shit about impressing nice girls?

Perhaps Halvorsen was thinking of his own precocious twelve-year-old granddaughter, Janelle; perhaps not. To Gary it was clear that this man liked to think things through, and that his decisions weren't as dumb as most. When Halvorsen left that afternoon, he carried a Food World bag full of tawdry loot Gary had dug out of hiding places, and a guarded promise that the Landis kid would think about organized sports to use up some of that extra energy. Halvorsen managed to return most of the purloined goods to stores in the area because that was the kind of man he was, the kind who is most satisfied when he can set things right with a gentle shove in the proper direction.

After that, Halvorsen saw the Landis boy often, sometimes with just a wave from the cruiser, stopping to talk or offering a ride only if he was in an unmarked car. Halvorsen's marriage had long since evaporated; his ex had custody of their only child, Martha, who'd been encouraged to drop the "H" on her way to the upscale life that Halvorsen could not provide while remaining a good cop. When Marta snagged a lawyer named Lance Betancourt in 1961 and had a daughter of her own, Swede Halvorsen was in his forties; no wife, no sons, no daughter who kept in close touch, though he sent cards and presents at the appropriate times.

By the mid-seventies when he befriended the Landis kid, Halvorsen had quit chewing on the barrel of his .38 on Christmas eves; had come to terms with his life and its limitations. A gun nut, he saw nothing amiss with collecting the occasional weapon that was not implicated in a shooting, and read his way through a library of Elmore Leonard and Louis Lamour. He was also a sports nut. Gary Landis did not know that, at his home games, one of his rooters in the stands carried an LAPD shield.

For years afterward, until his sophomore year at UCLA, Gary Landis did not realize what he owed to the big Swede. His scholarship as a defensive back carried him through school, though he rarely saw playing time on Saturdays unless the Bruins were well ahead. Then his dad, ordinarily the sort who let people handle their own difficulties, swung a bottle of Old Sunny Brook at the head of a kid in a liquor store who was pointing a target pistol at the owner and took three tiny slugs for his trouble. He never regained consciousness and, when they gave Gary the bad news, Halvorsen was with him in the waiting room.

After that, young Landis spent more evenings, maybe once a month, at the Halvorsen bungalow near a flock of those big metal Redondo Beach oil birds that pecked endlessly at the soil for the raw material of smog. They would swig from cans of Oly, sometimes twisting dials of Swede's multiband radio, a device so old it had tubes the size of dinosaur eggs; or tinkering with the blueprinted hemi engine of the Dodge police cruiser Swede had bought at auction and drove chiefly on fishing trips; or arguing politics; and always talking, talking, talking.

Then one day when responding to a loud domestic dispute, Halvorsen jumped a drug-zonked husband and took the point of a butcher knife near the knee from the wife who'd suddenly changed sides. He hobbled for a while and got a desk-sergeant slot where he didn't have to use his legs a lot, then went into plainclothes as liaison with an undercover police network called the Organized Crime Intelligence Division—OCID for short. After that career move, he never broached the subject of law enforcement as a career for Gary. The evening Gary mentioned that he'd switched majors from phys ed to criminal justice, Swede waited until he was alone before he would permit the tears to come. He wasn't sure whether he was crying more from satisfaction or from the knowledge that police work was a great way to dash the illusions of a kid with ideals.

Gary was a UCLA senior in 1981, the night he showed up with a six-pack to find that Halvorsen already had a visitor, one that Halvorsen hadn't expected. Before he could deliver his shave-and-a-haircut knock, Gary heard a firm husky female voice with a growl in it: "Sure I can crash somewhere else, Ampa. All you have to do is throw me out." And then Gary knocked.

Swede let him in, face flushed clear up to his fringe of gray hair, and waved aside Gary's offer to disappear. "Don't you run out on me when I finally need you," the older man warned, not without humor. "Damn kids, never appreciate parents as long as they have 'em." And then he indicated the young woman who stood defiantly, arms crossed, with a Nike bag on the floor beside her.

She was straw blonde, more muscular than willowy, with golden eyes like Swede's, the same strong nose too, not especially pretty in the conventional sense but—*So that's what they mean by striking,* Gary thought.

"Don't tell me; you're the jock," she accused.

"Um," he said, looking toward Halvorsen for help. Halvorsen had told him a little about Janelle Betancourt, as he might have yarned about court intrigue in Monaco. It had never occurred to Gary that Halvorsen, on the rare occasions when he saw his granddaughter, might have mentioned Gary to her.

"They say grandkids are your revenge on your kids," Halvorsen said. "I dunno, maybe they got it backwards. Gary, meet Jan. Gimme that six-pack if you're not using it." With that, he took the Olys and tossed one to each of them.

"You're offering me a beer," she said wonderingly.

"You're over eighteen," Halvorsen grunted. "What're you gonna do, tell your mom on me?" And when she smiled, Gary decided, she was simply bewitching.

Gary stayed longer than usual that night, uneasy over the issue of a young woman fleeing a wealthy home for freedoms that, Halvorsen kept insisting, were mostly imaginary. She was welcome to stay with the aging cop, he said, but only if she let her parents know. "He may be a lawyer, but as a father, I think Lance Betancourt's done okay by you. And if he's not worried numb by now, Martha will be," he added. "You wanta stay, okay. But call 'em, dammit."

Grudging it, she agreed. An hour later, they had made nachos and settled down to play hearts, a murderous game when three-handed, and between chuckling curses at the hands they drew, each of the young people learned oblique bits about the other. She was less dismissive on learning that Gary, his last football season over, spent time in ground school preparing for a private pilot's license. Her dance classes, he decided, accounted for the tendoned splendor of her throat, arms, and legs. In a way, she was more of a jock than he was; though he no longer wanted to be Nolan Cromwell, she still wanted to be Martha Graham.

Driving his old VW bug back to the dorm alone, Gary reflected on the facts. If Swede had been the sort to take revenge, he might have gloated over his granddaughter's defection. Instead, he had forced Jan to do the responsible thing, though it probably meant taking some unwanted phone calls, and probably some heat with them. Gary realized that he and Janelle Betancourt weren't exactly friends yet. But he knew that Jan's reason for leaving home was Fred Penrose, who played electronic bass in a rock group and who had been ordered out of the Betancourt home for reasons Jan did not mention. And if Jan wasn't exactly a friend, Gary thought, then why had the discovery of Fred Penrose struck him like a karate chop over the heart?

During the next few months Gary graduated, applied as a police cadet, and soloed in a Cessna. The day after his FAA examiner made the final sign-off in his logbook, Gary tried to interest Halvorsen in a ride—without the least sign of success. Jan, no longer a tenant but an occasional visitor, was at the house and took him up on his offer. It was the first of several quasi-dates between them, though she made it clear that Freddie Penrose was still The Man and managed to avoid any meeting between the rock musician and the police cadet. Swede Halvorsen knew Freddie by then, which made at least two households where Fred the Head was distinctly unwelcome.

Gary made it onto the force, then through his probationary period,

and managed to squeak through the mine fields laid down by generations
of cops before him because Swede had told him what to expect. Brother
officers had their own ways of finding out what a man was made of. Gary
proved he wasn't mouse meat, unwilling or unable to wade into a
donnybrook; or psycho, downright anxious to provoke one. He applied
for openings in various bear-in-the-air programs, though Vietnam vets
aced him out every time. Then suddenly it was 1984, and one day Gary
realized that he hadn't seen old Swede in, what was it, nearly a year? No,
over a year.

He carried a bottle of Bushmill's to the Redondo Beach bungalow as
his apology, showing up after his shift, and Swede let him in as though no
time had passed. It had, though; Halvorsen's hair fringe was thinner and
grayer, and now he walked more slowly, but in the same black shoes and
white socks. And Swede had retired, and Janelle Betancourt was now
Janelle Penrose, somewhere back east on tour, the last Swede heard.

They talked as peers now, mostly cop talk. Drugs had become such a
problem that the Narc Division had moved from Vice to its own division
in the LAPD. Already in plainclothes, Gary had worked with his opposite
numbers in the Drug Enforcement Administration and liked what he saw
of them.

"Don't tell me; you're going to apply," Swede guessed.

"Already did," Gary admitted. "I know I'm still pretty green, but I'm
getting good at street work. DEA street guys are more like us than like
Feds."

"With the risks, yeah, just don't forget they're Justice Department.
They all wearing their hair like you?" Swede's glance at Gary's ponytail
was eloquent.

"Thought that'd get a rise from you," Gary said.

"Hell, I'd run you in for it. Looks like a screaming bag of assholes."
A big hand went up, palm out. "I know, I know. It's supposed to. Well, if
it works for you, why not? But listen, just in case you make it: DEA shifts
won't be like ours. The older guys don't like night work, so they fill their
young bucks with bullshit and make nighthawks out of 'em."

"I can sleep days."

"Yeah? You'll come in after a shift at eight A.M. and do paperwork 'til noon. They don't pay overtime. With your degree and experience, you might get in as a GS–9—it's civil service, remember? So a lot of your paperwork will be just cleaning paper trails for fuggin' accountants."

Gary swirled the Bushmill's, sniffed, cocked his head. "You trying to talk me out of it, Swede?"

A short pause, deep breath, long sigh. "Nah. Maybe I'm just cynical. You dig deep enough into most law-enforcement bureaucracies, you turn up a lot of shit. Goes with the territory."

"OCID territory, anyhow," Gary said, making it light.

He would recall, years later, the way Halvorsen's face changed to expressionless, his gaze hooded. Looking away to avoid Gary's eyes, he said, "Don't joke about that around the force. And you know better than to quote me. But you know how Mr. Hoover stayed in place so long in the FBI."

"They say he had something on every president. Secret files."

"Just think of that as the rule, not the exception," Halvorsen said carefully. "Files, evidence, whatever works to get some kind of sweet-heart deal at the top. The game you play on the street may not be the game the suits are playing. You just never know, Gary. And that's all I ever intend to say about that."

"And you never mentioned OCID," Gary teased.

"God—damned—right I didn't. When your mouth gets too smart, you wanta watch your ass." Another pause, and a sip. Then: "So! You still flying those tinfoil airplanes around?"

"Keeping current when I can afford to rent one. Don't tell me you'd like a ride."

"I won't," Halvorsen said, and then suggested a fishing trip on the Arizona border. They did not speak again of law-enforcement corruption for years, but Gary would remember the older man's warning at the worst possible time.

4

SOME DEA APPLICANTS ARE HAPPIEST WORKING WITH computers and paperwork. The agency likes that. Others, like Gary Landis, would rather fly light aircraft or tinker with the engines of their Kawasakis, and the DEA likes that, too. Resident agent-in-charge Paul Visconti had run dozens of UC, undercover, street guys in his time but had never met one who needed as little supervision as this youngish retread, Landis, out of the LAPD.

The San Joaquin Valley wasn't Landis's first choice; but then, it hadn't been Visconti's, either. An enormous fertile floodplain created between California mountain ranges, favored by sunlight and irrigated heavily, the valley became a home to many ethnic groups: Latinos, Japanese, Armenians, Basques. Generations of them had tended their orchards and vegetables in relative harmony, and all this success drew more Anglos, and when sleepy little Fresno found itself choking on 600,000 people it also found that it needed men like Gary Landis because, in matters of population density, nothing fails like success.

Paul Visconti, a trim, onetime Chicago detective with ruddy features and a prow of a nose, found himself a victim of success when his handsome wife, Julia, refused a move east and he chose to turn down a DEA promotion. Thanks to a cool temperament, he had grown accustomed to the suit and the wing-tip oxfords, drove a gray Cimarron, and kept his straight dark hair carefully groomed. Sometimes he still envied the lives of his people.

Visconti might have a face-to-face with Landis twice a week, though he thought once a week would have been adequate. Visconti told himself the frequent meetings were to keep the division office happy, but he knew better: he simply liked to live the street life again, vicariously, through the yarns Gary spun about his cases.

Sometimes the story was funny: one perpetrator had brought contraband in from Mexico, all right, but the stuff turned out to be pre-Columbian art and, mistaking Gary for an addict, the man lectured him on the evils of drugs. He was so earnest about it that Gary used his discretion and did not turn this quaint perp over to Customs because, he said, you never knew when a guy that straight might be developed as an informant.

Sometimes the story was scarifying: Once Gary showed up with eight stitches high on his forehead at the hairline, after ducking away from a waifish four-foot-ten teenybopper who had been carrying a razor blade and a load of PCP. She'd been trying for his throat.

From all Visconti could discern, the Landis love life was an iffy proposition. Gary dated a secretary in Tulare, a real-estate broker in Fresno, a grammar-school teacher in Merced. If a lady objected too much to being preempted by his casework—as Visconti could have told him, the marriage-minded ones all did, sooner or later—Gary sought other ladies who did not object so much. Gary mentioned once that the Fresno broker was deeply into sculpture. Visconti, a family man now qualifying as a "suit" with predictable hours, said that was good.

"Yeah?" Gary had rolled his eyes. "You ever waste two hours watching a pretty lady slam clay against a wedging board?"

"No, but she's got something else that keeps her happy."

"So what's your point?"

"If you like things as they are, Gary, that *is* the point," Visconti said. He decided that his advice must have impressed the younger man because, afterward, Gary Landis occasionally asked his expert advice about the ways of women. And Paul Visconti would always reply that there were no experts in that field.

It became clear in time that Landis himself had uncommon street expertise. With his hair grown long, on a bike he *was* a biker. When he combed it and wore a fake Rolex, he *was* your average street scuffler looking for a connection.

As one of the more active young DEA nighthawks, Gary was tapped in May 1991, for an interagency task force, code name ENABLE. Working on loan to another Justice Department agency, the FBI, Gary earned a commendation and some friends in the Bureau in a monumental sting operation.

He was still a nighthawk, one of the street guys, but one night in 1992 he sprinted confidently after a young Latino crack dealer in Tulare. After fifty yards he had lost a step or two; after two blocks down alleys, he had lost his man. That night he called Swede Halvorsen to boost his spirits, and learned that Swede was moving to Bakersfield. A month after that, he visited Swede in his new digs, flying down just for stick time in the Cessna, and learned that Jan Penrose wasn't all that happy with Fred the Head anymore. According to Swede, she had become a health nut. "From what you tell me, she c'd run your butt into the ground, most likely." And he stuck an accusing finger into Gary's softening middle.

After that visit, Gary did his three-mile runs more religiously, but even the NFL's Nolan Cromwell had slowed down in his thirties. Gary began to rely more on subtlety than on his hawklike swoops. In a way, it was the subtlety that got him nailed.

The Merced schoolteacher had given up on Gary for a year when he called one evening early in 1993. He sweet-talked her into a round of miniature golf, then suggested a pizza delivered to her apartment. With a few limes and a fifth of Cuervo Gold to go with the pizza, he said, who knew what might happen?

She knew, she said; no, thanks. They compromised on the Pizza Hut at G and Olive: double cheese, pepperoni, while she explained about her new guy and her scruples about double-dipping. Gary had heard it all before but pretended he hadn't, taking it hard because she wanted him to, but scarfing down an awful lot of the Hut's best for a guy with a freshly broken heart.

Then, perhaps to change the subject, she told him about the sixth graders stoned to their gizzards in Merced. When he forgot the pizza, she knew she had his full attention. "I know what you do, kind of, and we agreed not to talk about it. But my God, Gary, now I'm seeing kids sharing samples in the schoolyard!"

It was like roaches, he told her; if you saw one, you had a lot more in the shadows. He asked what the school was doing about it, and she told him, and he promised to take a look. "You won't see me, but I'll be there."

"I don't want to see you," she said, blushing through her smile. "But I'm glad somebody's interested."

Soon afterward, he took her home, with a hand on her sleeve as she was sliding from the seat of his old Camaro. "Listen: about the schoolyard problem? Don't be too good a citizen. You've told me, but if you get too loud about it, you could get hurt. People who addict little kids don't give a shit who they destroy. It's not like the Mafia; women are fair game to some of these guys."

Her eyes got big, and she squirmed back into the seat, then gave him a Harvey Wallbanger of a kiss, maybe the best one she ever gave him. The kind that said, "good-bye," and also "see what you missed out on." And then he drove home to Fresno.

A few days later, a panel truck parked with its brush trailer less than a block from the schoolyard in question, with "Two Joes Landscape Management" on its sides in artfully aged lettering. One of the joes set about trimming trees near the street. The other joe, with a very long-lensed Nikon and a Porta-John inside the panel truck, was Gary Landis.

It took Gary a week to identify the young man who was supplying a dead drop for a pair of twelve-year-olds in his employ. The drop was a hollow pile of plastic dog turds placed below schoolyard bushes—not the kind of treasure your average kid would be curious about, and it was serviced at night. Once tracked to his Chevy Luv pickup parked two blocks away, the young man was easier to follow, especially with a tracer bug affixed by magnets to the Luv's chassis. A quick DMV check yielded the perp's name: Ralph Guthrie.

After following Guthrie to three more schoolyard drops, and another week of surveillance to learn who supplied the supplier, Gary removed the tiny transmitter from the Luv's chassis. Bugs of that sort are not cheap, and its discovery would have sent a wake-up call to the wrong people. Guthrie was Anglo, but he seemed to be tapped into suppliers who had all the earmarks of La Familia.

The DEA has a particular loathing for the Mexican drug organization called La Familia, in part because of Agent "Kiki" Camarena. It was Camarena whose gruesomely tortured body had turned up in Mexico, and La Familia that had killed him. The Mexican godfather of it all, Pedro Aviles, had already been submachine-gunned to death in Sinaloa by his own *tenientes* back in October 1978. Ernesto Fonseca and Caro Quintero, two of those lieutenants, may have grown too fond of their own products and were eventually put behind bars for their carelessness. Another of those top men, however, took over more territory until, finally, he seemed destined to wear the bloodstained mantle of Aviles. This was Miguel Angel Felix Gallardo, who had excellent connections to the Colombians and Mexican drug-processing plants of his own. Gallardo could hobnob with Mexican politicians while his torture experts clipped pieces from his enemies and recorded the screams for Gallardo.

In Mexico, La Familia operated freely and even intimidated Mexican federals with the old adage, *plata o plombo*, silver or lead; an elegant phrase offering silver first; and if you wouldn't take their silver, you would very likely take a few small pieces of their lead. Felix Gallardo and La Familia had connections in the United States, but it was not known to extend far up the San Joaquin Valley.

Paul Visconti doubted the Familia connection: too far north, he said, and it lacked the volume of a Familia operation. Maybe, Gary replied, they were using our grammar schools to build a hell of a volume. Though night patrols in schoolyards put an end to the original problem, Guthrie was still supplying street dealers; why not ease into the hierarchy through him?

So, in the summer of 1993, a long-haired, gray-eyed specimen took a small apartment in Merced. He cultivated a villainous mustache, drove a pickup, and put in a few weeks with a drywall contractor. His carefully groomed background included an old conviction for DWI and arrests— no convictions—for sale of illegal firearms and for grand theft auto.

Inquiries about his police record were flagged to DEA. He began to drink in a bar frequented by Guthrie, and he answered to the name of Chuck Lane. He also kept his face-to-face briefings, as usual, with Paul Visconti.

Guthrie was not an outgoing sort, and though he had a couple of sitdowns in the bar with Latino types during the following weeks, chiefly he kept to himself. Gary's intuition told him that his quarry must make the first overt move, but began to sense that it wasn't going to happen without some "accidental" arrangement. He arranged it by having two Fresno nighthawks wait for him near Guthrie's blue Luv, one with a bike chain and one with a lug wrench. The idea was to make it look good, but not so good that Gary would need stitches.

When Ralph Guthrie left the bar one night and moved into the parking lot, two guys were whaling the shit out of somebody right next to his wheels, the chain hissing as it flailed across the victim's leather jacket, but the victim was doing okay with his fists. Guthrie wasn't about to get involved, but the two toughs couldn't know that.

"We got company," one of them said.

"That's enough for now," the other said and raised his voice to the dude with the mustache who was now draped over the Luv's fender: "I catch you with her again, we'll be back, Romeo." And they walked away, straightening their jackets, stuffing hardware inside.

Guthrie did not step nearer until the attackers were gone. When he saw his side window smashed, he took an angry step forward, but didn't deliver the kick because now the beaten bozo was more-or-less upright again. "You broke my fucking glass!" Guthrie snarled.

The guy spat and ran his hands through his hair. "Them, not me."

"They gonna pay?" Guthrie's pitiless bark of laughter doubted it. He unlocked the door, swore, fingered the broken pane.

"Showin' up when you did, I guess I owe you. Don't have it now. Pay you back tomorrow. You know the bar around the corner?" The bozo was feeling himself over now to make sure his parts were still working.

"Sure I know it," Guthrie said. "Now I see you in the light, I know you, too."

"Chuck Lane," the bozo said, standing a bit unsteadily.

Ignoring the offered hand, sliding into the Luv, Guthrie gave another mirthless bark. "Naw, you're not." When the poor hammered bastard looked up at him in surprise, Guthrie added, "You're Romeo." And with that, Ralph Guthrie drove away.

"Chuck Lane" wasn't in the bar the next night as promised. But a week later, when legitimate bruises would have receded and with a smudge of eye shadow passing for a bruise on his cheek, he showed up. Guthrie hailed him as "Romeo" and bought him a beer to prime the pump, then reminded him about the window—$74.50 on the receipt.

Chuck Lane cursed good-naturedly and paid from a flash roll, twenties on the outside, consistent with the kind of scuffler who's never as flush as he wants to look. Guthrie understood, or thought he did, and let Lane buy the next round. Lane quit drinking after four beers, saying another DWI was trouble he didn't need, showing a dollop of caution along with a willingness to open up. Guthrie opened up, too, when it turned out they both felt that off-road racing was the best thing going on TV and thought Candlestick Park was a wind tunnel designed to destroy organized sports. Night after night, nuance by nuance, Gary eased himself into Guthrie's life.

Three weeks later, Gary could report that he was now a gofer paid by the Hermosillo Cartel, but perhaps not trusted all that much yet. Someone made discreet inquiries into Chuck Lane's rap sheet, but not discreet enough to avoid being ID'd by one of Visconti's men. It was the first solid evidence to the DEA that Felix Gallardo's people were expanding so far north. At that point, Paul Visconti told Gary just how far they wanted him to crawl out on the limb. Gary would be an essential probe in a sting operation in which *Los Hermanos Hermosillo* would make connections to U.S. crime figures in Las Vegas.

Gary's connection in Vegas was real, though the "criminals" were DEA men. The central plan was to lure Gallardo into a sitdown somewhere on U.S. soil. And because Gallardo was an exceedingly wary man, the DEA's game must be played without haste. That meant Gary Landis would be living out on that limb so long he'd grow feathers—if he lasted.

When a man goes all the way undercover, his life changes profoundly. Gary's meetings with Visconti would be fewer; he would travel and drink and carouse in new ways; in short, as felons put it, he must live The Life. He would have an emergency number to call, but most of his calls to Visconti would be through a scrambler circuit using a special frequency built into a commercial cellular telephone. It was an old trick borrowed from the CIA: when the antenna was halfway out, the special circuit energized.

The night Visconti handed over the cellular unit, Gary felt as if he were about to step into a moon rocket alone, and said so.

"You've still got me at Mission Control," Visconti joked, because Gary seemed more keyed up than usual. "I can't know who's next to you if I need to call, so it'll come in from a young lady, for Chuckie. If you can take my call, say so and deploy your antenna. If you can't, fob her off. If you're blown and you need help when she calls, cuss her. Any old curse will do. By the way: when your antenna's on the scrambler circuit, on or off it works like a tracer bug. Saves time looking for you. Simple enough."

Gary may have been thinking about Camarena. "So how likely do you think I'll need that feature?"

"Not very. You're positioned just right," Visconti told him truthfully, looking him in the eye. Then he added, "And we don't have a better man for it." This was only half a lie. Though more experienced agents could have been put in place, Gary had one special qualification: unlike Kiki Camarena, he had no family to mourn him.

5

NO ONE TOLD GARY THIS TIME THAT HE WAS INVOLVED IN another interagency sting because, Paul Visconti's chief warned, this street guy Landis not only lacked the need to know; if he were blown, he needed *not* to. But twice, at brief meetings with other agents on Visconti's orders, Gary sensed that the guys weren't DEA. They used the right jargon, but as if they weren't quite comfortable with it.

In fact, they were CIA, part of the task force. One of them was the nervous type, admitting to Gary that he "had a feeling" about this case. What kind of feeling? Just a feeling, he repeated, making clear that it wasn't a good feeling. What he would not tell Gary was that occasionally he felt a spectral presence hovering nearby, not necessarily a player, just—watching, like some alien anthropologist. Perhaps curious about his life-style, or perhaps about his contacts. They could have exchanged premonitions on that, though Gary chalked it up as the curiosity of La Familia.

Meanwhile, the fortunes of Chuck Lane were looking up. Flush from gofer services rendered, he took a better apartment in Merced, upgraded his stereo, bought a better grade of Scotch. He didn't bother with tricks that would tell him if and when his place got a toss, half-hoping they would, because he kept nothing there that Chuck Lane shouldn't have. He drove a little two-door BMW now with rallye tires; he took Ralph Guthrie and a Latino contact to Vegas where they enjoyed freebies offered by a pair of tanned, sleek, pinky-ringed, big-city-talking gents in buttery soft loafers and pastel shirts who were in on the sting. He was entrusted briefly by La Familia to hold sizable chunks of cash which he never, *ever* skimmed because he figured somebody was keeping tabs on that just to test him.

"Call it a basic course in staying alive," he told Visconti on the scrambler circuit one day. "Scumbag 101; you never know when you'll get the pop quiz that could get you popped."

"From all we can tell, you're running clean," Visconti said.

"Paul, you have no idea how dirty I'm running," Gary sighed. "But I know what you mean. It's nice to know; I feel a lot better."

But Gary quit feeling good the evening he returned from a gofer job in Bakersfield. He had two pieces of junk mail in his box, but that wasn't where he found the letter. He found that shoved under his door—no return address—in a cheap white envelope marked "DESTROY." He turned on the living-room TV and sat down, swinging his Nikes up on his new ottoman, holding the envelope up to a 250-watt bulb before opening it. He'd seen photos of guys who had opened the wrong letter without checking for a tiny spring detonator.

It was typed on plain paper, not from a word processor. *Somebody didn't trust his own computer terminal,* he thought, before the brief full-caps message really struck home:

PAUL IS TRADING YOU FOR BIGGER FISH. TRUST NONE OF US, THIS IS ALL I CAN DO. WE CAN WRAP HIM UP IN A FEW MONTHS BUT FOR NOW YOU ARE ON YOUR OWN. FIND A HOLE.

Unsigned, of course. No key phrase that would narrow it down, beyond the reference to "us." His first suspicion was another test by La Familia; but if they knew Visconti's name, he had already flunked. *One of the other street guys?* Possible; and if the note was actually sent by one of his fellow agents, then the cartel would know Paul, anyhow; in which case it was too late to think about testing.

Then: *Bullshit,* he decided. *If there's anything in this world I can trust, it's Paul Visconti.* His cellular phone was in the BMW and he needed to contact Visconti ASAP. He snapped off the lamp next to his chair and, in the dim illumination of the TV, headed for the door. That was when the big pane in his living room window disintegrated—a dozen slugs fanning through the room, two of them into the chair he'd vacated, others impacting the kitchen partition and its wooden trim. He did not think about the precise timing of it all. He was thinking that the muzzle blasts from outside came from the direction of the street, but weren't all that loud; an Ingram with a suppressor, maybe?

By the time Gary hit the carpet it was all over but he couldn't know it yet, scrambling in a fast crawl for the Beretta he kept between the cushions of his couch. Weapon in hand, he snapped off the TV, made it to the shadowed bedroom, risked a glance outside, along the path between apartment buildings. This wasn't L.A., where folks knew to keep their heads down, and some potbellied citizen in an undershirt was already leaning out into the dusk from an upstairs window next door, calling over his shoulder: "Shit, how would I know? Firecrackers, maybe."

Gary hurried back to the living room and, using the kitchen cleaver, chopped away the wooden trim where one of the slugs had impacted. It had mushroomed a bit but was still slender, its boattail longer than some, roughly .30 caliber. Maybe one of the 7.62 mm rounds from a Kalashnikov, certainly not one of the fat little slugs from an Ingram. And ever since the Cubans had fed Russian weapons into Mexico, La Familia had favored the lightweight AKM version of a Kalashnikov, an assault rifle with a folding stock so you could hide it under a coat, some with suppressors. That slug wasn't exactly a signature, but it was as strong a suggestion as Gary needed.

There was another number he could call—right from the phone in his apartment—and this was just the sort of occasion for it. And yet, Gary hesitated; could he really trust his life to Visconti's honesty, when somebody with inside information had just warned him about it? Old Swede Halvorsen had sworn that the suits didn't always play the same game you were playing. And there was the Irish saying: trust everybody, but cut the cards. Gary decided against making that call until he was on fast wheels.

Give the Merced police five minutes—you know damn well somebody called them. Do I want to be here? Maybe not. Chuck Lane would disappear in the Beemer, probably call Ralph Guthrie to ask what the hell was going on. *Yeah, and that BMW could be bugged by now, but I haven't been out of it long enough for a booby trap. Well, I can check it for bugs later.* Somewhere in the back of his mind was the question: *practical joke?* Agents had been known to pull some pretty raw stunts on guys they didn't like. But they'd been canned for less than this. . . .

While he thought it out, he was cramming his best pair of loafers, dark socks, dark pullover, and gray slacks into a flight bag, leaving room for his laptop and—*damn right, why not?*—the packet of hundreds and the one of fifties he was holding for those sweethearts in La Familia.

Roughly once a week, he rode his Kawasaki, but it was loud and gave no protection. The Beemer it was, then. As Gary Landis, he was one-third owner of a little Cessna, but it was hangared in a suburban Fresno airpark, an hour's drive away. He would decide during the drive whether to use it tonight. He went out the back way toward the tenant carports, cradling his Nike bag in his arms with one hand in the bag holding his Beretta, safety off.

He had one instant of adrenaline rush when he saw the old four-door Plymouth stopped in the parking driveway because it was blocking two cars and one of them was his Beemer. But the Plymouth's hood was up and he could hear a starter grinding, and its driver-side door was open, the interior light revealing a middle-aged woman at the wheel, lipstick bright as it outlined her imploring smile tossed in his direction. "I don't know what else to do, dear," she called as Gary swept past, safetying his Beretta, thrusting it inside his jacket against the small of his back.

Now he could see the younger woman, maybe a daughter, peering under the vast hood of the Plymouth in the gloom. He unlocked the Beemer; tossed the flight bag inside; shut the door and sighed.

"I'm awfully sorry," said the older woman as Gary appeared at her side. "It just died on me. Do you know anything about motors?"

"I can't see anything," said the younger one, coming around from Gary's left. "Are we out of gas?" At his quick glance, she smiled for him, too, smoothing long blonde hair with a casual hand, then added softly to him, "Her eyes aren't very good. What does the gauge say?"

And as he leaned in, his head brushing the older woman's cheek, he felt something like a dull bee sting in his left hip. Both women were talking at the time, and he saw that the gauge showed half a tank. And then he realized that the driver's right hand held a silenced handgun, and that its muzzle was under his chin, and that the bee sting was still stinging.

"Not a sound," the woman said, six inches from his ear.

As Gary moved back, he heard the younger one say, "It's all in him," but now in a huskier voice, and he lifted his hands hoping that someone would see this tableau, that the police would come, that he could slump convincingly enough to reach the Beretta in the small of his back. But after a long frozen moment, his eyelids began to flutter and his facial muscles seemed to dissolve, though he was still conscious.

Then his legs began to buckle, and he knew whatever he did he'd better do it instantly, because that sting at his hip was from an injection and he was losing it.

If the woman had been willing to shoot, she probably would have already. He recalled the old cliché that if you wanted folks to come running, you didn't scream, "Rape." "Fire! Pol—," he began, but the young one was a hell of a lot stronger than he could have imagined, clapping a wadded scarf over his mouth from behind with one hand, the other arm holding his own against his side. Now the Beretta might as well have been miles away, and suddenly so was everything else as the two of them fell onto macadam and his arms would not obey his orders.

A moment later, he knew he was being lifted by both women, but something was very, very wrong with his entire body as they tumbled him in the backseat footwell. The last thing he saw was a blanket the young one spread over him.

"Don't forget the client's bag. It's in his car," said the older one, and then a confusion of sounds that became muffled, and when the Plymouth's engine rumbled to life, Gary Landis's own life was ebbing.

6

ROMANA DROVE THE PLYMOUTH CALMLY, EXPERTLY, with one eye on the rearview, breaking no rules of traffic. She had driven that route a dozen times alone while Andy was at work during the past week, turning at West Avenue and then the few blocks to Grogan, where she had rented the old frame house for its double garage and the fact that it was two minutes from Chuck Lane's apartment. You learned to use your advantages as you found them, and one advantage in a town of Merced's size was that modern apartment complexes stood aloof, their skirts of lawn gathered around them, isolated from onetime farm homes by two minutes—and forty years. "Check his pulse again," she ordered, and Andy paused at his labor, leaning back between the seats, to fumble for the wrist of the dying spy.

"I still get one. Thready, but—no, wait. Stopped." Andy's words were hushed, as though the presence of death invested the corpse with a kind of purity. He set to work again, his upper body twisted back and down while she drove. She could hear the snick of his razor-edged little shears as Andy worked, filling a plastic bag with the raw material of his specialty. He was sealing the bag as Romana turned in at the old concrete tiles that defined their driveway. Andy peered at his tricky little illuminated Timex and depressed a stud. "One hundred forty-odd seconds since injection. And look what we have here," he added, pulling a 9 mm Beretta from the footwell. "Do we keep it?"

"You know better. We drop it with him, after you wipe it down. If the client is ever found, that makes it look more like an accidental fall. Put it away," she commanded.

He hopped from the car and raised the big overhead garage door to let Romana drive in, hauling it down again before she was out of the car. Romana noted that, where he had performed his jobs so quickly as to attract notice during their earliest commissions together, he had developed the proper casual appearance with practice. *We will make a professional of you yet*, she thought, *in a profession I created.*

Andy's Pinto had been left with its nose against the front wall to gain more room behind it and he had its little trunk lid open in seconds, his slender flashlight still in his teeth. The luggage space had been lined with a ten-mil polyethylene drop cloth, a cheap disposable protection against body fluids. Romana opened the right rear door of the big sedan and, using her own flashlight, flipped the blanket away from the client, donning gloves to check the pockets, replacing the coins and the pocketknife after swift, expert examination. She pulled the wire-stocked Kalashnikov from under the client and left it in the backseat under the blanket.

"Let's go, Mom," said Andy, standing behind her, betraying the impatience of his youth as she removed one of her gloves and rechecked for a pulse.

Nothing. A tug on the mustache produced no result. She lifted one of the eyelids with her thumb and saw the pupil already fixed in its dead stare, unresponsive to light. The fingernails were turning blue, the cyanotic hue of death. "A good drug," she admitted, tugging the glove on again, grabbing for the shoulders, letting Andy worm his way past her to help drag the body out. Because Andy seemed to handle the remains with something like reverence, she made a special effort to show the opposite; letting the head drop a few inches to the floor, giving the chest a swift kick for good measure. How many times must she show him that these corpses deserved no respect!

A truly dead weight seems to multiply, and they worked hard to lift the body up, then swung it into the Pinto's luggage space where Romana dropped her end—the head and trunk—heavily. Andy folded the legs in, smoothing the plastic drop cloth, prodding the body into a position of fetal flexure, then helped Romana arrange a waiting blanket over it. They did not use the same blanket because, knowing how police forensics could create a chain of evidence from microscopic strands of the same blanket in two vehicles, they were careful to minimize their risks. Later she would cleanse the Plymouth thoroughly of evidence, but before that, Andy would do the same with the Pinto. Not even a vagrant hair would escape that kind of attention.

Andy dropped the trunk lid and then they were changing roles, Romana wiping away the bright lipstick, roughening her eyebrows with her thumbs, removing her wig, slipping out of the low-heeled pumps and into men's bulky athletic shoes, shucking the frilly sweater and padded brassiere, all of her discarded role going into an opaque garbage bag. She slipped into a man's dark pullover of rough weave and followed it with a nylon windbreaker. The old slacks already had cuffs, and her wallet was already in a hip pocket. The battered hat over her own short, straight black hair completed the transformation; Romana Dravo was no longer a tall, moderately attractive woman in early middle age, but Roman Dravo, a fiftyish man of barely medium height and sharply chiseled, almost Asiatic cheekbones. The ID in her wallet was also that of Roman Dravo, male Caucasian, eyes brown, age fifty-three.

Andy's transformation to his standard identity, Andrew Soriano, took a few seconds longer, and Romana loosed a faint smile when he had to rip the bra off, failing to operate its hooks properly. She saw no point in remarking on that; she had been unhooking her brassieres for forty years, since her handlers had first decreed that she must wear them, and for the first year she had been as clumsy as the boy was tonight.

No longer a boy, she corrected herself, *not for years now,* watching Andy thrust clothing into the plastic bag. He was not thickset nor wide of shoulder, and his height was an inch less than her own—had not risen a millimeter, in fact, since he went away for his education in the mid-eighties. In the hard shadow of flashlights, the cords at his shoulders traced hollowed lines of strength to throat and to biceps, triceps, and those forearms were so powerfully sinewed that he could never pull off a female role in short sleeves, no matter how practiced his falsetto.

While he continued his lightning role change she moved forward and started the Pinto's engine. Its rasp steadied, still muffled because of the flexible metal hose that ran from the tip of its exhaust pipe to coupled sections of two-inch galvanized pipe. The pipe doubled back to run beneath the Pinto, finally to protrude out the front of the detached garage, so that the little car could idle for as long as necessary without poisoning their air. Andy had argued for this idea while still in his teens: if she had taught him that aircraft engines required a full warmup before performing with maximum reliability, why should they do less for their cars? It had been one of his earliest additions to her craft, a special source of pride to him.

In a day or so, Romana would return to the rental house and dismantle the pipe alone, erasing every shred of evidence of the two of them, a chore she actually enjoyed because each time she cleaned up after a "commission"—self-commissioned to be sure—she deliberately pitted herself against the minds of the forensics specialists who might come one day, seeking evidence. But the highest marks in her profession came when no one knew to seek evidence, nor where to begin that search. Far better than a cold trail was no trail at all.

Moments later, Romana backed the Pinto out in darkness while Andy closed the overhead door. The backseat was full of legitimate fishing equipment, canned food, cheap bedrolls, a two-man tent; everything they might want if they were starting out very late to stream-fish the tributaries that fed Millerton Lake, in the Sierra foothills near Fresno. Andy had, in fact, already mentioned such an outing to colleagues in the lab.

They had scarcely passed the Merced city limit headed south on Highway 99 when Romana glanced over to see what Andy had in his lap. "My God, what are you doing with that in here?" she said angrily.

"Spoils of war," he replied, unchastened. He held up a bundle of banknotes. "Hundreds—and there's more. Must be close to ten thousand in cash."

"You are an idiot, Andrew. It may be marked and if we should be stopped now, for whatever reason—"

"I'm carrying my lab ID, and this is my car. Nobody will notice the bag, and if they do, this will be something I spotted along the highway. And if they go digging into the trunk, it won't matter a damn anyhow, so what's the big complaint?"

We had agreed to leave the proceeds in the garage for now, but you changed a detail without asking, she thought, yet this was not a time to argue it. "Ten thousand? Hardly worth the trouble unless there is another treasure we can use."

"A change of clothes—not much else."

She knew what he was thinking; this was not one-tenth the value of most exfiltration kits they had taken. If they had waited and followed him, the spy might have led them to a much greater cache of goods. "It's always a judgment call," she said. "He had the bag with him, and I doubt we could have kept within range of that little car of his. Oh—you got the tracer from his car?"

"Of course. Switched off, in the Plymouth's glove compartment. Weren't you watching?"

"By now, I should not have to watch you every second," she said dully.

"But you do anyhow," he replied, mumbling it because the little flashlight was again clamped between his teeth as he counted money in gloved hands. He zipped the bag up and grunted in disappointment. "Only sixty-seven hundred to the penny, pretty much a waste of time. We could have given him more time. Wait—I have his wallet here."

She cursed under her breath; another unnecessary risk! Andy held too much stock in the identification badge he carried. One day he might run into a cop who remained unimpressed. The California Fish & Game Forensics Laboratory badge was convincing enough; for that matter, it was genuine. Though Andy Soriano did most of his work in the lab, sparse state funding meant that he was sometimes required to go into the field, and for that they gave him a warden's badge. Basically, a game warden was a peace officer, capable of arrests and authorized to carry a sidearm. But the time might come when the cop who checked that ID had once been harassed for a few undersized trout, and then . . . "Must I ask, Andrew?"

"Oh, sorry. Charles Alvin Lane, DMV license, Visa card and a MasterCard. Thirty or so in cash; don't worry, I'll stuff it back in with his change. Couple of snapshots of glamourpussy, Costco card, Triple-A membership, Social Security, a rubber in foil. No secret compartments I can find. We can do a better check back at The Place."

She did not respond, thinking instead how easily he dismissed the charms of young women. "Glamourpussy"; not a word she had ever used, but it implied the disdain she had worked so hard to ingrain in him. After all the training she had lavished on her foster son, an infatuation with some brainless beauty would mean utter disaster. If not for him, certainly for Romana.

"We may find something yet," she said. "I once deciphered a Luxembourg account number from a nonsense word printed on a postage stamp. The letters were—"

"Coded to a telephone dial, and you netted a quarter-million from it. You told me," he said quickly.

Am I some garrulous old fool, then, boring him with repetitious stories? That would happen one day, no doubt. She was almost—what was it?— sixty-one years old according to the calendar; nearer her late forties by the accounting of any mirror, with a slight resemblance to that tennis pro, Navratilova. Her thighs and buttocks were still firm. She could still chin herself, sometimes twice, and her weight had not fluctuated more than a few pounds in all her adult life. All that testosterone might have something to do with her muscle tone, with what she had come to regard as her unique good fortune.

Early in life, living as a boy simply because, even with no penis, she had been born with a vestigial scrotal sac and testes that never descended, she had been taught by her parents to keep her difference secret. Later, Soviet physicians had shown great kindness and greater curiosity, explaining that she had a structurally variant Y chromosome—a very rare phenotype—and that she must make the best of it as others had.

There were words for creatures with such genetic problems, most of them scornful: freak, hermaphrodite, freemartin. The Soviets were quite good at rearranging one's views. They explained that, as a female, she would have certain advantages: she would never have to bear children and would not enjoy the sex act enough to let it trouble her, though she could indulge in it. After the minor operation to remove that tiny scrotal sac while leaving the testes intact, she was taught to regard herself as specially gifted. With her inherent male strength and aggressiveness she might have been trained as an athlete; another Stella Walsh, perhaps, an XY female Olympic sprinter.

But the KGB handlers had a different life in mind for Skander Masaryk, and completed his/her education in operating in any sexual role that might arise.

Skander never forgot the kind advice of the doctors, however, and adopted femaleness by simple preference. Skander was so cautious about this secret that, even after the rape of her country by the USSR and her defection to the Americans, she used delaying tactics against a thorough physical exam. A good thing, too: to this day she had no doubt that the men who tried to garrote her on a Virginia campus were CIA. (Her physical strength and glandular responses had taken them by surprise.) It was really no great task to dispose of one body in a culvert and to leave the other in her place in a burning car.

That was when young Masaryk chose a life of vengeance, to prey on the predators, and no one was better equipped to identify an agent in the field; a client, as it were, from whom she took her deadly commissions. As she had expected, Soviet Bloc people rarely had much worth the taking; before her "death," she had avenged herself by giving up some of their operations to the Americans.

In a way, she felt, both sides had killed Skander Masaryk. But over the years, Masaryk's ghost had continued to extract a terrible price from the West. To her knowledge, no intelligence professional had ever grown wealthy by preying on veteran professionals in this way.

Now, enriched by the hoarded treasures of over a score of victims, she could retire at any time, while Andrew could carry on this unique pursuit by himself. Even after she died, this was a revenge she could keep on taking.

Long ago, Romana had realized that, in some respects, she fitted the definition of a serial killer. Because she kept herself current on such shared information ploys as VICAP, the Violent Criminal Apprehension Program, Romana carefully studied all aspects of this FBI program wherever they appeared in open literature. She studiously avoided tactics that became too routine, though there were only so many ways you could do these things. Her clients had been garroted, bludgeoned, bled, burned, shot, poisoned slowly—a mistake she had not repeated—and quickly; and in the case of a particularly irksome Iranian, left trussed with wire, gagged and weighted in marsh grass at low tide in a mud flat near San Francisco Bay. Tidal action erases footprints, but takes hours. That drowning had been a slow process.

So serial killers tended to be male loners, alienated from close family ties? Very well, she had obtained the best possible camouflage by posing as a health-services nurse and stealing a two-year-old from a bracero camp nursery. With that act she became a single mother with a toddler. She did not use the same method of client disposal twice until years had elapsed, and made an avocation of studying new ways to perform her lethal commissions.

It was Andrew who had discovered a humane injection used on rogue animals, called the Thomas Concoction. Essentially, it was an analog of curare injected with potassium chloride. In the briefest time, it stopped first the voluntary muscles, then the heart. It had worked so well tonight that she resolved to use it again in a year or so.

Without doubt, she decided, she had kept herself conditioned in part through her constant, long-term surveilling of potential clients and the deadly intellectual gaming it entailed. *I have kept this body in good repair,* she thought. But all the sun protection and creams and lotions in the world could not prevent those damned wrinkles from appearing at her eyes and throat almost imperceptibly at first, then so clearly that she had already paid for two sessions of cosmetic surgery in Mexico. Well, she could afford it.

Presently she turned off at Madera, then took the winding blacktop past Millerton Lake and the hamlet of Auberry, headlights spearing through the stands of scrub oak and, along creek sides, sturdy sycamore. Gray masses of granite shouldered from the soil here, with an occasional glitter of quartz reflected from the Pinto's lights. The road contained sudden twists and dips that took all of her concentration until, a few miles beyond Auberry, she slowed for the final turnoff.

The gate was little more than rusted barbed wire and posts secured by baling wire. The metal sign, targeted long ago by some idiot with a shotgun, proclaimed *"POSTED,* NO TRESPASSING." It had hung there for many years, a vain hope of protection for the miner's shack that squatted decaying not far from the road. She had not used this disposal site for years, but checked recently to make certain that it had never been discovered. During her hike to the site a week before, she had seen no evidence of recent activity on the claim, but Romana's small satisfactions lay in disposing of every tiny risk. And now she saw that no fresh tire tracks had preceded hers.

She switched off her lights and let Andy handle the gate, grinding forward in low gear, waiting for Andy to take his seat on the right front fender, a dangerous perch with the Pinto's front end bobbing through the underbrush. After careful consideration, she had left her night-vision goggles at The Place, vowing to buy a more compact unit. The one she owned was an ungainly device, and a flashlight beam could blind it temporarily. Andy's flashlight played along the path for her, though it was none too steady, and she found no unpleasant surprises on the way to the shaft.

For over a century, men had sought their big strikes in this region, some mining copper ore, a few following veins of gold into the earth, some with competent mine shoring, some innocent of the most basic safety measures. The shaft Andy had found here, long ago, had not been worked for generations. The original miner had cleverly elected not to run wagon tracks nearer than twenty yards from the shaft, allowing scrub oaks to remain as a final camouflage.

She helped Andy drag the client from the Pinto and took the ankles while he held the shoulders, flashlight again in his teeth, stumbling along toward the shaft. She realized that the grunts he vented were chuckles at his own clumsiness. "Break an ankle and you'll see how funny this is," she warned.

They stopped at the mouth of the shaft; not a truly vertical hole, but slanting down at a steep angle to follow an ancient vein. Some giant might insert a telephone booth down the hole, but nothing much wider. Once, in daylight, she had seen how the shaft leveled out some thirty feet down, and that water was standing at that level. Andy let his end go at the edge of the shaft. "Just a minute, let me replace those bills," he panted, clumsy with his gloves, forcing the small wad of money from the wallet into the client's pocket. If ever this one was found, even with the wallet missing, an accident would seem more likely than robbery.

"To the right, not in the middle," she cautioned, because the client might be caught on wooden debris toward the left side. Then she let go and let the weight tumble it down and down into darkness. The last sound was a sodden splash, far down the shaft.

"Thought I'd forget?" Andy shone his light on the client's handgun, displaying it like a trophy, then tossed it into the shaft and listened to its clatter and thump.

"You *did* wipe it clean of your prints," she said softly, more question than declaration.

"Oh, Jesus!" He gasped and clapped his hands against the sides of his head, turning to gaze into the shaft. She swore and took one step forward, and then, flicking her light toward his face, she saw the gleam of his teeth as his frame shook in silent mirth. "Naturally, I did," he said then.

"Stupid ass!" she burst out. "You do play the most deadly games!"

She turned on her heel and was halfway back to the Pinto before she heard his reply, good-natured as usual: "The acorn never falls far from the tree, mother mine . . ."

7

ANDY'S GOOD HUMOR WAS PROMPTED BY NECESSITY; HE had learned that relentless pursuit of a better mood could usually make it real. During the drive back toward Millerton Lake, he managed to infect his mom with it, aping the expression he had noted on the face of Charles Lane as the man felt Romana's weapon pressing beneath his chin, asking Romana to recount other commissions when a spy first realized he was to be, in her special jargon, a client. He had heard most of it before, knew her stories the way a Bosnian Serb schoolboy knows ethnic history. He also knew that the best way to improve her mood was to play student to her favorite role of teacher. So, when she launched into a memory fifteen years old, Andy's thoughts were diverted to his own boyhood.

He could not remember when she had found him, she'd said, a toddler abandoned by migrant workers in Southern California. She had always been severe with him, but had also taught him strict self-control. As a mother figure, she was not the sort to smother him with affection. His earliest memory was the terror he felt when she warned him of others who might take him away from her, despite the expensively forged adoption papers. After all, Romana was the only security he knew.

From preschool age, he had learned how to assume a role, to lie with perfect ease, yet never shade the truth to his mom. At five he could shed real tears at her command; at six, had served as bait for an Englishman who, Romana had discovered, was not only an intelligence agent, but was addicted to dalliances with small boys. Andy had not wept when he watched the man die.

Though Andy had grown up knowing his family life was vastly different from most, it had never seemed strange to him. In recent years, he had reflected that, had Romana been a cannibal, he would have shared her meals without a second thought. In a way, he now knew, she was exactly that; a consumer of a select group of men.

Yet he needed to fit into the world of convention, to understand ordinary norms. Romana's solution to the problem had been ingenious. She leased a home on reservation land and enrolled him in the nearest small-town school.

The Yomo Indian reservation, near Millerton Lake, adjoins another reservation and had been administered by tribal elders since early in the century. Some reservations are dirt-poor and look it, but when the Yomo sold much of their land for mining claims they held out for fair compensation. The upshot was that, as long as a Yomo Indian chose to live on tribal land, he did not need to work and could spend a modest tribal income as he liked.

Romana had shown the boy vendor stands in western Washington reservations where, on any day of the year, the passerby might buy fireworks the size of a trench mortar, illegal almost everywhere else in the Western Hemisphere. On Oregon reservations, the visitor is encouraged to risk a bit of cash in tribal casinos where the state government cannot prevent gambling. On California reservations, Asian card games add a modern touch; for a generation, Fresno's Hmong immigrants have cooled their gambling fever with the help of America's earliest immigrants. From the first time she saw the Yomo reservation and its casino, Romana had told him, she knew that ordinary laws and law enforcement stopped at the tribal boundary.

Because the courts tend to let a tribe keep its old ways as well, those Yomos who chose to live traditionally in half-submerged sod houses could do so, a stone's throw from a neighbor's mobile home or a standard ranch-style California bungalow. To a Yomo, building codes were a white man's bad joke. Romana discovered that a few reservation houses were for rent or lease, though the land was never for sale.

As it happened, a Yomo had built two modern houses of concrete block and wooden framing, in their own declivity overlooking the lake. The Yomo had then changed his mind, or simply lost it among empty wine bottles, and had died without ever moving in. The tribe, then, could do as it pleased with the structures. One house had never been quite finished and, decades later, sat with no connected plumbing, bundles of interior trim rotting nearby under tuft grass. Twenty yards away sat its finished twin, complete with three-car garage and served by a graveled blacktop that thrust into a meadow and simply stopped, as though in astonishment, with Millerton Lake stretching away below in the distance.

For Romana, the house, in such a site, could not have been a happier find. Here she had brought the boy and set up her workshop, had left him alone for days sometimes, could pursue her special calling with no worries about social workers or close neighbors. During those years, Romana might leave the boy alone for as much as a week, seeking her prey through connections in the Washington, D.C. area. She had used audio pickups in her visits to the Vienna Inn, a known hangout for CIA employees. The name of a Company-connected psychiatrist had been enough, after she spent three days bugging the man's office, to yield names of two agents stationed in the San Francisco region. And in California, newsmen had their favorite bars where Romana, paying for endless double Scotches, had engaged reporters in "casual" discussion about active intelligence agents. Never very far from her work, she was often far from young Andrew.

And, in his way, Andy had been happy with the place—in their phrase, with implied capitals, The Place. Endowed with a lively curiosity, he had enjoyed classes in the three-room grammar school a mile down Millerton Road from the reservation. The foothills weather was rarely savage enough to prevent his walking both ways. If his mom forbade him to play after school with reservation kids, or any others, for that matter, he could still enjoy classmates in school or at recess.

Forbidden to invite other children to The Place, often preparing his meals alone, Andy lavished affection on his pets. When Romana found the hamster he had stolen from school and the wire cage he had built in preparation for it, she praised him for his intelligent planning, then brought home an armload of translucent plastic cage modules. It did not escape her notice that the boy somehow recognized his kinship with small caged animals. She was amused, even touched, by the tubular plastic hamster tunnel he assembled; it was a deliberate copy of the tunnel he had helped her dig from The Place to the garage of the nearby vacant house.

She brought him books on burrowing pets. Then, when he patiently treated a white-crowned sparrow until its wing had healed, she brought the materials for him to build a walk-in cage and provided books, some of them advanced and expensive, on land birds. Long ago trained as an engineer, Romana taught the boy the rudiments of structures, of triangulation and, in the escape tunnel, of mine shoring. No wonder, then, with his succession of small birds and mammals, that his isolation did not seem impossibly confining to the boy, though he regretted it more in high school in the nearby town of Briant. He simply grew toward manhood without questioning the fact that the world was a lonely place— and that his mom spent a great deal of time searching out men who did not deserve to live in it.

While other children watched cartoons on television, Andrew Soriano had built cages in the family room, or stood beside his mom in the bedroom she had turned into a windowless workshop. He knew the fragrance of acid-core solder as she made deft connections in tiny transmitters; understood the workings of night-vision monoculars as she increased their magnification; learned how a vehicle could be tracked by a transceiver that, once emplaced with a magnet, would signal its location only in response to a signal she sent. At twelve, he was comfortable wearing a body mike; at fourteen, he could have built its transmitter. But the one time she caught him in her workshop without permission, he preferred not to recall. Some memories were too painful to . . .

"You're not listening," she said.

He snapped from reverie to the present moment: "Sorry," he said, seeing the Pinto's lights veer at the reservation turnoff. "I'm wondering how you pinpointed Lane in the first place." Phrased that way, not exactly a lie. He *had* wondered about that.

"His contact," she said. "He was part of a CIA group I've been monitoring. They're connected to a drug ring in some way. The tapes aren't very specific, but those people have a history of helping smugglers. Our Mr. Lane, though, seemed to be isolated from the others. And if he was that far under cover, he probably was experienced enough to keep a kit ready." From many hours of audiotapes they knew the term, "spooker"; but Romana preferred the earlier phrase, "exfiltration kit."

She went on, "Also, in such a job he might disappear for any of several reasons. I picked up several names; he was the best candidate, I thought. But sixty-seven hundred dollars!" Her humorless laugh suggested that Lane should have had more reasons than that; should have been more provident for a future that, thanks to Romana, he had not lived to enjoy.

She drove past the casino and parked behind a series of mobile homes, among the accumulated debris of Native American families who saw no sense in having junk hauled away when, in a hundred years or so, it would rot away anyhow. Andy waited patiently, understanding her tactic. For the next few minutes, parked in shadow behind an engineless Pontiac, she could spot any vehicle that turned off the main road. Perhaps the surveillance tail that she had evaded for so many years and was still awaiting with unflagging suspicion.

Meanwhile her eyes were growing accustomed to the dark so that, when she restarted the Pinto and eased it to the dirt road nearby, she did not need to use her headlights again. They were only a half-mile from The Place, and no one could be less inquisitive about such things than Native Americans. Their attitude, it seemed, was that people did things because they felt like it, and other people's choices were other people's business.

The little car trudged its way up a steep incline, down another, around several bends, Romana squinting more than she had a year previous, with a final turn onto gravel for the final hundred yards or so. She triggered the garage-door unit and drove in, wheels straddling a metal pipe tipped with flex hose, lights revealing old cages that Andy kept intending to dispose of. "I'll take the bag," she said.

He did not follow her into the kitchen immediately, but attended to his duties with the industrial-vacuum unit, first folding the filmy plastic drop cloth so that, whatever crumbs of evidence it might hold, the entire bundle would fit into a grocery sack to be tossed, anonymous trash, into a mall Dumpster on his way to his own garage apartment in Fresno. Had he found any blood, he would have burned that plastic in the fireplace. Working in the state lab, he knew only too well how DNA matching from a bloodstain could ruin the best of plans.

Then he clamped a work light to the trunk lid and vacuumed the trunk repeatedly. Next, wearing cotton gloves, he took a roll of duct tape from Romana's supply and smoothed strip after strip down against the rubber mat, inspecting the strips as he removed them. It was possible that some microscopic mote of evidence might escape this kind of attention; possible, but unlikely.

When he had finished wrapping used tape around the drop cloth to make a smaller bundle, he wiped the metal surfaces in the trunk area until they shone, then removed their camping equipment and stowed it all in assigned places on garage shelves. Finally he changed the vacuum unit's catch bag, dropping the used bag into another grocery sack for anonymous disposal.

When he entered the kitchen, the scent of fresh coffee beckoned. He poured a cup, sipped, let tension roll from his shoulders. "Mom?"

She answered from the workshop down the hall, and he detoured to the bathroom, relieving his bladder for a small eternity. He would not be thoroughly professional in this work, she had once told him, until he could finish a commission without feeling any special urges in body functions. Well, then, he wasn't a pro yet. By Romana's standards, perhaps he would never be.

He had been taught never to enter her workshop before knocking if the door was closed but she had left it open, a tacit invitation, the room suffused with a pallid ice-blue light from her ultraviolet lamp. "No UV marks. A few bills canceled but no counterfeits," she said. He saw her studying a bill using a jeweler's loupe. She had already set aside a small stack of bills near the UV lamp, those with scribbled notations that would not erase. Once, years before, they had relieved a client of an attaché case full of cash only to find that every bill was counterfeit, probably tumbled with dirt to give it a well-worn look. Romana had not been fit to live with for a week after burning that temptingly dangerous pile.

He picked up the bills that Romana had rejected and fanned them out, shaking his head as he saw what she classified as a cancellation. "Don't people know it's a crime to deface money?" he said. Perfectly legal currency, but they must burn—he counted it out—$450 on the off chance that some ballpoint scribble was a signal to law enforcement. On one bill was printed "bank"; on another, a cursive "Happy Birthday." As far as Romana was concerned, the words may as well have read "mass murderer." He restacked the bills and laid them on her work surface, then sipped his coffee. "It's really amazing," he said.

"Don't be cryptic, Andrew."

"Nothing less than a fifty. I can remember when you spent a week trying to bleach ballpoint ink out of a twenty," he said.

"Inflation," she murmured, then said to his retreating back, "Where are you going?"

"Milk," he called back from the kitchen. "You know how it is with me and milk."

Returning with his cup refilled, he reached into the client's bag and withdrew the wallet, now emptied of cash, setting its array of cards out as if playing solitaire, then directing the spot illumination of a small halogen lamp toward his work. Charles Lane's wallet would look very different after all that fine stitching was removed.

When he saw her regarding him he paused, the fresh X-Acto blade half-tightened in its holder. After twenty-some years, he still sometimes had trouble reading her expression. "Problem? You've shown me how a dozen times."

"More like two dozen," she said. "You should have asked, but go ahead."

He began to cut the stitches, teasing fine threads loose, opening the wallet out to its original pattern. Twice Romana had found useful information this way, including the address of a French safe house in Long Beach and identities of clients she had not previously suspected.

Roughly half of her success, she claimed, lay in patiently expanding her knowledge of a client until he led her to his connections.

And when occasionally she became certain that a potential client was exclusively a member of organized crime, Romana's interest ceased as fast as she could put away her night-vision glasses, her directional mikes, her tracer units. She had long ago made it clear to Andy that the Cosa Nostra, or a Latin drug ring, was not limited by law. In short, Romana Dravo did not like the odds, or their rules of engagement. They operated with the same merciless swiftness as she did.

"You know," he said, separating a nylon inner liner from thin leather, "you could just cut off the canceled part of a bill. Banks will make it good. Or keep it whole and use it on a trip."

She did not reply for a long time, typical of her. When she did, it was with that deceptively soft tone she sometimes used when he had said or done something stupid. "Is that what you will do when I have retired, Andrew?"

"I don't know. Maybe. It depends," he evaded.

"We have burned roughly three hundred thousand dollars in cash in all these years," she said softly. "Less than one-tenth of the total, most of which we still have in those ammunition boxes. Which does not even count the securities and the numbered accounts, or the stones and bullion." Her voice was hardening now, full of testosterone. "It is not worth the trouble, or the risk. Swear to me that you will never, ever take that risk as long as I live," she finished.

Some imp of perversity made him delay his reply. "Sure," he said at last. "No problem."

"*Swear it!*" she spat. He turned, and held the sigh he was about to vent. There were moments when Mom's blazing stare seemed more than human, less than sane, and this was one of those moments. That unblinking gaze signaled that he had somehow nudged a trigger in the mine field of her brain. Bearing down on himself, betraying none of his own exasperation as he failed to meet her eyes, he said, "I swear, Mom. I won't spend any canceled money, ever. Okay?" He drained his cup of milk.

She continued to glare at him for another moment, baleful as a trapped lynx, then turned again to her work without answering. Angry as always when he allowed her to dominate this way, he continued to hold it in, knowing he had outlets that usually worked. Masturbation helped, an outlet that Mom had endorsed for other problems. But this was a special kind of frustration. It called for an outlet he had discovered on his own, one that Mom did not know and probably could never understand. A few secrets were good for a man, their very existence a boost to the ego. He felt a bit easier with himself then, knowing that when he got back to his own apartment in the early hours, he would have no choice but to take one of his darlings.

8

IT WAS AFTER 1:00 A.M. BEFORE ANDY SORIANO DISPOSED of his grocery bags in Fresno and directed his Pinto down Olive, under streetlights that made him think of his mom's workshop, to the familiar turnoff near Fresno's city limit. His apartment over the two-car garage could be a noisy location, placed as it was in the landing pattern of Fresno's major air terminal. But that kept the rent down, and from there to the state lab, out Olive from town, was only a short drive. Andy had been trained to a frugal life for the best possible reason. Only months before, his mom had pointed to headlines, marveling aloud that the Russian mole Aldrich Ames could be clever enough to rise so high in the CIA, yet stupid enough to live so conspicuously beyond the salary of a government GS–14. Again, forever and again, Mom was right.

He knew he should be exhausted after the past few hours but it was almost like cramming for finals back at Cal Davis, you reached a point where you didn't feel tired, or worried; you felt wired. He had felt this way after his first commission, really his only one alone, while still a high-school student. He hadn't even thought about it as a commission until Mom had demanded the whole story. And you didn't refuse Mom.

When she had it all, she had sat for a long time thinking before she said, "Did you get what you were after?"

He had sought only justice for Briant High's most insulting bully. "Ohh, yeah," he had said. "If I don't get caught."

"I don't think you will. He was an unlikely client, from what you've told me, and it could have been an accident. I think," she said, with the

65

kind of smile that was rare for her, "you should treat it as a commission."

And she had hugged him close. It had been a wonderful moment, especially for a youth expecting to be thrashed. After all, he had done it all without consulting his mom. On later reflection, he had an idea why Mom might have chosen to praise him: it was either that or take a belt to him, and she had never beaten him from that day forward. Perhaps she had thought twice about the fact that he had taken that commission on his own. You might beat your dog, but you don't beat a wolf.

Obviously, she had liked his choice of a disposal site because she'd used it herself much later, once during his junior year at the Davis campus. And then again tonight. And he had performed as well as anyone could, almost as well as Mom. But two hours later, she was castigating him, making him feel like shit, like nothing, like a pussy. It was strange to think of Mom as, well, as pussy: a forbidden thought. Oh, yes, she would forbid him any thoughts on his own if she could.

He drove into the part of the garage reserved for his Pinto and lowered the overhead door, brushing past the milky film of plastic that defined the space he called his scenery shop. Andy's own woodworking space, with the drill press and radial-arm saw for cabinetry, and an old Frigidaire for storage of solvents, paints, cans of soda and usually a carton of milk, occupied half of the big garage. The ceiling-high partition of polyethylene kept the noise level down while it prevented wood dust from migrating away, and no one but Andy lived above. And he knew the importance of remaining on good terms with his neighbors.

A stair tread protested with a creak that might have been heard a hundred feet away as he trotted up to the landing. He would run a few drywall screws in from its underside one day soon and silence that telltale sound. No sense in alerting some neighbor as to the time of the night he came and went.

He could see his digital clock through the window. After that glance, he unlocked the door, pushed it open. Still in darkness, he inserted his right hand past the door facing to the wallboard; placed his palm flat against the wall. Behind that featureless wallboard lay a capacitance switch that sensed his mass and, with no audible click, disabled the circuit to a second capacitance switch set into his bookcase. Anyone who passed the bookcase while that circuit was live would trigger a relay set into the wooden base of his digital clock. Among amateur theatrical groups in the Fresno area, Andy was known for some very clever stagecraft.

He shut the door, strode past the bookcase, glanced again at the numerals of the clock which faced away from the door. It read 1:18, close enough. The relay advanced the hour readout. Had someone entered and left again, it would read 3:18. If someone had entered without leaving, it would read 2:18. If ever that clock was an hour or so off, Andrew Soriano would be forewarned.

He found the bedroom light switch by rote, sat down on his bed, toggled his answering machine for a replay. It was a source of quiet pride to him that Mom wasn't the only person who thought he had his uses.

A familiar contralto, mature and well modulated, made him smile. "Andy, it's Aletha from the playhouse, now Friday evening, ah, about seven-thirty. If you're there, how about a pickup?" His smile grew. Aletha McCarran was every inch a lady of status, but it had become her habit to toss Andy a private innuendo now and then. Did she really mean anything by it? Hard to say, dangerous to pursue, with a woman of such worldly ways and family money.

Andy sighed. His virginity did not leave him unaware of sexual wordplay. Quite the opposite. The contralto went on: "We're pushing the schedule on *Barefoot* rehearsals so I'm wondering how soon we can get together on the flats for the apartment scenes. I don't want to block it without your input. If you have any time this weekend, give me some of your input, pretty-please? *Ciao.*"

He sat perfectly still, thinking that pussy could always use some input, thinking that he would give Aletha a call in the morning and that it was scenery flats—not the other thing—they would focus on. Then, finding no other calls, he ran the tape back; played it again, running his thumb very slowly along his crotch, and still again.

Aletha had the voice of a gifted actress; as the star performer of the Valley Players, as well as its chief supporter, she could play the lusty young bride of *Barefoot in the Park* or the shrewish Martha of *Who's*

Afraid . . . with equal ease. Onstage, as Martha, she had reminded him of Mom. She had soft curves where Mom had sinew, but they both knew how to play roles. *Sisters under the skin,* he thought, still drawing his thumbnail back and forth, prompting a rise that no longer needed prompting. Soon, now, but not too soon, he would obtain relief from his frustrations. His gaze drifted toward the hamster cages ranged below his bedroom window.

He rose very slowly, his mouth dry, and squatted to survey his darlings, furry sleeping balls of life, in their tiny worldlets. Kong, stirring in the light; Gaia, an indiscriminate lump tucked among her babies; Freya, blinking alone, rousing herself, now climbing onto a treadmill as if performing for him. He liked it when they performed for him, pussy acts, acts of total submission.

He chose the silvery gray Queenie, a long-haired angora with a moody disposition. You never knew whether Queenie would curl up in your hand or bite you without provocation. For some reason, he respected Queenie more than the others. Queenie wanted to dominate you.

He reached down and stroked the somnolent female, who let him take her up without struggle. He replaced the lid and moved about the room, spreading a large double-thick white terry-cloth towel on the side of the bed, then opening a drawer, looking over the instruments he had collected during his undergrad courses in veterinary science.

Scalpels come in different shapes. The one he chose had a straight blade with an upward frontal curve, not so good for removing splinters or lancing abscesses, but ideal for deep incisions. His clasp knife's special blade would have worked as well, but was large for this work. He took Queenie by her loose neck scruff, filled his shirt pocket with her, constantly aware of the hard fullness in his briefs. He removed his shoes, socks, trousers, briefs, now moving faster. She was never satisfied, always dominating him, ever alert for some tiny deviation from her precious standards. He forced his memory to dwell on recent moments of Mom's behavior; snarling when he took the commission bag for immediate inspection, unappreciative when he played the fool for her, scornful at his suggestion for using defaced bills.

He sat down on the rough pleasurable terry cloth, touched himself, at first only with fingernails but then more roughly, teasing his maleness, his heart a trip-hammer that made his shirt pulse and began a faint roaring in his ears. Then he imagined Mom tied down as she had tied him down in earlier days, nude and vulnerable to the belt, a helpless pussy facing merciless power, and the focus of agony was not the physical pain, that was almost beside the point, but the recognition of your own insignificance, your impotence, but look who's helpless now, he thought, pulling Queenie from his shirt so quickly that she bit him.

He ignored the bite, now holding her expertly, Mom by the scruff as it were, and did what had to be done with a vagrant wish that Queenie might know why; and then he laid the scalpel aside and did more things, both hands sticky and crimson, and thrust himself into the still-warm furry hollow and thought that this, for Mom, would be the ultimate indignity. And thoughts of Aletha McCarran were suddenly mixed in now, though she had never done anything to make him want to get even but there she was, with her flirtatious smiles and winks for him, slipping from the open part of his mind into that dark catacomb where his frustrations and desires fought, writhed together like pythons in a crimson lake, and then he burst like a ripe melon falling and falling onto concrete, collapsing back on the bed.

He rolled the towel and its contents into a loose ball, washed his hands, found when he washed his penis that it was bleeding a bit—nothing serious, perhaps scratched by a tiny rib. He tossed the towel into his bathtub. A small eviscerated animal, he had found, would always keep until morning. He could sleep for a week, it seemed. If he fell asleep soon enough, the self-reproachment for his dark compulsion would not begin until tomorrow.

9

THE NIGHT PASSED FOR HIM AS A SERIES OF MOMENTARY agonies, each brief wakefulness bringing a flood of pain so fierce that at first he could not localize it. But by dawn, the receptacle of suffering that was his body had told him several things. His lower legs were numb because they lay in several inches of water that stretched away into a deeper dark, as if he had been abandoned at limbo's black shoreline. No wonder his head throbbed, with a swelling the size of an egg near the back of his skull and every time he shouted, he regretted it because the echo was tomblike, oppressive. He rolled slightly to relieve the pressure of a large rounded stone beneath his right side and grunted with fresh pain. He thought the left forearm must be fractured because he could not use it without a spasm. At some point, scrabbling with his good hand above the waterline, he grasped a familiar cold comfort that felt like his weapon; thrust it into his belt because it was too big for his front pockets. When at last he could see faint outlines around him and realized that the diffuse light came from far above behind his head, Gary Landis resolved to stand or die.

That issue lay in doubt for long minutes as he fought to get to his knees in soft earth, pulling his feet from muck, using his good right arm for purchase on anything he could grasp, snapping old sticks that lay beneath his lower back, buttocks, and thighs, rolling in the debris as he held onto a wooden pole that stretched, staunch as a root, down the sloping rock. Even when he began to feel cold tingles in his feet, he was not at first capable of climbing, though he knew now that the wooden pole was part of a rough-finished ladder, spiked into the rocky slope, with rungs of hardwood spanning two poles.

When he placed his foot in the center of the lowest rung, it cracked loudly enough to produce an echo of its own, and it was an echo from hell. He leaned forward against the poles, right shoulder nudging the side of the shaft, trembling with a cold that pierced to his marrow, skull pounding so that he feared fainting again. But if he fell backward, he knew, he would drown. Some shred of logic told him then that he must crowd the wooden side poles with each foot as he climbed, avoiding the center of the rungs, and in this fashion he began a one-armed climb that he could not have managed on a vertical ladder.

Once he vomited from the pain, swaying dangerously, and farther up he stopped again, fearful that vertigo would send him tumbling back down into that dark nest of dead sticks. But now, too, the light was much improved—not entirely a bonus because double vision made his dizziness worse. By shutting one eye, he handled that minor problem—the least of his troubles—and stopped looking up because it not only gave him vertigo but virtually blinded him.

By the time he neared the mouth of the shaft he was alert enough to realize that it was full daylight up there, and whoever had put him in that hole might still be nearby. Nearby *what?* He had no idea where he was, knew only that a small tree loomed above the shaft and beyond it, others formed a shifting canopy against sundazzle. But he was approaching the tag ends of his strength now, his left arm throbbing as though competing with his head. He came out of the shaft on hands and knees, drawing his weapon, threatening the area with an arm sweep like a man snaring spiderwebs as he fell—and then, for a time, he burrowed into a cocoon of oblivion.

The sun woke him, finding a midmorning hole in the leafy canopy to bathe his hands and neck. He jerked, moaned as his forearm did its painful duty to remind him that it was, by God, *hurt* and it wasn't going to get any better with abuse. And the handgun lying near his outstretched right hand was his Beretta, all right, muddy but a friend for all that—maybe the only friend he had.

He sat up despite the persistent double vision, checking himself over. His lower trouser legs and shoes were sodden, the shoes containing wet, sandy silt. But he would not remove his shoes because he wasn't sure he could get them back on, and obviously he was in the boondocks, so he would need to stay well shod. He still had his knife, coins, and a small roll of bills in his pocket that he didn't recall putting there. But that wallet— that goddamn old wallet—he liked so much and had stuffed with the talismans of Chuck Lane, was gone.

And he didn't have that little bag with his change of clothes and *Jesus Christ, six thousand in cash,* he remembered, but if he'd had the Beretta down in the shaft, who could say, his bag could be down there, too. But he didn't think so, and he did not want to go near that hole again; if he saw the bag and went down there after it, well, he was nuts, that's all. But he made himself go back and kneel at the lip and look hard.

He could see nothing down there in the gloom but the ladder disappearing into indistinctness and maybe a jumble of stuff at the bottom, and a glimmer that could be reflection from water. And then he patted the right-hand pocket of his jacket, wondering if he had a handkerchief or even a Kleenex in there. He didn't, but what he pulled out of that pocket stunned him, made him drop it like a tarantula.

He stared at it, closing one eye and then the other, and then—he would never be able to explain this act even to himself—put his hand to his mouth to be certain his chin was still in place. Because the thing that lay on the carpet of leaves was a human mandible—the lower jaw—with a few bits of mummified tissue clinging to it.

And when Gary put his hand to his temple in wonderment, he realized why his head had seemed so cool and sensitive to the breeze. He was virtually bald, with tufts remaining as though some drunken drill instructor had given him a recruit's burr cut.

"Well, Jeezus *Christ,*" he croaked, running his hand over the wreckage atop his scalp, wondering how many more revelations he would find in a mirror, finding small rips in his trousers that matched abrasions he could feel, dislodging the small stick caught in his trouser cuff. Only it wasn't exactly a stick, it was a piece of bone the size of a slightly bowed finger. A rib. And now he remembered that rounded stone against his side down in the hole—and realized that it was not a stone, but a skull. "So I'm not the first," he muttered aloud, pocketing the jawbone and the rib.

Suddenly he wanted very much to get the hell and gone from this place, and his legs were willing enough for a short distance, far enough to reveal a decayed shack that he detoured around, the Beretta in hand. But nausea swept over him, and he found a spot in sunlight where he could lie full-length. He may have fainted or simply fallen asleep. When he awoke again, he was in cool shadow with scents of pine and eucalyptus on the breeze, and the sun's position indicated roughly noon. *I'm not spending the night here,* he promised himself. A lot of things were coming back to him, once the pounding had subsided to a nasty little pulse in his cranium.

His lower trousers and shoes were still damp, but it was not so noticeable when he had brushed them with his one good hand. The double vision seemed to be lessening a little, too. He followed fresh treadmarks near the cabin, taking care not to mar the track with his footprints because this was evidence. *Yeah? And who'll be doing the forensics?* he thought, sticking the Beretta behind his belt and under his jacket as he saw ancient strands of barbed wire and, beyond that, a ribbon of blacktop.

He climbed between the strands and learned not to dip his head too quickly if he didn't want it to roll off; turned right, stumbling along beside the road merely because it had a downhill slope and he didn't feel like trudging up any more inclines than necessary. A hundred yards farther, he memorized a landmark; a black rusted-out car fender deposited ten feet off the road by God knew what, God knew when.

What next? Hitch a ride if possible. The terrain suggested that he might be in the Sierra foothills east of Merced, around Mariposa, maybe. He wasn't about to go back to the apartment, nor call DEA; not when he'd been warned by somebody who was definitely an insider—or a psychic. For that matter, he wasn't even sure that spray of bullets through his window had been from La Familia. *I can't believe Paul would be a part of this,* he told himself. *But I can't be sure he isn't, either.* Whoever it was, she sure played for keeps. *She!* Two of them, in fact. His short-term memory was full of gaps, but much of it had come back now, enough to make him wonder if they had really been women. He'd been hit by a hypo—he was certain of it. Not your standard drug-runner MO. *Let's see, there's something you're supposed do after taking a syringe load. Well, it can wait,* he thought.

That left forearm was swollen so much it nearly filled the sleeve of his jacket, the discoloration reaching to his wrist, and though he could move his fingers it was only an exercise in self-torture. He found the arm hurt less if he held it across his belly, but could not close the jacket zipper one-handed, so he gave up on using the jacket's closure as a sling.

One car went by, a woman with two kids in a Chevy sedan, properly ignoring the wave of a man who looked as if he spent his nights wallowing in ditches. Then two youths in an Isuzu coupe, blasting along the blacktop with the total confidence of kids who hadn't died yet, therefore could not die. Could not be delayed by hitchhikers, either.

The little old guy who stopped for Gary sat in an International pickup that Noah might have found after the Flood. "Hop in back," he called, nodding at the cab's other occupant. "He's not as friendly as I am." The big mixed-breed had its ears back, sitting up front where Gary wanted to sit, watching him through the closed window as if just hoping for a chance.

Gary tried to smile, nodded, managed to climb in over the tailgate one-handed. Then they were off with a gear crunch, and Gary found himself in a welter of ranch junk: chain saw, old rope, oak limbs cut to the length of firewood, gasoline can, big yellow-tinted chunks from a salt lick in heavy sealable plastic bags. And when he heard fuel sloshing in that can and saw the urine-yellow color of those slabs of salt, he remembered two things.

He had to take a leak in the worst way. And he remembered what you did after being forced to take unknown drugs: you saved urine for analysis.

Gary emptied the smallest of the bags, hoping the old guy in the cab wasn't watching, then spent five minutes of sway and jounce before he got his fly unzipped with the bag positioned. Then it was blessed relief; not such a blessing afterward, when he had to press the bag's seal with one hand while holding the plastic with his teeth, a quart of urine weighing the bag down. He couldn't get it into his left jacket pocket at all, and only after releasing half of it where it trickled away through rust holes did he manage to get it into the pocket with the bones. *Man, talk about compromising your evidence,* he told himself, but he felt a surge of hope. He was coping, coming back from the dead with thirty bucks, a Beretta, and a pocketful of piss.

He could get the arm checked out at any emergency room; yeah, that was Priority One, or so he thought until he saw the road sign as they passed the hamlet called Academy. Another sign claimed that the cutoff to Briant Dam stretched off to the right. Suddenly he tossed all his priorities into a pile and drew out a different one. The town of Briant, and Millerton Lake behind its dam, were folded into foothills, a hell of a distance from Merced but only a few miles north of Fresno and its suburb, Clovis. He recognized landmarks a few minutes later, and slapped the pickup cab as they neared Herndon Avenue. From here in Clovis, he could take a city bus to something better than wheels. In Fresno he had wings.

While he waited at the bus stop, he let his suspicions grow, now that he knew he'd been dumped so near to Fresno and his acting RAC, Paul Visconti. The arm ached so much he gave a lot of thought to calling one of the DEA guys just a half-hour drive away in downtown Fresno; McMilligan, maybe, a stand-up type who could get the arm tended to. *Right, and Paul Visconti's there, and McMilligan could get his ass in a crack if it was Visconti who burned me.* No, he decided, mounting the bus steps and returning the driver's curious stare; he would continue heading for safer ground, for somebody with no connection to the Department of Justice. He would try for Swede Halvorsen.

In the opposite northern edge of Fresno, far out Herndon to the west, was the hangar of a two-place Cessna 140 that Gary owned with two other men: Carl Michaels, a house builder, and Dave Nathan, a professor at Fresno State. Thanks to the lawyers and the liability insurance they scrabbled for, it was no longer possible for an ordinary guy to own even a Cessna by himself. It had become common for two, three, or more people to own equal shares in a small aircraft, and Nathan lived in one of those housing developments called airparks. In an airpark you could land on its airstrip and, without breaking a law, taxi down the street to your hangar-equipped home.

Dave Nathan owned a garage instead, but the airstrip had tiedown spaces and a ratty maintenance hangar of its own, and all three men knew where the keys were stashed. Gary's use of the old Cessna, one of the early all-metal stalwarts, tended to be in spurts when his caseload permitted. *Visconti knows I have it, but at worst case there's no way he'd expect me to use it because I'm dead,* Gary reflected, climbing down from the bus. All the same, he crossed Alluvial Avenue with a heightened sense of awareness, heading for the airstrip. Only a paranoid would imagine that anyone would expect a corpse to make a run for an airplane, but at this point Gary knew he qualified easily.

The place was deserted, the keys left as usual beneath the lip of the sliding hangar door. Gary cursed his arm as he shouldered the door wide enough to roll the little tail-dragger Cessna into the afternoon sun, its aluminum hide shining like a beacon. After a moment's internal debate, he rummaged at the workbench, running a strip of masking tape across the work surface. Then he printed a brief bullshit explanation in flow pen and sighed. Nathan or Michaels might be pissed about it, and Gary felt a pang over that; but each of them used the Cessna more than he did. At least they'd know the plane wasn't stolen.

He still felt rickety, but it didn't stop him from checking the fuel, making a cursory preflight inspection with a quick look through the logbook to make sure he wasn't trying to fly an unflyable machine, locking the hangar again. *Now for the fun part.* If even securing his lap belt was such a problem, flying a Cessna one-handed was going to be a real bitch. At least he could use his elbow to nudge the throttle.

The radio hadn't worked for a while, and there was no tower controller at the airpark anyhow. When his engine oil temperature came off the peg, he taxied over to the strip faster than he should have, uneasy over the body parts he carried in his jacket. *Calm down,* he told himself. *If you auger this thing in, it'll be somebody else's problem to figure out why there's a few too many bones in the cockpit.* Lightly loaded, the little aircraft sprinted forward at maximum revs, leaped off the ground as if it weren't as old as he was. Gary kept it firewalled until he had banked to a 165-degree heading, southeast toward Bakersfield following Highway 99, and then discovered that his elbow didn't have an opposable thumb and hurt himself again before he got the engine throttled back a bit. It was just over a hundred miles to Bakersfield, an hour for a 140 at fast-cruise setting. *Meadows Field? Hell, no,* he reasoned. It was close in to Bakersfield but, klutzy as he was today, the last thing he needed was to share airspace with commercial jetliners for the same reason he would not want to share a highway, not even under the best of circumstances, with those goddamned triple-tandem rigs. He would land east of town at little Rio Bravo. The runway was short, but last time he'd stopped there, they'd had a courtesy car. Rio Bravo it was, then—always assuming he didn't pass out from that resurgent pounding headache.

Be there, Swede, he implored. *For all I know you've died by now, but just for me, be there.*

10

THE TROUBLE WAS, RIO BRAVO'S COURTESY CAR WAS IN use. On the plus side, a landing of sorts can be managed one-handed. Shortly afterward, Swede answered his phone, sounding strangely buoyant after Gary mentioned where he was. "I think I can arrange to put wheels under you," he said. "Just a minute." And with that he put Gary on hold.

The two-minute wait was forever, with Gary's arm killing him after a couple of hard corrections in his crosswind landing over a hill near Runway 26. When Swede came on line again, he said, "Okay, no sweat. Look for a Datsun 260Z."

"You sold the heavy cruiser," Gary said. "I don't believe it."

"Then don't. You druther jog?"

"God, Swede, don't even mention it. You're talking to a man who's come in last in an ass-kick contest."

"I'm listening."

"Quit listening. Just hang up and come on, man. You're a half-hour away."

"Thinks he knows it all, doesn't he?" the old man said as though to himself, but he hung up in mid-cackle and Gary went outside to see if he could manage tiedowns by himself.

But he didn't have to. Within five minutes a car whrummed out near where he was fumbling with a tiedown chain, and he didn't look around until the door slammed, and she was standing there, arms akimbo, with that gremlin's grin he had remembered so often on lonely nights. "Still

79

clumsy," she said, brushing away hair longer than he recalled it. Same golden eyes, though; same carriage and bod, but perhaps less insolent confidence in them. Jan.

"Still homely," he managed to say, looking her up and down and trying to recover, but his astonishment was clear and he knew it. Then: "No, nonono," he added quickly, backing away as she approached with arms out, warding her off with his good hand, holding the other one against his belly. Even after all this time, he hadn't expected a hug. "I'm glad to see you, too," he went on, talking into her puzzled frown. "Can I take a rain check on that?"

"I suppose," she replied, focusing on the way he held his left arm. "Let me guess: a fight with your barber. Hurt yourself?"

He handed the tiedown to her. Its purpose was obvious, and so was the loop set into the wing. "Let me put it this way: if you'd bumped this arm, you would now be wondering how to lift me into your car." It was a 260Z, all right, though the daffodil-yellow paint job said there'd been a fire under the hood some time back and no one had repainted it since.

Jan clipped the tiedown in place and looked around. "Was that all, sahib?"

"Shouldn't be, but I can do the rest later. No kidding, Jan, I'm, uh, a little under par at the moment."

"News flash," she announced in portentous anchorman's tones, holding a nonexistent microphone to her mouth. "Vandals with large erasers have scrubbed the big 'S' from the chest of agent Gary Landis. Film at eleven." But her grin disappeared as he grabbed the tiedown chain for support and the wing bobbed. She stopped short of touching him. "Is it just your arm, Gary?"

He nodded, eyes closed, beginning to realize just how near he was to total exhaustion. "That and my head. And a bruise on my breastbone, and some cuts on my legs, I think. And there's—" And that is as far as he got before he sagged to his knees.

She took his good hand, helped him fold himself into the passenger seat, muttering tender little curses at men who take macho jobs while she got the Datsun under way. She lived in a mobile home within a mile of the airport, she said, but first she would take him to the nearest emergency room. He countermanded that; before anything else, he said, he needed a sitdown with her grandfather. And while she was telling him what a fool he was, he fell asleep, waking only as she shut the engine off.

Swede's place was in many respects like his old L.A. house, the old cop car filling half of his garage. Gary eased himself from the Datsun with help, Swede's welcoming smile a faded memory as he saw what came shambling in while Jan lowered the garage door. "I take it there was more'n one of 'em," he said. "Fuggers scalped you, that's a fact."

"More than that," Gary said, moving stolidly to the living room where he sat, rubber-legged, on Swede's lumpish ottoman. "This arm needs looking at, but I don't want any record of it—not yet."

He caught the look between the two of them; knew a few things had to be set straight immediately. "No, I haven't broken any law, and this isn't a gunshot wound—at least, I don't think so. I woke up this morning down a mine shaft where somebody dumped me last night. I have reason to think it *might* be, uh—Jan, maybe you don't want to hear all of this. Some of it could give you nightmares," he said.

She began to remove his jacket very carefully, good arm first. "We may have to cut this off," she began. Then: "Nobody who's lived with Freddie Penrose has any nightmares left," she told him. "You've said the magic words: you're not shot and you're not hot."

"I'm hot with somebody. They tried to cool me off about dark yesterday evening. I just don't know whether it was my own people."

With that, grunting at times while Jan got the jacket off, he described what he could recall: the note, the spray of bullets, the setup at his car, and a hellish jumble of impressions as, he swore, his paralysis got as far as his heart.

His arm revealed, Gary stopped his narrative for a time. No bone had protruded through the skin, but the flesh was too grossly swollen and discolored for any assessment beyond the fact that he had not been shot or stabbed. Then Gary descended into that pit again in memory to describe his awakening, the wallowing in what seemed to be brittle sticks, the long climb back. "And here are a couple of the sticks I was rolling in." He reached into the jacket Jan was now holding. He shrugged at her: "Well, you claim you're fresh out of nightmares."

She needed a moment to realize what he held in his hand. "Mother of God!" she moaned softly, with an openmouthed grimace that showed her teeth. She let the jacket drop with a shudder, rubbing her hands as though to clean them. Swede had made no sound, but took a long breath and expelled it.

"And by the way, there must be a pint of my p— urine in a Baggie there in my jacket," Gary went on. For Jan's enlightenment, he continued. "Sometimes they can tell what was in a hypo; some of it comes out again. It goes from your bloodstream to your blad—"

"Women pee." Jan cut him off. "I hate to dash your illusions, Gary, it's just something we do. Call us irresponsible." She swallowed hard, but she was smiling. Gary smiled back. *You're having to work at it, but you're tough enough,* he thought.

Swede moved over to his couch, set a cordless phone beside him, flopped a Bakersfield phone book on his knees. "Jan, bring us a pair of good Baggies for that stuff—it's evidence." His gaze on Gary now: "You oughta have X rays but that'd be tough without a record of it. I know a guy, disabled at Grenada, night security at a refinery. Claims the navy gave him great paramedic training in the SEALs. If that's a 'go,' I'll give him a call."

"No possible connection with DEA?" Gary said.

"One chance in a million. And he doesn't have to know who you are, I could say you're hiding from your ex. He'll identify with that," the old man added with a nod and wink.

"Go for it," Gary said. He raised his voice. "Jan, I know Swede hoards his old Safeway plastic bags. These should be new." *Now I get picky about bones left in a mine shaft for Christ knows how long,* he thought.

Jan returned with two fresh Baggies and, unasked, a dark brown plastic jar with a screw top. "Used to have those little plastic footballs of Vitamin E inside," she said softly, kneeling before Gary in a fashion so graceful, so unaffected, that his heart seemed to levitate toward his throat. "Better to store your pee in than the way you did it."

"I'll take it to the bathroom and—" Gary began.

"And fall on your face," she supplied, taking the urine-filled bag. She stopped on her way out of the room. "You know what's weird? After being on my own in the mobile home awhile, a little job like this has a nice domestic feel to it."

He supposed he would learn some details in time: how and why she was on her own, why Bakersfield of all places, and when she had developed this flair for domesticity.

Swede cut into his reflections. "That was Jim Marcus—he's got a graveyard shift and can come by shortly. He won't ask, but you might offer him a twenty. By the way, your name is Nolan Cromwell."

"I always knew that," Gary kidded back. "Listen, Swede, I've got about thirty-two bucks to my name. I'm happy to pay this guy but, uh, well, those bimbos took my wallet but somebody stuck its cash in my pants pocket. The only other things they left with me was my pocket-knife and sidearm," he said, pulling the Beretta from the small of his back.

The old man nodded, idly brushing a speck of grit from the weapon, handing it back as Jan reappeared with the brown jar full and capped. "I'm not sure how to deal with the evidence yet," he admitted, enclosing the grisly skeletal bits by turning the Baggies inside out, reaching inside them expertly, grasping the bones without leaving his prints, flicking the plastic right-side out again. "But I don't like the fact that they left you with a weapon and money in your pockets."

Jan: "Wasn't that a break for him?"

Swede: "Sure. What I don't like is how sweetly it would all fit together if he hadn't been found for fifty years. Armed, no gunshot wound, no cash missing. He could've just lost his wallet. A very well-planned accident."

"Sixty-seven hundred in cash missing," Gary corrected. "In my bag."

"So maybe that's what they were after," Swede replied. "I know, you think maybe it was your boss, but folks get killed for less than that stash you had. How many people knew you were carrying it?"

That put the turd back in La Familia's pocket, Gary said, but to most of those people, the money was small change. There was also Gary's job to consider: whoever might be dirty in DEA. If Gary played dead for them, too, his career with the Feds was over.

Jan's car was out of sight. When a car pulled into the driveway, Swede suggested she hurry to the back bedroom. "Marcus isn't an M.D. so let's not worry him with an extra witness," the old man explained, heading toward his front door.

It was lucky that Jim Marcus had such a winning smile because the scar across his nose and left cheek gave his face a villainous cast. Wiry, pale, and a few years Gary's senior, he carried a small fanny pack on a sling like a woman's shoulder bag, setting it down with care next to the younger man, doffing his own whipcord jacket. *I wonder if SEALs wrestle sharks for amusement,* Gary thought. The man's arms had taken worse damage than his own.

Marcus took a blood-pressure cuff from his little pack and used it on Gary's right arm. Its tinny electronic beep was the loudest thing in the room. "One-thirty over eighty-two, pulse sixty-eight. Good," he mumbled, removing the cuff again. After asking when the fall had occurred, checking the forearm over with tender care, Marcus took up a pencil, holding it at one end by bringing all the fingers and the thumb of one hand together. In his gentle baritone he said, "See this? Try to hold the pencil this way." Then a sigh. "No, with the bad hand, Cromwell. Sorry, I know it'll hurt."

Gary winced, but managed it. "Time to write my will," he hazarded.

"You'll live. Looks like you might have an angular fracture of the radius—the little bone—but it's not too bad and if there was any serious nerve damage you couldn't hold a pencil that way. 'Course, with such pronounced edema of the soft tissues it may be a little worse. What you need is a cast."

"What I need is about a pint of bourbon," Gary muttered.

"Maybe not," Marcus said with a lopsided grin that implied, "surely not." "I have a few odds and ends here, but I'd rather not be on the hook for dispensing them. If Duane, here, had some Tylenol with codeine, and if I were a doctor, I might suggest popping one or two. I'm not, so I won't."

"Got some." The old man rose. "I'll get it."

The onetime paramedic continued to study Gary, head cocked. "Why do you keep shutting one eye like that? Got something in it?"

"Got double vision in it," Gary said.

Marcus put his hands on his knees and laughed gently. "Well, Christ's little keepsakes! Why didn't you say so? Any more surprises for me?"

"Just scratches, nothing a little merthiolate won't fix. But I got this when I fell," Gary said, touching the back of his head. "And my chest is bruised."

"Fell into a running Evinrude, looks like," Marcus observed dryly, studying the goose egg on Gary's skull. Then he produced a flashlight and, with something like a jeweler's loupe, studied Gary's eyes thoroughly, so near that Gary detected bacon and garlic, reminding him that he hadn't eaten recently. Then, on command, Gary read various sizes of print from a magazine with each eye, then both eyes.

At last Marcus sat back, nodding to himself, unsmiling. "That's a concussion you've got, pal. Think of your skull as a bowl and your brain as Jell-O. Shake the stuff too hard and it can shear nerves. Has the double vision got worse? Better?"

"Lots better, but I still get a little dizzy using both eyes when I focus on things."

"No numbness anywhere?"

"Nope. I could use a little numbness about now," Gary admitted. "For the past twelve hours or so, in fact."

At this point Swede reappeared with a pill and a glass of water, and Marcus watched him swallow it with satisfaction. "You want a prognosis, I'd say a couple of days flat on your back will do you a world of good. You're not in shock. But I've seen guys walking around as lucid as you are, and thanks to a little depressed cranial fracture they were dying by inches and nobody knew it until the onset of coma. That's the bad news, and someone should keep an eye on you in case you start vomiting or sounding stupid. The fact that you seem to've gotten better for most of a day tells me you're probably going to be okay. From what you say, twelve hours ago I wouldn't have risked a guess either way."

"Me, neither," Gary said. "Uh, one more thing. If I had taken an injection of some kind, without knowing what the stuff was, do you have any way of finding out from blood or urine samples what it might've been?"

Try as he might, Jim Marcus was unable to keep a judgmental shift from his face. "No way. That's lab work, and I'm not into that, and I don't know anybody who is. It's the chance you take with needles."

"It wasn't his idea," Swede said protectively.

Another subtle change in facial muscles. "Well, all I can say is, one of your acquaintances has an interesting sense of humor. Any hallucinations from it?"

"Not that I can recall, but it put me down fast," Gary admitted.

"Just hope the needle was clean. Intravenous?"

"No, intramuscular. In my butt."

"Then whatever it was, if it had an immediate effect, it was probably strong as hell. You need an expert, and that's not me."

After a few more interchanges, Marcus slung his fanny-pack over his shoulder and stood. Gary offered him his only twenty-dollar bill, but it was refused, almost curtly. "I'm not sure I've done you any favors, Cromwell," he said, moving toward the door. "If you've got some foreign shit pumping around in you and you still don't know what it is, my advice is to find out. Without mentioning me. And soon," he said, with a glance toward Swede Halvorsen. The man left as if hurrying to avoid further involvement, speaking softly to Swede at the door.

When Swede had locked the door, Jan came back. "I was listening, and I've watched casts being made. Should I chase down some plaster of paris?"

"If it's all the same," Gary said, "I'd rather you chased down some bacon and eggs first, and maybe a beer. Later, I may need help shaving off this stupid mustache."

"I'm glad you said that. You look like Pancho Fuckin' Villa," Swede said.

"Amen," Jan said and turned toward the kitchen.

So it was old Duane Halvorsen who went after the plaster, while Jan crafted a four-egg omelet, with crumbled bacon and lots of diced green onions, Gary's favorite. Apparently, Janelle Betancourt never forgot anything.

11

SUCH A WILLING BOY, ALETHA REFLECTED, *AND OH, SUCH a* longing in those hooded eyes. That willingness had brought Andy here to the playhouse on a Sunday afternoon when the others had "engagements," as thespians were wont to say—probably engaged in reading the Sunday comics in the *Fresno Bee*. At the moment those dark eyes of Andy's were guiding a chalk line on the floor, upstage left, to locate a door which he would hang later. "The hinges should be stage right, Andrew," she reminded him.

She knew he was already a professional in his mid-twenties with a degree from a good school, a most attractive young man. Yet, like all of the other players, she thought of him as little Andy, too reticent to try out even for a walk-on part. But he had shyly told her of his preference in names once, and once was all it took. Aletha McCarran prided herself on a certain sensitivity to the needs of others, and duly called him by his formal name. Andy could be strangely touchy about that; one of the ingenues, clearly taken with young Soriano, had made the mistake of calling him "Candy." Quietly furious, he would not speak to the girl again for weeks. Crestfallen, she had finally left the troupe. *Still, I don't think our Andy is a latent gay,* she thought, toying with the single gypsy bangle earring she often wore. *Perhaps a mild fixation on mature women.* Women like herself, for example. And with a youngster so adroit with stagecraft, where was the crime in turning his fancies to her advantage?

Presently, lost in the complex scheduling of amateur troupers who had jobs and coursework, she realized with a start that Andy was standing

89

beside her as he shifted the leather tool pouch slung from his belt. "Have I got it laid out to suit you?" he said.

"We ought to put a bell on you, Andrew, you move so quietly," she said, tossing her long black mane, giving him one of those smiles he seemed to live for.

She found the correct page of graph paper and stepped down from her stool, taller than Andy in her three-inch heels, her gray slacks defying dust while they hid her legs. When she wore skirts, sometimes Andy Soriano paid more attention to her than to stage management. They moved across the stage, chiefly in silence broken by her murmurs of appreciation as she studied his work. "By George, I think he's got it," she said at last, adapting a line from Shaw.

"Can I take measurements then?"

"That's easy: thirty-six, twenty-five, thirty-six," she replied slyly. She would never have risked that quip if any other players had been within earshot, but she had handled innocent flirtations in private before. And, in the case of young Andy, she loved to watch the pupils of his eyes expand in mild shock.

For a long moment, he simply stood there, unmoving, as though awaiting a cue from the wings. Then: "Your timing is off," he said softly. "It's May—and April is supposed to be the cruelest month."

"Oh, Andrew, I'm sorry. You know me—I didn't mean anything by it."

"Exactly," he said with the faintest of smiles, then turned and drew a Stanley steel tape from his belt pouch. "I'll need to rip some two-bys," he went on, measuring between chalked marks as if they had not shared that brief moment of truth, a moment that now secretly shamed her.

Minutes later, she flashed on a mental picture of young Andy strapping two-by-fours to the top of his grungy little Pinto. "If you're going for wood, I think Lumberjack in Clovis is open today. You can use the station wagon; I'll be here at least another hour." She rummaged in her bag for keys.

He materialized beside her again with that wonderful spooky

noiseless stride, and reaching out for the keys he held his palm beneath them, a few careful inches from her touch. She dropped the keys and turned away, flustered for reasons she could not identify until she heard the Taurus station wagon scrunch gravel outside. Then she put down her pencil and folded her arms, gazing at nothing.

He might be terrified of touching her, but no, young Andy was no closet queen. Sensitive, even brilliant with a soft reply that could be all the more devastating for its gentleness. And what if she had taken his hand to transfer those keys? *Electric,* she thought, fearing the potential lightning of his contact, wondering if that was what she wanted.

After two years of Andy's tenure with the troupe, she had felt that she knew him well enough for the romantic byplay that so many actors enjoyed. Now, today, she was not so sure of his limits, or of herself. If she was right about Andy, he was a furnace tightly closed, his heat directed safely away, fearful that she would recoil from such energy fully revealed. Had any of her previous dalliances erupted in real passion, she would have done exactly that: pulling back with all the charm she could muster, controlling the damage with mature good sense, even with tender good humor. That's what you did when you were Caesar's wife, or at any rate a prominent broker's wife, not that Frank McCarran hadn't had a couple of hot little affairs himself.

Aletha had banked the fires of her own furnace, turned them to good advantage on the local stage. Casual letches had not been her style. But there was nothing casual about Andy Soriano, and a sudden magnificent hallucination overtook her: legs wrapped around his waist, his face buried between her breasts, her fingers gripping his hair, mutual thrustings to fan those flames until the final quenching—*Good God, and I don't even read bodice rippers! What am I thinking of?* she asked silently, knowing damned well, trembling with it.

"Yes, and he'd probably uncork in five seconds every time, or brag about it to all his buddies at Fish and Game," she said aloud, to distance herself from this delightful fantasy. No doubt he had his own fantasies, and more power to him. She would entertain her own, limiting her double entendres but enjoying them now and again with gentle, diffident Andy Soriano. There was a certain satisfaction in knowing that she was in control, that the risks she ran were safe ones. *It's too bad I can't read his mind,* she thought. *I'll bet his fantasies are really something.*

12

H E HAULED THE STUDS, EACH PIECE CAREFULLY CHOSEN, out of the Taurus and stacked them properly in his shop to avoid warpage. He had a companion for the moment, a gangling young Labrador female that often roamed the neighborhood in search of affectionate pats. Because he did not know her name, Andy called her "Princess," always giving her attention and perhaps a back scratch, never feeding her though she begged when he drank milk from the fridge, giving her a gentle shove whenever she got literally underfoot in the workshop. With any kind of encouragement, she would climb into his lap. But today he had no time to spare.

He stored the brads, the half-sheets of plywood for gussets, and finally he removed the ten-mil polyethylene sheeting he had bought to keep Mrs. Glamourpussy's upholstery clean and now folded away on a shelf for another day. Whatever you called it—Visqueen, ground cover, poly sheet—the stuff had endless uses. If Aletha only knew how he used it sometimes! He smiled as he lowered the garage door, shooing the feckless Princess aside so the door would not strike her, then locked the station wagon.

He took the stairs carefully, testing the drywall screws he'd installed, gratified by the silence of those stair treads. He unlocked his front door; disabled his noiseless alarm with a quick pass of his hand; locked the door again as usual. In a few minutes, he would be taking the Taurus back; but goddamn Aletha McCarran—she *would* set his imagination on edge, force him to seek relief as Mom had lectured him, and then he could face Aletha again with a steady gaze and hands that did not tremble.

In a way, aside from his constant learning experience with the Valley Players, he appreciated the woman for the temptation she offered, the testing of his self-control. Because he knew how to handle it. There was no real fury involved today, no self-loathing, hence no need to take stronger measures. Andrew was very much aware that those measures had gradually become more extreme. After a sacrifice from among his darlings, the tension would gradually return more pronounced than ever as he damned himself for needing outlets he could never explain to Mom. He was afraid that she would not understand.

He was afraid that she *would* understand.

He was halfway through the front room before his glance at the clock stopped him in midstride. He checked his watch. *One hour off.* It had to be an electrical glitch but *No, it doesn't, either,* he thought, a hot wave of apprehension climbing the nape of his neck. He went into a mode he had been trained for, a mode of deadly control: Mom's training.

You didn't give yourself away by showing fear, you kept on doing normal things but always strengthening your position, all senses hyperacute, waiting for your opponent to reveal himself.

And when he did, you'd better be ready. Hesitation had killed more people than bad aim ever did, according to Mom, and he knew that even if the intruder were armed with a search warrant, in your own home you could get a finding of accidental death by firing "in fear of your life" the instant you had a target. The little semiautomatic Ruger .22 with its folding stock and bipod—almost an assault rifle, though perfectly legal with its ten-round magazine—was stashed too far away, behind the false panel of his headboard. *Not optimum at close quarters,* Mom had cautioned. The tiny Davis Derringer, then, one of two that he owned, a half-pound palmful of death at close range; four inches long with a pair of .32 rounds, and it was as near as his videotape collection.

Feeling watched, he glided to the TV and snapped it on, audio muted, and plucked the cassette box labeled TAPE HEAD CLEANER from the stack. The derringer slid into his hand, half-hidden in his palm. And now, with the safety off, this was his home again, and he was master in it. But a soft footfall warned him of someone filling the bedroom hallway. As he moved sideways, he saw a face, impassive and shockingly familiar, and he came within a heartbeat of pulling the trigger.

"Very good," said Mom as he lowered the double-barreled weapon. "Almost perfect, Andrew."

"I—nearly. *Killed*. You," he managed to say, clumsy with the derringer as he replaced it in the cassette box, snapping off the TV again. The flood of emotion that washed over him was not relief, but frustration, confounded instantly by the pleasure of a rare, genuine compliment from Mom.

She seemed completely unshaken, moving into the big room now, nodding pleasantly to him. "You armed yourself immediately. How did you know I was here?"

You don't have to know everything, he told her silently, enjoying his moment. "I just—just knew somehow. That's all. I didn't know who, though. You think I would've shot my own mom on purpose?" His voice went high, thin—not the tone of command but of vulnerability. Frustration again.

She ignored his question, as she often did. "That sixth sense is something I've never been able to explain, either," Mom went on, crossing to the kitchen, taking her welcome for granted as she peered into his refrigerator. She chose a diet Coke, made an offering gesture to him, got a head shake, and popped its top for herself. "Just be glad you have it, Andrew." She moved back into the living room, swilling the Coke.

"I've got to be going," he said, sensing by the way she sat back on his sofa that she was in no hurry. "I borrowed a car to carry some stuff for stage flats." He did not need to ask why he hadn't seen her big Plymouth; she seldom parked within a block of a destination.

"I won't keep you long. I've spent the day cleansing the Merced rental and it gave me time to think about that scent-tracking device. How soon could we have one?"

Now it was obvious why she was treating him with such respect. She needed something that only he could provide, something she would not have discussed over telephone lines. He watched her drain the can, thinking, *You really don't know everything, do you, Mom?* Women her age didn't drink from cans that way, they sipped. When she dressed female, she should keep her gestures female; stay in character. But: *Tell you that? Try to teach the teacher? You'd bite my head off,* he decided. "The phero- mone tracker, you mean," he said. "Well, we're still doing field tests on it, and there's only one completed unit at the lab so far. It can't just disa- ppear, Mom. If it works out, in a year or so we might—"

"A year! Andrew, I'm surveilling two potential clients, and both of them like to play evasion games. One, in Sacramento, always goes through a big open plaza for foot traffic only. I think he's making contacts downtown, but if I can't get near enough to see where he goes—well," she said, shrugging.

Her surveillances were always cautious affairs, the sort of painstaking research that took several expensive people, or just one of world-class subtlety coupled with independent wealth. And that was Mom, all right. She might need several months of careful observing with a file folder of notes before she felt comfortable with her plans for a client. With Andrew's help and schematics, she had assembled a laser audio pickup that "listened" to the faint vibrations of a voice against a windowpane from over a hundred yards away. With the laser pickup, you didn't need the kind of electronic device that might be discovered by bug-finding countermeasure systems. It was advanced beyond anything she had known in the old days, she'd said, but now Mom had decided she should always be able to copy any new wrinkle.

"Well, you see, a pheromone tracker actually uses the antennae of a live insect," he explained, "and it won't work if you detach them. It has to be alive, and that takes some doing. The meters just amplify the natural signals picked up when a pheromone, a protein molecule of a certain kind, hits the antennae, but—"

"You've told me all that, Andrew. And I know the scent molecule isn't noticed by humans. That's why I've got to have this system."

"Mom, you've got to have it, but you don't even know if it's worth having. They're working on synthetic antennae, but so far, the live bug works best. We'd have to breed our own beetles to keep a steady supply;

I'd have to copy some classified schematics and buy sensors from restricted suppliers. I'm sorry I even mentioned the pheromone tracker now."

"Do they breed bugs at the lab? And do they count them? And if they do, couldn't one get loose now and then? Don't sensors overload or get broken? We need some positive thinking here, Andrew."

This was Mom at her worst: faced with an obstacle, suddenly and capriciously determined to scale it, willing to go to any lengths, make any demands, use any amount of her energies. And his. The trouble with his complaint was, sometimes all that endless research paid off; the laser audio, for example. And buoyed by one success, Mom would float past a dozen failures.

But that was Mom: picky, picky, picky. She would pick you to death, and she always had three more questions than you had answers so, "I'll do what I can," he said, not meeting her gaze, flushing and knowing it, unable to control this sign of his self-hatred which only made it worse. But he was the expert here, and he could be picky, too. "You'll have to be ready to feed the grub of the Malay beetle, *Popillia javanica*, that's what they're using; it's a pest they're starting to worry about, and it has big lamellate antennae that are easier to work with. The California Department of Agriculture provides the pheromone. Get some little avocado trees—five-gallon pots should do it. And you'll want grow lights."

"I'll just buy avocados," she said.

Oh, this was rich! He had some difficulty keeping the triumph out of his voice. "Mom, they eat the roots, not the fruit. That's why you need trees. And if the Malay beetle doesn't work out, they may have better luck with some other insect—no telling which one or what it feeds on."

Now she was staring at him, withholding her judgments, her little verbal lightnings. "Are you playing specialist games with me?"

"Just telling you what they're doing at the lab, and I'm not a specialist in this at all. If I can get specimens of everything, you'll have to be ready for them. It's not my fault, Mom." An old refrain, but this time with a new twist. He kept his eyes downcast, playing the role she wanted from him. Controlling her.

"I'll set the trees up in the annex," she said at last, referring to the unfinished house next to The Place. "I want us to get on this right away."

He nodded, jingling Aletha's keys in his hand. It occurred to him suddenly that it might be nice to have a spare key for that station wagon, just in case. Spares to all of Mrs. Glamourpussy's keys, in fact, a secret empowerment he would probably never use beyond his own satisfaction in it. He no longer needed to masturbate; his mood soared quietly now with small secret triumphs over Aletha and Mom as well. "I'll drop in on you Wednesday after work," he promised.

᛫ Mom started for the door, then paused. "I was looking at your pets when you came in, Andrew. Whatever happened to that big fluffy female?"

"They die," he said, shrugging as he opened the door. "Very short life spans, I'm afraid. Like your clients." He grinned to show that he was joking.

When Mom had walked off toward her car, he started the Taurus and sat for a moment, gunning its engine, enjoying the lusty sound. There would be time to get those keys copied. He savored the moment when he had told Mom what she'd have to do and then denied that he was, in her phrase, "playing games." He had carried off several pretenses before his toughest critic, all of them successful. That counted as a rave review.

Driving back to the playhouse, he thought about other roles. In Briant, there had been a grubby old fellow who collected bottles and rags. One baleful glance showing that white pupilless eye and people tended to shy away. And in Clovis, for a time, citizens had grown used to the pudgy young woman with the pageboy cut and singsong voice who haunted shopping malls, talking childish nonsense to anyone who made eye contact, capable of studying a potted palm for a half-hour; mildly retarded, harmless, with a sad, reproachful smile.

Occasionally, the old man had taken verbal abuse. Occasionally, mall-security folk had spoken with the girl. No one had ever penetrated the fact that, under the handmade wigs, both of these social rejects had been Andrew Soriano.

13

EARLY ON MONDAY, GARY HAD TROUBLE FINDING AN open barbershop in Palmdale; but the town has its military types, and the flat-topped butch haircut was a common request. When Gary tried his emergency number, Paul Visconti was out. Gary promised to call again from Palmdale at noon. He lied. Swede Halvorsen drove him, using Jan's 260Z, on to Newhall for the noon call because both towns were near enough to Los Angeles that his real base— Bakersfield—would seem a less-likely guess. And by using pay telephones, he made it easy for Visconti to verify that he was indeed calling from Southern California.

Swede still did not like driving the little Datsun. "Mountain roads or not, if this all turns to shit, your DEA boys are likely driving Broncos and such," the old man grumped. "In my ol' cast-iron Polara, we could bully 'em a little."

"Bullshit! You just want to light up the tires. Anyway, Jan's ten-speed wouldn't fit in this little bucket. She needs the Dodge more than we do."

"Couldn't light these tires up with a pail of gasoline," said Swede. "Good café in Saugus," he went on, pointing to a road sign along Highway 14.

"I called from a regular café before," Gary said. "Truck stop in Newhall changes our MO a little."

Swede's grunt was the nearest he would come to a compliment for this bit of subtlety on Gary's part. He shook his head. "Where's that dumb young shavetail I used to know and love?"

"Give us a kiss and I'll tell you." Gary warded off a backhand slap that would have caught him across his cast. "You wanta watch that," he went on and brought his forearm down on the car's shift lever to hear the gentle thwack of it. "This is the Dodge Polara of casts Jan put on me; brass knucks up to my elbow."

"She learned that with Freddie," Swede replied. "Pity she didn't leave him when he started getting drunked up, drugged up, beaten up."

"Fucked up," Gary supplied.

"Naw, that's what Jan did when she married him."

Gary held his ground. "Isn't he drying out in a funny farm back east? I'd say that's about as fucked up as it gets."

"Close. What's worse is Jan's being brought up Catholic, married to a Freddie who's not dead enough to qualify for a plot, and not alive enough to divorce. Dumb mackerel snappers," the old man muttered.

"You're Catholic," Gary reminded him.

"I say I am. Priest has his doubts." He pointed up the highway. "How's this look?"

In the distance, big semi rigs stood tall and inert against the rolling hills, awaiting fuel or drivers or merely the orders of some distant dispatcher. "They'll have plenty of pay phones," Gary said.

They did—a row of phones in a broad hall adjacent to a restaurant that smelled of yesterday's french fries and decades of cigar smoke. Gary established that a nearby side exit door was unlocked, and chose a phone from which he could see Halvorsen sitting at the fast-service counter, watching his back.

He reached his ASAC on the second ring. "I nearly got offed Friday night," Gary said without preamble and found himself interrupted. "When I say I don't know who, you're getting the benefit of some doubt." Pause. "Well, I'm banged around some, but what bothers me most is that, before it happened, Chuck Lane got a note saying it was one Paul Visconti who was setting me up for a long fall; literally, in this case. In a mine shaft! Paul, I've got to tell you I'm not coming in till I'm sure about that note."

This time he waited longer. He'd been afraid it would be like this, and now he did the interrupting: "Make it quick, mister. If you're tracing the call, that's cool but I don't intend to be here ten minutes from now. Just wanted to make it official and for attempted murder of this federal agent, the Fresno office is the proper conduit—I've got reasons to be out of the loop awhile. Put me on medical leave, vacation, compassionate leave, whatever. Or fire me if you have to."

Another pause, nodding as if Visconti were facing him. His management of the next moments now would be important; enough time for a call trace to place him near Los Angeles, not enough to get a tail on him. "Okay, and thanks. But check out Chuck Lane's apartment in Merced and you'll understand. A few minutes after my place was hit, two women nailed me in the butt with a hypodermic while I was going for my BMW. . . . Damn right, out in the open. Actually I'm not sure they were women. I've kept a urine sample, and I'd sure like to know what I was hit with. . . . Oh, I'm not *that* paranoid, I'm mailing you enough to fill out a Six. Also, just in case, I'm leaving duplicates and some evidence where it'll surface if I get taken down. . . . To the Bureau, Paul. Politically, it's the worst thing I could do, and by then I'll be past caring. I'm feeling a little hard-nosed right now. . . . Sorry, man. You can hope I stay healthy and this can all stay among friends. Assuming you're clean, you'll appreciate what I'm doing." *And if you're dirty, you'll be scrambling for a cover-up.*

After another pause, he laughed. "You're really not tracing my call? Sure, I can tell you: off I-Five near the summit, waiting for my ride to fuel up. . . . Just ask yourself what you'd do in my place. . . . When this is over, I hope I can apologize. I'll give you another noon call in a day or so. But don't expect me to take any more chances for a while, okay?"

Gary replaced the receiver and checked his wristwatch, nodding to Swede as he headed for the little car alone via the side exit. He'd been on the phone for a little over three-and-a-half minutes, long enough for a trace to verify his general location. If Visconti were behind the attempt on his life, he'd assume the worst; that Gary himself was running to L.A., a megalopolis where a man could hide indefinitely. Paul—or whoever it was—almost certainly would have help. *And if Paul Visconti knows I was dumped into a hole containing another body, right about now he'll be between a shit and a sweat wondering how to dispose of the evidence.*

A dozen sticks of dynamite down the hole would do it nicely, he thought. That was why he had given Jan Betancourt such explicit instructions before she'd left Bakersfield that morning for Fresno, driving the Polara. He did not have enough details of the land contours where he had gone through that fence, but all he needed was a report of sudden activity nearby. Jan had claimed she could do that much from concealment across the road, biking the last mile or so, hauling her old Peugeot bike into the woods with her.

When Swede arrived to unlock the car, Gary slid inside without help. The arm was mending, but it could still remind him that it was fractured. "We mail this package at the truck stop. Go back the way we came and call Jan first," he said.

But the old man was already driving toward the mail drop, pulling on gloves to handle the package. When he had pushed Gary's bulky package into the proper slot, he got under way again. "Hold on a few minutes," he urged. "I'm gonna go 'round the cloverleaf a couple of times and watch. Wouldn't it be interesting to see about three black-and-whites peeling off the freeway in the next few minutes, converging on that truck stop," he said, wheeling toward an on ramp.

"That would be good news," Gary said. It was beyond belief that the highway patrol would be on the wrong side as well, and it would probably mean Visconti was clean. "At least, I think it would." The two men shared a cynical glance at this final admission of uncertainty, then studied traffic as it swirled in broad patterns around the truck stop. When no marked cars approached after two circuits, Swede followed signs back to Highway 14, left Newhall behind, and stopped in the pass on a side road where the highway was both out of sight and almost out of earshot. Finally he lifted the cellular phone. Without the engine running, it was eerily quiet in the car, so quiet they could hear a constant breeze keening through the pass.

They had already agreed that Gary would not speak on their cellular link; and that, if confronted, Jan would link up to the Fresno County Sheriff's people instantly. Among the three of them, Jan had been the only one without a case of nerves over her part. "If I'm off the road, I won't be seen. If I'm seen away from the car, I'll be a biker on a back road. I do it all the time," she had said. "Besides, if I can't find a place to hide in a forest, I deserve to get caught."

Swede had demanded that they switch roles, with Gary seconding the idea; which only taught them for the umpty-umpth time that you didn't give orders to Janelle Betancourt. "I'm going to do it, Ampa," she'd said. "You can lump it, or you can like it."

Swede was lumping it as he waited for her to answer. "Hundred goddamn things could happen, her out there alone—Hi, Nellie," he said, voice shifting in mid-syllable to a sprightly tone. No one but her grandfather was ever permitted to use that particular nickname. "Can you talk?"

"Who is this, Joan Rivers? Never mind, Ampa, Trivial Pursuit was never your game. I've already found the gate, near that detached fender, but the phone won't work from there. I'm parked at the overlook to the dam on your map."

That would be Briant Dam. The way Swede held the phone, her words carried easily to Gary. "Good, that's miles from the gate. Tell her to get crackin'," Gary said.

"The call has been made. Time to grab your Ritz crackers and a book and hunker down," Swede told her. "Try and find a location where you can make a call while you wait."

"All set. And if I need to call and can't, I could pretend," she said. "Who's to know?"

Gary's quick grin said, *Smart lady* to Swede. The old man's return glance replied, *I don't like this one damn bit.* "If you have to strike out into the woods to avoid somebody, I'll buy you new wheels. You hear me, Nell?"

"Sounds like a good deal, Ampa. I may just fake it to get a new Peugeot. How's our one-armed bandit?" From her tone, Gary wondered if she were taking all this seriously enough. Like Halvorsen, he'd tried to impress on Jan that anyone she met near that gate of barbed wire might be as deadly as a Coast rattler, and that not meeting anyone was by far the best policy.

"He's dumb and he's ugly, like always, but I can't seem to ditch him," Swede said. "We're headed out now, and I want a call from you at three, even if you have to leave your post."

"Ten-four, good buddy, or whatever it is you guys say." And with that, she broke the connection.

Swede sat without moving for a moment except for the tap, tap, tap of his fingers on the steering wheel. Gary said, "You're thinking, screw this, I-Five is faster—right?"

"Yeah."

"You're right, we can do seventy-five on that racetrack and have folks passing us. Let's do it. I know the connecting roads around Fresno. We can be there before five."

"And what's more," the old man said, spewing gravel, "you're as worried about her as I am."

She called a few minutes after 3:00 as Swede was driving past a vast set of livestock pens. "Just checking in. I found a nice spot a quarter of a mile from that gate and I want to get back to it so's I don't miss anything. Nothing to miss, so far. Eleven cars up the road in two hours isn't exactly a crowded freeway. You two boring each other to tears?"

"Naw, but there's a rank smell in here, I can't decide whether it's the cattle pens or my partner."

She laughed. "I know exactly where you are, then." That stretch near Kettleman City in central California was infamous for its *eau de cowplop,* and Swede cursed under his breath. He could not have broadcast his location any better with compass headings. Jan went on. "Oh—the car will be parked off the road near a little culvert, about three miles your side of the, uh, spot in question. And the breeze is pretty crisp around there. I'll come back here at six, okay?"

Gary, leaning over to hear while Swede held the receiver to help him, flashed his right hand up, all fingers open. "Make it five," Swede corrected. "We'll see you there."

Favored with light traffic along the lesser Route 41 into Fresno, they took the arterial directly through town. Commuters and traffic lights had them cursing near Clovis at 4:30, but almost on the stroke of 5:00 they fled through the countryside northeast of Fresno, tires chirping, past a familiar vehicle near a culvert.

Gary: "You see your car back there?"

Halvorsen: "I saw it. She's late, goddammit."

Gary: "Well take it easy. If she's on the way, you don't want her for a hood ornament."

"Shut *up,* Landis," said the old man, but he slowed his pace and, minutes later, they passed Gary's landmark fender at a leisurely pace. "Still no Janelle," Swede said.

"But no sign of anybody else either," Gary replied, pointing at the sagging old wire fence.

"Recent tire tracks," Swede noted.

"They were there before. Let's find a turnaround. You might try the phone again," Gary said.

"In OCID, that's what they called micromanagement. Knock it off, rookie," Swede rasped. He found a wide spot moments later and made an expert one-eighty, passing the gate again at a crawl.

Swede had just picked up the cellular phone when Gary let out a loud "Thank God! There she is," finishing with a shaky laugh.

She was removing twigs from the front spokes of her bike and had obviously seen them, but made no outward sign as if to prove her coolness in the field. Moments later she was pedaling away briskly, bent over old-style racing handlebars, buttocks appealingly raised in tight jeans.

"I don't wanta know what you're thinking," Swede said, watching his granddaughter's fanny undulate at thirty miles an hour.

"Wishing I had a peashooter," Gary said.

"Sorry 'bout my temper, boy," Swede said after a moment.

"I had it coming."

"You did," the old man agreed. They maintained a hundred-yard deficit, speeding up as Jan did forty on the downhill sweeps. "She's really something, you know that," Swede said, low in his throat.

"I always did," Gary said, shrugging as Swede glanced his way.

"Dunno how to say this, so I'll just say it, Gary: she's not seeing anybody, and I guess I'm glad. But if she's gonna complicate her life with some asshole, I'd just as soon it was one I trust."

Gary managed to avoid a grin. "Is this your way of telling me what an asshole I am?"

Now it was the old man who shrugged. "Always thought you knew," he said. They rode in silence for a minute or so before Swede went on: "Young woman on a ten-speed, no weapon; you realize just how vulnerable she was out here?"

"Yep. Were you going to stop her?"

"Nope. Hell, Gary, that's your job. If anyone could change her mind, it'd be the boyfriend."

"It might, if I enjoyed that status."

Swede shot him a disbelieving look. "After two days, you don't know?"

"No, and she doesn't, either," Gary insisted.

Now the old man laughed. "You know, I believe it; I believe I'm the only one who sees that. Ever watch one of those nature specials that show flamingos and peacocks? Well, listen: birds don't do any more dumb-fuck mating dances than you two. 'Course you don't know how she was before you came back here all stove up needing TLC and a hidey-hole. When she came back from the East Coast she'd pulled into herself a lot, got that job teaching aerobics to old ladies, little mobile home I had to crawl around under to repair water damage; a lot of solitary shit. I know for a fact she gets hit on by guys at her health spa, which is half meat market in my book. Now all of a sudden she's cracking jokes. Wearing lipstick. Combing her hair. And by God I bet she doesn't even realize it. Flamingos! I bet they don't see what they're doing, either." He laughed again.

Because Gary did not know what to say, he only grunted. Soon they descended into the valley with its inevitable creek and pulled up beside the sturdy old Dodge as Jan removed the front wheel of her bike for stowage. "My God, you look like a football jock again with that butch cut," she said, and cocked her head. "Nice, in a Kojakish kind of way.

Anyhow, nobody stopped. Nobody even slowed," she said as Gary unfolded himself from the Datsun. "Dull city."

Swede heard, too. "Police work. Ninety percent of it's that way. And right now that's good news, Nell."

She managed to get her bike into the big car without help, then glanced at her watch. "I've got a late class tonight and I can just make it, guys." To Gary: "Still intend to take the night shift out here? You'll have mosquitoes for company."

"I figured on that. Can't be helped," he replied. "They waited till dark to dump me, and they might play it that way again. I've got to know."

Her peck against his cheek came and went so quickly that he almost failed to take note of it. "I know you do. Which car?"

"Leave the Polara right here," Swede urged. "Little neglect never hurt it. You mind the walk tomorrow, Kojak?"

Gary claimed he didn't. After Jan got into the big car and gave Gary the keys, she locked herself in momentarily while the two men drove back toward the surveillance site. Swede helped Gary haul Jan's old mummy bag and a sackful of amenities from behind the seats: sandwiches, coffee flask, flashlight, repellent, a paperback by Abbie Hoffman entitled *Steal This Book*. Then, with a thumb-up gesture, the old man zoomed away while Gary hurriedly climbed through the fence. He had his Beretta and his plan. As the Datsun's engine note faded, he was thinking, *If only I had a good camera with infrared film . . .*

14

RALPH GUTHRIE WAS SPOOKED. AFTER FAILING TO RAISE his cartel buddy, Chuck Lane, on Friday night, he'd tried again the next morning. Then, because Hermosillo hotheads like Pepe Luna didn't want to hear "I don't know" for an answer, he'd driven to Lane's place; see if he was hung over, see if his little Beemer was in its stall. The car was there, and squeezed ahead of it in the stall was that blazing-quick Kawasaki bike, but no amount of ringing Lane's doorbell got any reaction, and he wasn't about to pick the lock if Lane might be in there. Only when Guthrie walked around intending to toss pebbles against windows did he see the big pane shattered.

The old credit card–unlatcher trick failed him, and he could hear someone moving around in the next apartment, but that broken window drove his curiosity up enough notches to bring his lockpicks into play. It seemed to take forever.

Guthrie had already put his gloves on to wipe down the knob and the doorbell, and he was damned glad of it once he was safe inside. Maybe "safe" wasn't quite the word. Sure as shit, that living room had been very unsafe, very recently. Guthrie looked for bloodstains, Chuck's body, and a stash in that order, and did not find any of them. But Luna had said that Lane was holding a small bundle of cash for La Familia; quite small, in fact, for them. It might look a good deal larger to Lane. And if ol' Chuckie had bugged out with one cent of Hermosillo money, it was time for Ralph to downplay their friendship. Those bullet holes looked as if somebody on Luna's payroll had already taken an active dislike to Lane.

109

Another question loomed suddenly. A series of slugs stitching their way across a room in a crowded apartment complex should have made a hell of a racket. Why hadn't he seen a strip of yellow plastic across Lane's front door? Maybe because the apartment was now bait left out by cops and the noises in that next apartment were from big flat feet waiting for the trap to spring. If so, Ralph Guthrie had sprung it, but would not know for certain until he opened that front door again, or even the kitchen door.

Guthrie did not consider the fact that, if nobody is alarmed enough to call the police, they never arrive. He tiptoed into the back bedroom, cranked the window open, pulled its screen inside, and dropped fourteen feet, minus the four feet of hedge he fell into. It broke his fall, and his hide in several places, and eventually brought the police because a bright ten-year-old saw him coming out of that window and had always longed for a reason to dial 911.

So Guthrie had an interesting story to tell Saturday evening, but nobody to tell it to because dopers enjoy spending money, and instead of answering his pager, Pepe Luna was showering some of it around a private club that specialized in salsa music, but not in Anglo members. By Sunday morning there were plenty of yellow plastic streamers around Lane's apartment, and around his BMW and bike as well. Guthrie wore his Sunday sport coat and a tie to stroll through the area, feeling watched, but learned little more for his trouble.

On Monday, Guthrie was summoned by phone to the creek-side strip of Applegate Park in central Merced. When Guthrie arrived, a familiar black Lincoln slummed in a nearby parking space. Pepe Luna sat on a picnic bench getting his satin shirt dusty with powdered sugar as he swigged coffee from a big cardboard cup and scarfed *pan dulce,* a Latino equivalent of doughnuts. It was his broken knuckles that made Luna so maladroit; both of his hands looked as if they had, at one time or another, taken the worst of an argument with a boot heel. Though not much taller or wider than Guthrie, Luna positively towered over the pair of his wizened soldiers who sat by the boom box, wearing western boots and identical black jeans, snapping their fingers to music that was not quite too loud. Ralph Guthrie never got used to those slithery little wetbacks; seldom speaking, eyes always searching except to stare, evidently from the same clutch of snake eggs, straight long black hair with enough oil to lube the Luv. They were about the size of coral snakes, and roughly as much fun to deal with.

Not that Luna was any great joy. He listened to Guthrie's account quietly, stopping him only to ask a few questions in the soft, graceful accent of the Latino. From Pepe Luna that accent said, *We are a gentle people. Even our knives slide in gently.*

When Guthrie had finished, Luna thought it over awhile. Then he said, "I can learn what the local police know. Do you think your friend Lane has taken our money?"

"Hey, not my friend," Guthrie protested, his hands rising quickly enough to arrest the gaze of the snakes. "It might depend on how much there was, Pepe—Mr. Luna."

A judicious nod. "Have you received any warnings or even friendly contacts from—other businessmen? Bikers? Blacks wearing gang colors? Has he, you think?"

Somehow it had never occurred to Guthrie that drug turf wars against La Familia might explode in a town like Merced. "They'd have to be nuts."

"Some of them are. My question," Luna reminded gently.

"No, never; hell, I'd have come straight to you! Can't speak for Lane," Guthrie replied.

"Then find him, so that he can speak to us for himself. And do not let him know you have found him. Just contact me immediately; we will take it from there."

"If I ever see him again. Jeez, he's prob'ly still running." Guthrie punctuated his little joke by moving his forefinger, jabbing it as he made sound effects: "Puh-puh-puh-puh-puh."

Luna did not smile. "Make it your job to see him again. Visit every place he frequents. Keep an eye on his car. I will tell you what I learn to speed the process, but this is *el estilo de,* um, a tactic I have seen before. Frighten the little soldier into surrendering to another chief. But, deny it all you will, Chuck Lane was your friend. You brought him to me. Find him. You have one week."

"Jesus Christ! I don't know where to start, I've already stuck my neck out a mile, going into his apartment for you, I got Band-Aids all over from a sticker bush. A week?"

"If your Mr. Lane becomes an embarrassment to me, and you do not find him, Band-Aids will not cover your problems," said Pepe Luna. "You may use a thousand for expenses. I cannot be more fair than that."

You got some rough notions about what's fair, you spic bastard, but I knew that coming in. "I'll do my best," Guthrie said. "It'd help if I had a photo of Lane, but—" His shrug was helpless.

"You can describe him well enough. Aaah," Luna went on, disgusted; "I suppose it would help. Very well, I will supply a photo." Without turning, he uttered a rapid burst in Spanish.

"*Sí, patrón,*" said one of the snakes.

"He will deliver it to you at the bar—you know which one," Luna said to Guthrie. "Seven tonight. You may go," he added.

Guthrie wanted to back away, but he squared his shoulders and made himself grin as he walked back to the Luv, thinking hard. He would begin by checking hospitals, something he should have thought of before. And he knew several bars to try; he would make a pass twice a day to check on the bike, which Luna hadn't even mentioned, and the BMW. If Chuck Lane could do something stupid over a small bundle of cash, he'd probably take just as many chances to retrieve that sweet little set of wheels, cop warnings or no cop warnings.

It would be essential for him to keep in close touch with Luna to see what the spics turned up. If nothing broke for him in the next six days, maybe it would be time to move on without prior notice. Oakland or Denver might be nice.

But he might never again sit astride a money pipeline the way he did with Luna's outfit, and there was still a chance he could raise Lane. Even if there wasn't, somebody on Luna's payroll would probably be watching to see whether Ralph Guthrie was really beating the bushes, so he'd beat them.

Anything else? Not Candlestick Park—that would be one chance in a billion. Local sports events, dirt-track racing? Bike shops? Yeah, all definite possibilities. And then a submerged memory surfaced in his mind to pop its contents like a bubble: there was that receipt he had noticed, just a glance that prompted an instant of unspoken curiosity, when Lane was replacing a lever on his Kawasaki. The cycle shop that had sold that lever was not in Merced, but fifty miles away.

In Fresno.

15

MAY 1994

THE SAN DIEGO CENTER OF THE DEA IS ONE OF ONLY A dozen Division offices, and its secure lines to the local Fresno office stayed warm on Monday. Paul Visconti, in Fresno, had needed very little time to verify that Merced police had found Chuck Lane's apartment violated not once, but twice, in entirely different ways. Visconti's guess was that their Hermosillo connection in Merced had gone balls-up, but someone with a soft spot for agent Gary Landis had tipped him off in a way that would screw all parties, including DEA. Whoever it was had used Paul's name. Visconti had weathered serious leaks before, but this one had almost been fatal.

To make it worse, Visconti admitted to himself that he was monumentally pissed at Landis for entertaining a charge of treachery from above, giving credence to a tip from an anonymous source. *A few rounds through your living-room window could make a believer out of anybody,* a small voice responded in his head. *How calm would I have been in those circumstances?*

He covered Gary Landis's butt for officialdom, cursing under his breath as he did it, and began a computer search to discover which drug-connected hit teams employed women—or men passing as women. He knew that Israelis, Palestinians, and the IRA had all done it. Their connections to Hermosillo's La Familia, if any, were unknown. The Cali cartel was rumored to use a female courier named Nuñez-Moncada, but the woman was not considered violent. More likely this was a new wrinkle initiated by the Mexican dopers by themselves. *It's never been their MO. Perhaps they're getting more sophisticated,* he thought. He stayed late at the office that evening, telling himself it wasn't because he hoped for another call from the absent Landis.

On Tuesday Visconti drove to Merced wearing an ill-fitting old suit, heavy brogans, and no tie. In company of a detective and with all the plainclothes cops who'd seen that apartment in the past few days, he would pass to an outsider as another of the local brigade. Gary's neighbors had been canvassed; the time of the gunfire on Friday and the second-story man's defenestration on Saturday added more questions and no answers. Visconti learned precious little beyond a strong gut feeling that an extra faction was at work here.

When faced with knotty riddles, Paul Visconti tended to abstract the problem, to make it fit a more general case. This kind of intellectual chess had sometimes helped untangle a case. Just as often, it simply stole his time. Driving back to Fresno, he played his mental game and, from some forgotten source text, borrowed the notion of two factions. One faction, with a penchant for direct action, wanted Gary Landis dead. They had shot at him, kidnapped him, even tried to dispose of the body. Both times they had failed, suggesting a streak of incompetence combined with a violent nature. *For that we can substitute La Familia, but a lot of others as well. Too early for such substitutions—what's next?*

The other faction was friendly enough to Gary—or perhaps to the law enforcement he represented—to give him a sporting chance. They knew Visconti's name. So they had lied, warning Landis about his supervisor. *Someone who can operate out of the usual loops, an agent of change, of chaos. So we've got the direct action group and the agents of chaos, and a given individual might be a member of both groups.* Visconti grunted to himself in irritation. So far, chaos seemed to be winning.

In his mind's eye, Visconti was gazing at pictures of Ralph Guthrie in the case file. *Too early for that, I said,* he warned his inductive side. But at least one side of Paul Visconti thought it knew who had warned his street agent.

On Wednesday, his mail included a bulky manila envelope with plenty of packing. He had it opened remotely and the receptionist flinched when his "Good Christ!" rebounded from the glass front of her cubicle. McMilligan and another agent appeared at his side in moments. Paul Visconti was not the kind of man to exclaim at trifles.

They handled the human jawbone carefully inside its Baggie, temporarily ignoring the sealed bottle and the sheets of cheap typing paper covered with the cursive scrawl of Gary Landis. This was no recent victim, they agreed; probably dead for years.

"Not a lot of wear on the molars," McMilligan noted. "Very young, I'd say."

"Male," Visconti said, "judging from the pronounced angle of the jaw. But I could be wrong. Okay, this is what we were waiting for. Looks like priority work for Forensics. Don, you take care of packaging while I read this; save a little time."

In another hour they were less upbeat because by then, Visconti thought, he had read enough particulars to locate that mine shaft north of Clovis. And that meant overtime. By nightfall they'd found the place, contacted the Fresno County Sheriff's people, and identified the property owner starting with plat maps.

In a case like this, with the Feds claiming priority and willing to commit their resources, a county sheriff was smart to waive most of the responsibility, and Fresno County's sheriff was not dumb. He did, however, take time to make a personal visit to the site. "I guess we'll be clearing up an old missing-persons squawk pretty soon," he said, speaking over the distant rattle of an engine-driven water pump. Fifty feet distant, a big hose from the shaft spewed water which spilled through wire mesh before trickling into the soil.

"Two," said agent McMilligan, holding the big spotlight for him as they peered into the sloping shaft. "Could be more."

The sheriff squinted harder. "How can you tell?"

"'Cause I went down there with a damn rope around my waist to put that suction hose in place. And where the slope flattens out, farther in the hole just beyond where we can see from here, there's another body."

"Floater?"

"Has that transparent look," McMilligan said, "but this one hasn't been floating for a long, long time."

16

AFTER SPENDING MONDAY NIGHT IN A MUMMY BAG WITH-
out result, waiting to verify his worst suspicions, Gary returned to Bakersfield. And every time he recalled the patient
tone in the voice of Paul Visconti, he felt more and more like a
thoroughgoing asshole. Still, he knew it would take time for a competent
forensics rundown on the package he'd sent, and he refused to risk
another call until he could verify that Visconti really was doing what an
agent-in-charge should be doing. On Thursday he drove alone to the little
town of Fillmore and made that call.

It was too soon for a pathology report on the jawbone, Visconti told
him; or the urine sample either. "We only got your evidence yesterday,
Landis; give 'em a break. We've already put out an alert on Chuck Lane's
driver's license and credit cards. I'll tell you this: if anyone in the system
thought you'd gone berserk, they don't think so anymore. We found your
mine shaft yesterday, and you were wrong; there were two bodies down
there before you, not one."

"No idea who, I suppose," Gary mused.

"Not the bones; we think it was a young male. Just got a confirmation
on the other one, though, from prints."

Gary's paranoia flared. "How do you get prints off a skeleton?"

"You don't, but evidently the water level fluctuates in that shaft from
year to year. Some time after the youngster was dumped—long enough
for the body to decay fully—another adult male was dropped down there,
probably while the water level was higher. When the water receded again,

119

it took the second body a little way downslope with it. Since the water's cold down there—"

"Tell me about it," Gary growled.

"Well, it was a break for us. You know about adipocere tissue?"

Gary paused to make the connection. Adipocere was a transformation of soft body tissues into something between fat and soap, formed over a long period of time in cold, wet surroundings. It made a ghastly sight, but adipocere had been known to preserve evidence for years. "You're saying you've got a complete corpse," he said at last.

"Complete enough for prints."

"Whose?"

"That's a real eye-opener, and you can just get your ass back here and find out for yourself. I'm not going to cover for you forever, Gary."

A sudden tightening of his throat made Gary's voice husky. *Goddammit, what's wrong with me?* "I want to, Paul. I'd—okay, just one more favor. Who else could I call, just so I'll know this whole business is fully in the system and—you know."

"I know, you suspicious bastard." After a low, mirthless laugh, Visconti told him to call the group supervisor in the San Diego office. "Or, if you want to look like a putz, call the SAC and tell him you still suspect me. They both know you're running hurt; they just don't know you're running loose from me like this. That wouldn't look good on your record. You getting the picture?"

"In full color, with instant replay."

"So quit jerking us off; McMilligan could use some help," Visconti said, none too kindly, before he broke the connection.

Gary returned to Bakersfield before making his San Diego call to a group supervisor he knew slightly. It was good to hear he was ready for work again, said the GS; it wasn't every day that the DEA fell into cases that had remained open so long at Langley. And with both a skull from that hole and the mandible Gary had brought up, they had a good shot at a positive identification on those skeletal remains. Again, that sudden surge of emotion that almost blocked Gary's voice for a moment. But a different feeling this time: elation, even gooseflesh on his neck. He wondered if that whack on his head had scrambled his brains for him, after all.

Gary returned to Swede Halvorsen's place more bemused than ever. "So it's obvious that my RAC is straight-arrow, Swede," he said in summation to the old man over a beer. "I should'a known that—I feel like a dumb shit—and I'm flying back to Fresno tomorrow. They've taken two bodies out of the mine shaft."

Halvorsen sprinkled a smidgen of salt into his beer and Gary shuddered, having tried salted beer exactly once. Halvorsen sipped and smacked his lips. "They ID either one?"

"I think so. Uh, this is getting to a point where I'm not sure how much I should say to you," he said.

"Suit yourself," said Swede. "But if you ever wanta consider this a safe house again, and if you haven't already told 'em about me, you'll be smart to keep me and this place out of the loop. Janelle, too. *Especially* Nell," he went on. "You have any problem with that?"

"No problem." But he could see that Swede was not pleased to be treated as an outsider, now that a few partial answers were being teased from the evidence. "Okay, look, I'm just gonna review what I know, talk to my beer here, and if some old retired fart from LAPD happens to overhear me, I can't help it." They touched beer cans together, and Gary began his brief recitation.

When he had finished: "You don't mean the air base," Swede prompted. "Like in Langley, with the wind tunnels. You mean Langley, like in CIA."

Gary nodded. "Now, as it happens, I've liaised with a few of their guys, not much more than street contacts, but shit, often as not they play games against each other! You ever hear about the Howard Marks case?" The old man shook his head and threw him an interested glance. "Brit kingpin in the hashish trade; we called him Marco Polo. The sonofabitch was staying a step ahead of us for years 'cause a couple of his informants were in our loop. Fuckers had CIA connections. Anyhow, Marks finally went inside for a few years. Now I figure one of those bodies in that hole must be drug connected—not with Marks, of course, but I'm told it's closing an old Company file. Or reopening it—hell, I don't know," he shrugged. "When I find out, I'll most likely not want to pass it along."

"Don't suppose you will," Halvorsen agreed.

"It's for your own safety," Gary burst out.

"Put a lid on it, Gary. I'm satisfied," the old fellow insisted.

Gary could not know how far his guess had strayed from the facts. Sheepishly, he broached another worry to the old man; this emotional roller coaster that he found so unsettling. "It's worse than butterflies before the USC game, Swede! And very different, not like anything I've felt before. Shit. Do you know what I'm talking about?"

After a brief pause, a judicious nod. "Well, you never got took down like that before. I prob'ly wouldn't understand, if I hadn't lucked out once or twice from getting myself iced—and by pure dumb-assed luck, same as you." Almost whispering now: "It's a confidence problem." And a wry smile, followed by, "I'm not surprised that's a first, for you."

"Oh, horseshit! Me? Listen, DEA doesn't run psych profiles on candidates for nothing. The way Visconti tells it, an agent's problem is thinking he's such hot stuff the rules don't apply—which is why some agents get strung out on drugs or run games on the agency."

"But not you?"

Disgustedly: "Swede, you think I'm that stupid?"

"Not stupid at all. That's exactly why you're startin' to realize you're beatable, under the right circumstances. Problem you've got, kid, is that you realize just how lucky you were. All that macho 'I'm too good to take a fall' young buck confidence has been squeezed plumb out of your ass with an enema called 'reality.' It's no fun, Gary. It's hell till you get comfortable with the idea that you got set up, just like anybody else, and the rest of your life will be borrowed time."

For a long moment, Gary sat and blinked and thought about it, searching for a denial, finding none that would ring true. At last: "Yeaaaah, but meanwhile I'm not sure I'll be worth a damn as an agent, the way—"

"Wait." Swede held his hand up to halt these doubts. "I've been paying attention, kid, and it looks to me like you can't wait for payback time. Hell, you even went back to that hole in the ground. Some guys wouldn't have gone back."

"You think I'm looking for my confidence."

Swede Halvorsen grinned at him. "I think you're looking for that old *over*confidence, but good sense will keep you from finding it. I think you'll be a better cop for it. Best you can do is give it a few weeks and see."

Not completely convinced, Gary finished his beer in silence. It wasn't easy to admit your subconscious had been probing your virtues and, as Jan put it, scrubbing that big 'S' off your chest. He found his spirits rising later as he ironed his trousers near the kitchen pass-through.

"God, that's an awful job you're doing," Swede commented, watching from a kitchen stool.

"You could do better?"

"Blindfolded," said Swede, "but you need the practice. My expert powers of deduction tell me I won't have to cook for you tonight." A sheepish grin from Gary validated his guess. "And I guess it's none of my business where you're going."

Gary put down the iron and placed both palms flat on the ironing board, regarding his friend with a composite of amusement and exasperation. "Mr. Halvorsen, sir, I'd like your permission to keep a dinner date tonight with your thirty-something granddaughter, since we both know she has no mind of her own. I'll make sure she drives carefully, and I believe she has the hots—wups, 'scuse me, a desire, to see a picture called *Sunset Boulevard,* and if it's not rated PG, maybe I can talk her out of it. And I promise to have her home by—oh, September or so. Don't wait up."

Swede Halvorsen studied his fingernails, blushing. "Aw, go fuck yourself," he muttered.

Gary could not resist it: "You wish!"

Swede needed two beats to get the implication. "That's enough, goddammit," he said, scandalized. "I can remember when I bounced her on my knee."

"Yeah, and God help anybody else who'd like to, three decades later. Right?" Swede looked away, his ears glowing, and Gary relented. "I'm sorry. I know how you feel, Swede. She's had it rough enough; I intend to let her work things out in good time, and I'll be gone tomorrow. But I'll be back if she wants me around. I thought that was agreeable to you."

"It is." Bursting out: "Shit fire and save matches, Gary, she's my responsibility!"

Gary stood on one leg, pulling on his trousers. "No she's not, Swede. That's what I'm trying to get across. You're a great cop, the best I've ever seen, but Jan doesn't want you to be her cop. Be her friend. She may need help; hell, so did I, and I asked for it, including the better part of two hundred bucks you loaned me and some insights I'm still trying to digest. Jan just needed another kind of help. That's what friends are for, isn't it?"

Now, watching Gary zip up, the old man began to chuckle. "Somebody told me once, 'A friend who's willing to be understood is a joy, but a friend who demands understanding is a royal pain in the ass.' Was he ever right!"

"So which one am I?"

"Both. Nellie, too, and you damn well know it," Swede growled.

"Yeah, I do." And with two strides, Gary reached the old man, gave him the briefest of one-armed hugs. "Thanks—I think."

That was when Jan rang the doorbell. She brought a faint scent of orange blossoms in with her and left a light smudge of lipstick on the old man's cheek before doing a comic double take at the sight of Gary. "Wow," she said, "I must rate, guys."

Gary took in the tan wedgies, suede skirt, and short-sleeved yellow blouse that complemented her tan without following her contours too obviously, and allowed as how she rated, all right.

"He's been ironing," Swede said, as if conferring a vast secret.

"I smelled it," she replied, glancing at his clothing. "I always say, if you can't iron the wrinkles out, iron them in permanently. Grunge chic."

"I tried," Gary protested helplessly.

"And I'm impressed. Hey, if we want to make the movie, we'd better be going." Gary was easing his bad arm into his jacket when she called back to the old man who was still sitting, a bit morosely, on his stool. "Don't wait up, Ampa." And she wondered aloud why the two men laughed in unison.

Gary would not tell her. "Tag line to a joke," he said, and changed the subject. He was now satisfied, he said, that he could fly back to Fresno the following morning. It would be good to be back in harness, drive his own car out of the DEA lot behind the office, have a change of clothes, beeper on his belt, take the initiative again. *Beeper equals backup equals more confidence. I hate to admit it, but Swede had a point,* he told himself.

Jan tried to be happy for him and his announcement, but it didn't play very well. Gary was perversely happy for that; she might even miss him a little. They lingered over their dinner at a steakhouse near Highway 99 with a curiously mutual shyness, like teenagers on a blind date, with here a tentative smile at nothing, there an accidental touch across the table. He wondered what she would do if, after all this genderless buddy-buddy of the past week, he tried to put a move on her. *She's definitely laughing too much at my jokes,* he thought; *sending the wounded doughboy back to the front with fond memories, maybe even a good-night kiss.* But hell, at least now they shared a relationship, of sorts. A definite improvement over the past.

She had him laughing, too, over dessert. She was full, she said, as he ordered cherry pie. "But I'll take a bite when you aren't looking." Her voice shifted as the waitress moved away, to a faint, delicately tongue-tied accent, unmistakably a Hindu intellectual. "Pie. I love pie, I am obsessed with pie. I have meditated on pi ever since I learned that pi was a transcendental number." When he looked up, startled at her bewildering turn of whimsy, she went on. "I dialed three-point-one-four-one-six, but God hung up on me. I was in rapture; everyone is hung up on God, but God's hung up on *me*," she finished, as Gary rocked with silent mirth.

"Where the hell did you get that," he asked finally.

She looked down, with a negative headshake. "You don't want to know."

Through his fading grin: "Freddie," he guessed. She nodded. "Well, he must've had his moments. That's good; weird, but good."

"That was Freddie," she agreed, her smile working around old memories. "Or rather, it was one of a hundred Fred Penroses; you never knew which one you were dealing with. Intellectual Freddie, surly Freddie, the loving or the snarling or the plain overdosed Freddie. It was all too much, finally," she sighed.

"Too many Freds," he supplied.

Another nod, and an effort to brighten her moment. "He gave me a little aquarium once, with five little neon tetras in it. Said their names were Fred, Fred, Fred, Fred, and of course, Fred. Bright little Freddies to keep me company, he said, when he was really bad company.

"And," she went on, "one night he swallowed every damned one of them on a bet, during a party. Three months later, he was vegetating—a fugue state, they call it—in a sanitarium in Pennsylvania. He's still there, some of him anyway. Sometimes they let him call when he wants to, but he's nobody I enjoy talking to very much. The Fred I loved just got lost, I guess."

Gary's cherry pie arrived, with coffee. When they were alone again, Gary asked the obvious question, fearing the answer: "And you're still waiting for that one to come back?"

"Not really. Actually, I think the Catholic in me still is, even though I know it isn't going to happen." Her gaze toward him took on a sudden quizzical air, a buried thought exhumed. "I guess I'm waiting for hope to die, Gary. It's pretty sick, but it's still hanging in there." She blew her nose on a tissue, a glorious honker of a sound. "No, don't look at me, look out the window."

He obeyed, watching headlights spear down the highway a block away. "Wonderful. Now I've got you crying."

"Nope. I was stealing my bite of pie," she said, and giggled. And he saw that it was true and laughed aloud.

By now they knew it was too late to catch the film—"I'll have plenty of evenings to see movies," she said—and they agreed that she would drive him to his Cessna the following morning.

"Ah, how'd that old line go," she said, pursing her lips in a way that Gary found wonderfully unsettling before the real bombshell: "shall I call you in the morning, or nudge you?"

"Good God," he said, and put down his fork. "You've sure replaced my appetite for pie."

"No more cherries for you tonight," she agreed, grinning. He didn't get it until he was paying the check.

"You realize," he said as she drove eastward, "all during the meal I felt like some pimply kid, trying to figure out how to ask you if we could spend the night together."

"How were you doing with it?"

"Didn't have a clue," he admitted, laughing. "It seems I've developed a minor problem of self-confidence lately. Even so, asking you would've been easier if, uh, if it didn't mean so much to me."

Her right hand went up, limned by passing headlights. "Please. Gary, I don't want it to mean too much. I mean, okay, affection and appreciation and all good things, besides which I have always had a thing for the way your body was put together; but I'm not ready for *la grande affaire*. Maybe I never will be. I was trying to explain that over dinner. But I miss making love with a man I like, and I haven't seen any other candidates recently that I'd even slow-dance with, and I—like you very much. And horny as I've been, mister, I don't think you'll be disappointed." Again, that bobby-socks giggle.

"I can't believe we're having this conversation," Gary said in awed amusement. "Reminds me of a couple of pals before a golf date, working out handicap details."

"Aren't we? If we weren't, I couldn't possibly have just, just—"

"Propositioned me for a one-night stand," he finished for her.

"That—is—out—*rageous*," she said, in mock indignation. "It's also disgustingly accurate, only, um, I hope you don't expect to play nine holes."

Now that they had reached this level of playful comfort with one another, each vied to top the other's innuendo until the little Datsun turned off from the arterial east of town. "Don't expect too much from my nest," she cautioned, realizing that he'd never seen it. "Thank God it's dark, you can't see how I've botched my garden."

"I'll come back and help with it—if you still want me to after, uh—"

Suddenly she was no longer playful. "Gary: whatever happens tonight, no matter how incompetently we fumble, we're friends. You can depend on that."

"So long as I don't eat your tropical fish," he said, and she laughed.

Before she doused her Datsun's lights he saw that they had pulled into a carport attached to a dowdy, medium-sized Homette mobile home, not in the usual sort of trailer park but with fifty yards separating her from another similar place. "Almost half an acre. Ampa found it and fixed it up for me," she said, indicating the carport roof. "He spent a week crawling around beneath, replacing rotted bathroom flooring and stuff. You wouldn't believe how cheap it was."

Privately, Gary thought she might never know how cheap it wasn't because, if he knew Swede Halvorsen, the old man would have absorbed a lot of expenses himself. The front-door lock was a good one, sturdier than the flimsy door it secured; probably more of Swede's work, he thought.

She showed him the layout; living room at one end and her bedroom at the other, her living room cozy but surprisingly large adjoining the dining nook next to the kitchen which, in turn, was next to the bath, a bowl of nuts invitingly on the dinner table. The furniture was half built-ins, half Salvation Army, but it all had a nice, clean Jan smell. While she selected a tape cassette, he tossed his jacket on a shelf and used the bathroom, pausing to steal a tiny gob of Crest, using his forefinger for a toothbrush before rinsing his mouth.

When he returned, she was nodding to music, shoes kicked off, feet tucked beneath her on the couch. "I'm really glad you got rid of that Frito Bandito mustache," she said, grinning. "Makes you look like a different person—I mean, the one I used to know." She patted the cushion next to her and, as he sat down, she leaned toward him, sniffing appreciatively. "Aww, Gary, mint flavor; for me?"

"For both of us," he said, and their first real kiss was an artless gentle thing. "Nice," he said, his lips an inch from hers. *"Rhapsody on what's-his-name*, isn't it?"

"A Theme of Paganini," she supplied. "A cop with culture; I like it."

And this time the kiss lingered, her mouth softening, accepting his tongue joyously. They sat back then, relaxing, heads so near he could not focus on those frank eyes of hers. Their fingers entwined until she looked down in sudden concern. "I forgot your arm," she said.

"So did I," he said. "A kiss can be a great anesthetic."

"You're a pleasant surprise. For some reason, I always thought you'd come on like Tarzan of the Octopi."

"So did I. Usually I do—Jesus, how to explain it? You make me feel like a first-timer, and I don't care, and I don't even wanta think about it while I'm under anesthesia," he said.

She smiled, and anesthetized him again. Eyes closed, murmuring it: "Amazing, Gary. Have you ever noticed how, when you take up serious kissing with someone, it takes awhile to, you know, get accustomed? Like dance moves."

"Not with you."

"Exactly. I'd never thought about it either, until now. It was just something I took for granted. But it's as if you and I had been practicing for each other."

In a near whisper: "You are really, really something," he said, and began to scale the ramparts of a kiss that soared above them, now ardent, now softly sensuous as peach skin, each sharing the other's breathing until they became dizzy with it. Now his fingers found a long-held ambition; learning the delicious convexities of her breasts. She pressed against those fingers with a faint sound that said yes, without the word.

At last, she traced the outline of his lips with her tongue and lay a hand on his cheek. "I don't know about you, ol' golfing buddy," she said, "but I think it's time for bed."

"I'm happy here," he said.

"Me, too, but unless you came sneakily prepared, safe sex is twenty feet from here in my nightstand."

"Very careful planning," he said, swiveling up, pulling her with him. Why mention the condoms in his pocket?

"It's true; I've been planning this. I haven't had that many lovers, but a woman thinks about these things if she has any sense at all," she said, leaning against him, setting their course for the bedroom with a lightly furtive, unladylike grasp on his buttocks.

They undressed each other in semidarkness, unhurried, choosing special places to favor with lips and tongues. And encumbered by that forearm cast, they both fumbled now and again, accommodating it, and finally it was of no importance, and when Gary Landis fell asleep beside the faintly snoring Janelle at three in the morning, he was smiling, thinking, *nothing in the world that's this good should be this safe.*

17

BY FRIDAY, ROMANA HAD FIVE SPINDLY AVOCADO TREES arranged in the dining room of the "annex," the supposedly vacant house a stone's throw from The Place. Though she knew that Andy was as familiar as she with the tunnel's peculiarities, she led the way from the tunnel's entrance in her garage, hidden among storage shelves, in the hard shadows of low-wattage bulbs. They climbed the steps of padded concrete block and passed through the annex's pantry into its kitchen. The house boasted no water or gas service, though they had extended a heavy Romex electric cable through the tunnel for essential operations in the garage—which was no longer the usual article, its single window covered by foil-backed battens.

Their route was a nuisance that increased with the years but that was one of Romana's rules: both doors into the house itself were locked from the inside and you *never* came near it from the outside during daylight hours. In two of its rooms the windows were blocked by old construction materials, chiefly pieces of broken wallboard; a prowler would not be much intrigued by that. In other rooms the windows were clear, revealing bare floors, dust-covered and clearly untenanted. Andy had done this bit of stagecraft because there was no way to tell when some reservation kid might be watching, and thinking.

Andy nodded as he walked around the avocado saplings in their big containers, fingering glossy leaves that seemed too large for the trees. "Good thing they get sun through the skylights," he said. "You must've had a time wrestling these fellas up the steps."

"I didn't," she said, and saw his surprised glance. "I waited until

131

midnight and came in through the hangar." He stared at her for another moment, then shrugged silently. It was not a silence that implied praise. "Andrew, they were simply too heavy. It's not as if I had you here to help." Even to Romana, that sounded defensive. *Why should I justify myself to my assistant*, she thought. *I may break my own rules if I choose; and besides, the hangar door is not the same as the others. Damn him . . .*

"May I make a suggestion," he said into the oppressive quiet, kneeling on the wooden floor beside trees scarcely her own height.

This was proper deference. "Of course, Andrew."

"The tunnel runs below here. Water runoff from these pots can drip down through the floorboards, maybe do some damage."

"That is an observation, not a suggestion." Her smile was superior. She intended it to be.

His look, with that primly tightened mouth, was typical of him, these days. After a small pause, he went on: "I suggest we slide some plastic under the pots and border it with wooden strips as a dam. We can do it now. Don't you still have some of those spruce strips in the hangar?"

"Aircraft-quality Sitka spruce? I certainly do, and we're not going to waste it when any old wood will serve. Wait, I'm sure we have some leftover pine from the wing fixtures." He nodded, turned toward a door that led directly into the garage—now the hangar.

Romana followed, moving into the big arena that was entirely padded with batts of insulation, not so much against cold as against the sounds of electrical tools. The hangar was filled with evening shadows and, to Romana's ever-present satisfaction, with her one expensive toy: her Chamois, its wings spanning the entire area, its deep charcoal-tinted skin seeming blacker than black in near darkness. The place smelled faintly as always of gasoline and rubber and of the sweetish, artificial-flavor odors of expensive polymers. She inhaled with a pleasure that was almost sexual.

During two summers as an undergraduate, Andy had sweltered with her in the big garage of the annex, turning a score of kit materials including thin-wall alloy tubing and epoxy and precisely graded spruce, into her most prized possession. Now that garage was her hangar. It was true that Romana did not make as much use of the Chamois as she might; but the first time she had seen this site, she'd known what it could mean: her own private landing strip.

In early childhood, Skander Masaryk had been imprinted with the urge not only to fly, but to build and fly real airplanes. A technical education had only strengthened this resolve, but the goal had seemed unrealistic until the day the adult Romana saw that macadam roadbed next to a vacant house, and what she saw was a surfaced runway aimed across a meadow toward Millerton Lake. After that, it was only a matter of time, and of the perfect choice of designs. For all her expertise, Romana had always known she was not capable of designing a high-tech aircraft from scratch. Her Chamois was the nearest thing to it.

With a runway only a few hundred yards long, she had realized that takeoffs would be almost as dangerous as landings. For a traditional light aircraft, either would have been suicidal here. But the recent ultralight aircraft craze, with new materials and special engines no heavier than a child, had given hobbyists their choice of designs for very short runways.

Most of those designs looked more like kites than aircraft. Some could be purchased whole, ready to fly; some as kits, with plans; and some as plans only. The great majority of ultralights were limited to a single occupant, lacked a true enclosed cockpit, and could not exceed roughly sixty miles or so. But here and there, a Taylor or a LeGarre in America or a Shaw in England might create a design that begged for new definitions. Such a design was the Chamois, a two-place craft so unusual that most enthusiasts shied away like nervous horses. To date, only a handful of Chamois kits had been sold. Fewer still had been built. It couldn't be that good, said the wary; and who wanted to risk swiveling an engine while its propeller was gulping air?

Her expertise in flying had been rusty, but returned quickly after a few harrowing trials that used up a lot of that testosterone. Now, with several years of highly illegal flights behind her in this unregistered wraith, Romana knew that the Chamois *was* that good—though truly, it could kill you instantly if you swiveled that forward engine while moving too slowly. Named for a goatlike alpine antelope that could leap high into mountain air, the Chamois had a short fuselage pod with a slender tubular extension back to its inverted vee tail, its wing mounted above the cabin. Occupants sat in tandem. It was pushed by one engine mounted low at the rear of the cabin, and pulled by an identical engine mounted very high just ahead of the wing. Each of those engines weighed only sixty pounds, and even with a wingspan of twenty-six feet the Chamois was very close to the weight of an ultralight.

But the most astonishing thing about a Chamois was the ability, like its namesake, to leap from the ground at a trifling speed, yet cruise at well over a hundred knots. A Piper Cub will take off or land at fifty miles an hour; a Chamois, with that forward engine swiveled almost vertically, will do so at *twenty;* even less when facing a breeze. And once that forward engine has been swiveled back to the horizontal, the overpowered Chamois can outrun its competitors.

Because most of its flights were at night, the instrument panel of this particular Chamois had cost more than the airframe. Finding a suitable landing site without those instruments would have presented Romana with a genuine nightmare. By now, with over five hundred hours' flight time in this snarling little brute, Romana no longer feared it. Even Andy had developed a modest proficiency with it. But, as usual, Mom was the master.

Romana stood in reverie, lost in her reflections, as Andy rummaged among the materials ranged neatly on wall brackets. She turned only when he asked, "How's this?"

Though carefully chosen and milled on their machines, it was only inch-square pine in varying lengths. "I shouldn't have to tell you everything," she replied, implying, *it will do.* He mumbled something under his breath and stumped back through the kitchen, taking a cordless Makita drill and small screws from the workbench.

She followed silently, bringing a plastic dust cover for the job at hand, and did not ask him what he'd said; it would only end in delaying what she wanted him to do. And central to their relationship was—had always been—his uses to her. A frustrated cabinetmaker, Andy had become more adept with wood than Romana by the time she had given him his first flight instruction. No doubt that skill had a lot to do with the way those drama amateurs clamored for him—or, at any rate, so he claimed.

Romana gave the Valley Players some thought as she helped shift heavy containers and spread the plastic sheeting. She had attended one performance the previous year, making mental notes while watching the antics of a striking middle-aged woman in *A Flea in Her Ear*. Later, she had questioned Andy as pleasantly as possible, carefully complimentary, probing the depth of his devotion to this foolishness. Too much devotion could mean trouble.

How could they possibly make a profit, given the audience? As she surmised, they couldn't. That tight-girdled doxy with the funniest lines was also their financial backer. Why was Andy, a natural actor, kept behind the scenes? He had laughed at that, forcing Romana to hold her temper. No one kept him there, he said; he had refused even the smallest parts because he wanted no one but his Mom to know just how good he was when he took a role. He could learn much about the craft without drawing attention to himself.

She had always claimed he was expected to carry on her work; very well, he would become superb at it. *Your ambition is to be better than I,* she had added to herself. *Not in your lifetime, little man, no matter how I must manage that. It pleases me that you think of me as your mother, and that you imagine I consider you my son.* Always, always, Romana liked to have an edge. One never knew when it might be needed for cutting.

Another casual question: learning his craft behind the scenes, how did he like working with pretty young women, and attractive older ones? Surely one or another of them had set her cap for Andy—Romana had actually used that phrase, teasingly.

And he had smiled, and replied that their invitations were transparent enough but they were, after all, only "glamourpussy"—and Mom had lectured him on how to deal with that. No problem.

Not even an experienced hotpants who seemed to run the Valley Players? A thorough professional, Andy had insisted. She depended on him but, after all, he'd remarked, she was almost old enough to be his mom.

In some ways, the woman, Aletha Mcsomething, had seemed very familiar; sure of herself, body well maintained and erect, almost masculine in muscle tone, and then Romana had realized that if you described this queen bee in general terms, you were describing Romana herself. And Romana had thought about *that* for a long, long time. If any woman were ever to draw Andrew Soriano away from her, for whatever purpose, it would not be some vacuous ingenue or diligent worker. It would be a queen bee.

And now Andy was using the woman's car, working with her on weekends. Could he be playing with her as well? She watched him run a screw through a pine batten with the Makita, and knew that while she could surveil the two of them, it would take time better spent on that Sacramento client. Their discussions of sex, back in the days when they'd had them, had always been almost brutally matter-of-fact. He had responded well to that tactic.

"I can finish this later," she said casually. "Screwing pine can't be as much fun as screwing Aletha."

His mouth formed the word "whaaat," but no sound emerged.

"Never mind." But he did mind, flushing angrily as he flung the drill to the floor. "It doesn't matter, Andrew."

"You think I'm crazy? Of course it matters! If I were, wouldn't I have told you? *Christ!*" He stood up, trembling.

She thought for one terrible instant that he would hit her, and prepared mentally for a wrist-block maneuver. "I don't know," she said, wise enough to speak calmly. "Would you?"

"Until now I would," he replied, seeing her tower above him, rising now, trembling, but, always the dutiful son, imitating her as well as he was able. "Aletha McCarran is a friend, one of several. I couldn't study my craft without that. You think you know it all, Mom, but if you want to keep up with things in the lab, I have to live Outside. That means having a few outside interests. That's just the way it is."

Their eyes were level, yet he would not challenge her gaze. He attempted to stand as her equal, though his downcast glance and the faintly hunched set of his shoulders gave him away. She was still master/mistress here, and she knew it would be necessary to drain him of his anger before enlisting him in her next attempt at surveillance in Sacramento.

"You must maintain your contacts," she said agreeably. "I can understand that." She had not laid a belt over his shoulders for years, but that almost-imperceptible relaxing, lifting his head, verified once again that she could still punish him without a touch. "Let's go back to The Place, Andrew. I want you to hear a tape of our Sacramento client. If you can get a half-day off next Wednesday, this time I think we can get a step ahead of him."

He left the tools where they lay, breathing deeply, trying to recover his equanimity. *No, I don't believe you are fucking that woman,* she mused silently, *yet. She still stands on a pedestal. I wonder if it will be necessary for her to suffer a fatal accident one of these days. And if she does, I wonder how it could be done without your suspecting me. If someone shot her before witnesses, you would probably accuse me. You are a very bright young man, Andrew. Sometimes I wish I had stolen the child of some other migrant worker, one without your rage for independence.*

Romana led the way back through her tunnel unafraid of the soft footfalls behind her. Born of bracero laborers, Andy had no memory of any parent but Romana. Now she had become, in intelligence parlance, his handler, and he had become her asset, her creature, her physical extension into a modern high-tech laboratory. Despite that tense moment back in the annex, she remained fully confident. She was still unbeatable, would always remain in control of her creature.

18

WHEN GARY LANDED THE CESSNA ON ITS LITTLE HOME strip in the outskirts of northern Fresno, McMilligan was waiting as promised with a "G" government-furnished, hard-top 'vette. Mac waited until they had hangared the little aircraft to give his fellow agent a close inspection. "Love your perm," he joked, passing his hand an inch above Gary's scalp. As for the forearm: "Who does your casts: Frank Lloyd Wright?"

"Feels like concrete, too," Gary admitted. He started to add that he'd discovered it made a very abrasive third party in a bedroom tussle, but thought better of it. Somehow, making love with Jan was not a topic for sharing with his other friends. He admired Mac's choice of cars as they headed for the center of Fresno and Suite 200, DEA's downtown offices in an unobtrusive two-story structure. "We're seizing a better class of vehicle, I see. You just be glad this wasn't a ragtop." McMilligan smiled at this, nodding; by policy decision, agents did not drive convertibles. "Anybody keep my Camaro's battery up while I was, uh," Gary said, finishing with a silent handwave.

"Diggin' your way up from China," the agent furnished with a short laugh. "Yeah, your heap's movable." As he drove, the sturdy, sandy-haired McMilligan kept darting glances toward Gary; not furtive, but apprais-ing. "I've been out to that mine shaft. Want to talk about it?"

"Later, maybe. Don't suppose you know whether Visconti wants me back running our con on La Familia."

"He'll want to tell you. But my take on it is, you've done all the UC

139

work you're going to, for awhile. This one was too close. They got two deaders out of that hole, you know."

"I figured there might be even more," Gary said.

"So did we. County guy in scuba gear says that's all, though. I'm glad it was him down there in that muck, not me."

They pulled into the fenced back lot behind Suite 200 and went up the rear stairway, Gary grinning and speaking to several of the staff, all of whom seemed to be responding to some kind of radar that told them he was on the floor again. *Well, my little takedown is no secret from anybody*, he thought with a twinge that was pure shame. Mac peeled off into his cubicle with a light back slap in parting, and Gary knocked on a wall panel to announce himself to the vest-covered, erect back of Paul Visconti.

If Visconti was still angry over Gary's suspicions, he hid it well. "I feel due for a caffeine fix," he said, rummaging in a drawer, tossing a packet of powdered cocoa mix onto his desk. "Peace offering, Landis; I know you're a chocaholic." Gary smiled at him and as they moved around seeking spoons, hot water, sugar substitute, he made a mental note: to reduce tensions, spend a few moments doing something simple and familiar together. At UCLA they would call it displacement behavior. Visconti would call it good supervision.

When they were seated and sipping behind a closed door, Visconti uncovered a manila folder full of printouts with jotted marginal notes and, inevitably, forbidden doodles. "You can work up a real two-oh-two as backup for what you sent me," said Visconti. "But first: you ready for light duty?"

Gary said he wasn't sure and displayed his cast, claiming he'd done it himself—a half-truth at worst, and one nobody would doubt after seeing it. He wanted a physician's opinion, maybe a better cast as well, he said. His account of his odyssey of the past week was brief, mentioning an old friend from college days who had put him up without knowing exactly why—as phrased, not quite a lie though he intended to leave the impression that "down south" meant Los Angeles.

When Visconti asked him to tape his memories of that setup in

Merced, Gary agreed readily. "But hey, what's all this about a dead Langley man? I'm showing you mine; will you show me yours?"

Visconti had an easy smile for such requests, leaning back, enjoying the moment. "I didn't say he was CIA—not *our* CIA, anyhow. But they've missed him since 1989. They had a loose surveillance on him for almost a year, waiting for him to step too far out of bounds." He shuffled pages in the open file, made a quick scan. "Subject's name was Genet, French citizen, disappeared from his apartment in Cupertino in Silicon Valley without a trace. French consulate made official inquiries. We weren't much help, so they inquired harder. You know how it goes, pretty soon it's clear that Langley already knew Genet as an old hand in SDECE." Gary nodded at the mention of France's version of the Company.

Visconti continued. "The guy was a heavy spender, made friends around Santa Clara, almost certainly doing his bit for *la belle France* with—let's put it bluntly—industrial espionage. Frogs have a pretty good national expertise with semiconductors, but Silicon Gulch is where it's at. Genet may have been still on duty with SDECE, maybe not; they'd never have admitted it in any case. But he had twenty years' experience and, according to Langley, he was known as the kind of smooth player the French could trust with beaucoup loot. Very dependable and very tough, survived a few scrapes in his time. Doesn't seem like it would've been that easy to get behind him with a garrote wire."

"Shit!" Gary sat up straight at this.

"Shit indeed! Apparently, a wire breaks the hyoid bone in such a way that they can tell. And after those little mating dances we all get used to, we—Langley, that is—found out something like a quarter-mil in cash disappeared with him." With a thoughtful gaze at Gary's fast-growing crewcut, Visconti went on more slowly: "And when he's found—the second victim down that hole—he's missing his hair."

For a long moment, Gary sat still, rubbing his crew cut reflectively. Then: "Some sort of cult?"

"That crossed my mind, too. The similarities seem to be causing a flap among some Company analysts. One of their people from the Bay

Area wants to sit down with you. Could be tomorrow, so wear a pager and keep yourself handy. Evidently they think you were a mistake in more ways than one."

"You're sure this Frenchman wasn't the first," Gary said, wanting to understand it all, having his difficulties.

"Yeah. Times of the disappearances and the conditions down in that hole. We just got a positive match an hour ago from dental records, thanks to that mandible you sent: victim was an eighteen-year-old who's been a missing person since he disappeared from the family ranch in the Briant vicinity in 1986 or 1987. No leads at the time; big strong high-school jock named Steele Lowery, a six-footer who hiked all around. The ranch is only a few miles from your mine shaft, so it's a reasonable supposition the kid just fell in while the water level was low and never regained consciousness.

"Sheriff knows his parents, claims the father's a rancher with clout; sheriff will have told them by now. And that means the *Fresno Bee* will know, but I called in a favor and it won't make the papers before the middle of next week when the ID is, quote, positive, unquote, and it won't be front-page stuff. We want to keep this simple for the media, so we're hoping to keep Genet, and you, too, out of the news. It seems likely the Lowery kid simply stumbled into the shaft or fell while exploring. There's no indication he was put down there."

"But there might not be, when all you've got is a skeleton," Gary replied. With heightened interest: "Had he been snatched bald-headed, too?"

A head shake. "They found some hair at the site. Matches the description of the Lowery boy. There's simply no apparent connection with the second victim, any more than you'd connect two animals that wandered into the La Brea tar pits years apart. The boy was never in trouble, certainly not connected to organized crime or the intelligence community. They're going to treat his death as accidental, which is a plus for us and probably accurate. Damn shame, young man with a good life ahead of him, but it happens all the time. One slip, and accidental death."

"That's how I'd have looked, too, after a couple of years down there." Despite himself, Gary shivered.

"Probably, but listen: you really take top marks for keeping a urine sample." Visconti shuffled papers again, propping a pair of dinky little reading glasses on his nose, then turning back, removing them. "Ever hear of the Thomas Concoction?"

Donating a blank look: "If I ever did, it didn't stick," Gary admitted. "Refresh me."

"New to me, too. Used by veterinarians occasionally; an injection for big animals they want down and out right now, for good. A curare analog puts them down in a matter of seconds, and potassium chloride stops the heart moments later. That—or something very much like it—is what you took in your hip."

"Try my ass," Gary corrected.

Visconti's grimace was comically pained. "I don't suppose you'd like to rephrase that," he said.

"Wups, sorry. But they did try my ass, Paul, and it was fudge. And goddammit, *those were not women*," he insisted. "They grabbed me like a couple of wrestlers—wait a minute, so how come I'm still alive? Too small a dose?"

"You had enough in you, according to the lab report. I asked about that, and had two pathologists arguing over scenarios for half an hour. They finally agreed that *if* the victim was in top physical shape, and *if* he got shaken up hard enough within a short time after cardiac arrest—and I mean walloped on the chest, really rough treatment—it just might jump-start him again. By the way, when they inject a killer grizzly or something, they just let him lie there awhile." Visconti stared into Gary's eyes. "Maybe these two sweethearts of yours just didn't let their sleeping dog lie long enough."

"I wouldn't know," Gary shrugged. "But I knew I was paralyzed, and I think they bundled me down into the footwell of their car before I—Jesus Christ! Before I died." He gulped down his chocolate as if it were an antidote.

Paul Visconti nodded, swinging his glasses from an earpiece, sobered and thoughtful. "Then, I don't know, maybe they ran over a curb, kicked you in the chest—any suggestive bruises?"

Gary placed a hand at his breastbone, rubbing gently. "A little tenderness here, but it's not much to look at. I was more worried about the lump on the back of my head—had me seeing double for a while—but I'm okay now."

"That's what they all say," Visconti rejoined, smiling, pointing at the agent's breast. "All that stuff is going to get a thorough physical before the day is out. And tomorrow, if you're up to it, there's a Langley spook who wants some of your spare time."

"What was that phrase again? Spare time? I know I must've heard it somewhere."

"I'll give you odds you've had more spare time than any of us, the past couple of days," Visconti growled, then softened it with, "It's obvious what you went through, Gary. I want you to know there's no hard feelings. Firm feelings, maybe, but not hard." He stood up, stuck his hand out. Gary stood and accepted it with real gratitude.

19

EVIDENTLY, YOUR AVERAGE DESK-BOUND CIA "SUIT" doesn't do holidays, or so Gary concluded. The debriefing was set for Tuesday, thanks to the long Memorial Day weekend just ahead. With medical approval for light duty, Gary spent his Saturday morning on personal chores: choosing an apartment in North Fresno, fueling up his Camaro and the Cessna. His buoyant feeling was not solely emotional; compared to his new lightweight polymer cast, the old one had been a freeway abutment on his arm.

His belt beeper, a standard little Metromedia pager, sent him to the phone in his Camaro; Paul Visconti would spring for lunch at the Basque Hotel, an unlikely spot in a graffiti-laden part of downtown Fresno, boasting the best six-course meal in town.

As usual, patrons dining boardinghouse style at the long banquet table made enough noise to cover any conversations by pairs sitting quietly at the small tables. Gary had to grin at Visconti's attire: dress-shirt sleeves rolled back and a loosened tie were the man's idea of Saturday casual. Visconti, in turn, kept glancing at Gary's scalp. Finally: "You dyed your hair?"

"Me? No, why—oh. Too much chlorine in the motel pool, like swimming in Clorox. It's okay, this new cast is waterproof."

They automatically got the standard lentil soup in a big tureen, then oxtail stew and salad, already a full meal without the entrée, but a royal Basque feast with it. Visconti ordered chicken, Gary the lamb.

"Thought you'd like to know," Visconti said as they pursued succulent bits of oxtail, "I'm pulling the plug on your Merced operation."

Gary managed to look disappointed though his feelings on the subject were mixed. "A little La Familia cash is missing; fellow named Pepe is going to be suspicious," he said.

"So what else is new?" Visconti looked at the nearby wall, as if it carried a list of reasons for his decision. "No matter what story you gave him, he'd bounce his toes off your ribs for not checking in before this. And it's still very possible that his people were behind your problem; just not so likely anymore. Do I really want to bring in a team to keep at your back, about as inconspicuous as King Kong trying to hide behind a fence post, while you find out?" He answered his own question with a slow, and very decisive, head shake. "You've already got enough to nail Pepe Luna and a couple of others when it's time to testify."

"By which time I'll have a long white beard," Gary said.

"*C'est la guerre,*" said the RAC, pushing his stew away reluctantly and, as an aside, "you want to leave room for the lamb unless you've been starving for a week. Now, then: we've cleaned out your Merced digs. Forget the BMW—one of Pepe's boys might spot it. I take it you're driving your Camaro?"

Personal use of a "G" car could mean thirty days without pay, as Gary knew. "What else would I be driving?"

"Just checking. That damn velocipede of yours, though: we've got it here in an impound lot. It leaks fluids."

The waitress cleared away the debris of their first courses and Gary salivated at not one, but two lamb T-bones nested in French fries. "What've you got against my Kawasaki?"

"Against anything with two wheels and three hundred decibels," Visconti grumbled, attacking his chicken.

"Besides which, you think I must be an accident waiting to happen on a bike, just like you were," Gary jibed. "You said so yourself."

"I talk too much," Visconti said, chewing and smiling.

Their dessert, comically small portions of chocolate ice cream, was anticlimactic. They discussed office work that Gary would find during the coming week, using handy shorthand terms that made their phrases innocuous. Reading between the lines, Gary guessed that he would be focusing more on the drug channels of Fresno's Hmong Asians for a while. Thanks to his injury, Visconti said, Gary would definitely not be in on "the fun"—a major bust of an Asian drug house which had been pending for weeks.

A good bust, catching dopers with the product in a swirl of flak-jacketed action and shouted commands, was an emotional payoff, but it was not the place for a man operating at less than 100 percent. If the dopers made a fight of it and you weren't in top form, you could get some of your friends killed, along with yourself. Gary shrugged off his disappointment with "Doctor says the cast can come off soon. He didn't say I had to stay out of a pool or off my bike."

"Well, then, I do; stay off your bike, dammit, and don't quote me any regs about what I can't tell you to do on your own time. I've covered your butt enough for a while; now you can do me that favor."

Gary agreed with bad grace and let his boss pay the bill. They parted on F Street, among spray-painted legends announcing that this was Crips turf. The graffiti did not bother Gary; he knew whose turf it really was.

He made his final decision on an apartment late in the afternoon, a complex with a pool off Shaw Avenue not too far from the Cessna, and pondered another decision while moving in. According to Visconti, the local paper would not carry any story about that mine shaft until roughly Wednesday. It appeared that no one intended to do any serious checking on the Lowery youth, but after Wednesday, any inquiries would be in context of that news story.

Big, strong kid, narrow slanting hole. I could've grabbed for the sides if I'd been awake, and so could he. Accident, hell—that's an attractive excuse that we Feds can embrace to keep the rest of this business out of the news, he concluded. *So I have a window of opportunity here if I want to take it without asking permission.* He did not know exactly what years-old information might surface, but he feared that, after a few more days, it would be hopelessly embroidered in the light of the new discovery. Assuming he was going to follow an officially dead lead, it might be best not to discuss it just yet.

For his personal long-distance call, he used a pay phone on Blackstone. Jan answered on the second ring. "Oh, God, it would be you," she joked. "You must think I sit with sandwiches by the phone on Saturdays."

"Well, weren't you?"

"No sandwich. My Rachmaninoff is playing, though."

He groaned softly. "Boy, you really know how to hurt a guy. I've got a new apartment here in Fresno, and a cast that weighs under a thousand kilos."

She chuckled, setting his mind on edge. "You think that's what they mean by 'a cast of thousands'?"

"That reminds me, I owe you a movie."

"And free lodging for a night—don't forget that."

"Not as long as I live," he chuckled. "You just name the date, lady."

A long pause, then, and in a tentative voice. "How far is it from here to there, Gary?"

"You know as well as I do. Couple of hours," he said, a wild hope rising in him like the biggest trout in all creation.

It broke the surface and sunfished with joy as she said, "Well, I didn't have a workout today, and I'd really like to see your apartment, and, uh . . ." she trailed off.

"Jan. Jan, please quit making those dumb excuses, and jump in your rice rocket and bring a swimsuit. Who knows, maybe we'll even see a movie tonight."

She agreed and he gave her his new address, tingling all over like a schoolboy, and resolved to stock his place with edibles before Jan's arrival. As he eased into Blackstone traffic, he noticed a cycle shop a block away, a place he had patronized before. He knew the Kawasaki would need a gasket set if it was leaking fluids as Visconti said, but someone was closing the shop as he drove nearer, turning the window sign over to read CLOSED. No hurry; he could take care of it next week.

What he did not notice was the Chevy Luv parked near the rear of the shop, and the familiar figure rolling down a driver's-side window that Gary had paid for, not so long ago.

20

THEY WERE WAITING FOR HIM ON SUNDAY NIGHT, BUT
Ralph Guthrie didn't know it until he was lifting his big duffel
bag into the Luv's passenger seat. He hadn't learned much
about Chuckie baby, and what little he had found wasn't your basic upper.
It had cemented his decision to get the fuck out of Merced and onto
I-5 headed north while the getting was good.

Now suddenly it wasn't good anymore, it was awful. A moment
before, in his mind he was already halfway to Seattle. Now, as one of the
snake twins materialized from the dark to stand near his elbow, he was
nine-tenths of the way toward a shiv in his guts. *"Patrón* wants to talk,"
said the little guy, and pointed. Guthrie kept his motions cool, seeing the
other twin now, knowing he was flanked, locking the Luv again. The
dark Lincoln town car was a shadowed presence farther down the block,
and Guthrie walked to it as if he didn't want to break and run in the
opposite direction. In those run-down cowboy boots of his, he wouldn't
have gone twenty steps. He'd done all he could to find that frigging
Chuck, but time had run out, with only one slender lead to show for it
and it hadn't paid off by Saturday.

Once in the Lincoln's cavernous backseat, he realized the twins were
getting in front. Bad as things were, it wasn't as bad as it would've been if
one of them had got in back with him. Pepe Luna's face was indistinct, his
words too distinct as the Lincoln glided away. "Taking a trip?"

Guthrie thanked God the bag was his first load. "No, no, just my
laundry," he laughed. He wished he had that laugh back, it sounded like
somebody strangling a parrot. "I was gonna call you in the morning."

149

"To say what?"

"Got a line on Chuck." *Careful, don't promise unless you can deliver.* "Least I think so. And listen," he said, forcing a little excitement, hoping maybe it would rub off, maybe they weren't heading outside Merced to some farm road where neither cries nor gunfire would be investigated until too late. "Listen, there's a good chance his name isn't Chuck Lane." *There, stop and see if you've hooked him.*

After too many seconds, Luna responded. "Ralph Guthrie, do not waste my time. Tell me everything you know, without flourishes. You are going to tell me anyway. One way or another."

"Sure, hey, no problem. Smoke?" Guthrie fumbled at his shirt pocket and offered his Winstons.

"Neither of us will. You were saying." Softly, but with that edge.

"I haven't actually seen him; in fact I believe he's holed up somewhere. If we're lookin' for Chuck Lane, nobody's gonna find him. But maybe that's not who we should look for." *Right; we, us, you and me together, Lord Wetback.* "Lane had a cycle, one of those Jap screamers. That and his Beemer are both gone. Cops took 'em, but they aren't in the PeeDee impound lot. I found out Lane gets his Kawasaki parts from a shop in Fresno. Your guy gave me this snapshot—me and Lane at the downtown bar, how'd you get that without a flash, anyhow?—well, this snapshot, see, so I had a bunch of Xeroxes blown up of Chuck's face."

It occurred to Guthrie that he was talking too fast. Slow down and live, they say; well, by God, that was no lie. Draw it out a few minutes longer, at least. "Turns out that this Fresno parts man at a cycle shop recognized the picture, says he thought he did, anyhow, except for the mustache, I won't know till he shows—"

"The point, Guthrie."

"Point is, he thinks he knows Lane by another name and without the lip fuzz. Didn't remember what name—not even with a twenty to help jog his memory—but he said Lane's been in several times. But not recently. And not as Lane. So I showed him a hundred. Told him I'm keepin' it for him, for when he can give me a name and address without Lane knowing. Best this parts man could do was tell me he thinks Lane, whoever he is, is a Fresno guy. Couldn't say why; just his impression." Guthrie paused to swallow. "Mr. Luna, I think we could be onto a sting."

Silences are not all the same. This one seemed a little more friendly. Finally Luna broke it. "My name was not always Pepe Luna. Men in our business—I do not need to explain, I hope." A faint sigh, as of a schoolmaster faced by a student who may be honestly at a loss to add two and two. "But I intend to discover who he is. You, Guthrie, need to know who he is as much as I do.

"Because if he is connected to a business rival, you may hope to disappear, even retire from this line of work one day. But if he is government, then whether or not we could be convicted, for the rest of our lives we are already marked men, wherever the government of *los Estados Unidos* reaches. And that means everywhere. Do you understand now, Guthrie, why you need me?"

Damned if I do, damned if I don't. Guthrie took a cut at it. "If he's a cop, he'll want to testify sooner or later. Maybe there are ways to get him not to."

A dazzle of white teeth in the shadows of the Lincoln. "Very good. And toward that end, I have assets far greater than yours. In fact, *you* are one of my assets. It would be a shame if my assets should become— scattered. At best, you would be alone. Whoever fired into Lane's apartment might be luckier with you. And I would not be pleased with you either."

"Hell, I know that, Mr. Luna. That's why I'm still on the job. I've been scouting around Fresno a little, something else may turn up, hard to say—"

"But you will continue to look, and to keep me informed, in our mutual interest," said Luna. "And do not change apartments."

"Sure, no problem. You know me, Mr. Luna—"

"Yes, I know you, Guthrie. And *you* know *me*." He raised his voice, not much, rattling off something to the snake twins in front, then lowered it again as the Lincoln turned left. "When you locate our missing man so that I can reach him, my thanks will be worth ten thousand dollars. Perhaps then you can buy some deodorant."

Ralph Guthrie was too relieved to have any irritation at this, babbling on about his intentions for the immediate future. When the Lincoln pulled up within sight of his Luv pickup, he could have wept with pleasure.

Guthrie stood trembling on Merced's broken pavement, lit a Winston and watched that carload of trouble until it was out of sight, thinking, *Ten large! Not much for Luna, but it'll do. And the fucker's right; if I skip, they'll all be looking for me.*

Tasting the carrot, feeling the stick.

21

M A Y 1 9 9 4

BECAUSE MONDAY WAS A MEMORIAL DAY FREEBIE, THEY actually got to see a movie after all. Jan kept saying she should get back to Bakersfield, and Gary kept offering new reasons why she could wait until Tuesday morning: less traffic, another dip in the pool, more of his sparkling company. He loved that wistful quality in her statements about leaving, a hint that she didn't really want to, and it gave him a nice case of the pitty-pats just beneath that fading bruise on his sternum. It told him she did not want to outstay her welcome. Fat chance!

"Holy Mary, but I'm easy," she lamented Monday night after the film, having agreed to stay until the following morning.

Gary opened the Camaro's door for her, appreciating her legs as she tucked them inside. His melancholy was as bogus as hers: "Yeah. The responsibility must be crushing for you," he said, shutting the door, walking around to his side while she unlocked it for him.

When he was inside: "What responsibility," Jan asked, mystified.

"Role model for the world's bimbos," he said, and cackled as she pounded his right shoulder. "All right, then, just the Catholic bimbos." A muted squeal of comic outrage, and another mock pounding. "The blondes? How about only the gorgeous, evil-bodied, blonde Catholics from Bakersfield?"

"You forgot the 'bimbo,'" she reminded him.

"Not as long as you're with me," he said, and she fell against him, laughing.

It was like that through their late martinis, and their later midnight swim, and somehow their lovemaking was more satisfying than ever precisely because it became more languid, accommodating, no longer so desperately athletic. Another good sign: not once did either of them mention what Gary now thought of as the "F" word: Freddie.

He fell asleep wondering if this was what it was like to be married, a little nonplussed to find he was not uncomfortable with the idea, Jan snuggled spoon-fashion against his backside. His last waking thought was faint astonishment that, for the first time since he was old enough to grasp a steering wheel, he hadn't the faintest idea who had just won the Indy and couldn't care less. If God and Janelle Betancourt were very good to him, maybe he'd feel the same way the morning after the Super Bowl.

Jan left after scrambling up a big breakfast of chorizo and eggs for them, what she called her Once-a-Month Cholesterol Decadence Special. Gary's morning at work became an anodyne against a feeling of loss. There wasn't room in the DEA offices that morning for both his love life and the CIA's Graham Forster.

In his late fifties, Forster was a few pounds shy of paunchy, sported a Phi Beta Kappa key and an Ivy League accent, his wing-tip oxfords burnished a deep oxblood, his mane of hair only a few shades whiter than Gary's pool-bleached crew cut. Paul Visconti introduced the man to Gary and took part in the meeting, his casual elegance seeming almost grubby measured against Forster. The CIA analyst would have passed as a very senior attorney; Gary judged that he might be exactly that, among other things.

Forster began by saying he'd done his reading which included Gary's report, a "two-oh-two." He made it clear that his presence on the West Coast implied some urgency at Langley and went on, with an apologetic smile toward Visconti, "For the record, I've satisfied myself that Mr. Landis's only connections with Langley have been contacts under the aegis of DEA. Just clearing the air, Mr. Visconti. In the past, that hasn't always been the case." Visconti nodded; in a serious breach of etiquette, the CIA had placed a few men in other agencies from time to time.

"The circumstances of this debriefing would be quite different if you were one of ours," Forster went on to Gary. "The fact is, this isn't a debriefing at all in the classic sense. It's time to share some information. If you have the context of our concern, it may help you to help us."

Visconti sighed. "Hell of a note, isn't it, when one federal agency must explain why it's willing to cooperate with another." Not a question; a complaint.

"A sign of the times," Forster agreed, unfazed, and turned toward Gary. "We are now concerned that someone else may have concluded what I at first surmised, that you *are* a Langley asset. That could account for the attempt on you, Mr. Landis."

Gary frowned. "I thought the Russians had pretty much pulled back from that sort of thing—what's the old Sov term, 'wet work'?"

A frosty smile and a nod. "Pretty much, as you say. But Ivan's military intelligence, alias the GRU, is still in business. I don't know whether they're involved here. It wouldn't surprise me either way. A very long time back, we began compiling an entire file cabinet that's now backed by an armload of floppies, on an operation so covert, so deadly, we could not be certain it exists." Pause; a deep breath. "Have either of you ever heard of the Spooker File?"

Assured that they hadn't, Forster spun them a tale that activated Gary's scalp hairs: the twenty-five-year series of deaths and disappearances, all agents of Western powers, chiefly on the West Coast; the consistent pattern of missing funds; the conspicuous rarity of young agents from Langley's list of suspected victims.

"Of more than twenty compromised assets in several agencies—our British cousins, Israelis, French, Americans, and a few oddments—nearly all were old, experienced hands. In fact, only one or two were as young as you, Mr. Landis. The true total is probably higher because, as you will appreciate, an officially friendly nation hates to admit its less-friendly operations on our shores.

"The missing assets may, indeed, be taking their ease in Patagonia, or wherever. We don't think so. We believe most or all of these assets were terminated for their connections and, of course, for their spooker kits. It would help if you could repeat for me, in sequence, the events that provoked you to, um, exfiltrate."

Gary and Paul exchanged wry looks at this; the CIA seemed to have a nice, comfortable word for everything: "asset" for anything worthwhile, including human beings; "terminate" for murder; "exfiltrate" for a plain old panicky bugout. With Visconti's blessing, Gary spoke for a pocket recorder, detailing the note he'd received, its wording, the burst of muted gunfire that had made it all seem real and urgent, the doper stash of money he had taken along.

When he had finished, at Forster's request, he went over that harrowing moment when the slugs ripped through his window. "I remember switching off the lamp, getting up, taking a couple of steps. I was standing up when they shot at me."

"Shot at you. Isn't it possible that they intended to shoot *near* you? Not hit you, but provoke you into doing exactly what you did."

"I've thought about that," Gary admitted. "At first—well, hell, it's natural. I assumed the attempt was genuine. But I was walking diagonally across the room. My chair took a couple of rounds, and I figured my getting up made the shooter squeeze off a burst before he was ready. But maybe not." He turned to Paul as he repeated, "Maybe not. It could've been better shooting than I thought."

"That is the scenario we're entertaining," Forster said. "And, of course, a deliberate miss implies that they wanted some particular action from you. Let's assume that the same faction that sent that note also fired the weapon. Taken together, those actions should send an undercover man streaking for imagined safety, with whatever negotiables he had in his spooker."

"Interesting idea, Mr. Forster, but somehow I just never got around to putting such a bugout kit together." Gary's grin was openly dismissive.

"They couldn't know that. They may have known you carried fairly large sums in the course of your duties." Forster paused, inspected his flawless manicure. "You're relatively young," he said quietly. "Some people in our line of work—more than we'd like to admit—eventually do begin to take such precautions." He spread his hands. "Paranoia reigns. It's a human failing, one of the temptations that cause agents to hold back, um, some of the valuables passing through their hands. Cash, refined drugs, gemstones. He who would travel fast, travels light."

"Too damn light in this case," Visconti snorted. "Gary had less than seven-thousand dollars with him, and even that hadn't been squirreled away. It was pocket change to the people he was dealing with."

"La Familia," Forster supplied. "Don't forget, we're on that operation as well. Mr. Landis had passed samples of their drugs to one of our people for chemical workup. *He did intersect us in the field,* Mr. Visconti. Now it seems that someone, a very professional, hostile, subtle someone, was surveilling those contacts. Probably he or she thought you would be a much greater prize—forgive me, but we're talking about the money—than you proved to be. Your contact, our man, has asked to be transferred." His gaze met Gary's. "And I am assured that he doesn't even know about the attempt on you.

"He knows—or says he knows—he's been surveilled off and on for some time. Hasn't been able to pin it down, but twice before, in fifteen years of service, he has had those feelings. We used to give little credence to such vague apprehensions. We don't anymore, certainly not with him. He was right both previous times."

"If he's right this time," Gary said, "it sure isn't La Familia. Even if they thought I carried a bag of diamonds, they have their own way of handling UC guys like us. It was like them to use a noise suppressor on an assault rifle against me, but the rest of it—nahh. And your guy would be pushing up daisies, too."

"Our conclusions exactly," Forster agreed. "You intersected an asset who *was* ours. You came under suspicion by some faction that, for decades, has functioned very effectively as a kind of invisible terminator."

"I saw the movie," Gary said with an attempt to lighten the moment. This old guy had become too goddamned disconcerting.

Forster, without cracking a smile or shifting his gaze: "I hope you live to see many more films, Mr. Landis, and well you may; somebody out there doesn't like you, but you're evidently blessed with the devil's own luck. You were surveilled, perhaps since the first sample you passed over to us. The same hostile faction that surveilled you, and shot into your apartment, was waiting to take you when you tried to leave with your spooker."

Now Visconti grew restive. "We've checked out all of Gary's neighbors in Merced. No way."

"Not that way. As we all know, there are other ways. If that faction has no interest into how many pieces it shatters the law, several other ways come to mind. Phone taps, shotgun mikes, bugged vehicles, even laser resonators and motion sensors." Now the impeccable Forster turned to Gary. "How many times during your stay in Merced did you two talk on phones—land lines, cellular, whatever?"

"A few. Maybe four or five?" Gary looked to Visconti for confirmation; got it.

Visconti: "Our circuits are scrambled to TEMPEST standards, you know that."

Forster: "What does that matter if someone has bugged you and is, in effect, sitting by your side? On one or more occasions, I'll wager you called your supervisor by name, Mr. Landis. Someone was listening. It doesn't take much more than a name to make up a warning note, if the reader of that note has inside knowledge," Forster said.

They covered other details. Gary scraped his memory bare to describe incidents in which he might have been a target of surveillance. Visconti then brought up the likelihood of media attention, since the Briant boy's remains in the mine shaft were of local interest.

Forster agreed that, with good liaison between law-enforcement bodies, at worst the hostile faction would consider "Charles Lane" as a deniable corpse hidden from media spotlights. "We accept that the youngster's fate—Lowery?—was simply death by misadventure, years before that shaft was used by our hostiles as a disposal site. For one thing, his hair was not taken. But the hostile faction will be aware that his body could be found only with, ah, yours," he smiled pleasantly at Gary. "Langley is *very* interested in the fact that your hair was taken, as well as that of the Frenchman, Genet."

"Uh-huh. You've found some more like that," Visconti guessed aloud.

Forster looked quickly at the RAC. "I can't confirm that," he said, nodding nonetheless and raising four fingers, a silent and deniable way of saying, *yes; four.* "A hostile faction will have to suspect that M'sieur Genet's remains were also found, and all this will make them very cautious for a while. In any case, Mr. Lane's trail seems to have ended. It would be quite unfortunate if you reappeared in that persona, Mr. Landis. It could send that hostile faction scampering off permanently."

Now, for the first time, a hint of Forster's flinty resolve surfaced in his tone. "And that would leave a ragged tapestry of loose ends, all the way back to a Czech defector I met in my early days before someone terminated him. Rather admired the handsome rascal. We intend to wrap up this entire faction, gentlemen. Until now, we've never even been able to prove it's out there."

"Um," Visconti said. "I'm not sure it's proven yet. Beyond reasonable doubt, I mean."

"I suppose not," Forster conceded with another of those smiles chipped from ice. "Yet we have the outline of a pattern, left by people who have taken pains to avoid patterns. You have stared them in the eye at close range, Mr. Landis, and you lived. You may be unique in the Western intelligence community."

"They can pass as women," Gary said instantly. "Both Caucasian, one medium-blonde but dark complexion, maybe peroxided, a young woman. They're not women, though, unless they're on major steroids. Shit, not even then, I think."

Asked to relive the confrontation, Gary had to get past his anger before he managed, eyes shut, to recapture the moment. Both "women" had been of medium build, neither memorably large nor small. The one at the wheel had chestnut hair, shoulder-length and fairly wiry. "I felt it on my face when I leaned down to see her gas gauge," Gary said.

"That close," Forster murmured, with a touch of awe. "Well, I'm sure you know you'll be getting some VICAP questionnaires from the

FBI, now that this is looking like a special kind of serial-murder operation."

Visconti: "I'm surprised the Bureau doesn't have someone here. This is definitely not like the old days."

"A lot of streamlining lately. Since Freeh took over as Director at the Bureau, you don't even hear words like 'Feeb' much at Langley anymore. You do hear words like 'cooperation.' I wonder how long it'll last," he added with a wry smile. "Anyway, VICAP doesn't get a whole lot of victims capable of answering questionnaires, Mr. Landis. They'll want every possible detail: how they behaved, what they wore, how they talked."

"The driver's voice; I tell you, that bothers me because it was just a woman's voice. A little butchy, maybe." Gary's eyes flew open. "Not like the young one, the blonde who nailed me with that hypo. Her voice was really soft—you know, breathy, the old Marilyn Monroe thing. A guy in drag. I didn't get a good look at her face. Let's face it, I was thinking about other things."

"Blonde, you said."

"Not too blonde but yeah, fairly short straight—hell!" He shook his head in disgust, a quick guilty glance at Visconti. "While they were waiting for that poison to take over, the young one said something else. 'It's in him,' something like that. In a different voice, Paul. No breathiness, male, not very mature, but not a boy, either. Goddammit, it was a guy!"

"Do you know," said Forster in a dreamy tone, "I may have another piece of this thing. Genet's hair was straight and, according to his dossier, he wore it long. Unfashionably so. It was taken from his body—nearly all of it, scalp and all. It may have been Genet's blond hair the young one was wearing."

Visconti whistled softly. "I never heard of that as a part of Sov tradecraft," he said.

"Nor of anyone else's that I know of," Forster said.

Gary tried to ignore the gooseflesh on his body. "Some sonofabitch wanted my hair for a wig!" he said.

"And got it," Visconti added. "Be glad they didn't scalp you for it."

"Lots of blood involved," Forster said. "They may have discovered that while taking Genet's. I don't know, but my guess is that with every operation, they try to improve their technique."

"Going beyond proven procedures is definitely not professional tradecraft," Visconti said.

"Not as we know it," Forster mused. "But if they're gifted amateurs, they're awfully, *awfully* good." As he gazed into the wall, Forster's face was alight with admiration.

22

GARY FOUND IT DIFFICULT TO CONCENTRATE ON FRESH casework after Graham Forster's unsettling visit. The notion of a hostile counterspy group *not* connected to known intelligence services was good news and bad, said the CIA analyst. If freelancers, they would not have the huge resources of, say, Russia's GRU. On the other hand, they had been numbingly successful with limited resources, perhaps for the very reason that they did not play by the traditional rules of engagement.

Forster's next step would be another dip into the files of VICAP, the violent criminal apprehension program begun by the FBI against America's growing problem of serial killers. This, Paul Visconti had observed, would be something of a new spin on serial killings, in some ways akin to the old Murder, Incorporated. Forster left after he promised to send Visconti a report of his findings, inasmuch as the attempt on Gary spanned the current connection between the two agencies.

Gary signed out in mid-afternoon and, a half-hour later, wearing a tie and sport coat, strolled up a concrete walk to the smallish, many-windowed administration office of little Briant High School. A few youths were still in the halls, and young voices echoed from a nearby athletic field. He flashed his ID and his gentlest smile to the registrar, a formidable large-boned woman in a frilly white blouse and horn-rims. At the moment she was risking carpal tunnel syndrome, fingers flashing at the keyboard below a Macintosh screen. Using the name Garrett, which she was free to consider a surname, he mounted his diving board and took the plunge by asking how long she had been on the staff.

She'd been teaching part-time, he learned, in 1987, and the classes weren't that large. Did he have a particular student in mind? When she heard the name, a faint film of regret crossed her face. The Lowerys were very active locally, she said, and generous to a fault in funding school activities. She recalled the younger boy, Danny, who had graduated only three years ago. But Steele? Oh, yes, a wary aspect in her face as she reminisced, he had made his presence felt. She had not forgotten the furor over his disappearance. Had he finally turned up somewhere?

Gary replied obliquely that he might have been located. The registrar had given him fair warning of her bias; if the Lowery family was so generous to a small school, its registrar was wise to use discretion. Well, not to worry, he said easily; young Steele Lowery wasn't a wanted man.

At this, the woman relaxed visibly. "I always hoped he was destined for a military career; reasonably bright, carried himself like a general. Really a striking specimen—a natural leader in the physical sense— certainly the best athlete at Briant High in his day. He was due for graduation, just about this time of year."

Gary wondered aloud if he might look over the boy's personal file, note his special interests, health, behavior patterns. A slow head shake; not in these litigious times, she said, though a transcript was another matter.

In the 1980s, she remarked, Briant High had not computerized its files. The woman disappeared into a cabinet-filled room to return minutes later with a manila file on LOWERY, STEELE JAMES. "I'll be at my desk," she said. "Please keep the pages in order."

It was a transcript, all right, but it was also more. Visits to the principal, absences, records of immunizations. Some of those absences were noted as plain truancy, but no long-term pattern emerged. Young Lowery had taken part in several sports, 4-H, debate. Gary made a note of the family's address, a rural delivery route, and finally asked if he could pay for Xeroxing the transcript.

The woman took off her glasses and gave him a frank stare. "I don't think so, Mr. Garrett. You might ask the principal during school hours, especially now during dead week just before graduation. He is the one who approves transcript requests. Usually. I hope you understand."

The woman was clearly protecting her job and Gary nodded. "I think so, and I appreciate the help. But I wonder about a couple of things." He put his finger on the file. "Debate? Somehow that doesn't fit a jock profile."

She smiled. "No, I don't think Steele got past regional competition. But at Briant High he could be quite persuasive. Steele Lowery had a lot of charisma, a forceful way about him," she added, choosing the phrase with care, eyelids flickering with what could be wry humor. "Good family, lots of potential."

"One more thing, ma'am. Can you recall any special friends he had, either sex? Especially any who are still around?"

"Everyone wanted to be his friend, Mr. Garrett. It seemed like a good idea. I wasn't privy to all the gossip, but I gather he could select a girl as another boy might select a different chocolate bar. He was probably considered quite a catch.

"But Steele couldn't field a baseball team by himself or run interference for himself. He seemed to value a relationship with—" her brow furrowed, eyes shut momentarily. She attacked her keyboard and, in moments, smiled at the screen. "Kenneth Kirk. Heavyset young man, not the sort to move very far away from his roots. I know he works at the Shell station but the name escaped me. Sorry. It's been some years, and I trade at Texaco." And now she did smile, and Gary decided she should do it more often. "The school library down the hall isn't very large but it has yearbooks back to the Year One. And a Xerox machine that takes dimes," she added, pointing down a hallway. "I'm covering for the librarian, this late in the day." Wink. "And for myself."

Gary grinned back at her and checked his change pocket, moving quietly down the hall. Five minutes later, he found the yearbooks, slender volumes full of fond memories for most; for a few, reminders of lost potential. He noted that Briant's league played eight-man football, and that Steele Lowery rated a full page ". . . in our minds and hopes." The kid had worn a tie for his annual portrait: prominent jaw, unruly dark hair, strong nose. In the sports photographs, it was obvious the Lowery kid had been a stud: slender thighs and waist, well-developed calves, long trunk, good set of shoulders on him. *Not an easy mark to dump down a mine shaft*, Gary decided. He Xeroxed all four pages of the graduating-class pictures, replaced the yearbook, and left without speaking to a soul. The registrar did not look up from her screen as he passed; but as he waved, she nodded.

Gary drove to a combination roadhouse and convenience store at the edge of Briant. He was still officially on duty and, if his beeper insisted, he would use his car phone. He brought a carton of buttermilk and a pack of Fritos back to the car and, in the shade of a huge eucalyptus, took his time studying those Xeroxed pictures, swigging, crunching, guessing.

Two of the girls in the class of '87 had been active in everything, doubtless the socialities of their set. One, Ruth Madden, was a real knockout, the homecoming queen. The other, almost plain-faced with short bangs and a smile to fight tigers for, had been valedictorian. Gary bet himself that the beauty would have been Steele Lowery's choice—and that she would have parlayed those looks into a career in a bigger place than Briant. He would pursue these leads further with a phone directory that evening.

He studied other pictures idly. In quotation marks below the names, before their listed activities, were nicknames—perhaps nicknames invented by the yearbook staff. Steele Lowery's nickname had been "Hoss." *They don't always shoot horses*, Gary thought. This one had apparently died in a fall.

Kirk, Kenneth Robert, alias "Mongo," had been a big neckless fireplug of a kid, face innocent of malice—and of anything else worth noting. His portrait grinned back at Gary like Alfred E. Neuman, like a smiley face, ready for a joke or a pass-blocking assignment. It seemed that the Kirk boy had taken up exactly those activities that had interested Steele Lowery, and no others. Gary could not avoid grinning back at Kirk, the nickname an obvious reference to a comic character in Blazing Saddles, played by Alex Karras, another walking fireplug and an all-pro NFL guard of stupendous talent. Legend had it that Karras could show the wit of a pixilated genius. Somehow, Gary suspected, Kenneth Robert

Kirk would not quite measure up. "Well, Mongo, let's see if you're still pumping Shell," he murmured, and folded the Xeroxed pages away.

The Shell station was only a block from Texaco, advertising gas for identical prices. Gary drove up to the pumps, heard a bell resonate somewhere in the service bay where an old Volkswagen beetle was perched on the lift, rear wheels foolishly sagging like a broken toy. He got out and proceeded to top off his own tank, cradling his corn chips under one arm, then saw a pale round face emerge from beneath the VW. It sat atop the shoulders of a bowling ball of a man, unmistakably Kenneth Kirk with several years of accumulated fat.

"With you in a minute," Kirk sang out in a voice still boyish, using a grease gun on another fitting without haste. *No hurry,* said his manner, *I'll be here for the rest of my life.*

Gary took a bite of chips and pulled cash from his pocket, glancing at the pump, then at the overall-clad bowling ball who now sauntered up. "Eight sixty-five; uh, you could check the oil," Gary said and then, in pretended surprise as Kirk turned toward the Camaro's hood, "Hey, don't I know you?"

"Been here awhile," said the young man, wiping his hands on a red shop towel as he manipulated the hood. He glanced at Gary with a tentative smile. "I'm not that good with faces."

With a finger snap, Gary smiled back. "Yeah, you were a hot jock here a few years back. I used to do a little scouting for a friend, coach for special teams. He didn't always listen. You were Church—something like that?"

"Still am. Ken Kirk. Long time ago," he said, the smile fading like a fond memory.

"Yeah. Hell of a lineman," Gary said. "You had a great back, I remember. Big strapping guy. He do well in college?"

The smile had faded but now it returned in another incarnation, Kirk's dark eyes nearly closed in enjoyment. "Hoss Lowery. Naw, I don't think so. Or maybe so; jeez, man, who knows? He just dropped outa sight one day in April, didn't even graduate. It was in the papers," he added. "I thought maybe he got tired on one of his solo hikes, hitched a ride, maybe with some chick, and just kept goin'. That's what I told his folks, too. They didn't like that. Huh! Never were partial to me much, neither."

Kirk showed Gary the dipstick reading, up to the correct mark, and replaced the metal rod. Gary offered his half-empty bag of junk food. "Hands are greasy," Kirk said, but with a glance of longing.

"If it's grease you want, there's enough of it in these to lube a John Deere," Gary joked, and held a group of the curled chips toward Kirk's face. "Open wide, Mongo."

A startled look—not of pleasure—from Kirk, who nonetheless took the mouthful of chips. Gary did not miss that look, having tried for a friendly ploy and fallen on his face with it. "Wasn't that your nickname? Sorry, I thought I remembered—"

"Fuckin' Lowery. That was his idea, always playin' with your head. Gave everybody names, even if you didn't like 'em. Great jock, though, like you said. Yeah, we had some fine ol' times then." Kirk swallowed noisily. "I was his best friend. You didn't have to take a whole lot of his crap if you were Hoss's buddy."

"I'd think everybody was," Gary prompted.

"You'd have to think again." Kirk looked into the distance, remembering, and shook his head. "Don't get me wrong—everybody pretty much got along."

"Pretty much, but not always, huh?"

Kirk pulled his head down as if unconsciously ducking away from controversy. "You had to be there. Like with those numb-nuts nicknames, if you rolled with it, your day went smoother. Even with guys a year ahead of Hoss, they knew there wasn't no quit in him. Say you managed to put him down the first time, next day he'd come at you again. If he took the notion, sooner or later he would beat the shit out of you. Even if you won the first one, it wasn't no fuckin' picnic, I learned that as a sophomore. Kids just learned, if you gave him his way everything would be cool. Let the Wookie win, you know?"

"You say he just took off? Sounds like a mystery, Ken. Mysteries fascinate me." Gary offered another bit of chips and Kirk accepted like a tame hippo, opening wide. Knowing that a bit of misdirection sometimes elicited surprising tidbits, Gary said, "Anybody take off with him—maybe eloping, you think?"

"Not from around here—he played the field. Some Fresno dolly, maybe. His folks have money, and his little brother, Dan, would'a told me if Hoss had been in touch. Not these days, though." Kirk looked around him as if his surroundings explained everything.

Putting on his most innocent air, Gary nodded. "I knew a kid in L.A., skipped out. But he was running nickel bags of pot, and ended up running from some leg breakers. You don't suppose—"

"Not ol' Hoss. He'd take a toke now and then; me, too, if he wanted me to. But he could buy anything he wanted—booze or a joint—and he wasn't into hard stuff. Naw, I used to think instead of a chick, maybe he joined the marines, somethin' like that, just for the general hell of it." Kirk laughed. "That, or somebody finally run him off. Now that, I don't think he'd have told me."

"Why not, if you were buddies?"

"If somebody ever made him back down, he'd have kept it to himself. And maybe he wouldn't've stuck around, in case they wanted bragging rights. Nobody did, though, so it prob'ly didn't happen."

Kirk was showing signs of being restive, and now Gary handed him the pack of chips, shaking the bag suggestively. "Go ahead, I'm full. But I'd hate to see who'd be big enough to run that kid off."

Easily bribed, Kirk shook himself a mouthful of chips. "Maybe a bunch together. Hoss Lowery knew how to piss 'em off by the handful. They wouldn't'a told me, even if he did frost my ass with that fuckin' nickname." He glared at Gary over a mountain of emotional baggage, the pain still there. "Shit, I just wanted to be Ken, you know?"

"I give up. Who else did he piss off?"

"Guys whose girls he took out. Girls he dropped; boy, the names he laid on *them*! Loose-tooth Ruth, Dirty Dottie, Candy Andy."

Gary chuckled. "Briant's Don Rickles, huh? But he missed the boat on that last one."

"No he didn't," Kirk said, and paused to shake the last brittle shards of Fritos from the pack. "Andy wasn't a girl." Chewing, shaking his head:

"Hoss just let on he thought so. Naw, he wasn't queer," Kirk went on, seeing the sudden surmise in Gary's face. "Just blew kisses, grab-ass, stuff like that—always tryin' to get the kid's goat."

"Did he?"

"Nope. But if you knew Hoss, you knew he'd never quit tryin' to. Worst thing you c'd do to Hoss Lowery was shrug him off. Dunno why Candy Andy couldn't see that. Give the top jock his due, show him you know he's the boss hoss." Kirk balled up the empty packet, tossed it into a trash barrel in a perfect left-handed hook shot. "Maybe he's bossin' some bunch of roughnecks in the oil fields now. One of these days he'll show up and hand me a three-day line of bullshit about it all. I hope so. Well, look, I gotta finish lubin' the bug there," he said, leaving a smudge of grease on his chin as he wiped his mouth with the back of his hand.

Gary did not wait for his thirty-five cents' change, waving as he drove away. If Ken Kirk heard about the discovery of Lowery's body, he would recall that conversation. But he had already recalled enough to make this inquiry useful: if young Lowery had criminal connections, they weren't known to his best friend; but not everyone in Briant had been sorry to see the last of him, not by a long shot. *Loose-tooth Ruth? Dirty Dottie?* Steele Lowery had been one spirited kid. A mean spirit.

The drive back into Fresno gave Gary time to reflect on his next focus, and to mentally compose the notes he would make. If Steele Lowery had been such an arrogant bully, perhaps that yearbook comment about minds and hopes had been a careful insertion by the faculty, a gesture of sympathy toward the Lowery family. Well, by now the Lowerys had to know the worst even if the word hadn't spread. Wheeling into the graveled apartment-parking area, Gary decided not to contact the Lowerys. Whatever he was looking for, it wasn't a whitewash job.

His new apartment seemed vast and empty now that Jan had left. Sitting at his built-in breakfast nook, he unfolded the Xeroxed pages and sipped the rest of his buttermilk, jotting notes in his pocket-sized spiral binder. Then he rummaged in a box of still-packed books and came up with last year's phone directory. He did not yet have phone service in the apartment, but there was a pay phone near the pool.

Gary used his personal calling card several times in the next half-hour. He located the beauty queen's father in Auberry after four wrong guesses. Last he heard, Ruth was modeling in Nevada, he said. Used some stage name—she wouldn't tell him what.

Gary was too kind to tell him that a lot of Nevada models wore costumes they could hide in a dimple and if his daughter didn't want her stage name known, she probably modeled epidermis.

Her old high-school chums? She had shaken the San Joaquin dust from her heels fast as she could and hadn't kept up any friendships he knew of, said the father. Andy Anderson or Steele Lowery or Ken Kirk? Well, he remembered that spoiled punk Lowery, the father admitted, adding that he was going on vague memories of a big handsome kid with a great opinion of himself. The girl had dated Lowery enough to find another girl for him which, said the father, wasn't like the old days—but then, what was? And by the way, if the caller managed to track Ruthie down, would he mind asking her to drop Dad a postcard? Anything at all, he said wistfully, would be better than nothing.

Gary agreed and broke the connection thinking, *Poor bastard, it's as bad for him as it was for the Lowerys. Now they at least know enough to bury hope. For all this guy knows, his high-stepping daughter occupies a shallow grave somewhere in Nevada. Or a villa in Cannes; and he doesn't know how or where to start looking. Well, if she's doing that to him, I sure hope he deserves it.* Revenge, Gary decided, should at least be deliberate.

The name of the plain jane with the sunburst smile was SEIBOULDT, LINDA MARSH, nickname "Dottie." *Uh-huh; somebody smoothed over one of Hoss's little jokes for the yearbook. Probably because he had already disappeared,* Gary told himself. There was only one Seibouldt in the directory, but it was a bingo. Her mother answered. Oh no, Linda hadn't been home since Christmas. Had her degree from Fresno State, teaching third-graders in Porterville. Was the caller, perhaps, one of her old classmates? Pride was evident in Mrs. Seibouldt's voice.

Gary, as "Garrett," said he hadn't dated Linda, but liked her. Already he was asking himself whether to call or visit the girl—now a full-grown woman. If she lived more than an hour's drive south of Fresno, she might

very well miss whatever surge of gossip might attend the news of Steele
Lowery's death; perhaps he could wait a few days for that interview. Gary
was slightly familiar with Porterville, a farming and oil boomtown on the
edge of the San Joaquin Valley, bursting its old boundaries, some miles off
the main highway on an approach to Sequoia National Park.

Linda's mother hoped it wasn't unpleasant news, she said, that Linda
was married now.

Gary thought fast. "Not to somebody like the guys she talked about
from high school, I hope," he said. "Some guy named Lowery?"

A merry laugh. "Lord, I should say not! She married Gavin Tate in
Porterville." Settling comfortably into gossip on a prized topic now, in a
tone of confidentiality: "I take it you knew Linda in Fresno State, not at
Briant."

Curious but wary: "How'd you guess?" Gary asked.

"Well, Linda was a late bloomer, as they say. She wasn't always so
attractive, not till her junior year at State. Physically, I mean. She was
always popular with her friends, of course. But if you knew the Lowery
boy, you must've—"

Uh-oh, a little damage control needed here, Gary thought. "Never knew
him. I just recalled the name and made a bad guess. I gathered Lowery was
the big man on their high-school campus."

"Big *pain*, is what he was. When Linda found out he had dated her
just to settle a score with Andy, another boy she was dating—you don't
like to hear your daughter cry, Mr. Garrett."

"I believe it. Hey, you don't mean Andy Gossett," he said, picking a
surname at random.

"Anderson," the mother corrected. "Virgil, but we called him Andy.
Nice boy, but you wouldn't have known him at Fresno State. He got a
scholarship to CalTech, believe it or not. Even though they broke up over
that dreadful boy who later ran away from home, I sometimes wonder if
Andy still carries a torch for Linda." Her tone suggested that it would suit
her just fine if that were the case.

Gary passed a few more moments of pleasantries with the woman,
moving away from the Lowery focus, wondering aloud if Linda had

children, whether she was happy in Porterville.

Mrs. Seibouldt's last advice was a chuckled "You might as well give it up, Mr. Garrett. Linda's very happy, but thanks for asking. I'll tell her you called."

Gary left the phone and sat in fading sunlight by the pool, privately convinced that he had reason for a glimmer of suspicion toward the Anderson boy. And how many others? Hard to say; maybe Linda Seibouldt Tate could help. More likely, Andy Anderson could.

He found ANDERSON, VIRGIL PEASE among the Xeroxes; nickname "Andy." Dumbo ears, hair combed straight back from a high forehead, long slender neck, not merely smiling but laughing into the camera. Young Mr. Anderson had been salutatorian of his class, a member of the basketball squad, the band, the National Honor Society, and president of Mathpath. Gary caught himself, for the first time, faintly sympathizing with Steele "Hoss" Lowery. The Anderson boy had excelled in one thing that Lowery had not: dedicated scholarship. *I know how you felt, Hoss. Must've made you want to kick some butt. But I think somebody finally kicked yours.*

However, the Anderson kid had won a ticket to CalTech—Nerd City—for his education, and bright kids didn't become bright in Pasadena; they went to that ravine in Pasadena because they were already savvy and highly motivated. Nerd jokes aside, the jock who activated a brilliant techie's appetite for revenge was in effect a monkey with a meat grinder, liable to do his own tail some serious damage. Maybe Hoss finally made one smart enemy too many, one who was ready to test his manhood by the oldest trial of all; killing another young man. Maybe there would be a Virgil P. Anderson—more likely a dozen of them—listed in Southern California directories. Gary now had enough background on the Lowery kid to ask more intelligent questions.

At least that saccharine nickname, Candy Andy, hadn't worked its way into the yearbook, he thought as he hefted the big Fresno-Clovis directory. Chalk up one for the nerds of the world.

23

HE HAD WORKED LATE IN THE LAB ON TUESDAY, GETTING a little ahead in his work. On a disposition slip, he accounted for the tiny sensor relay he stole from lab stock, claiming it had been fried by accident in an overvoltage surge. Andy hated to look like a klutz, but he knew that Erwin Lockhart would only sigh and roll his eyes, and order another replacement. And make another dry witticism about exiling his maladroits to the Federal Wildlife Forensics lab in Oregon, where they could make their mistakes. Embarrassing for Andy, but it was the only way to expedite the parts Mom demanded.

He had seen from the chalkboard that Lockhart, the lab director, had scheduled a midmorning tour on Wednesday for some environmental group. It would be Andy's turn to play tour guide, a job he pretended to dislike because everyone else did. But, in truth, he enjoyed the way people on a tour of the lab listened to him with such respect, even with admiration. During a tour, he practiced speaking from a bit farther back in his throat, enough to suggest maturity, not enough to be a topic of jokes among the other staff. That was his Mature Andrew character, with the slow, sure gestures. If you couldn't afford to have close friends, respectful admiration would have to do.

Sometimes he would show them his office, not much more than a cubicle but with a few touches that made it uniquely his. The first thing he had brought in was his bookcase, an example of his cabinetry work in cherry wood and blond oak. About ten inches deep, standing some four feet high and five wide, its glass doors were secured by a hidden catch that only Andy understood. Roughly half of the shelf space inside was occupied by books, mostly hardbound, grouped with metal bookends so that the satin finish of the naked shelf, hand-rubbed lovingly by Andy, would show between the bunches of books.

The latest item sat atop the bookshelf as an example of his taxidermy: a hamster, relentlessly cute, erect on its hind legs with false intelligence in its tiny marble eyes, seemingly begging to be petted. The wooden base was inscribed QUEENIE, and within a week admiring visitors, with Andy's permission, had already damaged the pelt with curious fingers. Andy felt it was a small price for admiration from any quarter.

But there would be no admirers today; he had called in sick claiming a toothache, putting it on Lockhart's answering machine before the lab opened. Driving two cars, he and Romana had made it to Sacramento by 11:00, Andy wearing a watch cap with blond curls protruding and jeans with a jacket that matched, but reversed to become dark plaid. His lace-up shoes were fitted with tasseled lacing-spats, like golf brogans. By unsnapping the spats, shoving them with the watch cap–wig into pockets and reversing the jacket, he could complete a lightning transformation in ten seconds.

Romana's tailored jacket was reversible, too, with a dickey that suggested a lace-trimmed blouse when its gray side was out, but became a plain button-front with the black side out. Her smart little beret and wraparound sunglasses would cram quickly into her small shoulder bag, which could double as a purse. With her high cheekbones, cosmetics, and sunglasses, she could pass for fifteen years younger. It always made Andy uncomfortable to see his mom with her prettiest makeup on, for all the world like some glamourpu—like someone glamorous.

By noon they had a burgundy Olds for a rental, parked in the open near the railroad museum in the Old Sacramento district downtown. They had left Romana's Plymouth in a development on Sacramento's east side near Bradshaw and Highway 50, because the Aerojet rocket-development complex lay farther in that direction and Romana suspected that her client's domestic contact might be employed there; no one in the area needed metallurgical specialists more than Aerojet. If they managed to tail the client that far, an exchange of cars would be important. Back in the city's center, they parked Andy's Pinto in the public parking structure between the Capitol mall and Old Sacramento, a quaint jumble of brick-fronted shops in the 1900s style and something of a tourist trap.

Romana's problem was the evasiveness of her client, a well-dressed lobbyist named Hilton whose photos Andy had studied with care. She did not think Hilton was aware of her, but was merely using good tradecraft. Good, but not perfect, because he had developed a set pattern for his evasions that began among those old buildings now occupied by small shops: candies, clothing stores, a beer hall, a hobby shop. Twice before, Romana had followed Hilton from his office near the mall at times when she knew he had an exchange scheduled. On both occasions, he had left his office more than an hour before the scheduled time, walking at a leisurely pace along the mall, easily trailed, then presented her with a dilemma. Once he quickened his pace through the echoing pedestrian tunnel under the nearby freeway, the tunnel's length forcing Romana to hang well back. He had turned right as he exited the tunnel and entered the old town district, then simply disappeared. The second time she had worn running togs, jogging away far ahead of him and through the tunnel, expecting him to emerge from it a few minutes later. He never entered the tunnel, but she caught one glimpse of him soon after as he entered the old town district by another route.

Today, when she spotted Hilton leaving his office building, Romana would proceed to that alternate crosswalk at the limit of visual surveillance and would use their specially built radios to alert Andy, who would be waiting on the opposite side of the tunnel. Whatever he did next, one of Hilton's protective pawns would be swept from the board without his knowledge because there was no other practical means of reaching the old district afoot from the mall.

Hilton was a registered lobbyist in Sacramento, but his real wealth came from trading chemical-processing secrets to the Brazilians, who had a fledgling aerospace industry of their own. Romana had identified the man through that link, but his domestic connection was still a riddle and Hilton seemed to know the twists and turns of Old Sacramento better than the rats in its basements. By bugging his car and bungalow in suburban Fair Oaks, Romana had learned enough to pull his plug, but as usual she would not do it before she discovered the man's local connection in the rare metals–processing industry. The Brazilian connection which had led her to Hilton was only half of the puzzle. Once she had a line on his connection at the domestic end of this very profitable arrangement, she could flush Hilton and then, in good time, select other clients in the network. After a year or so, any resonant ripples of nervousness over Hilton's disappearance should have faded nicely.

The Pinto was cherry on this job, but Romana thought her big Plymouth could have been compromised when she had followed Hilton to work, early in the "relationship." Today, with a second tail on him, she might be more successful; and if that happened the Plymouth could become a liability. She suspected that Hilton, too, had a second car nearby because the tiny transmitter on the chassis of his Toyota proved that he did not use it for these rendezvous. If they could spot him in another car, with the rental parked two blocks away in one direction and the Pinto two blocks in the other, one of them could run to a car while the other waited to see which arterial Hilton took. Using their dedicated-frequency radios in the cars, they had a good chance at a breakthrough. Without Andy's help, Romana's chances were poor, at best.

Romana knew that Hilton gave himself that extra hour, having clocked him when she knew his rendezvous times. Andy's radio, built into a Walkman frame, had its lavalier mike set in the ornate cross hanging at his throat.

Andy was studying the workmanship of model trains in a shop window of the old district when his upscale Walkman spoke in his ear, inaudible to passersby. "Option A, solo brown wrapper, one-twenty or so."

He repeated it back to her in a murmur, continuing to study the shop display. If it had been option B, he would have set off down an alley to place himself nearer to that distant crosswalk, but option A was the tunnel. In roughly one hundred twenty seconds, their client should emerge from it alone, wearing a brown coat. Andy turned and ambled off to a candy shop across the street, stepping into its windowed recess where he could see the tunnel entrance through a window while inspecting old-fashioned stick candies ranked in antique jars. *This is the fun part,* he thought, feeling the surge of excitement under his ribs, confident of his prowess.

Andy's silent count had reached one thirty-two when a gent in tan sport coat and brown tie strode from the tunnel, turned right, and quickened his pace crossing the street a half-block from Andy's post. "Yes," said Andy, recognizing Hilton's general features, heading up the street as the client passed from view. He heard Romana acknowledge his message. She would be hurrying forward by now, perhaps within a block or two.

Before he reached the corner: "I say yes," Romana said, indicating that she now had visual contact.

"You say yes, I say no," Andy replied, turned on his heel, and retraced his steps in a brisk walk, avoiding eye contact with other pedestrians. Once he reached the alley he could lope along fast enough to watch Hilton's next move. If the man did not pass the alley, he would be isolated in one of a few shops in a half-block area. If Romana had him sighted, she would know which shop contained him. Their expectation was that he would head for a car.

Andy's blood was pumping pleasantly, his glands responding to the chase. Mom had trained him wonderfully well, teaching him constant awareness of available cover. That is why he did not literally collide with Hilton. Andy saw that the next block was an open greensward adjoining the railroad museum, and that Hilton would be easy to surveil from a distance. Andy had moved up behind a pile of flattened cardboard boxes that protruded from garbage cans in the alley, squatting to seek a hidden viewpoint, when the sport-jacketed Hilton came into view with the suddenness of a thunderclap. Hilton turned into the alley toward the waiting Andy, walking quickly back parallel to the street from which he had come.

Andy, fifty feet up the alley, sank onto the grime and turned his face to the shop wall, drawing himself as quietly as possible into the fetal curl of a comatose wino, one arm hiding his face. He heard footfalls on grit, approaching, then a subtle shift of their rhythm as they passed him, not stopping but perhaps a startled reaction to the drunk sleeping it off among the other garbage. Andy emitted a soft snore. The footfalls continued, the rhythm regained.

Ten seconds later, Andy said, very softly, "Doubled back in my alley. It's yours while I change." He did not dare look around yet; Hilton might be watching over his shoulder. Romana would realize that, if Andy needed time to change his costume, the pass had been very close. If she could not pick Hilton up now, perhaps their day had been wasted.

"Yes," he heard, Mom's voice betraying a quiet excitement as she spotted her client somewhere beyond the alley. After a subtle peek, Andy was on his feet, ripping away the spats, turning his jacket inside out, cramming the knitted cap with its blond curls into a pocket. He hurried back the way he had come—not twisting his head, but letting his eyes search fruitlessly for a sight of Hilton or Romana as he emerged onto the street.

"No. I say no, from my position one," he said, letting her know he was again window-shopping. There was no reply. Sometimes it worked that way, some metal structure impeding the transmission, or perhaps a situation where she could not afford to break her silence.

He wondered if Hilton had doubled back through the tunnel and was moving in that direction when she said, "Inside Rathcellar," very softly. "Hold your position." He knew then that Romana had followed her client into a corner microbrewery not fifty paces distant. She would be rummaging in her bag to speak, or inspecting her lipstick in her compact mirror. Andy realized that he might be seen from one of the Rathcellar windows and, if Hilton was judging passersby, Andy was one of the few to be judged.

Regardless of her orders, it was essential that he move on, and without delay. "I'll look for a parking place," he said. More of their jargon. He strolled away, then saw a pedestrian bench far down the block and finally settled into it, peering up the street now and then as though expecting to be picked up momentarily.

For ten minutes he sat, emotionally wired, noting that the

Rathcellar's side entrance was visible, realizing, too, that its service entrance was, by sheer luck, barely in sight. Then Mom: "Conference. Location?"

"Near the crossing at your position one." Almost immediately, he saw her turning the corner toward him, and he knew that stiff stride all too well. Something had gone badly.

He stood up and stretched, showing himself to her, then sat down again. She walked on, too wise to meet him face to face, stopping only when she had turned the next corner. "Can you believe," she stormed softly. "He tried to pick me up!"

"Not if he has a schedule," Andy said and made a serious mistake. "You followed too soon. He had to check you out." Divulging an unpleasant truth to Mom was *always* a serious mistake.

A long silence from Romana. She broke it with, "Have a sampler of beers. See if business is being done. Wait! Compromised?"

"Not after a change, and never showed my face," he said and crossed the street, mussing his dark hair into an unruly mass. He stopped just inside, waiting for his eyes to accommodate the gloom, and found a stool at the bar. He ordered a sampler, which turned out to be four squat glasses of the local products, paid, and let the bar mirrors help him survey the dark recesses of the place.

A man two stools away glanced over and grinned after Andy set his second glass down and muttered, "No." Andy made a wry face, then selected a third brew, fearful that Hilton had left by that front door seconds behind Romana. He did not spot the client until another man, returning from the men's room, took his seat alone at one of the small tables where a glass of beer sat, half-empty. It was then that the lobbyist revealed himself, standing up from his solitary lair in a shadowed booth thirty feet away, taking his coat which he had folded on the seat beside him, making his way to the men's room. Andy made a mental connection instantly.

He was watching a classic *dubok* pass, Andy realized, a transfer the Soviet bloc had perfected, something he had never actually experienced before: a dead drop in a public place where neither party made overt contact. Andy took a gulp from his beer and said, "Yes!" with great satisfaction, nodding approval at his glass.

"Finally got one that suits you," said the other patron.

Andy smiled and nodded, moving to the adjacent seat, glad of this chance to use conversation as cover. "I need only a few drops to tell," he said, knowing Romana was listening, hoping she would enjoy the pun. "But this may be the one, right here." With that, he held up his glass. "I must say it goes down very smoothly." Only Mom would appreciate these double entendres.   ·

In his ear, disbelieving: "The connection is right there?"

Andy took another sip, smacked his lips, set the glass down. "Mm, yes," he said.

Andy's companion began to talk of favorite brews: Sam Adams, Full Sail Ale, Kulmbacher. Andy needed to do little more than look interested, nodding, smiling, keeping his gaze centered on the bridge of the man's nose while his mind remained focused on his peripheral vision. Alone at his table, Hilton's contact tried to avoid being too obvious as his eyes searched the Rathcellar for signs of interested patrons. He seemed to take in Andy's conversation without really seeing it, his gaze passing on, birdlike in its intensity.

When Hilton came in sight again, he had his coat on and went straight to the side exit, leaving without pause or gesture. Andy leaned back, took up the darkest of the brews, sipped, and let the glass fall over in bogus clumsiness. "No! Well, it's gone now," he said, having spilled no more than an ounce. "No matter, I have a better one." At the same time, he saw what he had expected to see. The man who had preceded Hilton to the men's room stood up, draining his glass, and returned to the alcove too quickly. If there had been any doubt before, it was gone now. *Must remember to tell Mom he's the anxious type. Poor tradecraft; when it's his turn, she'll take him down like a light snack.*

The man was gone for perhaps a minute, barely long enough to fool any casual onlooker. *Probably still new at this,* Andy thought, making mental notes. He noted that this new contact was short and pudgy, in tan slacks and open shirt with wisps of dark hair arranged artfully across a nearly bald scalp. *No wig from this one*, Andy told himself.

When the short man emerged again, he made his way out the front door, walking with exaggerated calm. He could be seen through the Rathcellar windows as he ambled off down the street toward the railroad museum, stopping once to glance behind him. Andy looked at his wristwatch, shook his head, then smiled and nodded at his seatmate as he exited.

By crossing the street as he described his new quarry, Andy kept the man in sight, donning the watch cap, stopping behind a van to reverse his jacket again and to inform Romana of his progress. By now it was obvious that the quarry's goal was near the museum. "I say yes," Romana's voice intoned with something like grim satisfaction.

"Your location?"

"Rental," she said, and Andy laughed softly, elated with this twist after a near-disaster in the alley. If she were in the rental car, she had sensibly abandoned Hilton and was already in the museum parking lot. Their new quarry was actually walking in her direction.

He was curious about that drop location and its opportunities for hidden treasure. It would be an empowerment, somehow, to stand in that little space and survey it, guessing at the exact mechanism of the *dubok*. Of course he would not expect to find anything useful. In her anecdotes, Mom had cited loose bricks, light fixtures, even discarded soft-drink cans and cigarette packages left in trash receptacles. "Should I check the drop in the men's room?"

Now she cut in quickly: "Get your car. White Volvo, old sports station wagon." Moments later, as Andy sprinted back to the pedestrian tunnel, she identified the license plate. By the time he had reached his Pinto, out of breath with his own heartbeat pounding in his ears, Romana was already following the Volvo onto a freeway on ramp.

Andy did not see either of the vehicles until they turned off from the North Sacramento freeway onto Greenback, a broad straight boulevard on the city's northern edge with too much traffic and too many lights.

The Pinto's only air conditioning was an open window but, without his jacket or cap, Sacramento's humid summer heat was bearable. On orders, he overtook Romana in the Olds and settled into a practiced routine, a quarter-mile behind the old P-1800 classic with its huge, unmistakable rear glass. *Great taste in cars, but not for this work. Why doesn't he just tape a lit highway flare to his antenna?* He was not prepared when the Volvo pulled suddenly from the left lane and turned sharply right at a suburban corner. Andy was blocked from a lane change, giving his mom plenty of time to avoid a similar problem and calmly directing her to the turn. "Hazel Avenue," he told her as he passed it, looking for a place to retrace his path.

When he was delayed by an interminable traffic signal, and found that Romana had turned left instead of right on Hazel, Andy found himself laughing helplessly, too flushed with their partial success to feel much of a letdown. After all, it was Mom who had made that wrong turn. They spent the afternoon quartering the area, knowing that the effort was almost certainly futile, his mom admitting finally that they had "lost their tail."

Romana did not upbraid him then, nor while they recovered her Plymouth, nor by radio as they drove back to Fresno. She waited for that until they were back at The Place in twilight, Romana developing her telephoto shots of the dumpy little potential client, taken from a block away as he was unlocking his Volvo. "You treated the whole surveillance as a joke," she spat, choosing one of the negatives for enlargement.

He claimed otherwise, recounting his recovery in that alley. "And I kept you updated, I spotted what was happening, making his drop an hour before he'd said. He probably always does that. I even gave you the local connection," he protested.

"And didn't you love it, playing your clever word games! Pity you weren't clever enough to give me the right directions later. I could have had his base," she said in a quiet fury as the enlarger threw a magnified negative of their new quarry onto photo paper.

If he insisted he had steered her correctly, she would only deny it. "Hey, we have his face, his car, his plates; we're almost there with a new client, Mom. You'll have a name and address in a few days." He made his tones plaintive, accommodating. "Now you can set up this Hilton guy— he should be good for a nice piece of change. It was a pretty good day— wasn't it?"

She operated the enlarger with the adroitness of the expert, breathing heavily through her nose. "Let *me* tell *you* when we have a good day, young man. Don't think I haven't noticed how independent you're becoming, ignoring my orders as it suits you, enjoying my problems like some detached voyeur. I suppose you think you're ready to branch out on your own!"

Flushing with a humiliation as old as the relationship: "No, Mom, you know better than that. You've always taught me to improvise; I only did what I had to do. But what more could I have done today?"

"I'll tell you what you can do tomorrow," she said, ignoring his question, snapping off the enlarger. "You can get that damned pheromone tracker put together. Show me you can take something seriously. Now get out of here. I have a new file to start."

He left quickly, glad to be out of her sight, waiting until the Pinto was off of reservation land before he gave in to the temptation to pound the steering wheel with his open hands. It seemed to Andy that his relationship with Mom was worsening, not improving, and it was becoming more difficult to quell his demons. Maybe, by going over it in his mind, he could lower his frustration level by analyzing the ways he had pulled his mom's triggers; turned a good day into a bad one.

By the time he pulled up before his garage doors and doused his headlights, he understood the day better. He had made no errors; she had, and needed someone to blame for them. An old and infuriating pattern, he thought, made worse by the fact that he could see no hope of its ever changing. And he no longer had any of his darlings to sacrifice on this night. He was beginning to need them more than ever.

Well, he could still improvise, he decided, as a familiar presence nuzzled his shin. "Hi, Princess," he said to the Labrador bitch, a shape blacker than the deepest shadow of his garage, her tail thumping against his leg as he reached down to pat her head.

Andy got the garage door closed, murmuring to the dog, scratching her behind the ears, squatting before the old refrigerator he used chiefly for paint storage. The lone carton of milk, two weeks old, had not soured yet. He emptied the carton into a stainless-steel bowl to hold the animal's interest while he spread filmy plastic onto the workshop floor. The bitch might not follow him upstairs into his apartment, and if he left her enclosed in the garage for even a moment, she might bark. Well, never mind; he could clean up later. Here in the welcoming dark he soothed the friendly bitch with soft murmurs, sank down cross-legged on the plastic, pulled the knife with its specially modified slitting blade from his pocket and began to scratch the dog's flanks, pulling her nearer, then running a hand over her muzzle before pinioning her jaws, improvising a relief from his frustrations.

24

VISCONTI MIGHT HAVE SELECTED ANY OF SEVERAL AGENTS to check possible sources of the Thomas Concoction, but none of the others wore a temporary forearm cast so it was Gary who drew some of the least physical tasks. He began with the yellow pages under veterinary services, focusing on those that seemed likely to deal with large animals: herd consultants, practices limited to exotic animals, the Equine Clinic. Only one of the vets he canvassed had ever heard of that particular lethal injection, but she and another clinic both referred him to a local lab that manufactured veterinary supplies.

In all of these queries, he had a hidden agenda. Though the DEA could get just about anything it needed through official channels, there had to be other channels not so official. It was possible that, deadly or not, the stuff could be obtained easily. So, in these calls, Gary presented himself as a man with acreage in the Sierra foothills near the town of Sanger, a man whose liberal views had been sorely tested by coyotes. They ate his son's pet rabbit; the family dog had not been seen for days. He had heard of something quick and painless called the Thomas Concoction. How did one go about obtaining such a thing?

Ivy Laboratories accepted his story, but denied his petition firmly. "It's not a commonly accepted drug," the lab man told him. "I mean, not even in the veterinary community. Of course in Alaska you could probably get your hands on some, and the Canadians have used it in darts against polar bears that develop a fondness for people."

"You mean fondness, like in yum-yum?" Gary supplied.

"That's it. Some do acquire the taste, you know; and when something with paws the size of razor-tipped dinner plates is breaking down people's front doors, the Mounties tend to take extreme measures. That's what the Thomas Concoction is, an extreme measure; not that it's so much more deadly, but I understand it works quicker than other methods. The rumor is, a number of labs could brew up such stuff, given the correct proportions, but it would have to be for a state or federal agency, and I believe they concoct their own. Sorry we can't help you. What you need is Animal Control."

"Look, I've, ah, I can afford it, if that's the problem," Gary said.

Now the man's voice developed a brittle edge—not angry, but no longer accommodating. "Perhaps you can, mister, but we don't know what goes into it, and if we did, I do know that even divulging it is illegal; and we can't afford that. I hope you're not about to suggest something that we'd have to report because it's a pain in the backside. Am I being perfectly clear?"

"Perfectly," Gary said and rang off, not at all discouraged. He was pleased to discover how difficult it was for private citizens to obtain the drug and wondered whether there might be a black market in it. So far, he had gotten much the same responses he might have expected had he asked how to make high explosives in his kitchen; few knew, and those who did weren't helping.

That left his hole card: the state's wildlife forensics labs; one in Sacramento and another across town in Fresno. Those guys were law enforcement of a limited sort, much the same as the federal lab in Ashland, Oregon. On a hunch, he first called the Oregon lab, identified himself properly, and asked for what federal agencies called "mutual aid." The director heard his request, then asked for his office telephone number and promised to call back.

Gary knew the drill and was happy to see it used. Too many unofficial folks knew how to pose on a phone line as a DEA man in Fresno, and somewhere in Ashland, Oregon that director was checking Gary out.

He got his callback in less than five minutes from Director Goddard, a gent of rollicking good humor who frankly said he'd never heard of the Thomas Concoction until Gary asked about it. "But when I checked you out with DEA's crime lab in San Francisco, they asked me about the bloody stuff, too! Apparently, in their minds at least, you're already connected with it. What are you guys doing down there, tracking Godzilla?"

"Might be simpler if we were," Gary admitted. "The drug was used on a federal agent, but we'd like to keep that among ourselves. It's beginning to look like the perps could have an official source unless it turns out to be a precise mixture of commonly available chemicals. If that's the case, just the recipe itself might be enough."

"Maybe I don't want to know it," Goddard replied with relentless whimsy, "and don't tell my wife either. But let me redirect your call to our chief chemist—he'll know what's what. He knows the guys in both the Sacramento and Fresno wildlife labs too; may even know if they have this stuff on hand."

Moments later, the chemist was on the line, and his tone changed the moment he heard Gary's request. "You, uh, have some of the stuff with you?"

"Not anymore," Gary said.

"You want to be awfully careful if you do," the chemist warned. Asked how a private citizen might come by the Thomas Concoction, the chemist chuckled. "Theft, bribery, mugging a game warden, which I definitely don't recommend. Have I left anything out?"

"Legitimate texts, maybe?" Gary hazarded.

"Not in open literature. I can't discuss the proportions, and you aren't even supposed to know the ingredients, regardless of proportions; but I can provide a supply for a warden."

"Then it's not kept on hand?"

"No. Actually, I believe it has been, on occasion, in California; some problem with big mean seals along the California coast, as I recall."

"Well, it's not much, but it's something," Gary sighed. "This is sensitive information. A serious crime has been committed with the drug, and we'd like to know how the perps got hold of it."

"Good God! Just a minute." Gary could hear fingers tapping on a keyboard. After a long moment, the chemist went on: "I didn't think we had it on hand, and my records confirm that we don't. There aren't that many labs of our kind anywhere, but California and Alaska would be my guesses, in that order. Does that help?"

"It's a lead," Gary agreed. "So I guess what I need to find out is who keeps it or kept it, and where, and whether any of it is unaccounted for. Could you check on that without raising any eyebrows at the other labs?"

"Um, yes, I see your problem. If it was taken from a state lab, somebody in that lab may be very alert to this line of questioning. Tell you what: coming from me—better still, from one of our people in Fairbanks—a query might seem more routine. Why don't you let us work on it? Uh, Fairbanks is, what, an hour behind us, or two? Never mind—let me get back to you."

Gary made himself a cup of hot chocolate and drank it in Visconti's office, filling his supervisor in on the little he had learned. The resident agent's phone interrupted them several times and Gary opted for brevity, leaving quickly. The callback from Oregon hadn't materialized by lunchtime, but Gary did not want to miss it, so he sent out for a calzone and buttermilk. For all the good that did, he might as well have taken a long lunch at the Basque Hotel.

He was gnawed by a suspicion that the damned Thomas Concoction was an exercise in futility, what Swede Halvorsen would call a red herring. If the trail led to Alaska, where big predators were more populous than humans in some regions, the effective rules might be a lot different from those on the books. Alaskans tended to make their own rules, on the grounds that a federal statute cobbled up in a paneled room 4,000 miles away might not reflect the "real world" of one-ton bears, six-month winters, and killer whales that launched themselves out of the surf—huge torpedoes with peg teeth—to snatch a meal on the shore.

Late in the afternoon, Gary found and excised a brief piece in a back page of the *Fresno Bee,* about the finding of the Lowery boy:

YOUTH'S REMAINS FOUND

The skeletal remains of a Briant youth, missing since 1987, have been positively identified, says a spokesman of the Fresno County Sheriff's department. The body of Steele Lowery of Briant, aged 17 at his disappearance in April of 1987, has been found in a disused mine shaft northeast of Briant. Authorities say the youth died of accidental causes at the time of his original disappearance.

Everybody will buy that, thought Gary, *except the bastards who put me down there with the kid. And with any luck they won't see this piece.*

The telephone rang while he was running off copies of the article; Ashland, Oregon calling.

They had a bingo, said the chemist. "Of sorts, anyway. The state lab supervisor in Sacramento tells our Fairbanks guy that, according to their computer, their Fresno lab recently had a few darts charged up with Thomas Concoction for those big pinnipeds—ah, seals. Apparently they don't load the darts the way we do, they keep ampoules. It wouldn't make any difference except that the Fresno supervisor—name's Erwin Lockhart, by the way—reported they lost a load."

"Lost it?"

"Well, spillage, actually. Those ampoules are pretty sturdy; new ones are polycarbonate, just about unbreakable, but the old ones are glass. Lockhart verified to Sacto that he saw the debris, the load soaking into the concrete floor, one of the lab guys cleaning up with aqua regia—that's a mixture of nitric and hydrochloric acids that plays hell with any organic matter, including Dr. Thomas's favorite brew. It's a clear liquid, partly organic. The acids would've handled it right away."

"So it was really accounted for, after all," Gary said.

"No doubt about it, according to the records. Their tech—Andrews, I think his name is—spilled a few ceecees of it, but Lockhart witnessed it bubbling away as that aqua regia etched its way down into the cement."

"What was that name again?"

"Lockhart, or Andrews? I think it was Andrews," the chemist

replied. "They're pretty understaffed there, but you've probably seen their facility."

The moment Gary admitted he hadn't, he realized he should remedy that little oversight as soon as possible. He thanked the Oregon Fed for his help, rang off, and glanced at the wall clock. Not quite 4:00. Twenty minutes or so to the state lab; the opposite end of town from his apartment at the day's end, but whatthehell—

25

ERWIN LOCKHART LIKED DOORS TO BE KEPT OPEN UNLESS there was a good reason for them to be closed, so a closed door in the Fresno lab was a signal, of sorts. Andy Soriano preferred, at half-past four in the afternoon, not to signal that he was stealing a very small piece of advanced technology.

Andy hunched over his desk in the lab, a can of lighter fluid plainly in view as a decoy for anyone who might walk by his office. A stride in the concrete corridor made enough noise in the quiet of the lab to give a few seconds' warning. Instead of squirting fluid onto the spongy felt material of his old Zippo lighter, he was shoving his plastic-wrapped, handmade copy of the latest tracker subamplifier into the bottom of his lighter, between its felt pad and what remained of the cotton wicking. The little metal chamber, robbed of most of its cotton, retained enough fluid to light a few times and would pass any but the most careful inspection. Andy's only reasons for lighting an occasional cigarette were to justify that lighter in his pocket and, more rarely, as a mannerism for one of his characters. Though he did not flinch outwardly when the phone rang, his heart bounced against his ribs and, while answering, he smiled at his own inner reaction.

The smile died when Lockhart summoned him. Would Andrew mind showing a federal agent some of their special equipment?

"Oh, swell! He picked a great time for it," Andy grumbled.

Evidently, Lockhart was speaking for the benefit of the agent. "Good. Nothing like a full tour, Andrew. Just a rundown on some hardware. He's here with me," Lockhart added unnecessarily.

Andy pocketed his contraband, cleared his desktop, and shrugged into his Bright Young Andrew character for the visiting Fed as he walked toward Lockhart's office. Maybe this little command performance wouldn't take long. He had scheduled a couple of hours at the playhouse that evening, and after that a quick run to The Place to deliver his goods to Mom. She would probably complain about his lateness; *well, let her*. He turned the corner to Lockhart's office and almost bumped into a man standing in the doorway. For an instant, their heads were only inches apart.

The effect for Andy was dreamlike, hallucinatory, and then they both moved apart with the self-conscious laughs of men occupying a no-man's-land of personal space. To cover his confusion, Andy looked in Lockhart's direction, thinking, *I know this man beside me,* unable to place him but equating him somehow with danger. Meanwhile he put his gestures on automatic pilot while Lockhart introduced them, shaking hands, exchanging smiles with this DEA man, Gary Landis. He did not recall hearing the name before; could not place the short blond crew cut with the tanned, smooth-shaven face. As the moment passed, Andy realized it was entirely possible that this Landis fellow, with his alert regular features and easy grin, simply looked very much like several other men.

"If you're DEA, I suppose you'll be interested in our accountability procedures," Andy said, with a wave toward the hall.

"Good idea," said Landis. "But hey, this isn't a bust." He laughed to cement his denial. "We've heard you Fish and Game guys have some interesting delivery systems for tranquilizers," he went on with that infectious smile. "That's something we only hear about in the agency; high time we learned more."

"Carte blanche, Andrew," said Lockhart, and picked up a memo from his in basket to signify that Andy could take it from there, holding nothing back.

Andy led the way down the corridor, explaining that the lab's modest staffing did not allow a chief chemist. He showed Landis their pharmaceutical stocks, remarking that another lab technician, momentarily in another part of the building, doubled as chemist and microbiologist. "As you see, two levels of security," Andy said, "the receptionist where you got that green visitor badge is level one, the double-locked stockroom here for the more arcane materials is level two."

"I noticed the passes are different colors," Landis remarked.

"You betcha; red is for the press," Andy chuckled. "We're a little more careful with some dude looking for a good story." Picking up on his tour spiel again: "We still use the old key locks instead of electronic entry, it's cheap." *And they yield to a lockpick if your mom teaches you well enough.* "Chemist and director have keys, with a third set in the director's office safe. Want to see inside?"

Landis nodded, evidently not all that interested, and Andy's level of arousal subsided one small notch. "Nobody else has access?"

"Only those," Andy said. "We account for requisitions on a clipboard inside, backed with computer records and reports. Lockhart's a fiend for long-winded reports. Just a minute—Doug will have to do the honors." And with that, Andy walked a few steps down the corridor, tapped on the closed door, then entered. He found Doug Isaacs installing an insect specimen in the gold-plating fixture needed for the electron microscope. "Visiting DEA, needs to look at the secure stores," he said. "Lockhart okayed him."

Isaacs said nothing intelligible. He managed to be civil to a few of the staff, but for some reason he had never warmed to Andy. Grumbling, the chemist shuffled out, fondling his ring of keys like a priest with a censer. After brief introductions, Doug Isaacs opened the secure room and mumbled apologies about its untidiness. Landis glanced around idly, eyeing shelves, studying the contents of an ordinary Amana refrigerator. "Telazol? Triggers a memory," he said.

Isaacs: "I'm not surprised; it's one of the tranquilizers controlled by you folks. Some of the others like Ketamine and Xylazine aren't."

"It was mostly the tranquilizer hardware that's of interest," Landis said at last, shutting the refrigerator. "Can you really put a mountain lion out with this stuff in here?"

"Down and out, with some of it," said Doug. "Or a sea lion. That was something we had to do recently."

"Yeah?" Landis squinted with interest.

"Yeah—a big California sea lion can go six hundred pounds, and they're getting so aggressive, they challenge tourists at Fisherman's Wharf. In a few cases, the worst offenders were darted and towed away."

"Seems like they'd just come back again, when they woke up," Landis ventured.

The topic was not to Andy's liking. "I can show you some hardware," he began.

Isaacs, damn him, was not to be denied. "They *didn't* wake up. That was the point, but the tourists don't know that. We, uh, managed to kill a few square feet of cement floor while we were at it," said Doug, with a flicker of dour amusement toward Andy.

Landis cocked his head, glancing from one to the other. "Inside joke?"

Andy said, "What he means is, he overreacted to a little spillage—"

"My ass!" Isaacs scoffed. "That was the kind of stuff you don't fool around with, Andy." To Landis: "He did it; let *him* tell you about it."

They filed outside again, Isaacs relocking the secure room and disappearing down the corridor again with a parting mumble. "Sounds like I'm missing a good yarn," said Landis.

"Nah. It was just a glass vial of tranquilizer I broke," Andy replied. "But the stuff was special stores and Doug wasn't happy 'til he'd followed up with some acids that took off a millimeter of the cement around the spill. End of story."

It was, of course, only the end that Andy chose to explain. The other end of it, known only to him and Romana, was Andy's prior theft of a vial and its replacement with a plain potassium chloride solution. Andy had, in fact, dropped the damned vial once without effect. When he threw it down harder the second time, it had broken. And the pilfered vial had gone into the buttock of Charles Lane.

The thought of Lane, and his disposal, did not disturb Andy in the slightest. Lane had been a client—a thing that walked and talked like a man but, as Mom had taught him, was only prey. Yet Mom had also taught that dangerous topics were best avoided, and his theft of the deadly vial was too close to the present discussion.

To pass from the subject Andy said, "Want to see the dart pistol? That's the delivery system for the tranquilizer."

Landis did, and Andy produced it from a cabinet in another part of the lab. The two men moved into Andy's cubicle, discussing the weapon, lounging in swivel chairs.

Andy felt no reluctance to discuss the device, which had never been part of Mom's arsenal and did not look at all like a pistol. Its camouflage-painted brass barrel was easily four feet long, a half-inch in diameter. Andy showed how the barrel plugged into a pistol grip which had both a pressure gage and a steel reservoir fed by a common CO_2 cartridge. "You can also fill the reservoir with air from a foot pump," Andy explained. "You can even fit a mouthpiece on the barrel and use it as a blowgun at very close range."

Andy could tell that Landis was intrigued, as though by some expensive toy. As the instructor, Andy was in his glory now, genuinely enjoying the process, warming to Landis himself. He triggered the empty weapon once, producing its characteristic chuffing hiss that brought a smile to the DEA man's face. "There's a different rig for longer range, but this pistol is good up to twenty yards or so. And here's what it shoots."

He showed off a dart, a special syringe of clear plastic trailing a crimson stabilizer of soft, fluffy stuff. "You can get a gram and a half of Telazol in here, about six ceecees. That's enough to knock a brown bear out for awhile."

"Or that other stuff, I suppose," Landis prompted.

"Xylazine? It's for different animals. There's a dosage chart here somewhere. Coyote or bobcat go down easier than, say, a cougar."

Andy unlocked his handmade cabinet, extracting a text from it, checking a reference on tranquilizer dosages. Andy did this with practiced ease, hiding his most subtle work in plain sight. No one, seeing him take a book from that glass-fronted case, could have dreamed that the case might hide more than it displayed with shelves that were obviously half-vacant.

When Andy displayed the chart, Landis showed more interest, commenting on the fact that species of roughly the same size did not always get the same dosage. Andy explained that dosages had been determined partly by experience. Watching Landis's pupils, he saw them expand slightly at one chart entry.

"Thomas Concoction? Sounds like a cocktail," Landis said, looking up quizzically.

Knowing that vagueness was the province of the guilty, Andy said, "Well, I'm no bartender, but I can tell you one is all you'd order. That's the hard stuff."

Landis, reading from the chart: "Huh; says here, 'lethal in two to three minutes with correct dosage.' Was that the killing dose you spilled?"

Look him in the eye. You're innocent; nothing to hide, Andy directed himself. "Yeah, and I won't forget it soon. Doug will see to that," this last sally with a laugh. "There's more data on all the dosages there, if you need it."

But Landis was leafing through the book again, finally handing it back. "One of these days, law enforcement will be using this stuff on the scumbags," he said.

"Don't tell me DEA's considering it."

"Couldn't say. I can recall a few assholes who could've used a dose of that concoction stuff," Landis added. "But I can't see anybody pulling a quick draw with a pistol four feet long."

Andy knew there was a simpler way in close quarters but, replacing the text in the cabinet, did not suggest it. "I guess we don't think much in terms of fast draws here. You guys really have to do that stuff?"

Gary Landis admitted that it wasn't common. He went on to say that, as a Los Angeles cop dealing with gangs, he could have used something like the dart gun, which got them to swapping bits of their backgrounds as law-enforcement people will do. To Landis's mention of his UCLA days, Andy responded with his training at Cal Davis. Whenever Landis turned serious for a moment, his face sent little warning tremors through Andy's mind; but, for the most part, the DEA man's disposition was sunny and those moments far apart. If Andy managed to cultivate a friendship with Landis, he might also gain a better understanding of federal law-enforcement methods. Mom would worry. Jesus, no matter *what* he did, Mom would worry and bitch. *Worry-mom. Bitch-mom. The hell with Mom.*

At 5:30 Doug Isaacs strolled past, pulling on his coat as he glanced into Andy's office with that dyspeptic look Andy disliked so much.

With a glance at his wrist, Landis frowned. "Hey, Andy, I'm sorry; I'm on your personal time now."

"No problem. Tell you the truth, I'm enjoying it. Don't get to bullshit that much with, you know—"

"A world-class bullshitter," Landis picked up on it, chuckling. "Well, you drop in on me sometime downtown." He stood up and stretched.

"Maybe I will." Andy stood, too, liking this agent, honestly sorry to have the visit ended. The other lab people saw one another socially, but had long since given up on the diffident Andrew Soriano. Lockhart was decent enough, but always maintained a proper supervisory distance. As uneasy as if asking a woman for a date, Andy said, "Uh, Gary, you wouldn't, ah, have time for a beer?"

Landis raised his brows, then shrugged. "Gee, you caught me without an excuse. But then, I'm easy."

Landis surrendered his pass and the two parted in the parking lot where Landis, in his Camaro, followed the little Pinto to a local bar frequented by Doug and a couple of others. *I hope they're down there now. Let them notice me buddying up with a federal agent,* Andy told himself. *Let them see that Andrew Soriano can have friends anytime he wants them.*

26

IT WAS ALMOST DARK, THE MIDSUMMER SUNSET remaining only as a faint bloody smear crosshatched by bats in the foreground of the Sierra skyline, when Andy arrived at The Place. He paused to enjoy the stillness, leaning against the Pinto's warm hood, idly tossing the old Zippo in one hand, certain that its contents would bring praise from Mom when she returned. The tubular nylon kite that hung from the house TV antenna had been freed so that its tail streamers twisted lazily in a cone of light from a small floodlight at ground level. That told him she was aloft in the Chamois. She used the device as an illuminated wind sock; when she was not flying, the kite was secured downward by a Kevlar cord no thicker than fishing line. It was amusing, he thought, slipping the Zippo back into a pocket, how many ordinary things you could put to extraordinary uses.

All in all, it had been a fine day, full of little successes. He had spent a full hour with Landis at the bar, feeling the beginnings of a camaraderie that other men took so lightly. When Gary Landis laughed at a joke—laughing not for a group, but for him alone—Andy had found himself inexplicably misty-eyed with the fullness in his chest. Perhaps, at last, here was a friendship that Mom might cynically endorse as useful.

After that hour in the bar he had boasted modestly to Landis that he must soon put in an appearance with a little-theater group. It had been no exaggeration that they needed him behind the scenes as much as they depended on the actors to hit their marks among the scenery flats. He had spent an hour or so with Aletha and the others, basking in praise for such good work on short notice. He recalled that Aletha had preened her hair unconsciously when she saw him walk in. He had not felt so widely appreciated in a long time.

Years before, and not so far from this very spot, he had tasted moments of comradeship with schoolmates during his high-school years; even responded shyly to the first tendrils of romantic interest, extended by one of Briant High's most popular girls. Though not exactly a beauty, Linda had combined gentle wit with a quiet poise, a confidence in herself, that Andy envied without malice.

In a world just a little different from his own, Andy Soriano might have drawn confidence from Linda, might even have turned his relatively innocent fantasies into fact. But unable to borrow Mom's car for his own purposes, forbidden to date, Andy had let his opportunities wither. The girl had gravitated to an older boy, a basketball jock who even had the same nickname: Andy. In an odd, vicarious way, Andy Soriano had known a wistful enjoyment in their pairing.

And of course that horse's ass, Lowery, had to spoil it all. Andy had borne the "Candy Andy" humiliation like the stoic he was, staying out of Lowery's way, bottling his hatred, letting it settle and mature. Nor had Andy decanted the bottle when Hoss Lowery turned his attention toward Linda Seibouldt. If that was what Linda wanted, no doubt she had her reasons.

It was at the end of basketball season, when Lowery changed his mind again, that Linda's obvious misery had blown the cork from Andy Soriano's bottle. The coarse jokes, the newly minted "Dirty Dottie" nickname, all the little indignities Hoss Lowery was known for, had finally focused on a target to draw Andy's revenge.

The planning of it had taken much longer than the doing. Andy had known about the ruined cabin and its nearby mine shaft for years, one of his discoveries during solitary wanderings in the Sierra foothills. He had even mentioned it to Mom, who proved to have no interest in it. Once the decision was made, his first step was to check the cabin again, finding everything still more decrepit after added years of neglect. When he stood again before that yawning hole half-hidden by shrubs, Steele

Lowery became no longer the schoolyard nemesis, but a client: Andy's first.

Resolved to say nothing to Mom until his own client was history, he had used some of her tricks. Old gloves, hat, and canvas deck shoes— sometimes you had to make footprints, Mom always said, but you didn't have to sign them—bought at Goodwill in Clovis; a realistic Hong Kong copy of a Rolex worn briefly and consulted so that Hoss Lowery could not fail to notice it; a single admission to Hoss—nothing more—that Andy had found "an old cashbox" in a most unlikely place. Andy's roll of tattered bills, shown to Lowery, as if reluctantly, had done the rest. No one had ever accused Andy Soriano of being a big spender.

Hoss Lowery's methods of persuasion had always been heavily larded with coercion. Rough good humor with rougher jostling, murmured teasing while looming over the smaller youth, promises of good-fellowship if Andy would "give"—information, of course. A more thoughtful youth would have grown suspicious, or soon lost interest. Young Steele Lowery was made of somewhat different stuff. He seemed totally incapable of imagining that he might be in danger from a smaller youth—until the last.

After a day or so of the game, Andy had let himself be swayed to the point of a promise: to reveal the source of his wealth, but only to his new pal. After all, Andy had smiled his most innocent smile, how many ways did Hoss want to split the loot?

With his El Camino pickup and his princely allowance, Lowery needed another boy's treasure like a carp needed more bones. But once his curiosity was aroused, he took the bait—as Andy knew he would.

And on a Saturday afternoon in April, ten days after the most recent rain, Andy clamped a paper sack full of his Goodwill items in his bike's book rack and pedaled to his rendezvous, a roadside picnic table two miles from the cabin. Despite their agreement, there was always the chance that Hoss Lowery would bring a crony, perhaps Ken Kirk. In that case, he would have to cancel the operation. He arrived a half-hour early, as he intended, and checked his equipment carefully.

With his bike hidden and the deck shoes on, Andy had watched Lowery arrive alone; watched him fret and fiddle with his car stereo, and fret some more, and only when Hoss Lowery started up the El Camino again Andy trotted into sight, panting for effect.

So how the fuck come, Hoss wondered aloud, exaggerating wildly, Andy made him wait a half-hour?

Checking out the area, Andy replied, "We hike from here." How far? "About as long as you've been waiting." Grumbling, Lowery had locked the El Camino and pocketed his keys. Then the two had set off along foothill animal trails, Andy trotting tirelessly in the lead. Presently he withdrew a medical inhaler from his windbreaker pocket and, without pausing, raised it to his mouth. Then a burst of speed that forced Lowery to make up his deficit. Andy had been building his stamina with solitary runs in the hills, and it was working. The inhaler, clearing the alveoli in his lungs, was a distinct boost.

"You oughta go—out for track," Lowery had called a moment later. Andy had only grunted. And, some minutes later: "Hold up."

Andy had stopped to see Lowery, chest heaving, a new respect in his face as he walked the few steps to Andy. A lopsided smile before, "Andy-candy, you dickin' with me? I caught sight of the road just a couple hundred yards over there," he said, jerking a thumb to his right.

Privately, Andy decided this was only a ploy to take a breather. "It's a tumbledown cabin near the road. You want us to be seen on the way? Is there anybody around here who doesn't know you on sight? I don't know whose cabin it is, Hoss. If you want to, sure; we'll take the easy way. But we're nearly there anyhow. I just didn't want to take any chances, with so much money and all." And Andy used the inhaler again, pretending to revel in the dry, dusty taste of it. This time Lowery could not fail to notice, but said only, "Smart little fuck."

You know it, stupid big fuck, Andy had thought at him, and grinned. And a moment later, they had trotted on again at the same pace. At last, they could see the squat bulk of the cabin. Andy, first into the clearing, held the inhaler near his mouth and triggered its contents, breathing heavily but not as deeply as Lowery, who put his hands on hips and puffed, studying the decayed roof.

Smiling grimly, perhaps in triumph at keeping up, Lowery managed to say, "This better—be good."

"I guarantee it," said Andy, smiling back, and pocketed the inhaler which was no larger than a roll of quarters, set into a plastic mouthpiece. His fingers closed around the second inhaler in his pocket, the one with its plastic mouthpiece carefully ground away to admit a different thumb trigger. "You should open up your lungs a little, Hoss. Like I do."

"What is that shit, anyway?" Lowery asked, hands still on hips.

"Alupent," said Andy, showing the second inhaler with its carefully installed pressure cartridge that had never been intended for a medical inhaler. "Doctor calls it a bronchodilator. Just clears out the passages." They were standing twenty feet from the mine shaft.

"Some kind of—drug, right?"

"No, more like aspirin," said Andy, and let himself laugh at the larger youth. "It's how guys with asthma can be big-time jocks. But if you want to stand around gasping like a pussy, go ahead," he said.

A sudden glare from Lowery. "Gimme," he said.

"Open wide and breathe in," said Andy, and Lowery did so, and Andy brought up the little device and, from a distance of six inches, sprayed Mace directly into Steele Lowery's open mouth. Unlike Alupent, a cartridge full of malonitrile is not designed to stop with a measured dose—not as long as its thumb trigger is depressed.

He kept the spray directed into Lowery's face as the big youth slammed his own body backward with a single hoarse cry, arms flailing, falling into the leafy carpet with almost no further sound from his throat; his head, elbows, and heels drumming in fitful thuds against the ground. Andy, two paces away, made even less noise, watching analytically.

A whistling, tortured intake of breath said that Lowery was making his usual fight of it as he lay on his back, eyes streaming now, face livid. His mouth worked, but no words emerged as Andy leaned forward to use the spray once again. The violent writhing became weaker as Andy watched; yet somehow the client managed to roll onto hands and knees, facing the turf.

Andy thought that his client could probably see through those tears. He hoped so. Without hesitation, Andy drew the piece of raw potato from his pants pocket, took the single-edged razor blade from it, and knelt to one side of the client. With his knees clamped against the client's trembling arm to keep it steady, one hand buried in the unruly hair to position the client's head, he felt expertly for the carotid artery to one side of the larynx. It was Andy's conceit to avoid any marks on bony tissues because the larynx, Mom had told him, was easily damaged. Then he pressed very deeply and slowly, drawing the bright blade an inch toward the client's shoulder.

Andy was met with two surprises. First, that the spurting gush of blood did not make his client leap or stiffen, though its crimson spatter was audible against the leaves; and second, he had sprayed so much malonitrile into the client's unsuspecting face that, like an invisible halo, the stuff was beginning to affect Andy himself.

Andy thrust away, scrambling to safety on hands and knees. His hands were stinging a bit. He embedded the razor blade in its primitive sheath again and rubbed his hands briskly with leaves and dirt, blinking. No one had told him that a spray of Mace or its analogs could be *this* potent.

He removed his windbreaker and walked to a clearing to let the breeze bathe his face, blinking furiously, able to see the client in tree shadow only as a sprawled figure that was no longer trying to crawl. Once a car passed, unseen but terrifyingly near. After five minutes or so, Andy's vision and the tightness in his chest had returned virtually to normal. This was old, familiar business now, but without Mom to help. And to criticize.

He found the client rag-limp, no pulse or heartbeat, pupils fixed, fingernails more gray-white than cyanotic blue. It seemed he could have painted the cabin with all that blood, but little of it had stained the body. No matter. Andy fished the El Camino's keys from a pocket, then rolled the client by hips and shoulders, not leaning close enough to risk the remnants of that spray again, pleased to note that no deep scuff marks marred the leaves or turf. He pushed the legs into the shaft, then let the rest follow toward that deep blackness in a swift tumbling slide. His fake Rolex told him he had plenty of time before dusk. It certainly would never do to be seen driving that playboy's pickup in daylight; too many people knew it for Lowery's, and probably knew he never let anyone else drive it.

Andy spent some of the time with a short length of one-by-six board from the cabin, gently raking a cover of leaves and fallen twigs over the bloody ground. Then he shoved leaves and debris into the mine shaft. It might be true that no one else had visited the cabin for years, but, his training insisted, that was no proof it wouldn't be checked out when Steele Lowery was missed. When he could no longer detect any telltales except for the always-dependable biting flies, Andy put the board back and surveyed the area with a practiced eye. Why he sat down in the sunlight, then, suddenly overwhelmed with a fit of sobbing, Andy could not say; maybe a reaction to the spray, he told himself. He was thankful that Mom hadn't seen him fall apart that way. Clients, she would have reminded him, are not people.

Andy took his time walking back, avoiding the trails this time. He discarded the razor blade under one heavy stone, the Mace cartridge under another, a half-mile distant. He did not approach the El Camino until dusk. Wearing the gloves and hat, he placed his bike in the El Camino's carpeted cargo bed, listening for traffic, ready to duck from sight. Then he drove the vehicle to a gravel turnout near Auberry Road, where Hoss Lowery often left it when carousing with other jocks.

Andy could not remember ever moving with such speed as when he locked the El Camino and lifted his bike to the pavement with hysterical strength, keys in his pocket. He rode a hundred yards on pavement before he saw lights approaching and darted up a gravel road, terribly aware that he must not be identified this near to the car.

He was not seen. Andy exchanged the canvas deck shoes for his sneakers, tossed the canvas shoes far into a small culvert, and wiped the keys down before dropping them into a crevice in a rock pile near the culvert. Then he pedaled on in gathering April darkness, still nervously alert until he turned onto the reservation road. Mom was angry at his tardiness until he asked her to sit down, told her he had completed a relationship with a client, and waited for his punishment.

She had questioned him closely for nearly an hour, neither praising nor berating him, in the manner of a tutor interested in the project of some prized student. Finally she had smiled and nodded, making him promise not to do it again without her help. She had not beaten him then, nor ever again.

She had, in fact, taken him to DiCicco's for a celebratory dinner that night. He had never forgotten, from that day to this, her little joke after urging him to have the expensive veal scaloppine. It was the only correct choice, she told him as he ate: veal, she reminded him, is beef butchered very young. He had kept from throwing it up by thinking about other things, knowing that Mom's judgment rested on his reaction.

He was to learn how fully she approved of his work when she laid out her plans for that long-haired Frenchman—the name, among so many, escaped Andy for the moment. It was Romana's decision to use the mine shaft again, Andy's to try his hand as a wigmaker. The scalp had come away rather easily, but—from a client only two hours dead—messily. Andy had made a number of wrong initial assumptions about the craft; found that the scalp was an unnecessary complication to be discarded. After that, he snipped hair that looked useful and kept it; first for practice, eventually for Mom's operations as he learned the secrets of the professional wigmaker.

Though synthetic wigs of acrylic fiber were available commercially, the finest stuff was real, some of the best taken from obedient Belgian nuns whose long tresses brought a premium because they had not been ruined over the years by widely advertised chemical insults. Men did not pay so much attention to advertising, so their hair tended to be similarly healthy and supple. Natural hair could be woven into the interstices of a skinlike cloth cap by machine wefting, but the special equipment posed problems. Andy did his research and settled on the old way, hand-wefting two or three strands at a time with a needle like a fine crochet hook. It still took him forty hours to hand-tie a wig, and additional time to style it, pinned over a canvas form. Mom had teased him about his career as a hair stylist. But that did not stop her from using the wigs.

Andy could afford to smile about it now, as he heard a soft fluttering buzz overhead five minutes after his own arrival. He knew that sound well, a small high-performance engine fitted with an outsized muffler that robbed the Chamois of a few horsepower while making it very stealthy. The rearmost of the engines would be idling because its thrust line was low, urging a slight nose-up attitude that could let the Chamois float too far during landing. The forward engine, with its high thrust line, provided a slight nose-down moment. You didn't want it floating with only 200 yards of runway. Mom had drilled him on that, having sensed this eccentricity in the craft from her first flights on dusky evenings. *Mom's the master*, he thought, admiring, envying. He knew it was not good to allow those thoughts to fuse into something darker.

He saw the Chamois waft overhead and circle to its final approach, settling very slowly onto the gravel drive. Mom would have her infrared goggles on for this, the most crucial moment of flight. She cut the ignition an instant after touchdown, and with both props stilled, the loudest sound as she passed Andy was the brief passionate squeaks of disc brakes. She let inertia carry her near the converted garage before applying the brakes for a full stop and exiting through the flimsy door beneath the dark slab of wing.

With only a few words of greeting, Romana toggled the automatic garage door and let Andy help her turn the Chamois by hand, adjusting the nose wheel with precision, shoving the gossamer craft tail-first into its lair. These moments were crucial, too; every second during the hangaring process was a moment of vulnerability. Her attention to detail was astonishing. Andy had found his Mom scrubbing scuff marks made by those little tires from the driveway, one moonlit night.

Once the automatic door was secured, they entered The Place by the side door as usual, Mom ducking to check the tiny red eye of her silent alarm which was buried in the hinge framing, visible only if your eye was four feet above the steps, and if you knew the right angle to spot it.

Andy had lived in this house through most of his childhood and knew the routines intimately. Mom had brought the mail and newspaper from her mailbox at the reservation center before her flight, and now they awaited her scrutiny on the kitchen pass-through; she had previously loaded Mr. Coffee and now started its processing in passing; Andy withdrew two cups from the cupboard and set them out. He knew that she would light a Pall Mall just before filling her cup, take a couple of drags, and flick a tiny bit of ash into her coffee before dousing the cigarette. An old habit borrowed from Russians, she had told him once; its bitter tang was a taste Andy had never been able to acquire.

While Mr. Coffee gurgled and spat, she separated her mail, fully half of it going directly into the burn sack without opening. She looked up. "You're humming," she said.

"Was I? Sorry." Andy parked his rump on a kitchen stool and pulled the Zippo from his pocket, toying with it, smiling to himself. "Enjoy the flight?"

"Not much. Spotted the white Volvo in Orangevale about a quarter to seven, but I already had the address from the license tag; just off Hazel Avenue. Where would I be without good street maps?" Head shake. "It's too far to the Sacramento area for practical air surveillance, without a bigger fuel tank. I had to idle the forward engine while I circled, or get back on fumes."

"Then why fly?"

She smirked. "Polaroids of the neighborhood, of course."

"Mm." Of course. Sooner or later she would need a spot from which to park and bug the house, and the Polaroids might help. They could also be useful in planning a takedown.

Presently the coffeemaker gasped its last. As she pulled a Pall Mall from its pack, he tried his Zippo. It needed several flicks. "It should work every time," she said, inhaling.

"It does," he said, and winked. He pulled off the lighter's outer canister and teased the felt pad away, pulling the tiny assembly out by its flimsy wrap. "Your tracker subamp, ma'am," he said, placing it on the Formica.

"Wellll," she said, putting down the slender catalogs, suddenly focused on something he had brought her. He thought she was beautiful when she smiled like that. If he'd had a tail, he would have been thumping it against the stool. She looked up and smiled for him, and his heart melted. "How long now?"

"Maybe tonight, if I'm not all thumbs. I couldn't very well test it there in the lab. Listen, I met a guy today—"

"It doesn't have to be pretty, Andrew. We need to learn its range under breezy conditions."

He had explained that to her himself, weeks ago. "I know, Mom. This guy, he might be useful if I play my cards just—"

"Those beetles are busy killing my avocado plants. Should I bring a couple in while you do the soldering? I have to refuel anyway; you know I don't like to leave the Chamois on empty."

"Sure, why not?" He could tell her about Landis later. Once she tightened her focus on something she could be short-tempered as hell. *The time to discuss my friend will be after the tracker meter gives a positive register.*

He caught himself humming again after Mom went into the tunnel, relishing this chance to show what he could do without that critical presence at his elbow. As always her workbench was spotless, the small porcelain slab gleaming, lights positioned well, magnifiers ranked correctly on the shelf from the Rexall half-glasses through the two-power headset, on up to a 30X monocular with its own directed light source. He chose the headset because with his youthful 20/15 vision he could do most of the work without any artificial aids, and the subamp solder connections could be made best with binocular vision.

He was so engrossed in securing his components and emplacing heat-sink clips—the setup was half the job, as Mom said—he barely reacted when she returned, peering at his work for some minutes, then snapping on the little exhaust fan to remove wisps of soldering smoke for him and moving away as he used a light-duty soldering pencil. That silence, from her, meant more than consent: it implied a rare and complete satisfaction with his work.

For the next few minutes he worked steadily, fingers precise as a taxidermist's, as the occasional rustle of paper told him his Mom was leaving him to his work.

Andy did not know when the rustling stopped. He did notice when she removed an X-Acto knife from the shelf near him, but he was intent on a solder connection and did not look around, blinking, until he was finished.

She was standing, arms folded, in the middle of the room with a scrap of paper, perhaps two inches by three, sliced from the *Fresno Bee*. It was barely noticeable between two fingers of her right hand. He might not have noticed the scrap, but for the way it was vibrating in her grasp. Her eyes bored into him, and in them he read cold condemnation beyond belief.

"It's done. I didn't damage it—what? *What?*"

Her motion in holding the clipping out was jerky, and she made him come to her. She said nothing.

He took the clipping, dry-mouthed, and read it. "Skeletal remains . . . aged 17 . . . accidental causes" passed through his awareness like tiny lightning bolts and when he returned the clipping, his hand shook too. "But why didn't they find the others?"

"Use your head. They *must have* found the others. Unless the remains walked away by themselves," she said with a tremor that he hoped was rage in her voice. Rage, he knew how to deal with. "We're going to have to start using quicklime. I needn't tell you to avoid that site from this point on, permanently. If either of those others have been identified as intelligence agents, federal agencies will be involved. FBI, most likely. Did you expect them to release that to the media?"

Of course they didn't just walk away, he thought, remembering how Mom had identified the client, Charles Lane, and how Andy had kept his own face averted at first; recalled how Lane had weakened and sagged after the deadly injection during the few seconds they had stood close, Andy gazing hungrily at the man's long hair instead of his face. Andy's heart fell as he realized he must tell Mom about the DEA's sudden interest in the Thomas Concoction—*yes, that could be a frightening connection*—and then he saw the face of Gary Landis and, in a yellow-hot flash of recognition, he mentally stripped away Lane's mustache; added a tan. He had spent too much time judging Lane's hair. *"Oh,"* Andy said.

"And the fresh one may have told them a lot. Probably won't even have to use DNA testing for that one. Forensics pathologists may even know—"

"My," Andy said, substituting a bleached crew cut—a predictable move by such a shearling—for the long brown hair Andy had stolen.

"—how we put him down," Romana went on in a dull fury. "At least they can never testify."

Andy's eyes were bright and wide. *"God!"* he said.

27

"GO HOME," VISCONTI HAD SAID. "YOUR CAST DOESN'T come off for a week, and this weekend it's a multiagency bust. People will be stepping on each other's heels. Don't-call-me-I'll-call-you, only I won't."

Had Pepe Luna's people been the target, Gary might have tried to argue, having met Luna, wanting to be in on the takedowns. As it was, Gary had needed a minute to realize that, with luck, only a phone call separated him from two days with Jan. That and—he reminded himself while punching in her number from memory, a few hours of windburn on the Kawasaki—dodging bugs as big as parakeets. He could stash his bike at the airport on the outskirts of Bakersfield as a dependable ride when flying down, and on the way south he could nurse the engine and check that leak. Maybe stop in Porterville, on a dogleg off Highway 99, and look up the Seibouldt girl, now Mrs. Linda Tate.

He still hadn't told Visconti about his findings. For one thing, the impending Big Bust held his RAC's attention right now. For another, he had nothing solid to go on yet, maybe never would. In that event, Visconti might be pissed at his unauthorized—Jan's answer deflected the thought.

"Ms. Betancourt?" His gruff slimeball. "Miz Janelle Betancourt?"

Quickly guarded, not bothering to correct him. "Can I help you?" Cool to the touch, her mercury dropping with each word.

"This is the Murrican Terpsichore Foundation, ma'am. There's a lot of underprivileged girls need help for a career in the dance. I'm sure you know that?"

"Yes," she said, with "no, no, and *no*" leaking from her tones.

"Well, we wonder if you'd want to donate an old tutu or two to the cause," he said, improvising.

"I'm afraid not." Now solid ice.

"Or failin' that, one of your ol' bicycle seats," he wheedled.

"You appalling cretin!" she said, magma bursting through the ice.

Now lapsing into his usual tones: "Aw, c'mon, Jan, is that any way to respond to the underprivileged?"

A tiny squeal of outrage before: "Gary Landis, I'm going to—I was right, you *are* a cretin. If you were a woman you wouldn't think obscene calls are funny."

"If I were a woman, I wouldn't be making this obscene call to another woman," he explained.

"You"—and now she was chuckling, still angry but seeing his point—"you do that ever, ever again and I will hang up on you."

"You gonna hang up on me now?"

"That depends. Is this still an obscene call?"

"That, as you put it, depends. I thought I might bring the Kawasaki down tonight, if you weren't booked."

"And spend the night here," she supplied.

"Well, it crossed my mind."

"Thoroughly obscene. How's tuna salad sound? Or would you rather chew on a bicycle seat?"

"Gee, dessert, too!" And in another two minutes, he was on his way to his apartment to pack the Kawasaki. Its gasket set had not arrived, but he could have it sent on to Jan's; or he might find a set in Bakersfield. Swede would probably be happy to help him do the installation, if and when the parts ever came.

Once he got clear of Fresno's Friday-afternoon traffic, his trip was uneventful as far as Porterville. He'd found the Gavin Tate residence among the Porterville listings and hoped that Linda Tate would not regard him with too much suspicion. Perhaps it would be best to simply show his ID and trust her good judgment.

He found the Tate place in a settled development, a well-kept yellow bungalow with mature shrubs and a lawn that needed watering. *Lord help me, I'm getting domestic,* he thought without even a twinge of dismay. Helmet under his arm, he rehearsed his opening, but to no avail. The girl who answered the buzzer was in her late teens, alert, plumpish, and very much in command of the two preteen girls in her care. The Tates, she said, were attending a fly-in in Gavin's old two-place Piper. "So I get to corral the animals," she grinned, jerking her thumb over her shoulder. "Great pair of wheels," she added, nodding toward the Kawasaki.

"Thanks. Well, it was nothing important; maybe next time," Gary said. "You might run a sprinkler on that front lawn just to surprise 'em." She could just tell them, he added, that a Mr. Landis dropped by and would try again. He headed on down the state highway in an optimistic frame of mind. Linda Seibouldt had married a ready-made family, it seemed. If there wasn't room for kids in their Piper, it would be a classic Cub, and people who flew slow old tail-draggers always had common ground for a cordial talk: the ruinous price of avgas; FAA rulings that discouraged general aviation. With his Cessna, he'd have a built-in advantage.

Shadows were fading as Gary pulled the Kawasaki to one side of Jan's sporty "Z" car and dismounted. Someone had taken the Datsun's burned paint down to bare metal and applied a gray primer coat which was not fully feathered in; probably Swede's work. She'd heard the thrum of his approach; let the front door bang open as she twinkle-toed down the steps, helped him remove his helmet, planted a kiss on him in greeting.

He apologized for his previous call as he stepped inside and dropped his overnight bag on a chair. "I thought you'd recognize me right off."

"Wish I had, buster. I'd have strung you along like a mess of catfish."

"I just didn't think. It was, uh, I was just—"

" 'Simple-minded' is the term you're after," she said, and waved him toward her dining nook, set for two. "You're excused. Now wash your hands and take a seat."

They feasted on beer, chips, and a tuna salad made exotic by a hint of Roquefort dressing. Jan validated his guess about her car: "Ampa's repainting it. If you don't want to be wearing a respirator tomorrow, when he does the finish sanding, better have an excuse—like, your arm hurts after that ride."

"You're kidding, right? The arm's fine. Just keep the beer coming, and help us up when we fall down," he said. And the smile she bestowed on him said that his unfeigned answer was the perfect one. In the back of Gary's mind lurked a selfish motive: one of these days, that old "Z" might well be community property.

An hour later, he called Swede and offered his help for the sanding job. He put down the phone with a grimace.

"Don't tell me he turned you down," Jan said.

"No. I know what's eating him; he just doesn't like it that I'm staying here."

"He said that?"

"Didn't have to," Gary sighed. "It's—a guy thing."

"It's an Ampa thing," she corrected him. "He knows you won't be sleeping on my couch, Gary."

"That's a relief," he said. "I think Swede wouldn't be so grumpy about us if, uh, he thought we were, you know, going somewhere in the relationship."

"We're already somewhere, luv. We're together." She sat beside him, her fingernails gently massaging his scalp. Softly: "Isn't this where we both want to be?"

His smile agreed. "All the same, Jan, he'd feel a lot better if you were wearing my ring."

As if to an idiot: "I'm married, Gary. Are you saying *you* would feel better?"

"That, too." Then he was holding her, face buried in her hair, glorying in the unique scent of her. He felt the reserve in the set of her shoulders, a subtle stiffness she had not meant to communicate. He pulled back gently. "Is there something I haven't said that you need to hear? I do love you, Jan, and I'm not a boozer, and I wouldn't fool around or knock you around or—"

"I know all that, Gary. No, it's something *I* haven't said recently enough."

"The 'F' word," he growled.

"He called the other night. He feels lost, wants me there." A sudden laugh and head shake. "Really made me feel like hell because I'm not going back. Maybe I can someday, just to do the right thing, say good-bye when I can look at him without feeling guilty."

It was Gary's suggestion that she simply get a new, unlisted number. And Jan's reply that cutting Freddie off would be only a new cistern of guilt to fill. "Maybe I'm waiting for him to put me aside first, maybe—I don't know. Sometimes he *tries* to lay a guilt trip on me." That little laugh again, as though watching herself from some great distance. "That's good, because it pushes me away. If he'd just do that every time! Well, Ampa says I'll get over this eventually."

He nuzzled her again, gave her shoulder a squeeze that said, *support, affection, acceptance.* "I guess we'll just have to let it run its course. Like a fever."

"Catholic fever," she specified, with good-natured irony. "No, that's a cop-out, blaming my religion. It wasn't any priest who got me into this. But don't ask me to wear your ring, luv. Not yet."

"Not even to make Swede feel better? You don't have to—"

"Are we going to fight about this? *Dammit,* Gary!"

He showed both palms, giving her his caught-with-the-cookie-jar look, and after a long stare of exasperation she relented. If he promised to be good, she said, he could select a videocassette from her trove. Any naughty ones? She had a couple, she admitted. Her cassette machine was in the bedroom. On reflection, he chose an old Monsieur Hulot comedy instead, telling her that you don't need to sprinkle pepper on your salsa.

By invitation, Swede showed up for breakfast: chilled fruit, French toast, freshly ground almond coffee. His only reference to their shifting relationships was elliptical, when he sat back to pat his gut. "The way to a grandpa's *nihil obstat* is through his stomach."

Jan, amused: "Latin from my Ampa? Next you'll be doing 'The Bell Song' from *Lakmé*."

"Church Latin. Some things you never forget," the old man said, pushing himself away from the table. "I brought an extra respirator in the Polara, Gary." He took a final sip of coffee and went outside to face the promise of Bakersfield heat.

Gary looked after his old friend and said, softly, "He gave me the fish-eye when he came in. You think he's accepting us any better now?"

"You know him as well as I do," Jan replied. "Damn, I feel like I'm walking over month-old eggs with you two. Tell me: are guys really worth all this trouble?"

"Nope." Gary, got up, heading for the door. "But we take out your garbage and repaint your car. Among other things."

"Among other things," she echoed gently, and patted his rump as he passed.

Because it does not take a John Stuart Mill to feather a primer coat, the two men talked as they worked, Swede sensibly in a T-shirt, Gary naked to the waist, working mostly one-handed. They managed to generate extra warmth from an argument over football as played by the NFL and by the rest of the world, "I said—" being their most common phrase because they talked through muffling respirators. Gary supported the American game.

Swede Halvorsen claimed American football was a plot by middle-aged men to destroy the bodies of young men. "Soccer versus football is a contact sport versus a collision sport," he charged. "And football depends on three-hundred-pound freaks exploding in five-second bursts of energy that can't be good for your heart. Soccer builds stamina, and the players look like actual people."

"How the hell would you know?" Gary asked, forgetting that the old man watched a lot of TV.

"The Spanish-speaking channels—*claro que sí, cabrón*," Swede shot back. His squint said he was grinning behind the rubber mask. "Amazing how much of it you pick up. You watch a World Cup game in a week or two, ask yourself which game is healthier for the player."

When Gary found the logic of his own replies diminishing to helpless denials like "Oh, bullshit," he shifted the discussion. "I'm thinking about some maintenance on my bike," he began, and eventually added that the Kawasaki would wind up at the nearby airstrip, as of Sunday—tomorrow.

Swede understood the implications. "Gonna be a regular commuter, hm? Well, shit, maybe I'll even see you now and then."

"Count on it," Gary promised, eyeballing his work on the Datsun's hood. It would be so easy, he thought, to let the old man know that only Jan's reluctance stood in the way of his becoming a part of the family. It would repair the little cracks in their old friendship. *Yeah, and Swede would be leaning on Jan in my behalf, which would go over with her like a turd in her air conditioner. Bad idea. I'll just make haste slowly.*

By dinnertime, Swede pronounced their job complete and Gary's forearm felt tender. Jan's calls had turned up no appropriate Kawasaki gasket sets at local shops. Whatthehell, Gary said, he could wait. It was only a few minutes' ride to the "patch" of airstrip.

Both of the men were so full of beer that they downed only one of Jan's hamburgers apiece, and of course Swede stayed until Jan drove him away by insisting that they watch *Saturday Night Live*, which the old man loathed.

"You did that on purpose," Gary accused, as Jan waved good night toward the old Polara.

"It was that or have his snores collapse the couch an hour from now," she said. "Subtleties are lost on my Ampa. Now will you turn off that damned TV? I hate that program as much as he does."

Gary did as bidden. "Gotta drain my lizard again," he said, heading for the bathroom. "Still full of beer."

She eyed him suspiciously on his return. "Exactly how full of beer are you?"

"Too damn full," he admitted.

"You could've stayed in Fresno for that," she said, then kissed him gently. "And would you believe I don't care that you've drowned your lizard?"

"Not for a second," he said.

"Then we've reached perfect understanding," she replied, taking his hand, tugging him toward the bedroom anyway. "You can make it up to me tomorrow."

He did. Swede had the good sense to leave them alone on Sunday. When Jan looked up from the comics in midmorning and said, "Too bad you didn't fly down; this would be a wonderful day for it," Gary remembered that the little town of Taft was only a short drive to the southwest.

The thermal air currents of Taft, California, are famous for their ability to keep an airplane aloft, engine or no engine. Jan Betancourt got her first taste of sailplaning that afternoon, soaring over the valley with a professional. Gary had never seen her so awed by an experience, one that she claimed was nothing at all like the Cessna. "And that's okay, it's fun with an engine, yet somehow you're still aware that you're just, just buzzing around. But this was what birds do, Gary: this was *flying*."

And he claimed to be jealous, and she observed that he could always get a sailplane to compensate, and they had dinner at a Thai place and, with talk of buying aircraft and living together in an airpark, Gary began to realize that he might have the marriage, the life, the woman he wanted—all of it—if he would simply relax and accept their pairing without demanding that they "make it legal." It would require a different mind-set from him. *It'll damn sure need a different mind-set on Swede's part,* he reflected. But if Gary could manage "without benefit of clergy"—it was astonishing how clichés had grown like shrubs around the institution of marriage until the essence of the thing itself became obscured—he felt certain that, one fine day, Jan would turn to him and say, "I'm ready for the wedding."

Of course, their kids might be grown by then. *Ah, shit, why did I have to think of that?* He wanted children, and soon; and he did not want to have to wince at the word "bastard." A common-law marriage might satisfy Jan, but Gary knew he was a long way from accepting it.

He rode the Kawasaki to the airstrip, Jan tailing him in her Datsun, and left the bike in care of the proprietor. They spent another hour in her mobile home, Jan promising to drive to Fresno the following Friday. Then she drove him to the Greyhound station just in time to make the 10:25 express to Fresno. The talk with Linda Seibouldt Tate would simply have to wait. He dozed part of the way north, listening to strangers explain to one another why they were riding a bus instead of their Cadillacs. Now and then he wondered how Visconti's big bust had gone down, and why a nice-looking bright young guy like Andy Soriano seemed so starved for friendship.

28

THERE HAD NEVER BEEN ANY QUESTION, FROM THAT FIRST scalp-prickling instant when he realized that Chuck Lane was alive, whether Andy would tell Romana. She had reacted first to the news in flat disbelief, then fell silent as he explained. Finally, very quietly, she had gone alone into the tunnel. He had never known her to indulge in a fit of hysterics, but during the next few minutes he had heard her voice raised in hoarse shouts, using words he presumed were Czech. Or maybe Russian—he wasn't sure. He was quite sure the words weren't complimentary.

A long while later, she returned, her voice husky but calm, and asked him without rancor to help her in the darkroom. It was quite possible, she said soothingly, that Andrew had built a pair of coincidences into a fantasy. She had the look, Andy thought, of a slack-wire walker grimly focused on keeping a precarious balance.

She took photos of Lane from her files—the best was a telephoto of him locking his helmet to the Kawasaki—and created a matte-finish eight-by-ten head shot in black and white. Her Pasche airbrush rig was a specialty Andy had never mastered, but Romana had used it many times to manufacture false IDs. She spent a few minutes of practice while her hand became steadier, trying shades of gray paint from her Winsor & Newton greyscale kit, before beginning to retouch the photograph. Chuck Lane's mustache and long hair were obliterated with white. Then she filled in the upper lip area with a light gray tone.

He murmured, "He's bleached his hair, but it may just be the sun," before she began on the hair. She airbrushed a "butch" haircut over the

225

scalp in light gray, using a camel's-hair brush by hand on still-fluid spray to suggest individual hairs.

Her work was not a transformation intended to fool an expert, but one that made Andy tremble as he watched it take place. Finally, to her "Is this your DEA man?," he could only drop his gaze and nod. She continued to stare at the picture, now a near-perfect image of Gary Landis, for a long time. Then, suddenly: "Andrew, he doesn't know who you are."

He wanted to ask several things at once, so all he managed was a stammer. Tapping the photo, she went on; "When we took the man down, all three of us were playing roles. Yours was probably the best disguise of all, and he couldn't have had more than a few seconds with you up close. If he had known who you were today, they probably would have used a group to arrest you, instead of sending a single agent. Even if they hoped to draw you out, *they would have sent someone else*." A smile full of wisdom: "Almost certainly they would use FBI agents. They would have traced you here. And, as it happens, I was overhead in the Chamois when you arrived. If you had been followed, I would have seen them."

"How do we know they didn't bug my car?" he asked.

"Good point. We don't, but we certainly have the means to find out," she replied, rising to peer at the shelves behind her, taking her hand-held transmitter detector from its case. The device, a pricey little AID unit with a pistol grip and a digital readout, used a handful of nine-volt alkaline batteries which she tested before leading Andy outside, extending the telescoping antenna as she went. A week previous, she would have let Andy do the checking. Now he could see her trust in him slipping away.

Ten minutes later, lying on her side behind the Pinto with the detector, she pocketed her flashlight and struggled to her feet with the awkwardness of someone no longer young or supple. "You're clean," she said, collapsing the antenna, brushing dirt from her jacket as she led the way indoors. "And that's a strong indication that our Mr. Landis is still a few steps behind us."

"But after us," Andy said.

"Shut up, Andrew. He does not know *who* he is after." Romana poured herself a cup of coffee; lit and took one drag from a Pall Mall before answering. "We have to operate on that basis, Andrew. He has to know he was injected with a powerful drug; that's sufficient to explain why he would be checking on such things with a local agency that's publicly known to use them."

"The Thomas Concoction is something we don't share with the media, Mom. It can't be common knowledge."

Romana's nod was impatient, her mental circuits busy. Andy thanked God for that because it deflected her from raging at him. "He may not know what the drug was; CIA has used injections in the past. I had thought Mr. Lane *was* CIA. It is still possible that Mr. Landis is drawing two salaries, but if he is seeking information on injections from a state agency, most probably he was simply DEA working with CIA. They do that sometimes." Then, as if to herself, flicking ash into her cup: "I would give a great deal to know what went wrong."

"I put it all in him, Mom," said Andy, defensive but certain of his competence. "Maybe it doesn't work the same way on humans. There's no data on that in the manual." He backed this up with a smile.

"That's not funny, Andrew. Next time, we will use tried-and-true methods."

"Absolutely. From now on—" He blinked. "You don't mean we're going after Gary again."

"On first-name terms, are we? Yes, I mean exactly that. We can't be sure how much he knows, but we know it's too much."

Andy's mind protested against this line of reasoning, and he realized why: he had sought and won the friendship of this man. *No, he's a client. Keep that foremost in your thoughts.* The job would be easier for him at long range. "What about a remote detonation, or a scoped rifle?"

"Only if we must. That's obviously deliberate, and it would send dozens of agents backtracking his movements. Do you want more of them questioning you in the lab?"

Andy's head shake was vigorous. "He'll just have to disappear."

"Too suspicious. No, Andrew, what we need is an accident, something that doesn't set a full-scale investigation in motion."

Andy's open-handed gesture said, *tell me what.*

"We know he rides a dangerous vehicle. You said he mentioned that he's involved with a woman. It's up to you to learn more about him: his hobbies, his vices."

Andy drew a deep breath. Further face-to-face dealings with Landis were among the last things on earth he wanted now. "You taught me to avoid getting that close, Mom."

"You're already that close, Andrew. And this, you must admit, is a unique situation. It requires a unique approach."

"Any other time, you'd say I was compromised with this client," Andy insisted.

Something flickered in her eyes, the equivalent of an instant's hesitation. "But he came to you," she said, with that maddeningly calm smile. "It is he who is compromised. He would see your friendship as sheer coincidence. Anyone would," she said, "except you and me."

One forlorn hope occurred to him then. "How do you expect us to get on with the Sacramento work if we get involved with this guy?"

"You are already involved. You will just deepen your involvement while I pursue the Sacramento relationship."

Stolidly: "How many times have you told me to maintain focus on one thing at a time?" he said.

"How many times have I also told you that Mom knows best?"

"Too many."

Again that glitter in her eyes; then an elaborately slow sip of coffee. "You are collapsing now? You, who enjoy playing your roles, would turn down the role of a lifetime, Andrew? You would throw your responsibility onto the shoulders of an . . . old woman?"

He knew that the phrase had to be hateful to her, knew also that she was manipulating him with it. Yet somehow that knowledge did not lessen the impact. "No, Mom," he said, his voice breaking as he reached out to her.

She stood unmoving, echoing his tiny bleats of misery with her own, but at last he felt her free hand pressing oh, so gently, between his shoulders. That was when he felt the shudder coming, and he pulled away so that she would not feel it.

"This will take some time," he said, wiping his nose.

"Make it count," she said.

29

J U N E   1 9 9 4

PAUL VISCONTI HAD ONCE OBSERVED TO GARY THAT among the most profound changes in the life of a field agent is the shift from happy lone wolf to hearth-loving pooch. Generally, Visconti said, a woman becomes part of the sea change at some point. Sometimes the agent begins to lean toward domesticity and, as a natural part of the process, finds a like-minded mate; in other cases, a woman, already a part of his equation, urges him toward the hearth—often with a "me or the job" ultimatum.

Reflecting on his own case, Gary vaguely understood that the first scenario fitted him best. Perhaps because Jan Betancourt herself was only half-domesticated, she had urged no changes. And with no urging toward changes from her, Gary Landis had given it very little thought until recently.

What made him think about it now were little things. He no longer chafed so much over the paperwork that threatened to submerge federal agents. He was starting to chafe, instead, at the many little impediments to the life his "civilian" neighbors took for granted. It was a common irritant among many law-enforcement men that, in some ways, they lived like escaped felons. Gary had a personal Visa card, but its charges were handled by a standard Justice Department cutout that prevented tracing him. A few times, the delays had forced him to pay late charges he could ill afford.

In the mold of most other people active in the intelligence community, Gary knew it was good practice to keep himself out of the data banks of business, everybody's Big Brother, particularly American Express credit cards and volumes such as the Polk and Cole directories that were readily available in public libraries. In the blue-sheet numerical listings, his telephone number would typically be followed by a simple "Not Verified"; no name, no address. Nor was he listed in the "vanilla" white Alpha, or alphabetical, listings. In the green-tinted street listings as well, his apartment number had usually carried a Not Verified comment.

On one occasion some years previous, a naïve young apartment manager innocently gave him up to a canvasser calling herself a city directory employee. Finding himself in the listings during a routine check, Gary had demanded a change of apartment and raised hell to the man, explaining that while the telephone company had its own sources in the users, a "city directory" usually was a copyrighted commercial volume that might cost hundreds of dollars a copy. After that, he was careful to explain to apartment managers while moving in that, as a "revenue man," he wanted anonymity. If managers and landlords chose to interpret this as federal Internal Revenue employment, it had been no skin off Gary's ass, and it was simply amazing how anxious those managers became to keep him happy.

Even Gary's California DMV license and his vehicle registrations fell into a special law-enforcement category, maintained separately by the state. People empowered to check on those items needed the right ID— the kind that allowed backtracking. It was all quite rational and necessary, but for Gary it would be a major pain in the backside when he decided to trade his Camaro. Gary had accepted these and other circumventions as necessary evils, merely part of the territory. Only now had he begun to view them as problems.

For Romana, they were problems she had dealt with a hundred times. The simplest solutions usually proving best, she merely began with what she knew and gave Andy the tasks of broadening her file. She identified the Landis Camaro that Andy had described by driving past Fresno's fenced DEA parking lot, then followed the man home on Tuesday, giving him plenty of space. When he keyed himself into a second-floor apartment in Northwest Fresno, she made careful note. On Wednesday, while Gary was at work, a slender middle-aged fellow with Romana's aquiline nose and cheekbones walked through both of the vacant apartments in Gary's complex with the manager. The apartment layouts were mirror images of each other, so she had the approximate dimensions of his apartment as well. Romana did not rent either apartment; it was obvious from her notes that she could bug the edge of Gary's living-room window from the parking lot using an infrared laser pickup. In this way she avoided more dangerous ploys. At this stage of the surveillance, she did not know what datum might prove crucial, and of all her client relationships this one seemed fraught with the greatest potential for danger.

Because it was more dangerous, Romana was careful to make more use of her remote systems—and the best of hers, by far, was Andrew Soriano. The best thing about remote systems was that she could, if necessary, cut them loose leaving no trace of an umbilicus; in a phrase, unplug them. What Romana did not consider, despite her formidable background, was that Andrew was a self-monitoring system capable of fully autonomous operation. As she placed herself farther from the focus of danger, Andrew became more vulnerable. Because she had trained him very, very well to be paranoid, his mental circuits grew ever nearer to a constant overload. And, sensing this, Andy clamped down on himself more tightly. Sooner or later, that kind of feedback was bound to make Romana's finest remote system fail in unpredictable ways. Comfortably remote, unaware of Andrew's "relationships" with animals, she increased that overload.

Thursday afternoon, Gary took a call from the Cal Fish and Game lab. It was young Andy Soriano, saying he had rounded up copies of more data on some of the most potent tranquilizers. Andy claimed an appointment with the Valley Players after work but, he said with a chuckle, sometimes little problems in stagecraft took hours to fix. Would Gary be home that evening? Well, then, Andy would be happy to drop off the Xeroxes at Gary's apartment afterward. Maybe bring a six-pack if it wasn't too late, and what was that address?

Gary replaced the receiver with a sigh. Soriano had the friendliness of a puppy, the kind of guy you hated to deny. And whatthehell, Soriano was law enforcement himself, if you stretched the point a little. Gary's call to Bakersfield reached only Jan's answering machine. "Your turn to make a nut call," he told it. "I should be in all evening." Then he broke out the feta cheese and made a passable attempt at a Greek salad.

He was dozing in the gloom with a paperback around 9:30 when the door buzzer roused him. He opened the door to find Andy Soriano on the landing with a manila folder under one arm, a six-pack of Sam Adams, and a guilty smile. "I know it's late. I tried to phone you, give you a chance to say no, but you're not in the book," he said.

"No problem," Gary replied, then realized that Andy Soriano might stand outside forever without an explicit invitation. "Come on in. You'll get mugged standing out there with all that good yuppie brew."

Soriano was decked out in sport coat and tie, almost as if for a date, or a role in that play. At Gary's suggestion, he removed both items, folding them with conspicuous neatness. *So he's anal retentive,* Gary thought. *I could use a little of that,* stashing bottles in his refrigerator, opening the remaining two. "To crime"—he touched Soriano's bottle with his—"and punishment."

He accepted the manila folder with thanks, dropping it on his living-room desk without opening it. "I can study that tomorrow, Andy. Hey, I've got some old trunks if you want to take a few laps in the pool."

But Andy was not a swimmer, he said. When the talk proceeded to sports, it became clear that Andy did not spend much time with the sports pages. "I'm pretty good with my hands, though," he said shyly. "The scenery flats are looking great, she said."

He stammered when Gary pounced on the "she." "Oh . . . woman who kinda supports the Valley Players. Older woman," Andy added quickly. "Queen-bee type."

"They'd be in deep shit without worker bees," Gary retorted, with a glance toward the sport coat. "Why do I get the idea you've got your eye on one of the, uh, whatchamacallit, ingenues?"

Still shy, Andy admitted that he hadn't decided which of the pretty young players he preferred. The vague impression he left was that he dated them now and then. "I could probably fix you up," he said finally.

"No, no," Gary laughed, finishing off his beer, raising his voice as he retrieved another pair of Sam Adamses from the kitchen. "One relationship at a time for me," he claimed.

For some reason, Andy found this worth a laugh. "Well," said the younger man, "there are relationships and relationships. This one must be special."

And so Gary told him a few brief bits about Jan: their long-distance commuting, her status as a fitness freak, the basic fact that she wasn't as anxious to marry as he was. He had just mentioned Jan's first experience in a sailplane near Bakersfield when the phone rang. "That should be her now," he said, getting up.

"I need to use the john," Andy said, with a "which door?" gesture as though he had not already been briefed by Romana. He carried his second beer, barely tasted, with him into the hallway.

Gary pointed, then answered the third ring. "Hey, Wonder Woman," he murmured, and smiled at the response. "I dunno, I guess because I wondered who else would be calling, and I wonder about your plans for the weekend, and I also wonder if I can wait."

Andy's tactic in leaving the room implied that he was not interested in overhearing the conversation, which was true because tonight, Romana's laser audio link should be picking up every word spoken in that room. It also gave Andy a chance to give the bathroom a subtle toss. Some bathrooms tell little. Some tell all. There was no telling what little detail might prove useful, or to whom; had Andy accepted the offer to swim, it would have been obvious to Landis that he had shaved his legs during the past few weeks.

Andy shut the bathroom door behind him, careful to press the lock button quietly, and let the horseshoe of toilet seat make plenty of noise as it dropped. If Landis were one of those people who could split his attention expertly, Andy would give him a scenario to follow with innocent sound effects.

He placed a bath towel below the storage cabinet before opening it with care. On the shelves he found clean towels, a boxful of shoe polish and brushes, a supply of soap and toilet tissue, a toilet brush, and a scatter of uninformative odds and ends, and on the bottom shelf an old cardboard box half-full of clothes in need of washing. He rearranged the towel in the sink directly below the medicine cabinet, then opened the cabinet a crack, peering closely to be certain he was not about to commit a huge gaffe.

With one of her tragicomic little anecdotes about the old days and later with a harmless demonstration, Romana had warned Andy to always position a towel to muffle any possible falling objects from cabinets. She had discovered the hard way that some suspicious types will rig cabinet doors—especially a medicine cabinet—to let objects such as a child's marbles clatter out, an alarm against the prying guest who opens that seemingly innocent little cabinet door. The best way out of such an ambush, she had said, was a loud curse, followed by a laugh and "Now I know where you lost your marbles; but where do you keep your aspirin?"

But Landis was evidently not into such games and Andy made a brisk, expert survey of the cabinet. Bromo, ibuprofen, Vitamin C, rubbing alcohol, Band-Aids, and personal-hygiene articles were scanned without a touch. The plastic prescription bottles were of more interest: old prescriptions for antiinflammatory caps of Piroxicam, and Tylenol with codeine; another, very recent, for grooved white Percocet pain pills. Andy replaced each bottle exactly as he found it, closed the cabinet door silently and made a noisy production of tearing off several scrolls of toilet tissue with suitable pauses. Then he replaced the towel on its rack with his usual precision, emptied his bottle of expensive beer into the sink, and flushed while sitting on the toilet, undoing his belt. Finally he washed his hands to complete his sound effects.

Andy opened the bathroom door to the sound of flushing and strode out renotching his belt while his host was still on the phone. He retrieved a third beer from the refrigerator and took a brief swig, then strolled to the big living-room window with its view of the parking lot and West Fresno rooftops. Beside the window sat Gary's little Compaq computer with a scatter of software manuals, vehicle overhaul manuals, windowed envelopes; all strewn under the benign scrutiny of a young woman who smiled out from a color photo in a cheap cardboard frame. And one letter with a Bakersfield return address written in a voluptuous looping hand. No name. None needed, he surmised. The letter and photo were almost certainly from the woman talking to Landis at that moment.

He studied the photo more carefully. She sprawled barefoot on a poolside chair in shorts and halter, squinting up from beneath the bill of a baseball cap that was too large for her. Her grin was impudent. No guile here, nor self-consciousness, and no wonder, with the well-defined musculature of a young tennis pro. It seemed to Andy that warmth radiated from that photo as from a floodlight. As a sexual object, he decided, she would be perfection itself. He wondered how all that splendid tanned flesh would feel beneath a man's fingertips.

Because Landis was at the other side of the room talking, Andy leaned toward the window, craning his neck as though studying the view. Softly, he murmured the return address of the woman's letter to the windowpane. No possible way I can forget it now, he thought, smiling. But Mom will probably bitch that I took a chance in muttering to her toward the window. The prescriptions were firmly locked in his mind, even to the fact that a Dr. Bayless had recently given the Percocet prescription and a Thrifty pharmacy on Shaw had filled it. Mom salivated over little details like that, damn her. Strike that, don't think that way, we're the perfect team.

Presently Gary finished his call. "Sorry about that," he said.

"I can see how sorry you look," Andy replied with easy sarcasm because Landis was beaming.

"Well, she has that effect. If she'd canceled out on me this weekend you'd see one sorrowful sonofabitch," Gary said, and headed for the kitchen. "How you doing for beer?"

"On my third," Andy said and sat down. "My limit, long as I'm driving home." A pause. Then, "So she didn't cancel out. Gonna take her vroom-vroom on your motorcycle?"

Gary emerged swigging his third beer and smiling, but with a V of intensity between his eyes. "What motorcycle?" he asked.

Andy blinked, then pointed toward the desk with the mouth of his bottle. "Circumstantial evidence. Saw that bike manual and figured you must have one. Bad guess," he said, shrugging.

"Not so bad," Gary admitted. In the next half-hour, he told his earnest young friend about the Kawasaki gasket problem and about his old Cessna, and to explain that plastic cast but without the details, the fact that he'd cracked his forearm recently in a fall. With his third Sam Adams, Gary loosened up considerably. Young Andy Soriano was a very good listener, chuckling at all the right places, content to let his host ramble on. He didn't even pry for details about the fracture, and whether that fall had been from the Kawasaki.

Sometime later, Gary realized that he had dozed off while talking, and that Andy Soriano stood near gazing down at him with a gentle, almost beatific smile. "Long day at the lab tomorrow," said Andy, seeing Gary's eyes focus. "I came too late and stayed too long." He retrieved his coat and tie while Gary made his own apology, and paused in the doorway to promise he would keep his eyes open for a gasket set.

When the younger man had gone, Gary splashed water on his face and watched the end of *Nightline*. And thought fleetingly about Soriano. Odd young guy, anxious to please but, from most appearances, not all that interesting. Though already in his mid-twenties, he reminded Gary somehow of a college freshman craving acceptance from a big man on campus, eager to learn, or maybe to please. *I guess some guys just try too hard,* thought Gary. At least with Andy, he didn't have to play Scumbag Two to somebody like Ralph Guthrie, Scumbag One. A mistake with Guthrie could wind up getting you killed. In the company of harmless Andy Soriano, the only problem was staying awake.

30

J U N E   1 9 9 4

GUTHRIE WAS STILL SLEEPING IN THE SAME DUMP IN Merced so Luna wouldn't get antsy, but as he let himself in, the discovery that one of Luna's serpents was lounging on his couch failed to stab that familiar old icicle into his innards. Guthrie got the word on the street just like everybody else, and he knew about the interagency bust down Highway 99 in Fresno to take out some Asians who, in fact, were La Familia's competition. It was simply Luna's bad luck that one of his own boys was in the way, choosing exactly the wrong time to be making a small personal buy of something Luna didn't sell. Now there was only one snake to deal with. Guthrie wondered how the guy had got past his deadbolt; probably, he thought, he'd find one of his screens slit later. "Well, make yourself right at home," he said.

"*El Patrón* wonders if you have found your man."

"I've found out where he prob'ly isn't, for one thing," Guthrie replied. "Staked out the lot where the feebs park their cars, and hung around where they come and go. Not a trace, so I think that's a *nada*. The DEA has its own little building downtown on M Street so you can't hang out there, but I watched their lot too. No luck there either." He didn't add that while having a few smokes nearby he had spotted some dude in a big old Plymouth, sipping coffee and actually flicking cigarette ash into the paper cup between sips; now, there was a little pick-me-up to gag a maggot. He got the idea maybe this dude was on a stakeout of his own, maybe to snare someone like Guthrie himself. The idea had unnerved Guthrie enough to send him scurrying. Well, if necessary he could slip

239

that piece of news to Luna. It might not be worth much, but it was something. "Least we know Lane prob'ly isn't one of those guys," Guthrie said.

"*Quizás;* perhaps. And the cycle shop?"

That was different, and Guthrie was about to say so, but it was really a downer to be so far down Luna's list that he was now reporting to a snake. In fact, it was just a little off-pissing, now that Guthrie only had one snake to deal with. "I need to talk to Pepe about that," Guthrie shrugged.

The little Latino reacted as if he'd been waiting to reach some kind of decision, which pissed Guthrie off even more because it was unsettling. Usually this little reptile only followed orders. But maybe he was following them now. "You need to come with me," he said, and gestured toward the door.

Guthrie sighed heavily, but he put hands on knees to stand up, and that was when he found himself looking down the hole in the silencer of a medium-bore automatic pistol. "Hands behind, thumbs together," he was told. He saw the plastic strip, an automotive-wire-bundle tie, before it was drawn tight over his thumbs. It was really amazing how effective a wire tie could be; as good as clothesline rope, and a good deal more painful when used as thumb cuffs.

Guthrie let the Latino put his leather coat over his shoulders before they headed for the street, becoming a little less pissed, a little more worried. It was dark outside. Maybe Pepe Luna was waiting in the Lincoln. *Yeah,* Guthrie reminded himself, *and maybe generals cooled their heels in town cars waiting for privates to make decisions.* The car wasn't Luna's Lincoln, but within a few minutes after he was ushered into the backseat, Guthrie found reason to believe Luna had sat there. At first the little snake seemed to be headed for the Mex quarter, but picked up a main drag on the edge of town, proceeding due east out the Yosemite Road now, and Ralph Guthrie's intuition was hollering, "Deep shit! Deep shit!" as loud as it could. By then, he knew he couldn't reach the knife in his pocket but he'd scrunched down enough to get his hands behind the seat cushion.

Gum wrappers, a couple of coins, and a ballpoint pen met his scrabbling fingers before he touched a long, flat sliver of rough-faced cold steel with rounded ends that mystified him for only a second before he recognized it as a nail file, the kind of pricey diamond-surfaced tool Luna was always fiddling with. Fumbling with the damned thing behind his back, he dropped it too many times to count before learning that it worked best using only the fingers of one hand to saw at the plastic wire tie. It hurt when he pulled, but it hurt when he didn't, and by now Guthrie suspected he was heading for a world of hurt unless he worked something besides his mouth.

Meanwhile, he tried to get some kind of conversation started, but Señor Snake wasn't interested in anything but getting out into the foothills at a safe pace. Guthrie had almost given up hoping as the sedan nosed off the highway onto a gravel road, his fingers cramping now, but as the turn tightened and Guthrie rolled a bit, the plastic parted. "Luna's gonna be royally pissed if I don't get to tell him the latest," Guthrie said.

A low chuckle from the driver. "You have tol' him all you have to tell," was the reply. For Ralph Guthrie, it was as clear a death sentence as anyone needed to hear.

Because he didn't trust the little nail file's blunt tip and completely forgot his pocketknife, Guthrie got the heaviest thing he could reach. It happened to be his left boot, which he pulled off quietly, the car jouncing hard and slowing to negotiate the ruts. There were no lights anywhere through the oaks and madrones, and Guthrie knew he had waited too long by a bunch to make some kind of statement for himself. He made it by stuffing his right fist into the boot, then grabbing the driver by hair pomaded so thickly you'd think the lice couldn't get a grip, and simultaneously he drove the boot heel home into the man's temple as hard as he could.

Guthrie would never know whether it was the boot's impact, or the man's head rebounding from the closed window, that put Señor Snake into hibernation. Whatever. It was enough that the driver never made an outcry or a good defensive move before lolling against the door, the car making one final lunge before it stalled.

Ralph Guthrie was out of that car like a squirt out of a goose, and would have run off into the darkness if he hadn't stubbed his bootless toes hard enough to send him sprawling. The headlights still bored into the brush and with the back door open, the interior light showed that Señor Snake wasn't moving. Guthrie sat down, took the boot off his right hand, and put it on his foot. Then he limped back to the car and began to do a few things right.

The driver was breathing, but dishrag-limp, and blood was trickling from his right ear. Guthrie shut off the headlights, pocketed the silenced pistol, and found himself suddenly filled with a sense of godlike power; the elation of reprieve. He checked out Señor Snake's other pockets and threw his switchblade far out into the night, then thrust the little guy, who was almost pathetically frail, into a heap in the passenger footwell, closed the back door, and treated himself to a Winston while he sat behind the wheel and thought it over.

It was tempting to exult in the idea that he'd beaten Pepe Luna, but Guthrie wasn't that stupid. He had only clobbered a little snake with his boot; but clobbered him so hard there was a good chance the guy wasn't going to survive it. By the rules of the game, the snake and the car and oh, yes, the pistol, too, were Pepe Luna's property, and Guthrie knew better than to make any of them disappear because, sure as shit stinks, the snake had got his comeuppance while on a deadly errand for Luna.

"Wait a minute," Guthrie said aloud. There was no real proof that the snake had gotten Guthrie out here; none, in fact, that he'd even seen Guthrie, if Guthrie was careful to wipe down everything he'd touched. And that little toss of his victim's pockets had turned up a few little glassine envelopes—dime bags—in the snake's jacket. "Oh, man, he wouldn't like that at all," Guthrie told himself, chuckling, thinking about Luna's reaction if he learned that Señor Snake was found somewhere in Mextown, with traces of nose candy around his nostrils in a car that had been graunched by the wigged-out driver. Uncut coke could turn a driver into a cop magnet on wheels, which was one good reason why Luna didn't knowingly keep users around long. The elation was still singing in

Guthrie's veins, lending him optimism. He could even contact Luna as soon as he got home, volunteering everything he did have, which admittedly wasn't much, denying that he'd seen this murderous little fucker who was still breathing in brief snorts and snuffles in the dark down in the footwell. Chances were, after a setup like this, Señor Snake's word would be shit with Luna.

But if he had to—if the little guy woke up and gave him any static while he was setting this up—Ralph Guthrie was ready to put him away, kick his brains out if he had to. Shoot or boot, it didn't matter; Guthrie was on a roll. He'd never thought seriously about offing anybody before this, maybe because he'd never before actually believed he was seconds away from being murdered, but as he started up the car, backing to a turnaround, he marveled about a new insight into himself: given the motivation, he could waste an opponent in a second.

He could've opened one of those dime bags right then, smeared his fingers with it and stuffed them into Señor Snake's nostrils, maybe taking a tiny snort for himself, but he didn't need to feel any more cranked than he was and one thing he didn't want to do was jolt his victim awake too soon. He found his way back into town, cruising the edge of the Latino section until he spotted a few sturdy fruit trees near a little stucco place only a few blocks from the main drag. Headlights off, Guthrie eased the sedan off the road and so, of course, didn't see the shallow ditch until his front wheels nosed over into it. The noise wasn't as bad as it might have been, but the jolt had the feel of permanence.

In his haste to wipe his prints from everything, Guthrie nearly forgot the most important thing, but after hauling Señor Snake back into the driver's seat he got his fingers nice and powdery with white stuff before thrusting them into the nose, letting some fall on the guy's guayabera shirtfront as well, with still more on the floor mat. Anybody who couldn't draw the obvious conclusion from that and the rest of the envelopes— well, it wouldn't be Ralph Guthrie's fault.

Guthrie set out walking, cursing the local dogs, and splurged on a taxi from a nearby gas station. He wasn't feeling so hyper now, but he was still pleased that he'd resisted a snort that might have affected his judgment. Judgment, he knew, had never been his strongest suit.

His call to Luna wasn't returned for almost two days and, accompanied by two new guys who didn't seem to have any English, Luna met him at the park again. Luna sat across from him at a picnic table in bright, nonthreatening sunlight and if reading his eyes was any help, you'd think Luna was regarding him with new respect. It turned out that Luna told as much as he learned, and that was when Guthrie found out how wrong he could be about a simple thing, and how your luck could turn like a pinwheel.

As Luna buffed his nails, Guthrie began by describing his efforts, including the surveillance he'd noted near the DEA's place in downtown Fresno. "I don't suppose that was one of your people."

"No. I seem to be shorthanded," Luna remarked, making it a pun as he studied his fingers.

"You've got them," Guthrie said, nodding toward the silent companions. "And me."

"But not the Chiapas twins?"

The snake twins weren't really brothers, as Guthrie knew, but they were typical specimens from the distant state of Chiapas. "I heard one of 'em got took down by Feds in Fresno. You'd know more about that than I do."

"I know enough. And the other?"

Guthrie knew he mustn't even flutter an eyelid. Shrug. "Beats me."

"I don't think so. I think you beat him, Guthrie, and I even think I know how. Merced is not so big, and one of our good citizens recognized the man who, he thought, had driven a car into his orchard. By good fortune, he is of *la raza*. He contacted me. I caused the car and its contents to be removed. Observe." Luna pressed the blunt point of his nail file, exactly like the one behind the seat cushion, down on the wooden top of the table. A few twists made a permanent imprint. Then another imprint, three-quarters of an inch away, and another, and so on.

When he was finished, the table bore tiny depressions in a pattern perhaps two inches across. "Guess what that is," Luna said.

"A 'D'?"

"Now that you mention it; yes," said Luna, smiling. "Now show me the bottom of your boot."

"Prob'ly got dogshit on it," Guthrie objected.

"Humor me," Luna said, no longer smiling. Guthrie did it, showing his right boot instead of his left one. "It was doubtless the other heel, but the patterns are always similar. Did you know how a cobbler's nails will stick down through a heel when the boot needs resoling, Guthrie?"

The direction of this little discussion was not where Guthrie wanted it to go. "I guess," said Guthrie, whose run-down boots were practically a trademark.

"The pattern of your boot nails is almost exactly the same as the pattern found on the head of my soldier. I will be direct, Guthrie: I had sent him after you. Whoever took him down wanted to make it look like an accident, but those nails made nasty little depressions even though there was almost no blood. I can think of few people who would have left his money and his handgun, Ralph Guthrie, but you would know better than to take them."

"What does he say about that?" Guthrie said.

"He will not be testifying." Their eyes met, and Guthrie's didn't drop, though the implication was clear enough. "Did you plant the drugs on him?"

"Fuck, no!" It simply leaped from Guthrie's throat of its own accord. The possibility that he might be accused of planting the stuff had never entered his mind. Well, shit, it was obvious that Luna already had convicted him—on pretty shoddy evidence at that—so the least he could do was make a case for self-defense. "Look, what if he was all cranked up, waving a piece around, snorting that stuff to make him crazier, while he had *you* in the backseat? Whatthehell would you have done?"

"Was that how it happened, Guthrie?"

"Pretty much. I was gonna tell you about—"

"Stop. I am considering you to take the place of the man you bested, but not if you lie to me. You know better than that, Guthrie. Tell me how it happened and you will be rewarded. Lie to me and—" He shrugged.

So Guthrie told him exactly how it went down, including the nail file and his still-swollen toes, which was the first time he'd ever seen Luna smile like a human being. When he was finished, Guthrie added, ". . . the God's honest truth. How'd you know I picked his nose with that coke, by the way? I mean, it was his stash."

"Because, Guthrie, he could not possibly have been cranked up on it. I am actually touched, in my fashion, to know that you did not sample it. The Chiapas twins both developed a habit in defiance of my rule. You did not, it seems. That affected my decision about you, *hombre*. It looked like high-grade cocaine, powdery white. But," and now he was chuckling, "it was China White."

Guthrie's mouth fell open. What he'd thought to be an upper, La Familia's most popular product, was instead a world-class downer! China White wasn't cocaine, it was heroin—an Asian import so potent it could be snorted or smoked; no unsightly needle marks and, after a few experiences, no resistance to it, or to much of anything else for the rest of your life, amen. Asians had only recently begun bringing it in, the loudest smack that ever hit the street. Guthrie had only heard about it, wildly expensive stuff with a street price *ten times* as high as coke; before you snorted it, you picked out a nice soft spot to snooze because you'd be on the nod within seconds. No wonder Pepe Luna had figured out the real scenario so quickly. And knowing what the snake twins had taken to snorting, no wonder Luna was ready to have them replaced immediately.

They had a good laugh about Guthrie's little mistake, and then Luna repeated in detail what he had hinted earlier. His reasoning seemed to be that if Guthrie was capable of replacing a man, then he should be given the chance. That was how promotions worked. They didn't need to talk about how demotions worked. Guthrie himself had demoted Señor Snake.

Ralph Guthrie had heard that the snake twins made little trips now and then to places like Puerto Vallarta. He liked that idea. He also knew that if he turned down Luna's offer, he might not be so lucky next time, so he didn't feel the need to dicker about the job description.

But later that day, he bought new boots and shitcanned the old ones. New boots were a great confidence builder, especially when you can afford good ones. They settled him down nicely. It had given him the jimjams to know that, with every boot print he had made for the past three days, he'd been advertising a murder weapon.

31

J U N E   1 9 9 4

FOR GARY, THE WEEKEND PASSED AS A SERIES OF MOMENTS to be long remembered. Jan arrived late and, later that night, they quietly sneaked a forbidden after-hours swim in the pool, the chlorine-laced water astringent as mouthwash, warm as summer kisses with its lingering memory of the day. Later still, they shared a single doughnut over coffee at an all-night café, speaking rarely, smiling often. In his apartment, they exhausted one another sweetly to the murmurings of the compact disc Jan had brought him: love songs by Meredith d'Ambrosio.

They were up by noon on Saturday, and watched the sun's westering behind the whirling prop of the Cessna as they crossed Shaver Lake, a cerulean amoeba nested between Sierra foothills with its butterfly collection of sails pinned to its surface. Jan begged to see the mighty ramps of stone behind them, close up.

"You don't want to," Gary called over the engine's buzz.

"I guess I know what I want," she insisted.

"Okay, you have a choice. You either want to fly so high you'll freeze and fall asleep 'cause I don't have oxygen for us and probably can't get us high enough anyway; or you want to let the crosswinds and downdrafts through ten-thousand-foot peaks over there bash us into kindling. So which is it to be?" He began banking toward the white-capped peaks where winter kept its stronghold into August. She kept defiantly silent until she felt the first gentle buffets, many miles from those peaceful-looking spires of white which were already whispering of deadly violence. When her stomach began to have misgivings, she agreed to have Gary take them home.

They rented favorite videos Saturday night. Hers was *The Red Shoes*, a visual feast; his was, to her astonishment, Chaplin's *The Kid*. She cried during both and of course, Gary's comforting embraces changed character without premeditation. They fell asleep ruminating on the Chaplin film. "Is that really one of your favorites? A tramp fighting for a little kid?" she murmured, holding him gently.

"You're domesticating me," he accused.

"Domestic, but gooooood," she whispered, and held him more tightly, and then they slept.

On Sunday she surprised him by suggesting they investigate ads in the Sunday *Fresno Bee* for open-house inspections. They spent hours musing over fireplaces, bedrooms that opened onto atriums, and lease options. They did not mention marriage, though Jan worried aloud about how her Ampa would react to her moving away. Gary tacitly accepted the idea that they might begin family life without a wedding.

And Jan, driving her Datsun, never thought to notice the rental car that paced them far behind. She left for Bakersfield on Sunday night, alone, yet not entirely alone. She carried the tang of Gary's after-shave lotion with her and, sometimes a half-mile behind, that rental car.

Gary began his work week by getting rid of his forearm cast and spent the balance of the day requalifying with small arms. Tuesday was different. McMilligan brought the latest office scuttlebutt, which he called a rumor, to Gary as he was waiting for Graham Forster's fax message. "You knew we picked up one of La Familia's little Chiapas soldiers, right?"

"In the China White bust, you mean," Gary supplied, nodding. "Man, do I love it. Luna had a matched pair of 'em and if one was actually soliciting Asian product, he's got to suspect the one who's still running loose, too."

"Ah, shit! You heard, then." McMilligan's face was falling.

"Fill me in," Gary urged. "Don't tell me the other one turned himself in."

"Nah," said the burly agent. "I wish he had. I bet he wished the same thing while they were torching off his fingerprints."

Gary wrinkled his nose in disgust, shook his head. "Oh, Christ! Where'd they find him? I don't suppose he's still suckin' wind."

"You suppose right, Gary. He was found spread-eagled in the parking slot usually occupied by the Mercedes of a certain scumbag attorney. Took a little time to identify him; no teeth left, and his mouth was stuffed with pure China White. Now you get to guess which shyster's 450SL nearly ran over the body," McMilligan grinned, enjoying himself immensely.

"Not Luna's," Gary said, half-questioningly.

"Nope. Right here in Fresno."

"I must be slow this morning," Gary admitted. He suppressed a shudder, thinking of the agonies that drug-runner must have suffered during his last minutes of life. He had met Pepe Luna's wizened little soldiers more than once; saw them as deadly vermin. Still, even vermin deserved a quick end. "Which fine upstanding shyster was it?"

"Fong, of Batrachian and Fong," McMilligan said. "The selfsame bunch who represent the Asian triads here. I wonder if they got the same message I get."

Gary leaned back in his chair and squinted at his fellow agent. "Give me a sec . . . Well, hell, it's La Familia's way of giving their soldier to the competition. 'You want my guys? Here's how you get 'em. Stay off our turf.' I'd think the one that's still in custody would read it pretty much the same." Gary nodded to himself. "Yeah, but that just might turn him state's evidence."

"Dream on," McMilligan said, a cynic's twist to his grin. "Guys like Luna's would rather have his blowtorch than our handshake."

"Well, that's just what they'll get, most likely," Gary said, as his dedicated fax machine flashed a message. He reached for the sheaf of hard copy. "Thanks for the update. I still dunno why you called it a rumor."

McMilligan paused with his hand on Gary's door frame. "It's the implication, man. La Familia and the Asians could live and let live, pushing different product, but it doesn't look like they will for much longer."

Gary could see that his brother agent's eyes were dancing with anticipation. "Hey, there's a down side to that," he said. "Lots of bystanders get popped in a drug war."

McMilligan's answer was a shrug of agreement. Gary watched the man's broad shoulders diminish down the hall. *He's got a macho view of it,* Gary thought. *Like I used to have. He hasn't been a victim yet.* The label, Gary realized, ill-suited him; after all, he'd been a volunteer warrior, and decently paid at that. But you went into the DEA's kind of war with certain understandings about who your opponents were. To be blindsided by somebody fighting a war you didn't know you were in, was—he smiled at his own naïveté—it wasn't fair. Right. *Tell me about fair,* he challenged himself.

Graham Forster was as good as his word, but his word didn't seem to be as helpful as Gary had hoped. According to Forster, the newest VICAP analysis of the Spooker File plainly said that the CIA was not—and never had been—dealing with a classic serial killer. The differences were so great that, in VICAP's language, the serial-killer paradigm could misdirect law-enforcement theorists.

To begin with, VICAP had pointed out, serial killers did not ply their ghastly trade primarily for material gain. And they did not have a quota. Typically, though not always, the serial killer operated alone with a sexual motive. Such a monster did not grow overnight but began in youth as one who was isolated from peers, dissociated, with dark personal fantasies that grew darker with what VICAP termed "facilitators." Drugs, alcohol, pornography, all made effective facilitators; and vicious experiments on enemies or pets were more than facilitators, they reinforced the worst of violent sexual fantasies by telling him—it was almost always a male—that this was "it," the path toward satisfaction. The more specific a fantasy, the more dangerous the path.

The aftermath of a violent episode usually brought repulsion for the deed, remorse, a further lowering of self-esteem. The human monster needs to try again to somehow "get it right." The irony is that he cannot ever get it right in this fashion; and, sure enough, VICAP had a pristine clinical term for that: trauma reinforcement. Caught up in this ever-tightening spiral of psychic pressure, the killer often deteriorates into such mental chaos that he finally makes idiotic, calamitous mistakes. Now he may become more vulnerable—and very, very much more dangerous.

There was more, including the kinds of photos that are pornographic only to the mentally deranged. Gary forced himself to read it all. Judging from all this, the covers of detective magazines reinforced human predators by showing women in bondage. To such men, those depictions were the purest porn.

Another factor in VICAP's conclusion was the sheer duration of the Spooker File, suggesting that more than one generation of spook had been engaged in this bloody business. A third factor: the political implications. Even the most garrulous KGB turncoats could not point to any similar file in Moscow. Many a Russian agent had disappeared, but often they turned up in the West, or on neutral turf, alive—for the moment.

In summary, VICAP surmised much the same as had Forster: that some rogue faction in the intelligence community was responsible for the Spooker File. If so, its members were even more deadly than a serial killer because, while they might enjoy their work, they enjoyed it in a coldly professional way: patterned, patient, proficient.

Gary clipped the pages together and added a route slip for Visconti's attention. His eyes burned, and he closed them while considering Forster's report. There was damned little comfort in those pages. They implied anew that the "faction" that had reeled him in was unlikely to be caught except by dumb luck. Or—his eyes snapped open—if one of that bunch began to like his work so much that he crossed the line from professionalism to madness. But who could actually hope for that scenario?

He realized that Paul Visconti was standing in the doorway, regarding him with a mixture of amusement and pique. As Gary straightened, his chair squealed in protest. "Not so loud, Landis," Visconti said, a forefinger to his lips. "People are trying to sleep in here."

"Maybe I was praying," Gary said through a blush.

"Maybe you should pray for employment," Visconti smirked.

"Mm. Got Forster's input for you," Gary said, handing over the pages.

Visconti saw the time on the cover sheet; it had come in less than an hour before. "Aren't you going to read it?"

"Already did—while I was asleep," Gary said wryly. "It's trying to say, in so many words, the GRU or some similar bunch is getting rich off its vendetta against us."

Visconti nodded; closed his eyes for a moment, thinking that over. When he opened them, Gary had a forefinger to his own lips. "Your point is made," said the supervisor with a chuckle. "And fuck you very much." He moved off down the hall, still laughing softly to himself.

At lunchtime, Gary intended to call Jan from his personal phone in the Camaro. Trouble was, it wasn't *in* the Camaro. He was always misplacing the damned thing and suddenly recalled leaving it on his breakfast table that morning. He made his call from the pay phone in a nearby Russian restaurant while awaiting his order of piroshki, half-expecting her answering machine. After eight rings he was concluding she had forgotten to activate the thing again when he heard a clatter.

"Dammit! Yes, hello," she said quickly in a strained voice.

"Oh boy," he said. "What have I done now?"

A long sigh, and a pause. There was still an edge to her tone and he soon learned why. "Not you, hon. I seem to have pulled a muscle yesterday during Jazzercise." Her soft groan was convincing.

He suggested a doctor, a professional massage, and a soak in a spa, and she said she'd already tried the latter two. "Well, call Swede over," he said. "Get him to warm your soup, or something."

"He's still off fishing; I expect he'll be home today sometime, and I've already left a message for him. Meanwhile, I'm in bed with a heating pad. And this damn corded phone won't reach."

He advised her to ignore its rings, exchanged loving phrases, and went back to his piroshki. There was nothing he could do to comfort her further without driving down.

32

IT DID NOT OCCUR TO ROMANA INSTANTLY THAT SHE must get rid of her big Plymouth, inasmuch as one of her clients had finally survived and might have given out a fair description of it. Consumed as Andrew was with apprehension, she could understand how he might overlook that. Not forgive, but at least understand. Yet this same oversight on her own part frightened her more than the onset of crow's-feet at her temples, and the arthritic twinges that had begun, during the past year, to punctuate her exercises.

She could find no excuse for her lapse. Worse, contributing to a fury at herself that spilled over onto Andrew, she had to admit she had sought an excuse, a justification for failure. With an objectivity that finally did not flinch, she concluded that at long last, she was losing her mental as well as physical flexibility, becoming scattered in her thinking. Not badly scattered—at least not yet—but like other world-class competitors she had resolved to quit at the top of her form. In the game of revenge that Romana had played so well for so long, second-best would not mean a lesser prize. If she became a runner-up, she would *be* the prize joyfully held aloft by her enemies. And she fully intended to retire unbeaten.

Her long-envisioned plan had been to disappear wraithlike, without anything resembling close pursuit. The Chamois, an alter ego of sorts, would have been a tactical millstone around her neck with its short range and the difficulties in keeping it hidden. So it must become *hors de combat* but only as splinters and ashes, barely enough remnants to provide a goad to her enemies, proving that she had enjoyed the best and freest elements of the good life. That meant, when she set the timers, the circuit in her makeshift hangar must employ the blasting caps with minimal one-second delays because the unfinished house drew its power from The Place— which would ride another thundering firebloom into the clouds seconds later.

She had stocked the tunnel years before with hermetically sealed bags of fertilizer-grade ammonium nitrate, telling Andrew it was for a lawn that had never materialized. She doubted if Andrew had ever heard of the *Grandcamp,* a freighter docked at Texas City, Texas in April 1947 with a cargo of "fertilizer." When that cargo detonated, it flattened a small city and was heard almost 100 miles inland. This was the same stuff stockpiled in Romana's tunnel.

Easily poured and handled, the mealy white nitrate was even more effective when mixed with certain metal powders or soaked with the right amount of diesel fuel. Known as a relatively safe "ammonia dynamite," it was used in commercial blasting. Diesel fuel, too, was on hand. Romana had owned a diesel Volkswagen for a time and still kept a hundred-gallon storage tank almost half-full. At any time during the past ten years, Romana could have produced a crater the size of a gymnasium on the Yomo reservation. What she could not take, she could obliterate.

But what she *could* take amounted to almost half a ton of treasure in bullion, cash, jewels, identification sets, and other papers of almost incalculable value. In her original scenario, she would leave the country with a condom full of gemstones. It was somehow fitting, she felt, that the condom would be nested up into her body between those old surgical scars and the undescended testicles that had served her so well. She would pack her car with negotiable treasure—several million dollars' worth of it—in a storage unit. For this she particularly favored the town of San Bruno bordering SFO, San Francisco International air terminal, as her storage site while setting up her "legend"—her new identity—in Ottawa. That close to SFO, she could return occasionally for more spoils during layovers between Ottawa and, say, Phoenix or San Diego.

She had spent much of her childhood in Ottawa and, without once mentioning her fondness for it to Andrew, retained an appreciation of its river-flanked hills, its genteel parks, its gothic structures. It reminded her, a little, of Czechoslovakia.

Of course, she had never intended to bring young Andrew, her protective coloration whom she had crafted into a street agent and had now become troublesome in several ways. One of the few details still undecided was whether to terminate him or to leave him in place. Terminated, he could never betray her; but even if he should, he would betray a cold trail unlikely to lead to either San Bruno or a graying lady of leisure in Ottawa, Canada. Or, if it pleased her, a man of leisure.

Left in place, Andrew might continue the work she had taught him, perhaps indefinitely if he was clever enough to relocate ahead of pursuers. If anyone still kept an active case file on her, Andrew's work would make it appear that she was still active, and this idea had great appeal. It had become somewhat less appealing recently, as she noticed more frequent temper flares, more signs of what appeared to be a decay in his personality. Its appeal—and his—crumbled further the next time she visited his garage apartment in his absence.

She needed his help with the Plymouth. There were ways to sell it, but all of them involved some small element of risk. Under the circumstances, one more small risk would be like smoking one more of her Pall Malls in a fireworks factory. Instead, she used one of her ID sets and a cashier's check to buy a Chevy panel van in Stockton, and let Andrew drive it back on Friday.

Together, they disposed of the old Plymouth after sundown by driving it down along the dried-mud verge of Millerton Lake and sinking it. The method of its sinking was largely Andrew's own idea. He located a surplus twelve-man inflatable raft and a fisherman's cheap two-man version, and secured the larger one to the Plymouth's top by plastic tow ropes passed through the open windows. "It'll even look like an accident on our way to launch the raft, if anyone spots it," he said.

Though it was unlikely that anyone would see them in gathering darkness, she had agreed on the principle. A lake whose level rises and falls is a poor grave for an old vehicle because, some dry summer, the car's roof might break the lowered surface again. But driven into the lake, floating gradually away from shore beneath a rubber raft that can support two tons, even the great mass of the Plymouth could be towed very slowly out to deep water by a single-minded young man using paddles.

Despite her technical background, Romana voiced serious doubts that Andrew could tow anything as large as a four-door sedan any distance at all as he paddled alone in the general direction of the lights across Millerton Lake in a tiny inflated craft no larger than a couch. "We should have bought an outboard and put it on the big raft," she worried aloud.

But: "Too loud, too complicated. And it'd leave an oil slick bubbling up so some scuba diver might decide to salvage it. Outboard engines fall off or get sunk all the time; it's one way divers make expenses."

"For that matter, the car will leave an oil slick," she rejoined.

"The basic idea was yours." His shrug implied that he had long since abandoned arguing with her basic ideas. She bit back a scathing rejoinder as he went on: "Anyway, I've talked to scuba guys before. You can salvage an outboard easy, but I never heard of anybody going after two tons of ten-year-old car under a hundred feet of water, even if they find it. Not worth it. No, this is the right way. It takes forever to get started with all that inertia, but it'll work. Trust me, Mom," he said.

And, as he had promised, it did work: the Plymouth completely underwater, the big raft puckered by its bindings as it moved off almost imperceptibly into darkness. She had not even got her feet wet. Ten minutes later, Andrew had done the rest with a few slashes of a big razor-edged clasp knife modified in his favorite style, its tip curving like a linoleum-cutter's tool. His deft slashes pierced several airtight pontoon spaces before the whole rig sank with a bubbling rush that Romana heard all the way from shore. Her only complaint was the long walk back to The Place, climbing slippery grass slopes and slapped by branches in darkness, but she made the most of it.

The following day, with Andrew's help, Romana tried out the pheromone tracker again. Some devices were frustrating only until you developed a knack for them. This one, she felt, would never have become reliable enough for her purposes, and she used it now only as an intellectual exercise. A live and exotic insect instrumented as part of a hand-held device; the need to plant a smear of liquid, however mild-scented by human standards, on clothing or the porous materials of a car; the relatively short life of the components—all of it seemed faintly absurd to Romana, though she had to admit the pheromone would defeat electronic sweep devices, and the system did permit her to trail a car at considerable distance. Someday, better scent trackers might become standard equipment in the intelligence community. Turnoffs and inter-sections were the crucial problems, but weren't they always?

She had already abandoned her Sacramento clients—without a hint of her decision to Andrew, of course—but it was barely possible that she could effect perfect damage control by putting an end to Gary Landis and his woman as apparent suicides. Andrew spotted the lovers leaving Landis's apartment complex in a Datsun sports car on Saturday afternoon and, after their return, Romana anointed its rubber bumper stripping with a small squeeze bottle. After that it was only a question of Andrew's backtracking the woman, a confirmation of her address.

Using their laser audio pickup from a rental car, a bewigged Andy knew a half-hour before the woman left that she was bound for Bakersfield on Sunday night. He knew when their leave-taking became lovemaking, envious of Landis, remembering the woman's gracile suppleness as she had slid into her car. He knew her name; and now, with that pitiless audio pickup, he knew her willing sexuality.

And now, too, he fantasized about Janelle Betancourt as he listened.

On the long drive south behind her Datsun, he revisited his fantasy, cursing the vagueness of the pheromone tracker, finally seeing the woman turn in at a mobile home on the outskirts of Bakersfield. It would be so easy, he thought, to gain entrance; to put her at ease with some pathetic story; to—to—but that would completely ruin Mom's plan. And then Mom would know about his guilty secret.

Andy drove home quickly. He did not have a Janelle Betancourt waiting for him, but he did have a new pair of kittens.

Romana spent her Sunday evening in a rigorous appraisal of the tasks she had allotted herself, including items she would pack into her panel van. A trickle charger and extension cord, to keep the van's battery charged while in storage, was first on her list. She might, after all, want to drive it nearer to Canada someday. The replacement value of her tools and electronics was probably over $100,000, but no matter; all of that was behind her now, and Andrew must not notice any of her preparations.

She would have to give Andrew's apartment a subtle toss while he was at work, to make certain it did not reveal anything about her. That would be among the last things she did; meanwhile, she rearranged the items to be packed so that they could all be moved from tunnel to van in—call it an hour. Bullion low behind the seats, in sturdy ammunition boxes. Cash and documents farther back, and unset gemstones, the special favorite of her European clients, all transferred to one small metal lockbox inside a badly scuffed shoulder bag. Philosophically, it did not make sense for ten pounds of shoulder bag to be worth more than six hundred pounds of cash, but the fact was undeniable.

There was much more to be done, but she could do it all on Monday or, at the latest, Tuesday. By that time she would have worked out the details of bringing the star-crossed lovers together for their double suicide. Probably, she thought, the Betancourt client would be the more tractable; Andrew could simply bring her to Fresno, taking special steps to avoid signs of restraint. Forensics experts were very adept at detecting traces of adhesive tape or rope abrasions.

Should she do them in Landis's apartment? Probably not. They could just as easily "choose" to meet their romantic end in the Camaro or the Datsun in the small hours of the night. They would have to be put down within minutes or, better still, even seconds of each other. It should be painless; that would play better than violence. And because Landis was a specimen not to be taken lightly, he should certainly go down first, as quietly as possible. Perhaps they could both be blindfolded. She and Andrew must wear latex gloves this time.

A smile flickered at her mouth as she thought of prussic acid, liquid hydrogen cyanide. It could be squirted from a squeeze bottle. Against the face, it was fatal in seconds. Many suicides chose it, imagining that no pain at all was involved. Romana knew better than that: some of her clients had jerked and flailed for several seconds. But by removing the blindfolds and rearranging the clients as necessary—the squeeze bottle literally in Landis's hand—Romana and Andrew would only have to hold their breaths. In a warm Fresno night, the car windows could be open, the doors closed to avoid the Camaro's interior lights. Yes, it was all coming together.

Romana smiled again reflectively. The secret in all this was reiteration—thinking it out again and again—imagining the scene in detail, making those details change to take in all the possibilities. You might have problems, but a foreseen problem was already half-solved.

Well, she would play the suicides back to herself several times in the next few days, with Andrew's input. She had still not decided whether to tell Andrew that the first person to enter The Place, after she took leave of it, would be scattered halfway across Millerton Lake. She was estimating the time required to fill a hundred one-gallon plastic paint bucket with ammonium nitrate and diesel oil when her phone rang. Andrew had returned to his apartment after "delivering his packages." All was well, he said. Yet, as she put the phone down, Romana could not miss the tension in his voice.

On Monday, Romana met Andrew by arrangement for a picnic lunch in Fresno's Carozza Park, suitably distant from the lab. She had prepared his favorite sandwiches, thick with turkey, bacon, and cheese, and she did not forget the milk. They talked casually, even pleasantly, about her plans for their new clients. Andrew seemed a bit withdrawn, but no longer under so much tension. He did overreact, she thought, when she teased him about his call the night before. "You may not know it, Andrew, but you were jumpy as a cat," she said, and saw him wince as though she had struck him.

Because she wanted him thoughtful and unstressed, she changed the subject, asking him about his schedule for the next few days. He expected lab work to go as usual, he said, then recanted. "No, it won't, either, with Lockhart out of the lab. It'll be all spit and polish and nothing getting done because Doug Isaacs is in charge."

"We can rarely choose our supervision, Andrew," Romana said.

"Damn straight, 'scuse me, Mom," Andrew replied. "The guy's a nitpicker. The day he's promoted is the day I ask for a transfer."

A week before, she would have worried at any suggestion of Andrew's relocating. Now her retirement plans seemed to be developing a life of their own, a kind of rolling inertia that was carrying her happily along, like a stone downhill in a growing snowball. She did not care whether Andrew transferred to Oregon or to Mars. "Will you be able to take some time off?"

He rolled his eyes. "That's a laugh. It's eight to twelve and one to five; and if I'm a minute late after this lunch, I'll see a bitch slip. 'No goofing off on Doug Isaac's watch,' " he added in a crackling parody that sounded totally unlike Andrew. "I've got a little work on scenery flats in the evenings but I'll leave at eight. See you tonight by eight-thirty without fail."

Romana did not want to tempt fate by complaining about the McCarran woman; not with Andrew so increasingly volatile these days. "Go over what we've covered on your own," she told him, handing him a napkin, accommodating him in her occasional role as Solicitous Mom. "Come over late Wednesday as well."

He agreed, and Romana was soon cruising back to the reservation, estimating the time available for her tasks. Because she had never actually set up a large-scale ammonia dynamite blast by herself, she had allotted ninety minutes for the circuit and explosives around her beloved Chamois. After that she would know exactly how long it would take to mine The Place itself, gallons and gallons of damp chemical lined up and down the hall in plastic containers. Andrew would have no reason to visit the Chamois and, if he had one, she would simply forbid him. Was she still master in her own home, or wasn't she? Those were her thoughts on Monday afternoon.

All those thoughts changed radically Tuesday at midmorning, after she had parked a block from Andrew's apartment and let herself in, hoping that Andrew's temporary supervisor was as unyielding as he was painted. Of course she had an excuse for being there, if Andrew did come gliding up those stairs.

Wearing surgical gloves that made her hands sweat, she spent an hour querying his computer, and most of another searching his files: coursework from Cal Davis, articles on taxidermy, more on stagecraft. Then she put in some time searching stash-drops, places she had taught him to hide things. His sugar and salt containers held nothing but sugar and salt; none of his books were hollow and she already knew about the videocassette that hid his derringer. Checking the time before heading for the kitchen again, she had a brief fright until she realized that his desktop clock was an hour ahead. She chuckled at herself while ascertaining that Andrew's ice trays held only ice.

And then she checked in the meat tray and saw what was wrapped in bloody butcher paper, and something told her that this was not an ordinary exercise in taxidermy—not the way the tiny bodies had been mutilated.

She saw, still not entirely mixed with other body fluids, a milky substance; knew what it was by sheer intuition. And now, for the first time in her life, she trembled in honest fear at what she had created. Romana could not stop her hands from trembling as she refolded and replaced the pathetic, sickening evidence of Andrew's decay. She pulled the front door shut behind her before stripping off her gloves and, shortly after noon, drove the new panel van into her garage thinking furiously, no longer content with her previous schedule.

Her schedule now had a deadline of 8:00 P.M., because the little monster had promised to leave his scenery work at eight "without fail." Thanks to his training, Andrew's punctuality could be depended on. If she left The Place as he was leaving the playhouse, he would miss her by a safe half-hour. She smiled grimly, knowing that he would elect to come in as usual, and if she were still within ten miles she would know the moment he did it.

The need to cut her timing so close was repugnant to her as a professional. Still, there was a certain satisfaction in knowing that, though a stunning new circumstance had curtailed her schedule, she was equal to the challenge. She might have to leave some of the papers if she was to set the circuitry to her blasting caps—but perhaps not. The inexorable sweep of her chronometer would make that decision.

Arranging the explosives took her nearly three hours because the heavy containers grew so heavy after the first fifty or so. The circuitry itself would be the last thing.

So intent was Romana on noisily dragging the last bullion box into place inside the van, shortly after 7:30, that she did not hear the vehicle that pulled into her driveway.

33

AGENTS WADE ECKERT AND NEWTON JESSUP SHARED A single mood—foul—as they left their Fresno FBI office Tuesday afternoon under the baleful glare of their supervisor, Senior Agent Walter Hildreth. That mood did not improve for either of them as they drove into the parking lot of the state fish-and-game lab.

The morning had not gone well, especially for Newt Jessup, whose savage hangover was still hanging in there. Walt Hildreth, one of the old spit-and-polish guys who had become an agent when law or accounting degrees were required, showed little sympathy for the foibles of younger agents. As one wag put it, Hildreth had been in the Bureau so long, he could remember when Jedgar Hoover was too young for high heels.

Nowadays, Hildreth just wanted his day to run smoothly. When it didn't, he tended to steamroll the lumps. During the morning's monumental ass-chew, Hildreth had placed agents Eckert and Jessup on notice. He'd wondered aloud whether Heckle and Jeckle, as he called them, would give him a coronary before his impending retirement. Then he sent them out on a call and his parting words were still ringing in their heads: "Even you two can't screw this up—it's too picayune. But if you find a way, you'll both be on unpaid leave tomorrow. Count on it."

Newt Jessup got out of their sedan too quickly for his aching head to assimilate the motion. Because he didn't intend for Eckert or anybody else to intuit what his Tic-Tacs were hiding, Newt leaned back against the car in an attitude of deep thought. What he was thinking was, *I'm about to throw up.*

Eckert gave him a disgusted glance. "Christ! You forgot your piece. Or your ID."

Somehow Newt Jessup, who had skipped lunch, kept his breakfast eggs and bacon down. "Those are your tricks, not mine. I was just trying to remember the statute that sent us here." With that, he set out toward the building.

"Effective as of August, 'ninety-one," Eckert furnished, keeping pace. "Vandalizing research animal facilities is now a violation of Federal statute—"

"Okay, save it for the perp," Newt snarled, and made his face presentable for the receptionist. Both men flashed their ID at the same instant, identical badges in identical cases.

The lady seemed impressed but, "Director Lockhart is out for the week," she confessed. "Would you like to see Mr. Isaacs? He's Acting."

Newt blinked and turned to Eckert. "An actor named Isaacs?"

Eckert, muttering to his companion: "Acting director, putz." To the lady: "That's fine, he was the complainant anyway." As the receptionist consulted her intercom, Wade Eckert took Newt's arm and steered him aside. "Goddamn, you got bombed at lunch, didn't you?"

A violent head shake nearly shook Newt Jessup's brains loose. "Swear to God!" he whispered furiously. "That was last night. Now leave me the fuck alone—I'll make it."

Moments later, a balding specimen fussed toward them, removing a long lab coat and offering clip-on badges. "Douglas Isaacs." He beamed nervously. "You guys really respond fast, I'll say that." And he ushered them into the director's little office, shutting the door.

Newt Jessup collapsed into a chair as though someone had extracted his spinal column; Wade Eckert stood and took the initiative. It was the Bureau's understanding, he said, that a lab tech named Andrew Soriano had been caught vandalizing the lab. Would Mr. Isaacs care to fill in some details before they accosted the man?

Sensitive to the fact that the FBI men's aspects were not exactly benign, acting director Isaacs did a lot of lip licking and eye darting as he talked, like a man wondering whether this whole thing was shaping up into a mistake. With each moment, Eckert became more convinced that it was exactly that.

Eckert interpreted the scenario as follows: a second banana named Isaacs takes the reins of a small state facility for a few days while the boss is on a junket; had seen a lab tech kidnapping—or was it catnapping— some stray kittens from the lab the previous Friday; obviously doesn't like the tech, Soriano, anyhow; realizes he has the power, momentarily, to stick it to Soriano because those stray kittens were there for certain lab tests for a disease believed to be mildly communicable. And theft of lab assets of this kind was now a federal offense. Of five kittens, two had disappeared. Isaacs swore he'd seen one of the furry mites struggling from the vee of Soriano's jacket as he left the building after work on Friday. Isaacs's firm conclusion was that the tech had taken both.

Newt Jessup suddenly came to life. "Five P.M., late June in Fresno, and the guy's wearing a jacket?" His brows jumped in a kind of facial shrug.

"Warding off the heat, maybe," Eckert put in. "Ah, you sure it wasn't a fur-lined jacket?"

"With a cat's head sewn on the lapel? I don't think so," Isaacs said, quick to see the direction of Wade Eckert's query. "Even though I happen to know Andy does pretty fair taxidermy. And correct me if I'm wrong, but those were, technically speaking, research animals. Their theft comes under the heading of vandalism. Technically."

"Technically," Eckert agreed, though his tone denied it. "Even if three of your research animals are still in the cage."

"Well—two," said Isaacs. "One of them is, um, at another facility for—observation."

Eckert had his notebook out. "What facility?"

After a moment, Isaacs brazened it out: "Our receptionist's facility." He saw something in Eckert's face and added with some heat, "We'd done the serology tests, and the kittens weren't infected, after all, and she'd already named it, and . . . and dammit, it was my responsibility."

Eckert: "So what happens to the ones you've got left?"

"Humane Society," Isaacs said.

Newt heaved a long sigh. "Let me get this straight, Mr. Isaacs. The kittens were okay, and you'd already given one away—"

"Loaned it," Isaacs insisted, flushing.

"But a couple you hadn't given—*loaned* away were taken, maybe on the same kind of loan, by one of your other people. And yet you want this guy, Soriano, picked up on federal charges."

"The case of the purloined pussies," Eckert murmured. "Excuse me if I don't take this too seriously, but don't we have a simple matter of, say, lab rivalry here?"

Isaacs folded his arms. "I hardly consider the young man a rival. Andy stole those animals. Technically, it's a form of vandalism, which is now a federal offense."

Newt Jessup, eyes closed against a particularly vicious pang midway between the furrows in his forehead, put up one hand. "And you want us to do—what?"

From the fast blinks Isaacs gave them, it seemed that question had never occurred to him. But Doug Isaacs was a quick thinker. "Whack his balls. Get those cats back. Let him know it's serious."

"But it's not serious," Newt said, his pain transmogrified into irritation. "It's"—he recalled a perfect word for it, the very word old Walt Hildreth had used—"it's picayune. Guy brings the animals back, you send 'em up the river for a little therapeutic carbon monoxide; or he goes to the Humane Society and gets 'em back anyway; or now he's afraid to, and they go to that big sandbox in the sky. Where does that leave us?"

"Doing your job," said Isaacs.

"Doing what your own director should do when he gets back," Eckert said, "busting the guy's chops a little. Isaacs, you don't really expect us to snap the cuffs on this tech, read him his rights, take him downtown, lay real charges on him, all that?"

"Wouldn't hurt him any," Isaacs said. "But I'll settle for your telling him who's in authority around here and why he can't vandalize this place at his pleasure."

Newt Jessup stood up, took his bearings, headed for the door. "We hear you: shake him up, throw the fear of God and Douglas Isaacs into him, see that he doesn't track mud across your turf again. You're demanding that we do one of those things we don't do, but we can sidle up close to it if you don't get in the way." Any other time, Jessup would have stopped the charade here and now. But Hildreth wanted it handled, and Isaacs was the sort who'd bend Hildreth's ear again; and if Walt Hildreth's ear got burned, he would chew on Jessup's like a goddamn ferret. Newt Jessup sighed. "Now let us do the talking, Mr. Isaacs. Just show us to your Mr. Soriano."

Isaacs put on his lab coat again and led them down a hallway past one bend, pausing to frown toward an open door from which issued several voices, their echoes indicating a cavernous room. Jessup and Eckert would have walked in, but Isaacs shook his head. "Tour group," he said. "That's the repository for warehousing of specimens and evidence." He motioned them forward and walked on.

Newt Jessup got a glimpse inside that lasted only seconds, but would remain with him forever: a room two stories high and, in it, a motley group of women wearing clip-on badges. They listened to a lab-coated assistant and gawked at metal shelving piled high with animal pelts, carved walrus tusks, cowboy boots tipped by real cobra heads, pharmaceutical extracts of bear gall, rhino horn, and tiger penis labeled in English and Chinese: a stunning display of the outrageous and expensive trivia that compel grown men to hunt other creatures to extinction.

Presently Isaacs pointed in silence toward a half-open door down the hallway. "Let us handle this, Mr. Acting Director," Wade Eckert said in a second warning.

"Okay, but I wouldn't miss this for the world," said Isaacs.

The Bureau men stood together to confer in soft rumbles. "We're not gonna take this guy in," Newt said, mindful of the paperwork.

"Nah, but we can get him as far as the front door," Wade said. "Weren't you listening? We also remind Isaacs of all the hassle the charges would be for him, and then let Soriano off with a scare. Shit, we haven't any proof the guy took the animals anyhow, and I don't feel like getting a search warrant to turn the poor guy's house inside out for two pocketfuls of puddytat. Jeez, Hildreth would never let us hear the end of it."

"And we keep the office caseload down." Newt nodded. "What do you think about cuffs?"

"Oh, come on!" Wade scoffed. "Just dangle 'em on your pinkie—they'll get his attention."

And, with that, agents Eckert and Jessup stepped smartly into the little guy's office.

Soriano nodded brightly when his name was used, a friendly smile forming. He saw the proferred IDs and the smile began to die by millimeters as he looked back and forth at these large, formidable Feds. He also saw the stainless-steel handcuffs Jessup held. And Wade Eckert managed to make it sound like this was the most important bust since Bonnie and Clyde. ". . . Serious breach of federal statutes . . ." and ". . . theft of multiple assets from a research facility." At no time did Wade Eckert make specific reference to animals—especially kittens—because he feared he might start to snicker. "I'm afraid you'll have to come with us," he ended, avoiding the more formal phrases that spelled out "arrest."

Eckert decided he'd done it just right because young Soriano's face went dead white, hands fidgeting slightly, before he took control of himself with a valiant effort. "I can't imagine what you mean." He stood erect, squaring his shoulders, spotting Doug Isaacs in the door frame. The apprehension on Soriano's face told Eckert that the little guy was lying; he was busy imagining exactly what the agent meant. "But I'm sure we can get this straightened up," Soriano assured them with a new, imposing calmness. He stepped to the door, waited for the agents to follow him into the hall, and closed the door behind him. He flashed them the smile of a man disdaining a blindfold. "I'm ready."

By God, I think he is, Eckert thought. *Tougher than he looks.* He felt a pang of sympathy for the little guy. They walked together down the hall until, at the turn, Soriano stopped. "Oh hell, let me get my jacket and shut down my screen. You've got me a bit flustered, guys."

Jessup would have gone with him, but Eckert tugged at his companion's sleeve. "Where can he go?" he said softly.

Where, indeed. Soriano's windowless office had only one door, and the little fellow stepped through it, then shut it again. It was on the tip of Newt's tongue to remark that this was a failure of standard procedure; you didn't accost a suspect and then let him out of your sight. *Whatthehell, this isn't a real arrest*, he thought, and leaned against the wall and waited.

And waited. Ten seconds stretched to thirty before the two agents made eye contact. Eckert: "What's he doing in there?"

Jessup: "The lambada. Go ask him." But both agents hurried to the door. It would not open.

"Locked," Eckert said in disbelief.

"Can't be—there's no lock on his door," Isaacs protested. Wade Eckert did an "after you, Alphonse" hand-wave and Doug Isaacs, after trying the door himself, kicked the thing open. A small steel ratchet lock, favored by people who frequent cheap motels, clattered across the floor as the agents crowded into the room.

Jessup marched to the coat locker in one corner, obviously the only place in the room where anyone would be hiding. It pained him more than anyone could know to pound on the locker with his closed fist; but he did it, hoping the noise would hurt their trapped fugitive more. "All right, Soriano, you want to add unlawful flight to it? You're under," he began as he swung the locker door wide.

The locker was untenanted.

"I knew it, I *knew* it," Isaacs stammered. "I've never trusted that bastard, it's always the quiet ones that—"

But Newt Jessup's silent pointing finger stopped his tirade. Newt had scanned under the desk; peered into the glass-fronted bookcase with its half-empty shelves; studied the cement-block walls; then noticed that one of the big acoustic ceiling tiles over Soriano's desk was now awry in its metal frame. "There he goes," he said.

"Hold it," said Eckert climbing onto the desk, lifting the two-foot panel out to peer into the space above the false ceiling. He hopped down again with a head shake. "Mr. Isaacs, please usher all the civilians out of this lab and secure it. Now!" he added. When Isaacs disappeared down the hall, Eckert laid a hand on Jessup's shoulder. "Okay, we've already lost procedure when Soriano waltzed out of sight. My next posting may be Point Barrow, Alaska, pawprinting polar bears. Let's not make it any worse, I can hear Hildreth now. . . ."

"Heckle and Jeckle ride again. I know, you don't have to tell me," Newt moaned. "You're senior to me; what's the drill?"

"I'm going up into the ceiling. You find the rear entrance from the hallway, secure it, see if you can gain access above the ceiling from there. Sumbitch's gotta be here somewhere." And Wade Eckert hopped onto the desk again, struggling to gain handholds above the false ceiling.

"We oughta be calling in backup." Newt trotted down the hall. "But you want to keep this just between us, don't you? Settle it all down, keep it off the caseload. Fat chance," he said, but he said it all to himself. Isaacs was the sort who would raise a stink, and a letter of censure was the very least they'd see out of this fine fuckup.

Eckert had crawled ten feet on hands and knees above a ceiling that swayed, and Jessup was one second down the hall, when the shoulder-height bookcase swung open, all the shelves swinging as one because they had been framed that way with thin aircraft plywood. Andy Soriano had always felt just a little safer with his masterpiece of cabinetry so near, not even seriously fantasizing that he might ever have to use its most special feature. Though each shelf had its separate glass drop-front, all of the shelves could be made to swing out together on hidden hinges. And while a few real books occupied the cabinet, most of the books on the shelves were false, mere shells cemented together. The groupings of the false books seemed casual, but coincided generally with the shape of a small wiry man, perched on a bicycle seat rather like a monk in a cloister, but kneeling on one knee. A wide-angle door-viewer lens, set into a book spine, allowed Andy to watch the entire room while huddled within arm's reach, mouth open to silence his breathing, hoping the hammer of his heart did not carry three feet to the nearest FBI man.

And they had bought it. This wasn't the time to wonder whether it was the Thomas Concoction, the pheromone tracker hardware, or some of his other thefts that had finally set the Feds on him. This was the time to disappear. Knocking that ceiling tile askew had been an inspiration of the moment, sending one of those two-hundred-pound lummoxes overhead and out of sight, into a maze of ducts and wiring.

Andy shoved the bookcase facing aside and scrambled up, dialing the combination of his lower-left desk drawer. He drew out the clothing he had put there two years before: gossamer cotton, strap sandals, other items that he had chosen as his own personal survival kit, his spooker.

His shoes, socks, and trousers went back into the drawer though he transferred items from his pockets to the purse in his spooker; the shirt was okay because he had always fastened his blue-and-yellow Cal Fish & Game patches on with snaps and the patch came off instantly. Still, he needed a button undone to emplace the falsies, nice obvious C cups, with their adhesive. *Twenty-five seconds,* he told himself, ramming his feet into the sandals, snapping the wraparound skirt out, then cinching it with Velcro. He could hear women's voices down the hall, raised in confusion and mild protest.

The blonde wig and the hat went on together. He hoped his hand did not tremble too much when he applied lipstick without a mirror, and as his silent internal monitor said, *thirty-nine seconds,* he remembered to snatch up the cloth purse that emptied his spooker. Forty-four seconds after he cracked open his bookcase, Andy Soriano was moving swiftly down the hall, donning wraparound sunglasses and trying to hold the purse under one arm because it contained fifty $100 bills and a few smaller ones, a few quarters, false ID, and a derringer that would lob a pair of .38 caliber slugs with fair accuracy across an average room. He clipped on his stolen visitor lab pass and turned the corner, slowing his pace as he approached the tour group filing out past the receptionist, some of them murmuring little expressions of dismay.

"I still don't understand why," Andy said in a soft falsetto that carried, turning his face away and dropping the lab pass onto the counter, adding to the scatter of passes.

Douglas Isaacs paused in his furiously whispered conversation with the FBI agent, whose cursory glance ended when those C cups registered. "Just a routine matter, ma'am," he said to the back of the head of the lady with the blonde hair and the funny little hat, and resumed whispering. The agent set off down the hall again. Andy shrugged, swayed his hips in a flirt of bogus irritation, and filed out with the others into the warm afternoon.

He couldn't believe his Pinto would not be under surveillance and, spotting a gray four-door Chevy with the keys still in it, Andy slid inside giving a little twiddle-fingered wave to the tour-group women, just in case he was being watched.

Beneath that fall of blonde hair, Andy's forehead was damp with sweat as he accelerated slowly from the parking lot. Very soon now, if not already, agents would be dismantling the little garage apartment, finding his weapons, his notes, and the remains of those two kittens which would tell more about Andy's problems than any outright confession could say.

They wouldn't find the real contraband he had stolen because he had given it all to Romana. He wondered if she had made her escape. But who could have known of those stolen lab assets? Isaacs or Lockhart, the punctilious creeps, would have blown their whistles long before this if they'd known. Which left just one person—the one who, he suddenly perceived, could have burned him as part of some deal and might not have to escape at all. Mom had said, if they ever came for him, it would most likely be FBI. Mom had known, all right. Of course Mom had known. . . .

Andy's mind leaped from point to point at fever pitch, not pausing to consider how unlikely his suppositions had become. Stepping-stones of hard logic remained, the first one being his need to ditch the car he had stolen and then to hot-wire another car downtown.

And that is why the Fresno police found Wade Eckert's government-furnished Chevrolet sedan after it was towed from a parking lot off Divisadero near the city's center, wiped of any useful prints. That matched up perfectly with the auto-theft report from a woman whose Oldsmobile had been stolen from that same parking area.

34

AMONG THE BEST PLACES TO DITCH ONE CAR AND hot-wire another in broad daylight is a private parking area without an attendant, but emblazoned with terrible warnings to the trespasser. Andy chose one such area, reserved for staff, behind a clinic. He wasted no time on recent makes, which were harder to hot-wire and more likely to have alarms. He lay down in the seat of the first old American sedan he found unlocked. Its bumper sticker proclaimed: LOVE A NURSE. STAT! After scaring himself witless by grounding the wrong wire for a brief blurt of the Oldsmobile's horn, he found the right connections beneath its steering column.

Once he had driven the car away, he calmed down enough to check himself in the rearview. The room for cosmetics in his purse was minimal so, as a woman, he was the frazzled wrath of God. As a white male fugitive, he was well disguised. At the moment, his mind was ablaze with juggled priorities.

First he must remove that package he had left in his refrigerator before the apartment was searched, if indeed it hadn't been already. He could not say why, but he would rather be sought as a violator of federal laws than as—as whatever he had become when in desperate need. The car he was driving would do for the moment, particularly since he could approach his apartment as a woman and perhaps spot stakeouts in time to walk away.

But the car might be reported stolen at any time, so he needed safer wheels. He checked into his purse quickly, and, on his key-ring, found the key he had duplicated to Aletha McCarran's Taurus. If Aletha was out as he hoped, please, *please* let her be driving her little Fiero. He could leave a note and, with any luck, keep her from reporting the Taurus for twenty-four hours. He did not want to meet Aletha now. He *liked* her.

And if Aletha were home, he must sweet-talk her into lending him a car. He would not be seeing her again and that was a shame because some of his most briefly satisfying fantasies in recent weeks had featured her, but there must be other Alethas in the world. He had more pressing priorities centering on Mom—Mom the Empress, Mom the Treacherous—the only person alive who could have known he had stolen those things from the lab. *The only person alive.* The phrase stung him, but he could turn that sting around.

He parked the Olds around the corner from his apartment and became his brisk female, wishing now that he had shaved his legs more recently, knowing also that some women didn't. First he would get a change of clothing, and then do what had to be done. He consulted his purse and paused to look at his own address numerals, just in case he was under surveillance, then trotted, with hips swaying, remembering to take one riser at a time, up to the landing.

He opened his purse for his keys and then saw the numerals on the clock inside, and was not certain whether he was an hour off, that was possible; but not two. Someone had been inside already, and Andy heard the roaring of blood in his ears as he trotted down those steps again. He kept the purse unsnapped, focusing on the derringer, determined not to draw and fire it until he was approached at point-blank range. He was truly astonished when he reached the Olds without a hint of pursuit. Well, he had more clothing at The Place.

He made several switchbacks, watching for a tail, and once he stopped the car to listen for helicopter surveillance. There was one chance in ten thousand that the Olds had been bugged during the few minutes he had left it, and that slender thread of chance seemed to be choking him as he sped toward the midtown freeway, a hair-triggered bomb wrapped in skin, yet still in tenuous control.

He left the Olds, wiping it clean of his prints with the edge of his skirt, not far from the McCarran place. The Taurus was in Aletha's driveway, and he used his key to enter it, moving quickly, rummaging among her scuffle of papers and ballpoints so that he could write the note that, with luck, might buy him a day. He felt a mixture of emotions now at the idea that he would not have to face Aletha. Relief, yes, but in his present state of mind, a black frustration as well. There was much unfinished business there. . . .

"Excuse me? What are you doing in—" a familiar voice inquired in no-nonsense tones. He turned to see Aletha McCarran, in red shorts and white halter and deck shoes, standing nearby with a gardener's trowel in hand. She was sweaty and smudged and haughty, and altogether fetching.

"Oh, Jeez, am I glad to see you!" Andy whipped off the hat with its wig. "I was writing you a note," he said.

"My God!" Aletha's eyes widened; then she began to laugh. "Andrew, you would not believe the things that flashed through my mind! But what on earth? Weren't you going to the playhouse?"

The *dramatiste* in her was never long in surfacing, and Andy realized suddenly that it was her way of maintaining superiority in her world. He wondered how Mr. McCarran dealt with that. In the bedroom, for example. Because, in any game she played, Aletha was certainly a woman who would want to be the dealer. In that, Aletha was a lot like Mom. Too goddamned much like Mom.

One brow arched, bringing up the corner of Aletha's mouth as though they were linked by wires. "Well, they say cross-dressers are usually straight," she said. "I do hope they're right, Andrew."

He could have proven her correct by lifting his skirt to show the erection that he had grown upon seeing her. The momentary temptation was almost irresistible, but sanity intervened. He clapped the hat and wig back on, stepped from the Taurus, and struck a model's stance with a smile he hoped was just winsome enough for Aletha. "Do I pass?"

"As a woman? Um," she began, and was overtaken by giggles. She stepped nearer; moved a tendril of hair from his eyes; shook her head. "I suppose that depends on the effect you want. You wouldn't exactly prod my lust, if I were a man. Luckily, I'm not." Then: "Damn, I thought I'd

locked that car. Well! As long as you're here, come on in. I was just going
in for limeade, it should be cooling off, but it's hot as Romeo's codpiece
out here."

She kept up her banter while leading him through the house to the
kitchen, a vast airy room in which blinds kept the windows protected
from Fresno's late-afternoon brilliance. Mostly her jabber consisted of
questions he scarcely heard and did not bother to answer—like did he like
his drink with ice, and why wasn't he at the playhouse, and what would
his note have said. Something told him she wasn't so much full of
questions as full of nerves. Well, he had cut loose from his pursuers for
the time being. Another ten minutes or so wouldn't matter.

He improvised. He had always wondered how it would feel to wear
women's clothes, he said, and was finding that it was more titillating in
public. Men sometimes waved, or honked, he added.

"Does that excite you?" She handed him his limeade and the question
at the same moment.

"Kind of, but not the way you think. It's even better when women
make eye contact and smile."

"A wonder they don't laugh. You need to do some things." She
sipped her limeade, set it down, stepped so near that he was immersed in
the musk of her sweat. She took his chin between gentle fingers, tilted his
face for a profile. The little finger of her free hand traced a small scar on
his cheek. "A bit of concealer here, first. You don't need much, with that
lovely gypsy skin. Then a good foundation; we call it 'blush'—it's really
rouge in a powder form. It takes a very good brush to apply perfectly; not
many women seem to understand that. And some liquid eyeliner is more
dramatic to the folks in the cheap seats, or in the next lane of traffic. If
you're going to do this, do it right. You need to be taken in hand," she
murmured.

He found his tumescence going away now as Aletha took charge of
the moment, handling him. Momming him. He allowed it, while she told
him things he had picked up long ago as he watched Mom and, later, had
watched Aletha herself prepare for a performance.

Finally she took him by the hand. "Andrew, darling, come upstairs and let me show you how it's done."

"Wait, I don't know," he said. "What will Mr. McCarran think?"

"Frank? He will think"—she tugged as she led him upstairs—"that he should push Nike and Bell Atlantic, or whatever they tell him to think. By now he has left that fey oak-paneled whorehouse they call a brokerage downtown, and he will not think about things he doesn't know about. *Capisce?*"

"But if he comes in unexpectedly," Andy said, topping the stair behind her.

"Not until after his visit to the club while afternoon traffic dies away, and that means seven-thirty on the dot after three slow martinis. My dear husband does *nothing* unexpectedly. Ever. There are times when I honestly believe he will drive me up the wall." Now they entered a room that might have been staged as a set in *Manon Lescaut,* draperies on the four-poster in bordello crimson and white that matched her outfit and, its mirror surrounded by lights, a table with a huge disarray of cosmetics and sable-tipped brushes. He knew those brushes; they were outrageously expensive. It was an Aletha room, he thought: melodramatic, but with nothing missing, and a class act all the way.

"That's some vanity," he said as she snapped on the lights.

"When you're this serious about hiding nature's oversights, you call it a makeup table," she replied, smiling. "Now sit down, Andrew."

Something in her tone was just that faint shade too peremptory for him to accept. "Maybe some other time, Aletha." Because her hand was pressing on his shoulder, he laid his own hand atop hers, smiling at her in the mirror, feeling himself hardening again. "There are other things I'd rather learn from you."

"I'm flattered," she said, "though I doubt I have much else to teach you. Perhaps we could discuss this at your apartment sometime soon."

"I've got another place. Bet you didn't know that." He turned to face her; wondered why he was telling her this but a part of him knowing, all right. He was probing the edge of the envelope by sharing his secrets, but that wouldn't matter because he would not have that secret for long anyway. "A really nice place in the country."

"I didn't know," she said. "On your salary? Don't tell me you're one of those kept men." Her smile was provocative.

"No. I've never, uh, done that." It sounded timid, spiritless; the pendulum of their relationship was swinging to her and to shift the balance he tried a deeper tone. "It's on the Yomo reservation. You'll probably find out about it anyway, sooner or later." *Sooner than you think, and on the front page.*

"It sounds nice, Andrew. Was that—is that the real reason you came here today? To talk about us?"

"Not to talk." He was empowered, seeing the uncertainty in her eyes. "We've done too much talking, too many times. I'm going to do something about it."

It was true; if he were ever to learn those delicious secrets of mutual pairing that all lovers share, this would be the time, and the woman, and the chance for him to share them in traditional ways. He tossed his purse ten feet to her bed.

She stepped back, and he snapped off those pitiless lights that showed the tiny wrinkles at her throat. "Andrew, until now I never really thought," she began, taking another step back, one hand touching her own cheek. She seemed hesitant, vulnerable, and now his erection could have scratched crystal.

"What didn't you think, Aletha? Every time you teased me with words, you must have thought." He took a step toward her, and she moved back as if doubtful. Ohh, and it was fine. "When you reminded me of your body, reciting your measurements, and then told me you didn't mean anything by it, you were thinking."

"You have a wonderful memory for dialogue," she marveled.

"A wonderful memory for Aletha McCarran," he corrected her softly and let his skirt slide away. "It's not as if I had memories of other women, you know. I want my first memories of that sort to be of you."

She saw his maleness fully ready as he pulled his briefs to one side, to brandish his threat. "You're really a virgin, darling, in this day and age?

And you're offering yourself to me." Her eyes grew moist. "And why shouldn't you, after all?" Something almost coy surfaced in her gaze but, as if abandoning one interpretation of a role for a better one, she became forthright, her voice husky. "I admit I've thought of you, of us together. I'm more than flattered, Andrew. More than touched. I believe I am"— she smiled again—"persuaded." And with this, her hand on her breast, that hand began to undo the knot that held her halter together. Her breasts, he saw, were ripe, not yet pendulous, with a tan line that stopped near nipples that seemed to be staring at him. They were magnificient.

They were daunting.

She readied herself with a sinuous wriggle, letting her shorts and panties fall to the floor, and removed the deck shoes quickly. Then she took him by the hand again, leading him to the bed. Controlling him. Momming him. He saw her lick her lips, head back, with a voluptuary's smile. And he felt himself ebbing now, knowing at last that he would not be able to take her—or any woman—this way.

As she sank onto the bed before him, deliberately sensual and tempting, the roaring began in his ears again, and beneath it a litany of despair. He could not be a man for her because her consent unmanned him; and when she realized his failure, she might try to console him, even hold him. And later, after he had gone, she would laugh.

But she would not laugh if he took her without consent, the way he had taken his other darlings, the way he had fantasized taking her recently. It would be far better than any previous sex he had ever known because while he indulged his fantasy it would be real; was already real. His erection was becoming resurgent as he grasped the purse lying near her; unsnapped it; withdrew the knife he had modified and honed for similar purposes on lesser darlings.

"Andrew? What the hell!" Her protest had grown almost to a scream as she saw his intent, and the upcurved eviscerating tip of the blade. Legs scissoring wildly, she rolled away before he could find her center with it, the blade slicing harmlessly into bedding. "What's wrong with you?" Standing on the floor now, the bed between them, she pulled a corner of a sheet up to cover her as if hiding her nakedness was somehow proof against him. He was wonderfully functional, potent in his mastery of the situation. "Listen, buster, you're scaring the shit out of me!" she yelled. "If you're not out of here in five seconds, I'm going to bring the neighbors!"

"Scream like you did before." He moved around the end of the bed, bringing a frilly edged pillow with him as she dropped the sheet and moved another step backward. "Go ahead, Mrs. Glamourpussy."

"That was a scream? *This* is a scream!" she raged, and unleashed a shriek that set her chandelier to tinkling in the closed room. Ears ringing, he knew capitulation when he heard it. He smiled and she saw her obliteration in it, and her throat worked convulsively without result.

There was going to be a lot of blood, he realized, but he could wash his shirt out before he left. Despite the thudding pulse in his head, he felt that his mind had never been so sharply focused. "But I promise you won't feel anything but a nick at your throat. Really," he insisted. He honestly and truly did not want Aletha to feel pain. After she had bled out unconscious, what he needed would remain warm. He would still have plenty of time.

He did not have as much time as he thought, however, as Aletha backed against her ridiculous spindly legged little bedside table and, fumbling at its single drawer without looking, produced a businesslike and definitely nonridiculous .380 automatic. He paused, judging his options, and she might have brought it off had she not begun to fumble again in that drawer.

He was only six feet away when he saw that she had kept the weapon separate from its magazine of heavy-caliber rounds. And as their gaze met, they both knew he was not going to give her time to shove that magazine home.

35

JUNE 1994

GARY LET THE TIME GET AWAY FROM HIM AND DID NOT leave the office until nearly six, driving directly to Highway 99, giving more time to his thoughts as traffic lightened south of Fresno. Perhaps he should have checked more thoroughly on Anderson, Virgil Pease, after a single call on Monday afternoon had verified that young Anderson had graduated from CalTech and was now, they believed, with Hughes–El Segundo.

Even CalTech's records clerks were high-tech, he had found. Because Anderson's course records showed he had been "heavy" in computerized visual display, the young woman suggested that Anderson's work at Hughes might be involved with Hughes's parent company, GM, developing virtual-reality maps for automobiles. That was not military work, so Mr. Garrett should have no difficulty in contacting Mr. Anderson.

With his second call, Gary had found that Andy Anderson could be reached at an extension in the El Segundo facility, unless he was temporarily visiting the test lab at GM's test complex in Arizona. Mr. Anderson's schedule was a very crowded one. At that point, Gary had postponed further checking.

Now, he decided he had done the right thing to wait. It was only an hour to Porterville and, with any luck, he would soon have more pieces to fit into what might, or might not, be a puzzle. And after that, it was less than an hour to Bakersfield.

The lawn at the Tate place looked like it wasn't so thirsty, he saw as he parked the Camaro at the curb. His knock was answered by one of the kids he'd noticed on his first visit: a blonde with a tight helmet of curls. "Which one you want?" she chirped, answering his question with another.

"Maybe your dad," he said, because both men flew old aircraft and that might gain him a few points at the outset. The girl bounced from sight, and Gary heard a brief burble of conversation among sounds of dinner preparation.

Gavin Tate came from the kitchen with the sleeves of his open-necked dress shirt rolled up, drying his hands on a small towel. Erect, taller and older than Gary with curly graying hair and a direct blue-eyed gaze, Tate thrust out his hand with a smile. "Mariette tells me you're the lawn police. Trust a realtor to forget his own turf," he said in a low musical baritone.

"I dunno what made me say that when I came by before," Gary replied, coloring. "None of my business, actually; that wasn't even why I came. Your Piper wasn't the reason either, but I bet it's an old Cub, right?"

Tate nodded, his face lighting up. In moments he was describing his old tail-dragger's pedigree and how he inherited it from his father. He backed into the room, waved Gary to a couch and parked his own rump on the arm of a chair as he spoke.

Without remark, Gary noted the faint patchwork of lighter skin at the older man's throat—hardly more than a shadow, but suggesting old skin grafts, expertly done. The living room was furnished in well-worn American Second Mortgage style, as unprepossessing and friendly as Tate himself. On two walls were family photos. Gary recognized Tate and his girls at various ages. Two different women were represented, though, reminding Gary that Linda Seibouldt had married a ready-made family. The earlier photos showed a conventionally pretty young woman, roughly Gavin Tate's age. The most recent one revealed that Mrs. Seibouldt had been right: her plain-faced Linda had lost enough youthful pounds to reveal elegant cheekbones and the serene features of a Venus. Not pretty, but handsome.

Gary told about his jointly owned Cessna and, unknowingly, spent too much crucial time cementing his new aquaintance. By now they were "Gavin" and "Gary." Apparently, they had both attended several fly-ins without meeting. "Your name was vaguely familiar though," Gary admitted, and then took his plunge. "The real reason I'm here is, well, it's my curiosity about something your wife might help me with. I'm not the lawn police but, in a way, you nailed me." He showed his ID.

Gavin studied it carefully, then handed it back, grinning now. "Not lawn police, but serious grass police," he said. "Haven't seen one of you guys in a while. I was with BLM for fifteen years."

Gary shared his grin and nodded. The Bureau of Land Management had discovered many a back-country glade managed by people who took care of their illicit patches of marijuana more carefully than the BLM could ever manage timberlands.

"This isn't a drug problem," Gary said. "In fact, it's not even official. It's about one of your wife's old schoolmates. You and Mrs. Tate will be within your rights to tell me to go peddle my papers."

"Then let's see if we can tear her away from that lamb casserole she's salvaging." Tate sallied off to the kitchen and Gary was pleased that the conversation from there did not sound stressful.

Linda Tate had a voluptuous bod; that was Gary's first inevitable impression as she strode into the living room because he had thought of her only as a face and shoulders. She gave him a Gioconda smile that must endear her to kids in school. It said, "Whatever it is, it's okay."

After introductions, she asked him to stay for dinner. "It's really just leftovers. My kids have taken over the kitchen. They say you've got, and I quote, 'bad wheels,' so of course they'll want a ride. And don't you do it," she said with schoolmarmly firmness. It was hard to remember that Linda Tate was years younger than Gary himself.

Gary pointed out the window and confessed that he'd driven his car instead of the Kawasaki. "No bike, so no problem, Mrs. Tate." He warmed to her because she'd said "my kids," as though she had borne them. "Tell you what: let me give you a little background and then, if you still want me to dinner, you can ask me again. If you don't, I'll understand."

She turned serious at this; sat down, taking her husband's elbow so that they sat together, a supportive team. "Fair enough," she said.

Gary began by asking her if she recalled a kid called Hoss, and if she minded talking about him. It was possible that she might not want the Lowery boy discussed in Gavin Tate's presence.

At the name, a faint hint of distaste bracketed her mouth. "You mean Steele Lowery, I take it." She turned to Gavin. "Before we met. A real bastard." She virtually whispered the last word, but with considerable feeling.

Gavin nodded. "Fresno State?" Exercising the smile lines at the corners of his eyes, Tate went on: "Lot of young guys milling around her there, Gary. I thought maybe I'd have tripped over him at some point," Gavin said gently.

"Briant High," Linda said. "He just pulled up stakes and dropped out one day. Never graduated that I knew of." She turned back to Gary. "Or did he? I'm afraid I haven't kept up."

"No, he didn't, Mrs. Tate. He couldn't." And he told her of the single column in the *Fresno Bee,* trying to avoid seeming to watch her reaction.

Linda Tate closed her eyes and grimaced sadly. "Oh, Lord, it must be a blow to his parents. And his little brother Danny, who thought Steele was a god incarnate." Now she shook her head, her gaze fixed on things far away, long ago. "Somehow it's hard to think of Steele Lowery falling into a hole."

"That was my impression, too," Gary said. "And I'm wondering if he simply fell."

Linda Tate, startled, gave a humorless *huh* of denial. "I'd like to know who could have pushed him," she said and turned again to Gavin with a few well-chosen phrases. Big strapping man on a little campus, mean to the bone, briefly her date simply to add to his conquests—which didn't happen, she added.

Gary kept silent on that one. Perhaps by now she remembered it that way.

"Do you honestly think someone put him down there and let him die?" She seemed to have trouble with the concept.

"Maybe not in that order," Gary said. "But this is only my idea, Mrs. Tate. No one but me seems to doubt it was an accident."

"Linda! Please, Gary."

He nodded. "I've done some casual checking, and I know it seems pretty extreme but if any high-school hotshot ever built up more ill will, I never heard of it."

"Oh, I think that's putting it too strongly. Hoss Lowery had more friends than enemies."

Gary: "Friends, or cowed victims?"

Linda, after a pause: "You've done your homework. Good point."

Gary shrugged. "It didn't take much digging, Linda. And what I'm wondering is, which of those friendly victims might have been victimized once too many? Maybe gotten ol' Hoss drunk, teased him into that hole—something like that."

"All of them," she said suddenly. "Oh, not really, he had his sycophants. And I don't think any of us could have deliberately—" She mimed a push with both hands, and shuddered.

"How about the parents? Ruth Madden's or Andy Anderson's, or even Ken Kirk's? I admit that's a reach," he said.

"A long one," Linda agreed. "Lordy, I haven't heard those names in eons." She thought about it for a long moment. A brief squabble emerged from the kitchen, centering on the words, "rosemary" and "garlic." "Pardon me," Linda said, and whirred away. The next sounds from that quarter were more subdued.

"Domestic tranquillity, it's wonderful," said Gavin Tate. "And she's its linchpin, believe me."

"My mother died young, but I imagine your kids are lucky."

A slight pause. "She's not their first mother, you know."

Gary nodded. "Her age. The photos. I figured."

"They were running wild after—after Marian died. It didn't help that I was back in Fresno State for the degree I should've finished up before I joined BLM. But when you're twenty-one, who can tell you how important that goddamn sheepskin is?"

Gary smiled reflectively. "A role model, I suppose. Luckily I had one."

"You a family man?"

To his own surprise, Gary found himself nodding. Well, dammit, Swede and Jan *were* his family. The family just wasn't official yet. "No kids yet, but—call it a family nucleus. Works for me," he said.

"Take care of it," Gavin said earnestly. "It has sure taken care of me."

"Liar," said Linda, who had issued from the kitchen under the noises of two nymphets ordering each other around. She sat down and patted Gavin's knee. "It's Gavin who gives the care," she said, speaking to Gary but gazing at her husband. "That's what drew me to him, the way he cared about people. He was a man among big, beer-swilling boys. One who'd stood up for his principles, and had taken some awful consequences. I don't suppose he's told you. Or did his name ring a bell?"

"C'mon," Gavin said softly.

"Jogs a memory, but forgive me," Gary admitted.

"This is the Gavin Tate who blew the whistle on those timber poachers in 1986 to his BLM bosses."

"Ohh, yeah," Gary said. "Something about copter lifting of logs from public lands, at night. Was that the case?"

Gavin nodded. "It was the helo that cemented my suspicion. The pilot kept honest maintenance records, he'd have been nuts not to under the circumstances. I claimed an interest in his big Skycrane and sneaked a peek. That damn helo was flying twice the hours it should've."

"So you kicked over a can of worms in the boss's office," Gary guessed. "Bet you didn't win any popularity contests," Gary said.

It was Linda who replied. "Well, let's just say they didn't want to hear about it. Pick your own reason," she said.

"There were no indictments in our office, and you were a kid at the time—so be careful," Gavin warned her.

"No indictments. Just a firebomb under the hood by some space-age timber thieves to silence Gavin. It would have, too, but his wife chose that morning, of all days, to start their car." A silence, as the little team of two gazed at each other. "He almost saved her. It cost him two years of recovery. When I met him, he was building himself a new career safely out of all that."

"I'd had enough," Gavin said. "Going back to finish school saved my sanity, and Linda Mujjer here saved my kids."

"Linda Mujjer?" Gary's face reflected his confusion.

Gavin grinned. "Bonehead Spanish; *linda mujer*," he said, pronouncing it properly.

Gary laughed aloud. *Linda mujer* meant "pretty woman."

The two Tates went on for a time, recounting the days at Fresno State when a tragically injured man courted a blossoming younger woman. Gary did not have the heart to bluntly interrupt because they seemed to enjoy reminiscing. By now the odors from the kitchen had him salivating.

They did not return to Gary's Topic One until Linda had recounted the fact that she'd had her eye on the widower Tate for some time. "Yeah, but I couldn't use an apostrophe for sour owlshit," said Gavin Tate. "So this twenty-year-old with the great shape helped me pass English, and the rest is history."

"And biology," Linda amended with a smile.

Gary's glance at Tate was admiring. People like himself sought dangerous work, but Gavin Tate had simply been doing an honest job and had stepped unaware into a high-risk situation. And had kept slogging through it to the end. To shift the topic, Gary said, "I suppose that's what I'm fooling with now: ancient history."

"It certainly is," Linda replied. "You mentioned Ruth Madden; I hadn't thought about her in ages. So pretty, and so trusting, and she didn't have a clue. Do you know if she's doing all right?"

So Gary told what little he knew about the Madden girl's move to Nevada and described the greasy niche Ken Kirk had found for himself.

"Poor Mongo," Linda said, smiling. "Or maybe not, if he's satisfied."

"And how about Candy Andy?" Again, Gary was alert to Linda Tate's reactions.

"Plain Little Andy will do," she corrected. "Such a sweet kid, and bright as a button—but very shy. The truth is, Gavin, he was the one I had a sort of letch for. Though I think I probably just wanted to mother him. He seemed to dote on his mom, but I never met her and if I ever knew anybody who seemed to need mothering—anyway, there was a sort of quiet determination there under the shyness. A depth. Especially the way he shrugged off the worst of Steele's day-to-day insults. Bastard," she hissed again, then recovered her easy manner. "If anyone had a special reason to rejoice when Hoss ran off, it was Little Andy—oh, Lord," she said. "Hoss didn't run off at all."

"Nope," said Gary.

The eldest of the Tate girls poked her curly head from the kitchen. "The microwave dinged and Marlys set the table," she said, glancing shyly at the man with the bad wheels.

"And you're invited. Again," Linda smiled at her guest. "We usually eat on the sun porch in summer."

It wasn't a feast, but there was plenty for five: salad, a piping casserole of lamb with brown rice and a ton of garlic, with ice cream for dessert. Gary met Marlys and Mariette officially and knew he had set the right tone for Linda's taste when he claimed that his Kawasaki was more trouble than it was worth. Most of an hour passed at dinner before Mariette brought the Butter Brickle and Marlys added a bowl of diced strawberries.

"My lady, Jan, loves this stuff," Gary confided, dumping a dollop of the strawberries onto his ice cream.

"Bring her next time," Linda said.

"In fact, you two can fly down to Porterville Municipal," said Gavin brightly, "just south of town. I can pick you up, put you both up for the night. And we can get in some formation flying, if you trust me not to get paint on your wingtip." Gary agreed, though they set no specific date.

"I don't know that we've been much help, Gary," Linda said as they picked at the last of the strawberries. "It seems so long ago, and Steele Lowery wasn't really worth—the trouble," she said with a darted glance toward the girls. "Except to Little Andy, perhaps," she said with rueful amusement.

"I wonder if you've heard from Andy Anderson since those days," Gary said.

"Andy Anderson," she said, as if he had changed the subject, brightening with that sunburst smile Gary had seen in an old school annual. "His real name was Virgil. He was my guy for a while, my senior year in Briant, but I was stupid. Never mind. My mother and his kept in touch for a while, and I gather that Virgil set new standards at CalTech. Of course, that's his mother talking. But it might be true: he could play the class clown one second and stump the teacher the next. I don't know what ever happened to him, but I'll bet he didn't flunk out."

Gary decided against telling her where an old beau had gone. Gavin just might not take kindly to that. He did have one more question to ask, and it was a corker. "About Andy: you say he was bright. And you say he might have had more reason to, um, shove his troubles into a hole than anyone else. Did he ever indicate that he had what it might take to do something like that? Think back."

"Oh, good heavens, I don't need to think back," she replied, laughing. "What you saw was what you got with Virgil, and he was a star basketball player as well. He and Hoss played on the same team. They got along."

"Even with that name, 'Candy Andy'?"

She stared blankly at Gary for an instant. "Not Andrew. We're talking about Virgil—Andy Anderson."

It was Gary's turn to stare. "There were two Andys," he said, detecting a cold lump in his guts that was not Butter Brickle.

"I'll show you," she said, and left the room. She was back in a moment with a twin to the school annual he had copied in Briant High. "This," she said, "is Virgil—Andy Anderson. Was," she corrected. "He could be fat and bald by now. Wait." She flipped a few pages farther, to the smaller junior-class photos. She placed her finger triumphantly beneath a picture. "And this is Little Andy, the one Steele named 'Candy Andy.' Big difference."

Gary read the brief legend. "Andrew Soriano," he said, very quietly.

"Little Andy," Linda explained. "He was small and quiet, and too shy to be popular. But very sweet."

He still is, Gary thought. It was the face of the same Andy Soriano who worked in the lab. And had access to the Thomas Concoction. And had ingratiated himself into Gary's apartment. "Look, I need to make a call to Bakersfield, and then I've got to be going. I'll pay for the call," he said to Gavin.

"Don't be silly—it's practically a local call," Linda said.

36

BY LATE AFTERNOON, HIS HANGOVER HAD SIMPLY GIVEN up on agent Newt Jessup. It was replaced by the memory of Hildreth's latest tirade still ringing in his ears after he had reported losing their man, and their car as well. He tooled the replacement Chevy to a stop shortly before 8:00 in the evening, blipping its engine impatiently while Wade Eckert stepped inside the Yomo tribal headquarters not far from the casino. "If they hate our paleface ways so much, why does their casino have a marquee like God's personal pinball machine," Newt asked himself idly. Their backup still had not shown in Jessup's rearview but was expected momentarily.

Each shadow on the reservation hillsides was stretching to extravagant lengths as Newt waited and wondered how Eckert was doing. You had to be careful how you stepped on tribal land, unless it was to throw money around in the casino. Sheriff's deputies seldom sought perps on the reservation because the law was very persnickety about that. Many tribes had their own ways, some of them fairly rough and ready, of handling their native-grown troublemakers or anybody else's. Federal agents had clearer access, but Eckert was checking in with the elders anyway. Besides, neither of the agents knew exactly where the hell they were going. Maybe the elders would know.

It was a good thing old Walt Hildreth had developed a decent relationship with Fresno's county and city cops, thought Jessup. When Eckert phoned in the APB on Soriano, naturally all the law-enforcement groups got it. But locals often seethed at high-handedness by the FBI; sometimes with good reason, sometimes not.

This time, it wasn't long before Fresno's Finest shot back a rocket of their own. Young Mr. Soriano had been a busy boy, and a very bad one at that, said the police. And it looked like just the kind of job for their good friends at the FBI because the word was that Soriano's apartment was untenanted, but his fridge was of considerable interest. And Soriano had hinted about a second hideout somewhere on the nearby reservation, which was tailor-made for a Fed followup. The CHP was on alert, and copies of Soriano's state lab photo were in the hands of agents dispersing to air, rail, and bus terminals. The fugitive was considered armed and maniacally dangerous.

From what Jessup gathered by car phone, Soriano had stolen a tan Ford Taurus station wagon after attacking a Fresno woman in her home. She'd thrown down on him with an equalizer. Unfortunately, he saw her trying to cram its magazine in. Fortunately, there was already one round in the pipe. Unfortunately, she missed him with it, so close to his face the muzzle flash had sent him spinning, perhaps with flash burns. And while the woman was fumbling the damned magazine into the butt of her pistol, Mr. Soriano was grabbing his skirt and purse. The game had then been called on account of mutual avoidance, but the tan Taurus was missing.

His skirt? His purse? Uh-huh. Newt Jessup nodded to himself, guessing how the little fucker had got past them at the lab. Newt would never look at women quite the same way again.

Wade Eckert came hurrying out of the little building and flung himself inside the Chevy. "Straight up that surfaced road," he said, pointing. "Left when you're past the cut, but take it easy and stop after that—it's a dead end. We've gotta wait for Reid and LaRusso anyhow, and the perp can't get back past us." Ordinarily, the term would have been "suspect." In their own minds, Jessup and Eckert were far beyond mere suspicion of a perpetrator.

"On foot he could," Jessup said as he drove, studying the hillside with its cover of sparse trees and high grass. "Or a boat. Fuckin' lake is right over those hills somewhere. Is the lake on the reservation, too?"

"By God, I think a synapse just fired in you," Eckert said suddenly, grabbing the dedicated-frequency car phone. Jessup eased up on the pedal to hear. Eckert got patched into the Fresno County sheriff's quickly enough, suggesting they bring some heavily armed gents in small boats to lurk near the lakeshore bordering the Yomo reservation. Anybody who tried to launch from that shore might be of interest. He might also be packing artillery—a knife, at the very least.

Newt turned left past the hill, then pulled over to the verge. Two or three hundred yards away, the surfaced road simply stopped facing Millerton Lake, a few hundred feet downslope. "Well, well, look who's here," Newt said softly.

Wade Eckert nodded, already giving exact directions to Tom LaRusso, who was still a few miles from the reservation in another Chevy sedan. Newt was pointing toward two ordinary ranch-style houses— 3 BR 1–1/2 B types with big garages—and to the tan Ford Taurus station wagon parked in the driveway of one of them.

"Can't make the plates from this distance and angle," Newt complained. "Could be a wild coincidence."

"Yeah, or it could be that wild hair up your ass," Eckert muttered as he put down the phone. "Let's assume that's our boy in there, and try, for once, to keep procedure. Now here's the word on the place ahead, according to the chief back there. One house was never finished. The other's been leased by a woman, one Romana Dravo, and her boy for over ten years. Chief thinks the son's name is—would you believe—Andrew. He's grown and gone now."

"Shit he is," Jessup said. "He's in drag and crying to mama, right over there in front of us."

"Cool your jizm, Newt. We don't even know if mama's home. LaRusso and Reid are five minutes from here and we don't wanta color outside *any* of the lines from here on out. You realize, if we take this guy right, Walt Hildreth will forget every effing thing that went wrong today."

Newt: "Maybe there *is* something to live for. Man, I hope you're right."

"Mark my words, fair-haired boys. Ol' Walt will hug us so close under his arm we'll be snorting his Brut for a week."

Then, because Newt had let the window down and the breeze was right, they heard it: a long, faint howling cry, a demon's wail that sent gooseflesh up Newt's arms to his hairline. It did not sound quite like anything human, yet it could hardly be anything else. As the agents stared at each other, a different cry erupted from the near distance. It lasted several seconds and could have been from a different throat, even a different species; a low-pitched scream of unearthly rage, or perhaps of terror and pain, neither identifiably male nor female. Later, neither of the agents was able to characterize it more closely; but, Eckert was to say, you don't expect anybody who's made that sound to ever make a sound again.

The Chevy's engine roared to life. "Awright, goddammit, that's more than probable cause," Newt Jessup snarled and started the Chevy rolling.

Wade Eckert's larynx bobbed twice as he held onto the armrest. "You know what you're doing?"

"Not exactly, but I know I'm not waiting to hear anything like that again," Newt Jessup called over the engine's thump as he hurled the Chevy forward.

"Man, I'm with you," Eckert breathed, dry-washing his face with his hands. The search-and-seizure regs let you go in with unequivocal signs of violence. They didn't have to specifically mention the shrieks of the damned. Eckert had no time to raise LaRusso in the few hundred yards of Newt's rush.

Jessup went over the curb and stopped crosswise behind the Taurus, giving it no way to back up and banging his door against its bumper as he exited the Chevy. He had never had a situation quite like this in his career, and knew somehow that he must rely on old training, without giving himself time to think it over and maybe let discretion mature into plain chickenshit. He took his old Smith Model Ten in hand as he set sail for the back door. "Take the front," he called to Eckert who was a few paces behind. That, too, was procedure.

The front-door locks—Romana's work—stopped Eckert cold and stopped his shoulder, too. The back door was already ajar and Newt went through it fast, announcing himself, squatting and popping up once he was inside, stepping over wires and blasting caps strewn on the floor, so pumped that fear seemed as irrelevant as bikini briefs on a fat man. Newt could hear Eckert bashing himself silly against the front door and announced himself again, listening for other noises in between the body slams of Eckert, scoping out the living room, releasing three locks on its door and Eckert nearly shot him then but calmed down a little and they went from room to room, taking more time than Newt liked, finding a dresser drawer full of men's clothing dumped onto the floor of one bedroom and another room fitted out like a wealthy hobbyist's workshop, stumbling over plastic buckets full of goop in the hall that filled the house with an odor like kerosene; and Eckert pointed out that a muzzle flash might ignite the whole place, which dampened their enthusiasm a bit, but it didn't slow Newt down much until they heard some kind of distant thumping, and that was when Newt Jessup's free hand went up for silence.

It sounded like a lawn mower, faint but distinct. Then like two lawn mowers, or gasoline-driven generators. They might have been automatic systems somewhere behind the house. Eckert pointed toward a door from the kitchen and opened it for Newt, who went ducking through into a big shelf-lined garage, and what he saw lying in front of a panel van made them forget that distant thrum for the moment, and while Eckert lost his lunch in a corner Newt tried to determine whether it was their perp, part of him anyway, opened like something that should hang in a meat locker, but whatever had done this work had done it only too well and incredibly fast. The jeans and shirt were unisex, slashed and soaked with gore; the shoes were loafers. The victim was roughly the size and build of Soriano. There was no sign of a bra, but Newt had seen men with bigger tits.

Newt Jessup had once watched a pro dress out a three-point buck in under a minute, leaving the hide on, the head attached. But he had hung the deer up first. This butchery had been done faster, with great economy of motion. The head was missing.

Newt looked around him, searching for the head, gooseflesh marching in columns up his spine. It did not seem possible that this ghastly business had been done in the thirty seconds before he entered the house, but a new possibility made his arms shake. What had begun as he drove toward the house might have continued more quietly in that garage as he went from room to room only a few yards away. If that was the case, they weren't dealing with anything that should be treated like a human being. Newt saw no need to step into the great crimson pool on the cement to establish vital signs.

And what if the slasher was *still* there, hidden among the shadows of that cavernous garage, silently waiting? The garage door hadn't been opened, and there was no other door Newt could see but the one they had entered. Newt Jessup studied the nearest shelves closely before sidling up near them, then squatted to peer beneath the big panel van. "Find the light switch, Wade," he said.

Eckert apologized, coughing, and tripped a toggle near the door. The place flooded with light.

The two men began moving slowly along the shelves, standing well back, ready to fire at the first sign that somebody or something— anything at all—might be moving among all that stuff. Newt pointed to a bloody partial footprint on the floor beneath one big set of shelves. Then it was Eckert who snapped his fingers for silence. Somewhere in the distance, a mechanical scraping had begun, something homely and familiar as a garbage disposal, or—

"Garage-door opener," Newt said, not bothering to look because he knew it wasn't the door of *this* garage, bounding back to the kitchen and then to the outside door. Wade Eckert had said the second house was unfinished, but what better place to stash some kind of hot wheels. With LaRusso and Reid still en route, they could all wind up looking like the "duhh" factor was kicking the bejeezus out of them all when some CHP throttle jockey made the collar.

And because there was no breeze, it did not matter which direction an aircraft used to take off. By the time Newt burst outside he saw, passing behind his car, a slab-winged craft all in charcoal gray with a short pod of fuselage, not much to shoot at, one engine pointing upward as if broken though its prop was a blur. The big garage behind it had all the appurtenances of an aircraft hangar, with gallon-sized containers lined across the floor. Two of the containers rolled lazily down the driveway slope, one trailing what looked like cooked oatmeal.

The aircraft was gaining speed like a rocket, so Newt stopped and took an approved two-handed aim, knowing small airplanes didn't get off the ground without considerable roll, aiming at the front of the canopy for Kentucky windage. Just as he squeezed off, so did the little plane, which left the ground as if jerked aloft by wires, climbing without much tilt at all. Newt sent five more rounds after the first one. Wade Eckert was firing too, now, and Newt reloaded in record time, faster than he'd ever managed on the firing range.

As the plane banked overhead, a dark, boxy Chevy sedan smoked its wheels around the corner, LaRusso and Reid braking to a stop in time to lend credence to the idea that either a homicidal maniac or his mother had just fled from a garage in a fucking airplane, taking off within fifty yards, while two FBI agents emptied their service revolvers at it.

Newt stowed his Smith and looked toward Eckert, who still had glop on his chin. "You think we got it?" he asked.

"If by 'it' you mean Walt Hildreth's warm embrace; no, I don't think we got it," Eckert said glumly.

Newt: "Now I've gotta find a head."

Eckert: "Me, too. I've got nicotine stains in my shorts."

Newt: "No, Wade, a *real* head. We don't know yet if that was a man or a woman in there."

Eckert sighed. "I hate it when you're right."

"I wish I was following that thing," Newt said, nodding aloft.

Eckert began to reload his piece. "Why? Where d'you think it's going?"

"Far from Fresno—that'd be good enough for me."

"Oh." Eckert sighing, and stowing his piece, "I don't think either of us has to worry about that. Did I ever mention Point Barrow?"

37

JUNE 1994

IT WAS HALF-PAST EIGHT BEFORE GARY NOSED THE Camaro toward Route 65. He told himself repeatedly that his anxiety was nothing more than a reaction to Linda Tate's little conversational grenade. When he had called Jan from the Tate house, she had felt well enough to answer and, now that she knew when to expect him, she had sounded almost chipper. On the outskirts of Porterville he checked his fuel gauge and cursed the thirstiness of that engine just ahead of his feet. Like all pilots, he had a horror of an empty tank.

Paying for his fuel, he asked for the nearest phone and was directed inside the station where he used his calling card. Okay, maybe he wasn't paranoid enough to alarm Jan over nothing. Swede was another matter.

The old man's answering machine growled, "I'm feeding the attack dogs and cleaning my Uzi. Leave a message of any length—or not." Swede owned neither dogs nor burp guns but, with a welcome like that, he wasn't as likely to be burgled while off drowning worms.

At the beep, Gary said, "Swede, I just got a line on the guy who may have put me in that mine shaft. If I'm right, he's still serious trouble, and he knows me. He may know—well, I'll brief you later. I'm in Porterville on the way to Jan's. I don't think he knows how to get to me through her, but you never know, and I don't want to scare her or blow this out of proportion with our people in Bakersfield. So look: just to be on the safe side, if you get home before I raise Bakersfield, I'd feel better if you staked out her place. She doesn't have to know. See you there."

After that, his drive through the twilight seemed to take no time at all because he was focused on his discoveries about quiet, sweet Candy Andy

Soriano, whose friendship had seemed wholly coincidental until now. In fact, it had been Gary—not Andy—who made that first friendly contact.

Yes, but why? Because Andy had access to the Thomas Concoction at the state lab. After that it had been Andy who promoted the friendship in that shy, deferential way of his. And both Linda Tate and Mongo Kirk had implied that Candy Andy was anything but sweet on the Lowery kid. Recalling Andy Soriano's ways, Gary found it hard to imagine him overpowering Lowery. *Yeah, it was probably hard for Lowery to imagine it, too.* With a little more imaginative paranoia, maybe Gary could avoid getting his ass pumped full of the Thomas Concoction. Again.

But what had Linda said about Andy's mom? That he doted on her, but he still needed mothering. Then the phrase *"two women"* popped into Gary's mind, jolting him with the connection. The older of his attackers had been a woman, but the younger one could easily have been Andy. Soriano in drag? Maybe; Andy had mentioned being part of a theatrical group.

Christ, it was almost too pat, now that he thought about it. He'd even wondered briefly if some parent had taken Steele Lowery out. Now it seemed a lot more likely; with those two working as a team, they had nearly bagged Gary himself. And maybe a hell of a lot of other people, over the years. Yet somehow the idea of an aging woman and her son as a team of contract killers was so bizarre that Gary found himself ridiculing his own suspicion.

Well, first thing tomorrow morning, he would sit down with Visconti and lay it all out for him: Gary's inquiries in Briant, his follow-ups at the state lab and later with the Tates, and that visit Andy Soriano had paid to the apartment. There was simply no telling what part, if any, Andy's mysterious mom had taken in all this. Maybe none.

Or maybe she was the puppet master.

One thing he could depend on: if he passed his suspicions on to Graham Forster, with or without Visconti's blessing, both Andy and his mom could never sneeze again without some Company spook muttering "gesundheit" somewhere nearby.

And if Gary were totally out of his tree in this guesswork, some part of his fiasco would work itself into his file. His best tactic would be to offer the idea as highly speculative, a tissue of circumstantial evidence that he was offering only to cover all possibilities. *But without proof to the contrary, I intend to make Andy and his mom a hobby of mine,* he promised himself.

It was fully dark as Gary parked beside Jan's little Z car, emotionally warming himself in the glow from her shaded windows. He blipped a faint bleat of his horn for her and for Swede, who might be sitting somewhere nearby with his back against an apricot tree. Recalling his paranoia, he locked the Camaro, though now that he was with Jan, his worry seemed groundless.

His knock got an immediate reaction as Jan opened the door a few inches, red-eyed, her hair in need of brushing, wearing nothing that he could see. He was already grinning up at her, taking the steps, as she blurted hoarsely, "Run, Gary—get help!"

A hand, with a knife in it, slid into view at her throat. A soft female voice said, "And if you do, Gary, she'll die. I promise." It did not sound like anyone Gary knew. He noted that Jan's shoulder was averted and realized that her hands were probably tied behind her.

Gary stopped with his hand on the doorknob. He had slammed against partially open doors before; they could send big men sprawling. But he'd had a weapon in hand. And nobody had been holding a knife to an innocent throat. Was Swede on stakeout? On that supposition, Gary spoke so his voice would carry. "If you hurt her, lady, you go down hard. That's *my* promise."

Now the voice changed cadence, timbre, everything; and it was the voice of Andy Soriano. "Let's be honest about this: I've already hurt her. Not much, and I think she enjoyed it, paaal." The last word drawled sarcasm. "But she won't enjoy it if I—but do come in and shut the door."

Gary did as he was told, moving deliberately, no longer in doubt that this sly little changeling was capable of premeditated murder. Gary's entire body sang with adrenaline, and he knew the sensation well but had learned how to keep it on a tight leash until the proper moment. He managed to close the door without depressing its center lock and turned, hands out and empty. He saw that Jan was entirely naked and that Andy was as well. Andy Soriano might not be interested in sports, but completely nude he was a healthy, wire-muscled specimen you didn't jump without thinking twice. He had pulled Jan back, staying close behind her, using her as a shield against any weapon, keeping the tip of that knife blade against her throat. On closer inspection, it was not quite like any blade Gary had seen on a big clasp knife before—ground down near its end so that the tip, honed on both edges, would slash catastrophically either way it was guided. "I'm not armed," Gary said, and tried to give Jan an encouraging smile. Her eyes seemed listless, devoid of hope.

"That's for me to find out," said Andy, now in a teasing singsong parody of cuteness. "And I will. When she told me that big bad Gary was on the way to the rescue, it simplified things a lot."

"I'm sorry," Jan said, her eyes pleading toward Gary.

"It's okay, honey," Gary said softly.

Andy chortled at that. "Is it? We'll see. Take two giant steps back, Gary. The first order you disobey, I twitch. Do you want me to twitch?"

Gary shook his head and stepped away, facing his dilemma. He'd left the Beretta in the glove compartment before entering the Tate residence because such weapons added an unwelcome presence to a friendly discussion.

"Take off everything. Shoes, too. Turn your pockets out," said Andy. His voice seemed to exaggerate his mood of the instant, varying from childlike to peremptory. At the moment, it held a hard edge of command. Gary began to take his clothes off, doing it slowly, hoping to give Swede time to shift the balance before this batty little bastard really hurt somebody again.

"Got an idea, Andy," he said as he sat on the couch to remove his shoes, pausing. "It's me you want anyhow. She looks pretty tired. You're probably getting tired holding her up—"

"Keep taking it off," Andy demanded. "Like us, naked like the rest of us, the best of us, and the best of me is rather good, isn't it, Janelle?"

Jan's mouth moved twice before she managed to say, "Wonderful," in a tone that denied it. "He's got a little gun, Gary." Now Gary noticed the scatter of clothing across the living-room floor, some of it Jan's, some of it obviously Andy Soriano's. But he doubted that Soriano had a gun on him. There was not even an ankle holster in sight.

Gary forced himself to breathe regularly, muscles aching with need to grapple, throttle, smash. He took off the shoes, then began to turn his pockets out, sitting naked. "But there's nothing more she can do for you, Andy. If I lie down facing away from you, and you can see I'm not carrying anything, why not let her go out the front door? Then you'll have me like you wanted."

"For a start," Andy said, "she can do the same thing for me she did before. See?" He moved to one side and Gary saw the erection he was meant to see. "But maybe I won't, not yet, because you're my friend and I want to make this easy for you before I—well, anyway . . . Besides, I don't have to bargain; you'll lie down facing any way I tell you to. You'll bite off your dick if I tell you to. Won't you?"

This guy is completely off his trolley, Gary decided. Even if he had raped Jan, keeping his own clothes off was a sign that he didn't care about his own vulnerability afterward. Maybe he didn't think much about being vulnerable. Maybe he wasn't thinking much, period.

"I asked you a question," Andy said, and Gary saw the tendons tighten in his knife arm.

Oh, yes, he was thinking, all right. "Sure, anything you say, Andy. If I can. 'Course, it won't help if you ask me to do something I can't. Because you don't want to throw away your advantage—"

"Don't tell me what I want," Andy demanded. "I know what I want."

Jan was crying now, a silent heaving of her poor lovely despoiled body that was without tears. "What do you want, Andy," Gary asked, still sitting. He knew that if he gathered himself for any fast movement, his muscles would betray him before they could launch him. Andy had known that, too.

"I'll tell you when the time comes. Maybe." Andy's tone teased again.

"Maybe you'll tell me how you found the lady. Or maybe you'll tell me why you set out to kill me, dump me down that goddamn shaft with the others. What had I done to you, Andy? Or was it something I did to your mom?"

"Fuck mom! Fuckfuckfuckmom, fuck her dead." Saliva formed at the corner of Andy's mouth. His eyes danced—not in hatred, but with blazing triumph.

"Boy, you really get off on that, don't you?" Gary said in awe.

Andy licked the spittle away. "You have absolutely no idea," he said with a death's-head grin that generated visible gooseflesh on Gary's legs.

"If you hate your mom, why help her? How long have you been helping her?"

"Too many questions," Andy said, sobering for an instant, and then smiled again. "I bet I know why, Mr. Chuck Lane, Gary Landis, whoever else you are. I bet you're counting on help. I think you actually believe that poor clod out there near the drainage ditch can save you, but"—his eyes grew large in false wonderment—"who was going to save *him*? Lucky I landed off in that field while there was still a little light. I don't think he even saw me go over, but I saw him. And I can be very, very quiet."

"You flew?"

"Like a birdie. Your friend's neck will bend ever so far over backward now, he could lick his own asshole. But no, I don't suppose he could. I took his ID; always take their ID," he advised, winking like a conspirator.

Gary could not help the tear that found its way down his cheek. He was trembling now, knowing it showed, not much caring. He must not think about Swede now, lying alone in a ditch with his throat laid open. If this little ghoul was a practiced killer, maybe he wouldn't make the mistakes Gary had been counting on.

"I think you'd better give me a better reason than her to keep me from disobeying you," he said.

"Really?" The arm twitched. Jan made a soft noise, and a small trickle of blood appeared at her throat beneath the knife's tip. "What I think is, you'd better go to the bathroom. Go on; we're right behind you,"

Andy said, his voice strained because he was half-lifting Jan from behind with his free arm.

The bathroom had never been designed for three, but Andy solved that one easily. Standing in the doorway, he made Gary step into the tub. Then he withdrew the knife from Jan's throat, thrust her toward Gary, who embraced her, and switched the knife to his free hand while the two held one another. "Get into the tub, Janelle!" he commanded, and burst into laughter.

As she complied, a faint metallic *clink* sounded from somewhere nearby. Gary saw that somehow the naked man had produced a medium-caliber derringer, and it was cocked. "Neat, huh?" Andy said in a tone as rational as a politician's. "You can hide one under your arm without a holster, even move the arm around. Mom showed me that. Mom was the master," he added, nodding at his own words, smiling as though at some faintly pleasant admission.

Now he leveled the ugly little weapon at Jan's breast; closed the clasp knife one-handed; tossed it four feet to Gary, who nearly failed to catch it. "Now," said Andy Soriano, "you can do the honors. Let go of the curtain!" he barked to Jan, who had grasped the shower curtain to keep from sliding down into the tub. She swallowed and stood upright, hand to her throat, leaning against Gary, who could feel her body trembling against his.

"You don't think I'm really going to use—" Gary began.

Singsong, teasing again. "Yes I do," Andy interrupted, speaking in the slow cadences of sweet reason. "I think if you have the choice, you'd rather do her quickly. It doesn't hurt much, honest—not if you do it right. Or, you can make me put a round or two into your belly, and then I can gut her very slowly while you can see and hear it. You're both going bye-bye, you know. There's positively nothing you can do about that. Oh, you may think you could take my little slitter and try for me, but think about it: I can't possibly miss, and nobody functions well when he's gut-shot, and surely you don't expect her to be much help. And when you tried and failed, then I'd get to do it my way." The face was gleeful, eyes intent on Jan's unprotected torso.

Knees shaking uncontrollably, eyes closed, Jan slid downward until she was sitting on the back lip of the tub. The derringer was now pointed at Gary's very center. "If I have to do you first, Gary, I may just wait awhile for you to enjoy that new navel. And you won't like that, will you, Janelle?" The face changed. *"Choose!"* he snarled.

Jan laid her cheek against Gary's naked thigh, leaning forward. She did have a few tears left, it seemed. "I don't want to hurt anymore, Gary." To Soriano, then: "Why must you do this vicious, horrible thing?"

"Horrible? If Gary weren't my friend, Miz Glamourpussy, you wouldn't be in that tub together. You'd get to see him die, and you'd hurt more than you can imagine while I made a new cunt for you. This was Mom's idea, fuck her in hell, but she was right. This way it will look like you—"

And the world exploded, a dark spray of debris filling the space between Soriano and his victims, peppering them with splinters, Soriano hurling himself backward to rebound from a wall. A second blast erupted beneath the doorway, the sound deafening Gary, more debris cascading from the ceiling.

Soriano, on one knee, blinked hard and swung the derringer toward Gary, who flung the closed knife into his teeth. The muzzle blast stung, but the slug went into the ceiling and then Soriano was pounding toward the front door, Gary flinging the first missile he could reach as he followed. It happened to be Jan's bowl of unshelled almonds on the dining table, scattering in the air as Soriano wrenched the door open, turning to fire again but ducking away instinctively as the almonds pelted him. And then Soriano leaped into the darkness, Gary hard on his heels.

The open door threw a rhomboid of light into the yard. Soriano, fleeing from it, turned sidelong to find his target in the light, and he did not see the nose of Gary's Camaro until he impacted against its hood with a squeal that was more anger than pain.

Gary's vision was equally poor, but he saw Soriano roll back into the light and regain his balance; but not before Gary slammed into him, managing to grip the derringer with one hand, twisting Soriano's wrist ferociously and, when the weapon fired, feeling the heat of it against his palm, knowing he might have the slug in him now but not feeling that at all, not with Andy Soriano butting him in the face, not with his hands now beneath Soriano's chin, both men rolling on the gravel as Gary shook and gripped his opponent, slamming the head against gravel repeatedly, not stopping until long after the legs had stopped churning against his, not until he found himself strangling a rag doll.

Not, in fact, until a beloved gruff voice beside him said, "Overkill. I like it," and Gary looked up to see Swede Halvorsen, a sawed-off pump shotgun hanging from one hand. The old man was disheveled, baseball cap askew, and on his face was a look of terrible satisfaction. He reached down, helped Gary pull himself to one knee, looked back toward the mobile home. "Did the sonofabitch hurt my granddaughter?"

"Not much," Gary said. Let Jan tell him if she wants to, he decided. "He sure would've if you hadn't showed up." To tell Swede of the obscenities that involved would not have been a kindness, and Gary left it at that.

Swede waved his hand toward Soriano and Gary himself. "Don't tell me this was the uniform of the day," he said.

38

"THE UNIFORM WAS ANDY'S IDEA. LOOKS LIKE HE'S ALL out of ideas now," Gary said, inspecting the palm of his hand.

"Shit, no wonder," Swede said, kneeling, pressing his fingers against a bluish depression oozing in the faint light on Soriano's muscular little chest. "You popped him here."

"Popped himself," Gary replied, rising, hugging the older man.

"Hey; the neighbors," Swede growled, and Gary realized he was outdoors, naked, embracing another man.

He began walking toward the light. "He said he had cut your throat out here, Swede. What happened?"

"Well, he lied. I just got here, and saw your Camaro, and started to knock. But then I heard what was coming down and worked my way under the floor. Believe me, I know every inch of that bathroom layout upside down. Especially upside down," he chuckled. They closed the door behind them, and Swede raised his voice. "It's us, Jan. It's okay now."

"She'll be dressing," Gary said quickly. "Wait—Soriano said he had your ID." He knelt at the rumpled jeans Soriano had left on the floor.

Swede fished his old wallet from his hip pocket with two fingers, held it up. "What the hell are you talking about?"

Gary pulled two wallets from the trousers, tossed one down after a cursory look, then flipped open a slender, flashy eelskin wallet. He laughed in disbelief. "Christ! Looks like my old buddy Ralph Guthrie is out there somewhere in a ditch, bled out. Couldn't happen to a nicer guy—but how'd he find this place?"

"DEA guy?"

"Scuffler for La Familia. Somehow they got a line on me after all." He stood up and shrugged. "Well, Andy Soriano, you'd say you got the wrong sentry. I say you got the right one."

At this point, Gary's knees began to shake and he sat down, regaining his own shorts and trousers. "Jan? If you're decent, I am," he said, hoping this moment of reaction would not become a fit of the shakes. He had shot men in the line of duty before, and knew to expect that rushing mixture of dread and elation, *I've taken a human life,* and *he would've taken mine but I won,* that had followed. It didn't follow this time. Only the dread was there, a dull ache of uncertainty, not of whether he'd been justified according to every law of man and Providence, but *what kind of a cynical Providence would give us this kind of free choice?* There had been an Andy attentive to a friend, meticulous in his work, almost pathetically congenial. And another Andy full of a demonic force that lusted to kill and far worse, to torture, even to force a friend to murder his own mate. And how many more Andys had there been? To kill one, you eliminated all the Andys.

It was all too metaphysical to unravel this quickly. Gary stood up, forcing his knees to obey him. He would know the elation he sought when holding Jan close, feeling her vibrance, glorying in what he and Swede had saved from shy, friendly, hellish Andy Soriano—or from chaos, or perhaps from Providence if that was the way it worked.

And when he arrived at the bathroom, stepping past a two-inch hole in the flooring with its splintered plywood edges, Jan Betancourt sat in the tub looking past him with an unearthly calm. A small runnel of blood, like a tear, had trickled down her cheek from the inner corner of her left eye, and as he knelt and tilted her face in his hands, then held her still-warm body in his arms, Gary knew that one of those metal pellets—probably double-aught buckshot—had struck the orbital ridge just above her eye and—Providence again?—deflected inward, into the brain, instead of out. She was not breathing. For all practical purposes, death had found Jan instantaneously.

—

Gary was not worth a damn those next two days, but Paul Visconti helped him through his debriefing. Graham Forster's congratulations sounded hollow, perhaps because it was the FBI, not the Company, that had begun to unravel the secrets of that hideaway on the reservation, including the discovery of Helmut Klemmt's gun cabinet which was an outstanding datum in the Spooker File. But the central discovery was that the fingerprints of Romana Dravo were a perfect match with those of Skander Masaryk.

Some of those secrets might never be resolved, said Forster. Very few would have come to light if someone had taken five minutes more with a few dynamite caps. As for Romana Dravo's head, it had been found in the rear seat of an exquisitely constructed Chamois kitplane, in an open field near Bakersfield. Evidently, Andrew Soriano had not wanted to leave his mom entirely behind.

Gary sat at the rear of the sanctuary, alone, the Betancourt family huddled together in the front pews as if hoping for security in numbers. He had offered his sympathies, but Jan's mother had said only, "If it weren't for you," in a choked whisper, and the father's stare had been eloquent with silent hatred.

Swede had witnessed this in silence, standing a little apart before filing into a pew with the family. After a muted buzz of furious whispering among them, Duane Halvorsen stood up and strode to the back, seeming suddenly very old, reseating himself near Gary without word or glance.

Gary only half-heard, and later would not recall, what the priest said. The place smelled of incense and sweat, the odors of penance, and later Gary drove alone at the tail of the short procession to the brief graveside service. Swede drove just ahead of him in the old Dodge Polara that Jan had once driven into the hills, demanding to be part of the action, utterly incapable of imagining how serious the consequences might be, what part she might ultimately play.

At the graveside, Swede stood well apart and Gary took up a position near him, both of them sweltering under unrelenting California sunshine.

They could hear nothing but distant murmurs. *Probably just as well.* At no time did the Betancourts give any sign to acknowledge the presence of Gary or Swede.

When the obsequies were past and the others had driven off, fat tires grinding gravel as if it were guilt, Gary sighed into a blinding sun. "Why isn't it raining?"

The old man looked at him. "In Bakersfield?"

"It rained for Amadeus. It should be raining for Jan," Gary insisted.

"Amadeus?"

"Never mind. Shit. Who said, 'The world isn't like they told you it was'?"

"Ever'body who knows anything worth knowing," said Swede.

"That'd make a damned short list," Gary replied. "And if they know, chances are they won't tell you. Reminds me: you said once I'd be different after realizing I'd come within an inch of winding up on a slab, Swede. Remember?"

"Yeah."

"Well, it's not true. Did you know it wasn't? For a few days maybe; it shakes the hell out of you. But in the long run, the feeling of reprieve wears off. That little monster almost took me down twice. I know I was lucky but—you don't change that easily, Swede. At least I don't. Did you, really?"

Swede Halvorsen's gaze stayed on Gary for a long moment, then strayed to the ground. At last he sighed and shook his head very slowly.

"Then why tell me it works that way, if you knew it doesn't?"

Another silence. Shrug; then, angrily, "Well, goddammit, it *ought* to. It would, if we had the brains of a tapeworm." And when he looked up at Gary again, his face held a plea for understanding. "Guess I just hoped you were smarter than I am, Gary."

"I'm a cop, is what I am. And I *am* smarter than you are—hell, I'm meaner, too. Maybe I forget that for a week or two after a major dustup, but sooner or later I remember. Just like I'll bet you did."

"Oh, you're a cop all right." Swede turned toward his car. His words floated back: "I'll get in touch, one of these days."

"I understand," Gary called to him, knowing with leaden certainty that he really did understand the old man's subtext. Swede was saying, "Let me be the one to get in touch, and I probably won't." *Too many memories, too much pain in them.*

Gary noticed the two men in work clothes waiting patiently near a backhoe for him to leave. He trudged off another fifty yards, saw Swede's old Polara dwindling along the drive, then sat down beneath a shade tree. He would not leave until the backhoe had done its final work, heaping earth over his hopes, his devotion. *At least,* he thought, *we know how to do something right.*